I0544281

THE BADDIES

For Bravo and Charlie

© 2025 Victor Tango Kilo
All rights reserved.
ISBN: 979-8-9990041-0-9
ISBN: 979-8-9990041-1-6
This is a work of fiction (duh). Any resemblance to actual persons, living or dead,
or actual events is purely coincidental and kind of hilarious.
Cover design by: Nervous Pop Bottles

NARRATIVE UNITS

Prologue: The First And Last Day Of Spring I

1.0   Some Other Beginning's End 1

2.0   Bad Feelings & Dark Asides 9

3.0   The Wages and Benefits of Sin 17

4.0   Scum and Scullery 25

5.0   Breakfast at Star-Killer's 33

6.0   Burning the Polaroids 41

7.0   Modern War Fare 53

8.0   The Phantom Menu 61

9.0   Carnage Over Cocktails 69

10.0   The Imperium Retaliates 75

11.0   Forbidden Danger Zone 87

12.0   Hopeful One 99

13.0   Rogue Solitaire 111

14.0   Villainous Journey 123

15.0   Apocalypse Wow 133

16.0   The Butler's Jihad 145

17.0   A Sudden But Inevitable Betrayal 155

18.0   In the Court of the Crimson Deathlord 163

19.0   Apocalypse How 169

20.0   Misplaced in the Cosmos 179

21.0   Until Morale Improves 187

22.0   Rebel Without a Clue 197

23.0   The Horde Unleashed 207

24.0   Forceful Awakening 215

25.0   Reunited – And It Feels So Forced 227

Prologue: The First and Last Day of Spring

The planet Katarina had been untouched by the interstellar war, so far, but Kataranians who paid attention to things had begun to sense that their reprieve was over. The Red Scorpion Fleet—long stalled in a brutal ground war on Carpathia—had recently mopped up the last remnants of that planet's resistance. Its army of Deathwalkers was wiping the mud and blood from their combat boots, its battle cruisers preparing to mobilize for the next conquest. The Black Scorpion Fleet had likewise been kept busy suppressing a rebel uprising in the industrial zones of the Mechanus Forge Worlds but would be freed up as soon as they finished reducing the surface of Mechanus III to smooth radioactive glass.

With both fleets wrapping up their respective operations, Katarina was looking more and more like their next conquest. The only question was which fleet would strike and when. Some cycles earlier, the Kataranian High Council had sent a delegation to Scorpius Prime to negotiate a peace agreement. They returned in failure, also body bags.

In one of Katarina's outer provinces, Ogden Kevitch—known as 'OK' within his rather small and diffuse social circle—knew his planet was in peril despite the best efforts of its information services to suppress news of the war in the name of preventing "widespread panic." It was a futile gesture. Everyone knew an invasion was coming, no matter how many government officials declared it "misinformation."

OK likewise understood the Scorpion Imperium was evil, relentless, ruthless, merciless, malevolent and ten or more additional diabolical adjectives, but he faced a more immediate dilemma: his financial solvency, or rather, the alarming lack thereof. His credit was extended farther than a spaghettified space suit at a black hole's event horizon, and his bank account was no longer a binary number; it began with a zero, ended with a zero, and was nothing but zeros in between. His business partner had been good at finagling loan extensions, but alas, every credit line had been stretched until they now involved more theoretical math than the physics behind wormholes. OK couldn't even glimpse the far side of the financial chasm he was staring across.

It was an unseasonably warm evening—which coupled with the imminent threat of cosmic obliteration should have been a real boon for the tavern business, but only a few scattered and not particularly thirsty patrons occupied the tables of his rundown bar, sipping on cheap ales, watching the regional rollerball tournament on the buzzing holoscreens.

Then, suddenly, as if the universe decided to throw OK a bone—his dingy bar was suddenly flooded with a gaggle of attractive young college women. And right there in the center of them was Anya Halleck. To OK, she was nothing short of perfection. Her hair poured over her shoulders like rich, dark molasses. Her green eyes sparkled with secret mischief, while her perfectly symmetrical nose led daringly to the delicate sprinkle of freckles playing hide-and-seek across her cheeks.

As a teenager, he had filled an entire notebook with odes to her, using phrases like "her complexion is luminous as moonlight" and "her smile made starlight envious." He had never intended to show it to anyone, but his business partner found it and read from it at an open-mike night at the bar. OK would have been humiliated had anyone but a few of the usual drunks been there to hear it.

OK's worries about invasions and unpaid bills faded when she came in. "That's my brother's friend, he owns this place, Hi OK!" Anya called out. She and her friends filled in a corner booth while OK drew a couple pitchers of one of his better ales from the tap and carried it to their table.

Anya had been majoring in Zero G Hospitality at Tranquility Minor College in hopes of landing a job as flight attendant on an interstellar starliner. "How are your studies?" OK asked her.

"My studies are over," she announced, filling her glass. "Father says the Scorpion banner will be flying over Katarina City by the end of the year, so we're getting out."

"Getting out?" OK repeated, as if expecting her to clarify she meant something other than leaving their homeworld possibly forever.

But no, she meant exactly that. "He sold our house, sold the business, and liquidated my education account. Converted everything to Antarean money." Antarean Aurea were the only hard currency in Scorpius, the only cash that would be accepted in other constellations.

"When are you leaving?" OK asked. "I mean, maybe we could hang out sometime before you go."

She fixed him with tragically soulful eyes. "We're going to the spaceport tomorrow. With the government's new travel restrictions, we can't even get on a starliner. We had to bribe our way onto some old rusty trade ship. The kind where your in-flight entertainment is waiting for the airlocks to blow."

"At least you're getting out," giggled one of her friends. Another lamented that none of them had the means to become refugees. And even leaving was no guarantee, the Scorpion Horde was not above shooting down civilian transports.

"Where are you going to go?" OK managed to ask. He clung to a flickering hope that maybe, just maybe, there'd be a moment for them to steal away, to say goodbye properly. And perhaps, to speak the unspoken feelings that had been fermenting in the vat of his heart.

She shook her head. "Father says it's best we don't know." She sighed, "I just hope it's not some barren mining colony, or one of those planets with slime creatures."

"Or one of those ice worlds the atmosphere freezes and you have to cut open an animal to survive the night," one of her friends suggested.

"Gross!" all of them agreed.

"What about you?" Anya asked OK. "Are you going to stay or try and get off-world before the Imperium comes?"

Getting off Katarina would require a lot of money and a few Government connections. OK had neither. He didn't even have an Interstellar Passport. Even if he had the choice, he wanted to believe he would not flee in his planet's time of need.

"I'll stay and fight," OK answered. "For Katarina!" he added, imagining himself, pulse rifle gripped in his hands, drawing a bead on an advancing column of hulking, cyborg, Scorpion Horde Deathwalkers. He had never even seen a pulse rifle outside of HARVEY—the Highly Advanced Recreational Virtual Environment thingY he used to play in after school. He had no idea how to acquire one, or any of the other intermediate steps before he could become a rebel freedom-fighter. But he knew what he had to do when the time came.

"My hero," she giggled, then passed back her half empty ale glass. "Bring me the strongest *drutt* you've got. I plan to get absolutely annihilated tonight!"

1.0 SOME OTHER BEGINNING'S END

On a balmy night in early summer, the peace-loving planet Katarina ceased to be a free world. The Red Scorpion Fleet, led by the infamous Deathlord Damocles, brushed aside the planet's defenses like an atomic bulldozer through a bed of petunias. A single trans-orbital warhead obliterated the capital—Katarina City—undoing centuries of sensible, smart-growth-oriented urban planning. The other major cities were pounded to rubble within an hour. Then, the Horde followed up with another orbital bombardment to pound the rubble into dust—just in case the first round of devastation had failed to make the point. Finally, they ignited the dust with gamma ray weapons, setting off firestorms that filled the skies with toxic smoke and transformed vast swathes of land into radioactive hellscapes.

The fact that the Katarina had surrendered three days earlier was a moot point at best.

On the following Friday, OK stood in the shattered doorway of his tavern, looking toward the radioactive glow that had been the city of Tranquility. Imperial invasion was no longer horror stories from distant worlds, but the terrible reality of his own. In the outer suburb where he lived, every door was smashed, and every window shattered. Fires burned in the shells of buildings. His street was an obstacle course of debris and abandoned hovercars.

The Scorpion Horde had not bombed his neighborhood. This devastation was from the panicked fleeing and opportunistic looting that took place as soon as their battle cruisers appeared at the edge of the system. Kataranian Government officials referred to this as, "the orderly evacuation of the urban core." Also, this had been a pretty bad neighborhood even before the invasion.

A year before the Horde came, OK had been persuaded to invest his paltry inheritance in a bar rather than engineering courses at Tranquility City Technical College. It was called 'Driver's Bar' after the friend who had talked him into both purchasing the bar and that 'Driver's Bar' was more marketable than 'OK's Bar.' The establishment had never been profitable and a few days before the invasion, their creditors had moved to foreclose on it. In that one respect, OK thought, the complete annihilation of his planet's civilization could not have come at a better time.

Completing the post-apocalyptic urban wasteland, a man was coming down the street pushing a motorcycle between the post-apocalyptic gauntlet of smoking rubble and hovercars. OK was surprised to see anyone still around. The man drew closer and propped the hovercycle against a cyber-hydrant. He wore a battered leather jacket, a black toque, a chartreuse scarf around his face, and bulky aviator goggles. He looked rather dashing until he took off the goggles and scarf and ruined the effect with his face.

OK recognized him. "Halleck?"

"OK, old sport, I knew if anyone were still around it would be you." Halleck pulled the rest of his scarf from his round, puffy face. He wasn't an ugly guy, unremarkable, nondescript, ordinary, bland one might say if one had a thesaurus at hand. The goggles and scarf had given him a certain rebel élan, but when he took them off, he looked like the assistant manager of a men's clothing shop, which he had been until the shop was burned and looted during the orderly evacuation of the urban core. Somewhere, there must have been a camp of very fashionable refugees in smart business suits.

"I can't get this thing to start," Halleck explained, pointing at the bike.

OK offered a guess. "The electromagnetic pulse from the gamma ray warheads probably fried the control circuits."

"I didn't think it would affect something this old."

The hovercycle was a classic; a Faron Fury with dual xPulse™ power jets. OK pulled the cover from the engine compartment. "There is one advantage to these older models. You can bypass the control circuitry and run it on full manual." He pulled two plugs from the circuit board. "Try it, now."

Halleck touched the ignition. The engine roared to life. There was no reason for it to make the roar, except Faron motorbike customers liked to announce themselves with a lot of noise. "How did you do that?"

"I learned a few things from my dad. There's no automatic collision regulator, now, so don't accelerate yourself into a tree or something."

Halleck cuffed him on the shoulder, "Very nice. The Pact could use someone like you."

"The what now?"

"The Pact of Rebellion Against Imperial Supremacy—PRAXIS for short."

"Where do you get the X? There's no X there."

"Without the X, it could spell PRAISE, and that would be off brand. We're regrouping in the eastern hills to take our planet back!"

"We?"

"Me, what's left of the Kataranian Security Forces, the Tranquility City Patrol, some other survivors. You should come and join us." He clenched his fist in front of his chest. "For Freedom, Justice, and Equality! For Katarina!"

He turned his gaze upward at the thousands of tiny block dots that punctuated the formerly aqua blue sky, each representing an orbiting Scorpion Horde battle cruiser. Colony after colony had fallen to them; Karelia II, Rodina III, Novaya IV, Zeta Zeta V, and even mighty Carpathia. But their relentless onslaught had also inspired a fierce resistance. Across the constellation, rebel forces were organizing to fight the Imperial tyranny. They were outgunned and outnumbered, but they were noble, brave, and on the right side of history, at least according to their public relations department.

"I don't know how good a fighter I would be."

OK was hoping that Halleck would respond with, "Nah, you'll be great," but he told the truth instead. "You aren't cut out for combat, for sure, but you're brilliant with machines, and engineers are just as important as combat fighters to the Pact!"

An engineer? Halleck knew that it had always been OK's secret ambition to be a space engineer, ever since they were little kids. Which reminded OK of something else. "Did your family make it off-world?"

"Yes, they are safe. It took every crown we had, but they managed to bribe their way onto a Serpentinian freighter. Anya made it out with them." Anya was Halleck's sister. OK was relieved that she had made it off-world, even if their last night together had ended not with mutual attestations of love for each other, but with her drunkenly punching him in the nose when he tried to help her into a hover-ride.

"Do you know where they went?" he asked Halleck.

"They were trying for Cellador... they should be safe there, if they make it." Cellador was probably the only safe world in the Scorpius constellation.

"Can the Pact count on you, comrade?" Halleck asked. As if to drive the point, a Horde troop transport passed overhead, trailing black pillars of smoke, the roar of its transorbital engines rumbling the landscape.

"Of course, I'll join you," OK agreed when the roar diminished to a dull distant thunder. Fighting back with the resistance—even just fixing engines—would pay back those Scorp bastards for what they had done to his planet and countless others. "I'll need to grab a few things. Will I get a pulse rifle?"

"Don't take too long, the Deathwalkers will be marching through any minute." Halleck wrapped the scarf around his neck and pulled the goggles over his eyes. Once again looking the part of a rebel, he aimed the hovercyle down the street and rode off. OK watched him until he disappeared behind a burning pile of rubble that had once been a branch of the Bank of Tranquility. The banks had been the first places to be looted, even though Kataranian crowns became worthless the moment the Horde arrived.

OK turned toward back to the bar, wondering if there was anything he could salvage to help survive the bleak days ahead. Someone else was inside already, its namesake and co-owner, Driver Stoat. Stoat was a tall, wiry fellow OK had met playing roundball back in middle school. Stoat had an advantage in height over the other kids but never put in much effort. OK spent most of the games on the bench trying and failing to capture the attention of the cheerleaders except for the one male cheerleader who had intercepted a wink meant for one of the girls and made things awkward for the rest of the season.

"The looters didn't leave much, Friend-o" Stoat said. "Just the caffeine-free cola and the alcohol-free beer." He held up one can of each. "Your choice?"

OK wondered which would be less disgusting at room temperature. "I'll take the beer I guess."

Stoat tossed it to him and opened his warm caffeine-free cola. "Have you come to terms with the end of the world as we know it? Everyone and everything we've ever known, gone. Our beer distributor... gone. That banker who turned down our credit extension... gone." He grinned. "I also think we can ignore that pile of health department violations."

"Not everyone is gone. I just ran into Adam Halleck. He's heading off into the eastern hills to rendezvous with the resistance."

"Well... good for him."

"He said we could join him, and fight against the Imperium."

"I guess he doesn't want to die alone." Stoat took a slug from his can. He had always been a cynical sort.

"Our planet is worth fighting for!" OK argued.

"Is it though?" Stoat sighed, "The Scorpion Horde is the biggest military power in the galaxy. 10,000 battleships. Hundreds of thousands of death fighters. Millions upon millions of Deathwalkers. Sorry to say, friend-o, but they aren't going to be defeated by a bunch of tatterdemalion rebels running around in the woods with surplus military rifles and patriotic slogans."

"The Carpathians put up a hell of a fight."

"Yes, the Carpathians were a proud warrior race that fought to the last man. Which is why there are no more Carpathians."

Before OK could retort with a strongly worded appeal to patriotism or an admonition against the broad cultural stereotype about Carpathians, a message boomed out from the holoscreen behind the bar, which had been silent since the night of the invasion.

"Inhabitants of the planet Katarina. Prepare to receive an address from your new lord and master, Deathlord Damocles of Scorpius; Supreme Commander of the Red Scorpion Fleet."

The Imperial anthem erupted—a tempest of shrieking guitars and thunderous timpani, underscored by glass-shattering operatic vocals—at just the moment Deathlord Damocles made his grand entrance.

Clad in gleaming black battle armor, he ascended above the smoldering ruins of Katarina City on twin pillars of fire from his rocket boots. Hovering ominously in the sky, he addressed the vanquished populace. His voice boomed out—deep, resonant, and flawlessly modulated. If he weren't a genocidal warlord, he could have gotten voice-over work on hovercar insurance commercials.

"Inhabitants of the planet Katarina. I am the Scorpion Imperial Deathlord Damocles– the Sword that Hangs Over Your Head. If you can hear my voice, you have been granted the privilege of continuing to live—for a time. However, make no mistake, your life as you knew it is over. Your pathetic, insignificant world belongs to the Imperium of Greater Scorpius. You will survive for so long as you are useful to the Imperium.

As a tribute to our Imperial Victory, you are ordered to provide one million of your strongest men and women to serve in the ranks of the glorious Scorpion Horde that vanquished your weak and pitiable planet. You are commanded to deliver the first 100,000 within 100 of your days as a gesture of submission. Failure to comply will necessitate further reduction of your population. Obedience ensures survival. Disobedience will bring annihilation. Heed the words of your new masters!"

Deathlord Damocles's announcement was followed by Scorpion Horde recruiting video. It opened with a massive fleet of enormous battle cruisers lit against a vast starry expanse. Dramatic heavy metal music swelled in the background. A deep, theatrical voice provided narration.

"In the Way of the Scorpion, it is written, "Conquest transcends conflict; it is an art to be mastered only by the galaxy's most adept." The video showed a group of recruits in training, marching in formation, handling the deadliest weaponry in the galaxy with precision and alacrity. Then came a montage of Scorpion Horde fleets conquering planets, raining down trans-orbital warheads as populations fled before legions of Deathwalkers and the brutal war machines of their cyborg infantry.

"The Scorpion Horde is more than the projection of the Overlords' infinite power, it's your opportunity to fulfill your potential, become more than you could have imagined, travel to exotic planets, meet interesting people, and subjugate them in the name of the Imperium!"

The narrator concluded, *"The Scorpion Horde, it's not just a job, it's your obligation as a subject of the Imperium!"*

In the closing shot, a tremendous scorpion fleet flew toward a supine, presumably peace-loving planet, until it was fully eclipsed in their shadows. The screen faded to black, and then there was a brief, almost subliminal flash of bare breasts before the Scorpion Horde's logo appeared; a stylized scorpion with oversized claws raised aggressively, its stinger poised to strike. The message was followed by a hastily assembled map of local recruiting centers.

As the Imperial anthem faded, Stoat crossed to the smashed front window and surveyed the devastation outside. "He's right, you know, our lives as we knew them are gone. But this could be a fresh start for everybody! Well, everybody who survived, of course."

OK agreed, "A new life… fighting for the liberation of our home world."

"That would be a rather short new life, wouldn't it, Friend-O? And pointless. There's no way we're going to defeat the Imperium."

"Well, what then? What fresh start are you talking about?"

"I was thinking we should sign up with the Horde."

OK could not believe his brain was correctly interpreting the soundwaves reaching his ears.

"Are you insane? Join the Scorpion Horde? They just killed a hundred million people... probably..." He couldn't remember what the population of Katarina was. One hundred million seemed like a fair, horrifyingly genocidal, guess. OK's brain rejected the suggestion of joining those bloodthirsty tyrants like an algorithm rejecting an imaginary number.

But Stoat had a knack for talking people—OK in particular—into doing things they didn't want to do. "I know this idea is so far out it never would have occurred to you. But our options in this situation are limited. Join up with the rebellion and be killed. Surrender to the Horde and get sent to a labor camp and then killed. Or avoid both of those terrible options by joining the Scorpion Horde."

OK sputtered. "The Scorpion Horde is evil!"

Stoat pressed both hands downward in a subtle, calming gesture. "Let's set ethics aside and try to be pragmatic. The Scorpion Imperium rules our planet. We're never going back to a life of tending bar and giving away free drinks to the ladies..."

"You gave away free drinks to women? No wonder we went bust."

"Men don't go to bars for drinks, they go to meet women. Giving free drinks to women was just good marketing."

"Obviously, it wasn't."

"It's too late to worry about that, now. We have a choice to make; serve the Imperium and live or resist the Imperium and die." He grinned with the kind of smile that could part a fool from his money. "We don't have to mean it. We could stay in the Horde just long enough to hitch a ride to some other, better planet and then make a break for it."

Stoat knew that going into space had been a lifelong dream of OK's. But not like this! Never like this! In a gesture as futile as it was furious, OK slung his empty can of not-beer into the shadows of the bar, where it clattered with a metallic clang that resonated with his boiling over fury. "I will never be a part of the Horde! Never. Nothing you can say will make me change my mind."

OK stormed out of the bar and into the wreckage of the devastated street outside. The air was thick with dust and smoke, but he barely noticed. His chest hammered with the raw, helpless rage of a man faced with nothing but unthinkable choices.

Steadying himself against the stump of a vandalized streetlamp, he cast his eyes again at the looming silhouettes of the Horde ships hanging above the sky. Join them? How could Stoat have even suggested such a thing? The trauma of the invasion must have driven him out of his mind.

Just then, a Scorpion trans-orbital warhead came screaming out of the sky; a blazing spear of annihilation that detonated not far away from the ruins of city. The skies ignited with a blinding flash followed by a thunderous roar. When the shockwave hit, it slammed OK back through the open door of the bar as a cyclone of dirt, fire, and debris hurtled through the street, tossing aside rubble and hovercars. The very ground shuddered beneath him, as if the planet itself had winced in pain.

The maelstrom passed, leaving in its wake random gusts of hot dusty wind and fluttering ashes. Stoat offered him a hand and helped him to his feet.

"That was close," OK said, his voice muffled by the sharp, merciless ringing in his ear canal.

"Yes, it was," Stoat replied. "Eastern hills, unless I'm mistaken."

OK watched the red mushroom cloud rise into the sky over the eastern horizon. The Scorpion Horde had just emphatically made Stoat's point for him.

2.0   Bad Feelings & Dark Asides

Beyond the western edge of the city was a former Kataranian Security Forces (KSF) base where the Scorpion Horde had set up their occupational headquarters. As Katarina was a quiet and peaceful world, the KSF had been more of a police force than a military. One of their largest deployments had involved rounding up a herd of genetically modified cattle that had escaped from a research facility; difficult because they were aggressively carnivorous, easy because they glowed in the dark. As the Scorpion Imperium became more aggressive, the Kataranian Congress made a belated and underfunded effort to build up KSF military capabilities. Many people in Katarina's political class believed that military spending was waste of money because if the Imperium ever invaded, they wouldn't be able to stop them anyway. This turned out to be pretty much spot on.

The base was where the Horde would be recruiting survivors into their ranks, so OK and Stoat set out to reach it. As they made their way through the devastated exurban landscape beneath the constant shriek and boom of transorbital warheads, OK began to see the logic behind Stoat's plan. The Horde was too powerful to fight from the outside. He would have a better chance fighting them from within. Failing that, he could defect to the Rebel Pact once the Horde got him off-world. Stoat agreed that these were good ideas. "Trust the plan, friend-O."

Late in the day, they reached the gate of the base. The sky-blue/sunshine yellow flag of Katarina had been supplanted by the banner of the Imperium— an emblem of a black scorpion outlined in white against a deep red background. It was so on the nose OK wondered if it was the product of a design committee. "We envision a predatory arachnid on a field of blood. Red and black are power colors! Its minimalist authenticity will grow the brand."

The automated guard turrets swiveled and trained red scanning beams on them as they approached. Stoat gave them a little wave. "Hello, there, Scorpion conquerors. Is this where we sign up to join the Glorious Scorpion Horde?"

"This is the Occupation and Transition Base for Sector 81! You will identify yourself and declare your loyalty to the Imperium of Greater Scorpius or you will be terminated"

"I am Driver Stoat and standing right next to me is my great friend, Ogden Kevitch. We are loyal Imperial citizens. New citizens, but tremendously loyal. The most loyal you'll ever meet. We have come to present ourselves for service with your awesome and mighty Scorpion Horde."

"Proceed to the recruiting area! Mind the doors! Hail to the Imperial Victory!"

The heavy gates creaked open, revealing legions of Scorpion Deathwalkers marching in formation across the grounds. These were no mere soldiers; they were merciless cyborg killing machines built around the husks of human victims; or so the propaganda said. Squads of them loaded onto rumbling troop carriers and moved out to assert authority over the conquered planet.

Stoat grabbed OK's arm and pulled him forward. "Remember, we're joining the horde out of loyalty and duty. Got it? All right, here we go."

"Into the belly of the Imperial beast," OK thought. A voice inside of him desperately screamed that joining the Horde—even to bring them down from within—was the worst decision he would ever make in his life and that included the time he let Stoat talk him into eating a live parasitic cephalopod.

But he forced himself forward. A hover-drone inside the gates directed them to the building that had been the base's dining hall and issued them red paper tickets with numbers on them. Stoat was A-64 and OK was A-65. About forty other people waited, spaced out among the plastic chairs. Overseeing them were a pair of armed guards and an angry woman whose face resembled a cross between a Rottweiler and a failed genetic experiment.

"Alpha-22, proceed to the interrogator!" she barked into her microphone.

OK imagined the Interrogator as a dark metal machine whose blunt appendages would probe his mind and possibly other places until he was forced to confess he didn't support the Imperium.

"At this rate, our appointment won't be for hours," Stoat lamented. OK parked himself in a hard plastic chair that had a jagged crack where the back met the seat. He surveyed the room; curious what kind of people would betray their world so soon after it fell. Most of them stared at the floor, as though shamed at the desperation that had brought them to this place. Some large, tattooed men seated in the front row wore neon green prison jumpsuits, marking them as former inmates of a Kataranian prison. The government had freed thousands from prisons to fight for the planet. Most of them had instead joined in the orderly evacuation of the urban core.

The convicts sat with their arms crossed, anxious to get on with the next part of their violent lives, probably as Deathwalkers A small clot of obnoxious young men stood in the corner smoking deathsticks and laughing. They had decided to sign up for the Deathwalker infantry. "The rebels will be like, 'Oh no, don't kill us,' And we'll be like, 'Eat charged plasma, rebel pansies! Pyoom! Pyoom!'" There was also a pale young woman in black clothes who sat by herself, muttering, "Look at me, now, dad! I'm joining the Horde. I'm going to kill, kill, kill! What do you think of that, dad?"

To OK's disappointment no one here appeared to be joining the Horde to fight the Horde from within. When the nasty woman up front called a number for interrogation, he realized he would have to hide his intentions from his interrogator.

Stoat stood up. "I'm going to go chat up the guards. Wait here," he said, as though there were another option. If OK had tried to bolt from the room shouting, "Sorry! Changed my mind! Good luck with the occupation!" he was sure he'd be shot before he made it to the door.

OK practiced repressing his hatred of the Imperium as more numbers were called. The convicts were A-33, 34, and 35. The thin girl was A-36.

Before they reached the forties. Stoat returned. "I talked the guard into letting us cut in line. Let's go."

"What? How?"

"Never mind how, she's going to let us go right now, so let's go already."

The woman bellowed. "Alpha-64. Proceed to your interrogator!"

"See Friend-O? We're up." Stoat picked up OK by the collar and all but dragged him to the front desk. "Hail to the Imperium. Lorraine, would it be all right if my friend and I did our interrogation together?"

"Alpha-64 you may proceed to the Interrogator with your significant other!"

"Called it!" shouted one of the smokers from the corner.

The automatic doors swung open. "Proceed to Interrogation Cube 9."

"Thanks, Lorraine, you're a sweetheart" Stoat said. He patted one of the large burly guards on the shoulder. "Bialas, good luck with the marksmanship practice. I'm sure you won't just wing the next human target."

"Thanks, buddy. That means a lot," the guard growled.

At the end of the hall, a piece of cardboard with "Interrogation Room" hand-written in black marker had been taped over a plate reading "Staff Dining Hall." Walls of curtains divided the room into makeshift cubicles. Another taped up and handwritten square identified Cube 9. At a makeshift desk sat a heavy-set, jowly man with receding, salt-and-pepper hair identified by a small black sign on his desk as "Death-Adjutant Pang, FIST Interrogator."

OK had pictured Scorp officers as trim men with perfect creases in their uniforms who barked clipped orders from beneath their pencil-line moustaches. The portly man in the sloppy uniform didn't have a moustache of any kind. "Have a seat, you guys," he said.

Stoat greeted him with great gusto. "Hail to the Imperium."

Pang corrected him, "We say hail to the Imperial victory, now. So, you gentlemen are here to sign up for the Scorpion Horde, is that right?"

"Yes, sir," Stoat replied, again with great gusto. "I look forward to honorable and service in the glorious Imperial Scorpion Horde."

"Fantastic," Pang replied, perking up. "I like your enthusiasm. Guys like you make my job so much easier. Let me tell you, the last world we took out, I was assigned to the unit that processed people to the Voluntary Residential Production Facilities. There was not a lot of enthusiasm with those guys."

"Voluntary Residential Production Facilities," OK wondered aloud, as was his habit. Then he realized, "Oh, the labor camps."

Pang bristled. "There are no Labor Camps in the Imperium. Our Voluntary Residential Production Facilities provide food, clothing, health care, and shelter in return for productive services offered voluntarily by labor units... sorry, I meant valued civilian workers."

Stoat smoothed things over. "Forgive my friend's choice of words. You know how wartime propaganda can be. Everything was 'labor camp' this and 'genocide' that."

"Quite all right, people have called us worse. Of course, we shot them for it," Pang laughed. Stoat very quickly laughed with him. "Name, please?"

"Driver Wesley Stoat."

Pang slowly punched it into his computer. "S-T-O-T-E..."

"S-T-O-A-T," OK corrected.

Stoat assured the recruiter, "However you want to spell it is fine."

Pang then took down OK's information and led them through more questions—planet of residence, educational background, state of health. At one point, they were interrupted by rifle shots from outside.

"Every damn day," Pang muttered. "All right, what kind of service were you thinking about? And before you ask, you don't want to be Deathwalkers."

"Why not," OK asked, not that he had been considering it.

He leaned over and pointed to the back of his balding head. "When they make you a Deathwalker, they surgically remove parts of your brain ... snip... gone. You wouldn't even remember what cake tasted like. Do you like cake?"

Stoat answered, "I like cake a lot."

Pang snapped his fingers. "You know that reminds me. You know what we need? Kitchen sanitizers! I know it's not the most glamorous work, but there's been an outbreak of mutant E. Coli and we have desperate need of kitchen sanitizers." Wherever humanity settled in the cosmos, E. Coli, cockroaches, and bureaucracy inevitably followed.

"Kitchen Sanitizers?" OK repeated. How could he possibly aid the rebellion as a kitchen sanitizer? He had been hoping for a job as a technico which would give him opportunities for sabotage.

"Half of the officers on the *Attila* are down with space diarrhea. They say it was the birthday cake at the first officer's birthday party. So, can you guys sanitize a kitchen? 'Cos if you can, I can get you a billet right now, a good one, on one of the big cruisers."

Stoat jumped into the opening. "Well, until very recently, Mr. Kevitch and I ran one of the finest dining establishments in Tranquility city."

"You did?" said Pang.

"We did?" said OK.

"Well, I imagine you used to have to keep your kitchen sanitary."

"Oh, absolutely we did. We were well known at the local Health Department for the sanitary quality of our kitchen, I can tell you that."

It wasn't quite a lie. OK could remember a health inspector who had a mental break after looking into their cold storage unit.

"Well, that's just terrific. Let me see what openings we've got. Some billets are better than others. Sometimes, a recruit is even willing to offer something of value in exchange for a better post."

This monster cannot possibly be suggesting a bribe. Anything I had of value was burned or looted when those guys showed up, OK thought.

Stoat took off his shoes and pulled out a pair of silver disks from the toe. "Antarean palladium, 200 grams total." He slid the coins over the table.

Pang discreetly pocketed them. "I'm going to post you to the *Subutai*. Second rank battle cruiser. Really good ship. Great crew, very progressive captain. Much better than a waste-processing ship."

"Couldn't we get a first rank battle cruiser?" Driver asked.

"A fleet command ship? Impossible. Do your job really well, make some friends in high places, and maybe in ten years you can transfer to a command ship. All right, I will enlist you as kitchen hygiene technicos, with the rank of Deathfinger Third Class—No, Second Class, in light of your experience."

Pang pulled out a pair of electronic forms and a sharp lancet. "Now, all that's left is for you guys is to thumbprint these forms wherein you swear your loyalty to the Imperium and affirm that you are not joining to spy on us or take down the Imperium from the inside or anything like that."

OK opened his mouth, and unfortunately, a series of words came out of it. "If I were a spy, wouldn't I just sign these anyway?"

Stoat elbowed him hard in the ribs, but Pang helpfully explained. "It's a termination offense to lie to the Imperium, meaning the penalty is death."

"But isn't spying already a terminal offense?"

"It is indeed. You can be terminated for spying, or sabotage, or fomenting dissent. Pretty much anything, really, if you cross the wrong guy."

OK still didn't see the point, but Stoat interjected. "I will vouchsafe my life that my friend here will be a loyal and obedient servant of the Imperium." OK wondered where Stoat had learned the word "vouchsafe."

Pang waved him off and chuckled. "Oh, no need to go that far. We'll just shoot him if it doesn't work out."

OK and Stoat jammed the lancet into their thumbs and pressed their bloody prints on the forms.

Just then one of the other recruits jumped up from his seat and ran for the door, shouting "I can't. I can't. I just can't!" He was about to run straight by them when Stoat casually stuck out his leg. The man tripped on it and tumbled over onto the floor, landing in a heap.

A pair of guards hoisted him up and dragged him toward the parade ground as he begged, "Please… I don't want to die…"

"Nice reflexes," Pang said to Stoat.

"Just glad to be helpful."

If either of them had looked at OK's face, they would have seen a mask of horror.

Pang handed them each a thick data packet. "These are your orientation packets. Whatever you do, don't lose them. And especially don't lose these." He handed them each a black disk about 5 centimeters across.

"What are they?" OK asked.

"Your bond coins. Everyone in the Imperium carries them. They monitor and record all your interactions with people or technology. The medicos will synch them up with your biochip once you're on the ship."

"I don't have a biochip," OK said.

"You'll get those on the ship, too. I cannot emphasize this enough, do not ever lose your bond coins."

"What happens if we lose them?"

"If you're lucky, 20 hours in the Cubicle of Torment. If you're unlucky, you'll get a view of your ship from the outside without a spacesuit."

"What is the Cubicle of Torment." Stoat poked him with his elbow.

Pang shuddered, "It's something you definitely want to avoid. It looks like you're all set. How soon would you guys like to leave for the training ship?"

Stoat answered, "How soon is now?"

Pang grinned. "I really like you guys. There's a shuttle leaving tonight. Help yourself to some Black Scorpion coffee… the Fuel of the Imperium!"

Black Scorpion Coffee was a trademarked blend of dark Jovian coffee beans and Geminian narcotics. Dark as a black hole and as bitter as divorce proceedings, it both woke you up and induced moderate existential crises.

Pang gave them directions to the departure station where a hoverbus would take them to the spaceport. It was on the far side of the base, past the range where Deathwalkers were doing target practice against holograms of fleeing civilians. Most of the holograms were making it to the far side unscathed. Stoat and OK gave it a wide berth anyway.

They continued hiking as the twilight gave way to darkness. Imperial troop carriers rumbled past, their antiquated halogen headlights searing into their eyes, blinding them as they went by.

As they approached the station, the crackle of firearms and the thunder of trucks faded. When it was quiet enough, Stoat offered some helpful advice. "Friend-O, you need to be, about, a thousand percent more watchful about what comes out of your mouth. You're in luck I was there to cover for you."

"Sorry."

"It might help to imagine that you really are joining the Horde out of patriotism or whatever."

OK agreed that was a good idea.

He had to ask, "Where did you get Antarean palladium."

"Oh, that? I thought we would need some hard currency if the Scorps ever invaded. I've been skimming from the till for the last year. Aren't you glad I did that, now?"

OK felt a brief sensation of anger, a passing vexation. No wonder they were always months behind on the rent and could only afford cheap liquor. But he conceded to himself that it didn't matter now. Today, they had joined the ranks of the Scorpion Imperial Horde; and the only way OK could reconcile himself to that grim fact was by vowing to make it a day the Horde would come to regret!

3.0   THE WAGES AND BENEFITS OF SIN

As the first pink light of dawn poked through the smoke and dust that choked the Kataranian sky, the shuttle roared off the launch rail and shot into space. The devastated planet of Katarina fell behind it as it shot toward the massive fleet of black-armored warships that had devastated it. The flight had been delayed supposedly due to weather, but OK privately doubted there was weather in space. It would be just like the Imperium to lie about such a thing. It was a very full flight and of course OK was stuck in a middle seat between Stoat and a large, sweaty man who smelled like sausages.

Despite the circumstances, there was cause for excitement. "This is my first time in space," OK said out loud.

Stoat replied with a dismissive grunt, "Big whoop. Humans have been in space for a thousand years. Quiet down before people think you're a tourist."

OK didn't care if he sounded like a tourist. He had dreamed of star travel since he was a young boy, watching the early seasons of *Sexy Space Rangers* (before the AI showrunners ran out of ideas and just rehashed old plotlines with celebrity guests). He had always thought Caledonia, the chief engineer of the star cruiser *Vanguard,* was the real heroine of the show for keeping the ship in good trim even though every week something broke down at the most dramatic possible moment. She was his role model, although he didn't think he would look as good in a tight miniskirt. The point was, OK thought space was cool, he thought spaceships were cool, all of it was cool except for the part where he would be washing up dishes for genocidal galactic tyrants.

The excitement wore off at some point during the two hours the shuttle was kept in a holding pattern due to what the pilot announced was "some sort of problem with the docking mechanism." But eventually, they were able to enter the landing bay of the training ship and disembark.

OK didn't care if he looked like a tourist as he gawked at the landing bay. It was his first time inside a starship, and even if it looked like a space-going parking garage he was still impressed by it. Next to the airlock was stenciled *Imperial Training Vessel S3-88906/T66 – Yao Wenyuan.* Below it was the ship's inspiring motto. "The voice of the Overlords shall prevail over the wind!"

The words felt like a command, a promise of something vast and unyielding awaiting inside—lectures, drills, maybe worse, all meant to forge him into the Horde's tool. He forced a neutral expression, hiding the spark of defiance in his chest.

They checked in at a desk occupied by a troll-like woman who seemed to resent their existence. "Report to Indoctrination Center Beta." They asked her how to get there and she responded by spitting at them. So, they wandered the ship's labyrinth of corridors until they found the training auditorium. It held were a hundred and fifty seats but only about thirty were occupied. Patriotic imperial music—a cacophony of blasting guitars and pounding drums— blasted from the sound system. The music halted for a safety announcement.

Horde Command reminds you that in the event of emergency, the ship's lifepods are for officers only. Any unauthorized use is punishable by immediate termination!

A woman took to the podium, around 40 standard years old, moderately attractive but making the best of what she had. "I am Death Lieutenant Viduus from Imperial Inhuman Resources. I'll be leading your orientation today. Does anyone not have their orientation packet? OK, I see three hands. If you will follow the enforcers into the corridor, you'll be taken care of. Off you go. Now then, this training course is for non-combat assets of the Horde. You will not be killing the enemies of the Imperium, but your work is still important, whether you a technico, a logistics specialist, or even a lowly kitchen sanitizer." She was interrupted by three distinct blaster shots from the corridor. "Reminder! Do not misplace your orientation packets! You will now give your full undivided attention to the indoctrination holofilm."

OK gripped his orientation packet until his knuckles turned white. The lights dimmed and the orientation holofilm opened with zooming spaceships, columns of marching Deathwalkers and heaving breasts (for some reason), accompanied by driving rock music and a title in blazing red letters.

"Welcome to the Scorpion Horde."

The title faded. A small rectangle appeared at the bottom of the screen.

"Brought to you by Black Scorpion Coffee – The Fuel of the Imperium."

An image faded in of a terra-class planet that even from space looked aloof and forbidding. Cold, gray nimbus clouds shrouded the planet in overcast save for a few ragged breaks of pale blue sky above jagged, shark-tooth mountains.

A deep male voice intoned, "Scorpius Prime—seat of the glorious Imperium of Greater Scorpius—founded some 900 hundred years ago by exiles fleeing the tyranny of the Old Earth, now rising to become the greatest power in the Orion Arm!" The holofilm panned out to a fleet of thousands of imperial starships; brutal looking cylinders, covered with armor save for some geometric cutouts on the side and pointy bits coming out the front.

"The ship you are on today is one of ten thousand in the invincible fleets of the Imperial Scorpion Horde. Your mission is to serve this mighty force. You are no longer a native of your weak and pathetic planet. You are a citizen of the Imperium of Greater Scorpius. Do as you are ordered with no hesitation and no mercy. The Imperium asks no more of you, and no less."

The hologram ended, and the training officer led them through a long presentation on properly filling in time reports. This was followed by another long presentation on the rather complicated Imperial benefits package. The health care plan was provided by the Scorpius Health Administration Ministry and covered all medical needs provided your Imperial social credit score justified maintaining your life. "Are there any questions?"

OK wanted to ask if benefits were deducted from his military salary of 1,000 Imperial Monetary Units per cycle but another inductee rose first. "Why is our rank Deathfinger? The soldiers are Deathwalkers and Death Runners. Shouldn't we be Death-crawlers, or something else ... *movement* oriented. You can't just arbitrarily go from a Death anatomy reference to a Death action verb. There's no consistency." He was promptly taken into the hall and shot. There were no further questions. Part of the secret of the Horde's success was preventing idiots from bogging down meetings with stupid questions.

The next instructor took the through the Scorpion Horde "Pincer" salute, which involved raising one arm straight up and out while making a sort of crab-claw with the hand. When the training group practiced it, they looked like they were raising a small crowd of invisible hand puppets. This was followed by an hour-long presentation on 'Ethical Behavior and How to Avoid It." Afterward, Viduus returned to the podium and concluded the orientation session. "Are there any questions?" Of course, there weren't.

Next, the group was taken to the ship's medical bay for blood and DNA sampling. After extracting half a liter of blood and several centimeters of skin from his upper arm, a stout unsmiling woman injected a bio-monitoring chip in OK's shoulder and a bionic communication link into his wrist. OK hugged his orientation packet to his chest through the whole painful ordeal.

From there, they were sent to the ship's quartermaster for their Horde uniforms. The quartermaster was a slight, tired, annoyed little man who issued them each two training uniforms, two regular uniforms, five pairs of underwear, and two sets of coveralls and aprons for sanitizing the food preparation areas; all wrapped in plastic. OK wondered what they were supposed to sleep in but was afraid to ask. The Quartermaster directed them to changing rooms and incinerated their former clothing.

Inside the changing room, OK turned on a holo-mirror and saw himself in an Imperial uniform for the first time; sort of a black coverall with a red scorpion over his left pectoral and his Horde serial numbers on the shoulder: OEK-085582-050K. There was a patch on the left sleeve reading "*Subutai* S3-117806/HCSV2" beneath the ship's crest of a scorpion driving a sword through a flaming skull. The right sleeve had the Red Fleet's motto, "Malevolence to All!" embroidered on it. The cap likewise had a flaming skull on it. The sight of himself in the livery of his oppressor shocked him. "This is not my uniform," he reminded himself. "It's my disguise."

Stoat emerged from the dressing room and admired himself in the holo-mirror. "This outfit looks amazing! And the fit is a dream! Look how slimming these buttons down the front are." The buttons were embossed with flaming skulls.

"That uniform represents terror and oppression across the entire galaxy."

Stoat was still admiring his reflection. "This uniform stands for power… respect. All the people who used to look down on us, if they were still alive to see us now, in these uniforms, they would have to show us respect."

"They'd be terrified," said OK.

"Terrified like insects fit to be crushed beneath our boots!" Stoat gave himself a turn to check out his backside. "But not these boots. They look smashing and I would hate to get insect guts all over them!"

"Driver… you're starting to scare me a little bit."

"You must learn to suppress that. If any of our fellow Imperials even suspect that you are less than completely loyal, you're going to go for a short walk into the hallway." A grin spread across Stoat's cheeks. "How was that? Do I sound like an Imperial? Or do I need more practice?"

"It sent shivers up my spine," OK assured him.

Beginning the next morning, OK and Stoat underwent grueling training in ship's operations. Their instructors were irate, battle-hardened men and women who favored them with a torrent of furious reprimands for even minor mistakes, like opening a radioactive plasma conduit instead of the bread cooker. The intense atmosphere made it clear that in the Scorpion Horde, there was no room for error; or maybe they just enjoyed shouting.

Their kitchen sanitation training centered around the dangerous mutant E. Coli bacterium. Part of it was in the form of an animated holo-film where the mutant E. Coli bacterium rapped about itself. *"Yo, yo, yo, it's your boy E. Coli, I'm a mutant strain/I'll get into your guts and cause you pain/ I'm a tough little bug, I ain't gonna lie, if I get into your blood, you're probably gonna die."*

There was also a short safety lecture about safely handling the various caustic and highly toxic chemicals used to eradicate the mutant E. Coli bacterium. They lost four members of their class to chemical mishandling.

To OK's tremendous disappointment, there was no instruction on weapons or military tactics; knowledge he could one day turn against the Imperium to avenge his conquered world. The Horde considered combat training non-essential to food service workers, which showed how little they understood the restaurant industry.

They also were forced to study *The Way of the Scorpion*, a quasi-religious text and the only legal belief system within the Imperium. On pre-war Katarina, it had been treated as something of a joke, like Jovian Scientology. Its text was impenetrable, essentially 200 pages of vague analogies between a desert arachnid of ancient Earth and the Overlords of Scorpius.

The scorpion is the master of survival, the champion of strife, resilient beyond measure, a creature so worthy of respect the ancients gave its name to the stars. The scorpion is the king of the desert realm, and like unto the overlords of the stars, the scorpion's venom is feared wherever it is known.

After thirty grueling days of relentless shouting, backbreaking labor, radiation exposure, and an alarming amount of body cavity probing, their training was finally complete. Cleared for transfer to the *Subutai*, they packed their belongings and made their way back to the landing bay. As they passed the same lecture hall where their ordeal had begun, they saw three new inductees being led into the corridor for losing their orientation packets. OK couldn't be sure, but they looked like the same ones from his own orientation.

Upon disembarkation in the *Subutai's* cavernous main landing bay, OK and Stoat were met by a quote glowering from the bulkhead above the airlock:

"They are the Four Wolves of Temujin. In the day of battle, they devour enemy flesh. Behold, they are now unleashed, and they slobber at the mouth with glee. These four dogs are Jebei, and Kublai, Jelme, and Subutai."

"They named the ship after a slobbering dog?" OK found the thought amusing. Stoat had no time for the history lesson, he was getting directions from the automated kiosk under the watchful… well, bored and disinterested … gaze of the ship's security enforcers.

Their assigned quarters were on Lower Crew Deck; Section U-13. There was a map next to the tube dock. The *Subutai's* internal structure was complicated but all sections could be reached via the central transport tube. The transport that arrived for them was a fat metal cylinder with built-in benches covered in well-worn, reddish-black, industrial carpet.

Stoat confidently tapped the Destination Panel. "Deck U-13, please."

"Brrrt, Brrrrk, Bllllt?" a voice responded.

"Deck U-13," Stoat repeated.

"Brrrt, Brrrrk, Breen?" Stoat scowled at the thing. "It's broken."

"It might be a problem with the vocal input processor," OK suggested Stoat try speaking clearly and slowly.

Stoat enunciated slowly. "Deck. U. As in Ultraviolet. Thir. Teen."

"Brrrrk, Brrt, Ultraviolet, Thirteen." The transport jerked into motion, knocking OK to the floor. It zipped through the ship's internal tube network, sometimes zipping along, sometimes grinding to a near halt, but it eventually found the way to deck U-13. The Deck Officer barely looked up from the holo-porn he was watching as he scanned their bond coins and waved them to their new home: Compartment 13-U-13—a tiny metal cell large enough for two stacked bunks, two small lockers, and a small desk with a holoscreen.

There was a door on the far side of the compartment that OK thought was a closet. He opened it to find a young woman sitting on a toilet who screamed at him, and he slammed the door shut again.

OK turned to Stoat. "There's a lady leaving a dump in our closet."

"It's not a closet; it's the hygiene unit we share with the next room."

OK tapped on the door. "Sorry about that. I thought it was a closet."

The door opened again, and the red-faced woman also offered an apology. "That compartment's been empty so long, I guess I've gotten lazy about locking the door." She offered a hand. "Qi'Anna."

"Did you wash up, because I didn't hear a sink?" said OK.

"Oh, don't mind him," Stoat interrupted. "I'm Driver. This is OK. We're Culinary Operations Hygienic Condition Supervisors."

"Kitchen sanitizers! Oh, I'm so glad they finally got some guys to do that," Qi'Anna's accent was an unfamiliar combination of harsh vowels and a nasty head cold. "With those Red Fleet squirts, I've been spending more time on the throne than I spend in my bunk."

"Don't be gross, Qi'Anna," called a similarly accented voice. Another woman came through the hygiene pod and introduced herself as Rue. OK would have described them as in the middle between plain and cute.

"What do you guys do?" OK asked.

"We're Death Support Technicos."

Before OK could call time-out on the Horde's insistence on appending "Death" onto everything, Rue explained. The *Subutai* carried 10,000 Deathwalkers in its trooper holds. Transporting a dead body in stasis took only 10% of the energy required to sustain a living body in suspended animation. So, when the Deathwalkers aren't needed, the Horde simply killed them and put their bodies in status. Which may have been where the name came from. It was Rue's and Qi'Anna's job to terminate their life functions, mind their cryo-chambers, and resurrect them as needed.

OK's jaw dropped open. "You mean all those Death Walkers are actually walking dead? And you … have the power of life and death over them?"

Qi'Anna shrugged. "Yeah, they call it 'Non-Life Stasis' or NLS. I was appalled at first, but after a few months of scream-myself-awake nightmares, it was just another job."

"How do you kill them?"

Qi'Anna and Rue made simultaneous gestures like flipping a switch. "Put 'em in a tank, click the red button. Easy as taking off your underwear."

Rue deadpanned. "Yes, that does come easily to her."

OK noted that information for future reference.

"So… I'm new to the Horde. How do I…?" OK tried to come up with a more diplomatic way to say, "cope with being a cog in a genocidal war machine of tyranny and terror" couldn't think of one and ended up saying something that sounded like *"hafffla fuh fla luhluhza."*

Somehow Qi'Anna and Rue understood. "The Horde ain't so bad. Just do what you gotta do. And whatever you do, stay away from FIST."

"FIST?"

"The Imperial secret police… fleet security. They are embedded everywhere and always looking for subversive influences."

OK managed a nervous chuckle. "Well, I'll make it a point not to be a subversive influence, then."

After some more conversation, the women wished them luck, said they should get drinks sometime, and retreated to their compartment. Stoat and OK decided to get rested before reporting for their first shift the next night.

OK lay on his hard bunk staring at the gray metal bulkhead. Well, here he was, in an Imperial bunk, on a Horde ship, wearing Horde pajamas that he had to pay for because they weren't part of the standard issue kit. Katarina was a million miles behind him, and he doubted he would ever see his home again. But here he was, a virus in the bloodstream of the Imperium. How would he make something of that and strike a blow for the rebellion?

He thought about the 10,000 Deathwalker carcasses in the hold. If he could get to them, he was pretty sure he could sabotage the containment pods and destroy the entire battalion. It wouldn't stop the Horde, but it would be a little bit of payback for what they had done to his world. He remembered that complicated map of the ship next to the transport station; a madman's labyrinth of corridors, blast doors, and trigger-happy enforcers standing between him and them. Qi'Anna could get in, of course. Perhaps he could somehow gain entry by seducing her. His mind rendered a tawdry and overly optimistic seduction scenario for him. And then he stopped thinking about the Imperium entirely. And then he fell asleep.

4.0   SCUM AND SCULLERY

OK and Stoat were ordered to report to Death Chief Socordia, the supervisor of the Lower Crew Ingestion Facility (LCIF). Their job was to clean and sanitize it before 2,000 lower crewmen came for their morning meal. They could smell the problem before they could see it; a septic stench, faint at first, but nostril-stinging by the time they reached the galley. The tables where the food was prepared were splotched with gobs of brownish green liquid, some of which had hardened into sticky black patches. The sinks were full of rotting veg and both putrid odors and swarms of tiny insects rose from the drains.

A woman shaped like a traffic bollard waddled toward them from the back of the hall, a deathstick pinched in her withered lips. She let it drop to the deck and didn't even bother to snuff it out. "You must be the new *drutt*-kickers from that *drutt*-ball of a planet they just bombed to *drutt*."

OK and Stoat snapped her the pincer salute. She barely acknowledged it. "I have one question for you *drutt*-brains. What is your job?"

They answered per their training. "Our job is to serve the Imperium, to do whatever is demanded for the glory of Greater Scorpius."

"Bull-furking-*drutt*!" she snarled back at them. "Your job is to clean this *drutt*-stain of a galley." OK could see that her curse vocabulary was limited. "You got six hours to make this *drutt* clean enough to pass inspection or else you two *drutt*-kickers are going to eat off the floor. Are my words penetrating the thick layer of *drutt* encasing your last two brain cells?"

Stoat answered with a sharp recitation of the military affirmative. "Ia! Ia!"

She leaned forward and her eyes narrowed to razor thin slits. "Prove to me you're worth the oxygen this ship's life support system makes to keep you alive, or I'll make you regret the day you joined the Horde."

"I…" Stoat began. Before he could get another word out, she picked a wet rag from the counter and threw it at them. They ducked just in time. "Stuff a glove in it! Cleaning supplies are in the back. Don't drink any!"

She turned and waddled away from them. "She seems nice," OK said when the hatch to the mess hall closed behind her.

Stoat tossed OK a pair of thick rubber gloves. "Find a scrubber. I'll work on the sink. Let's get to work and whip this place into shape."

"Get to work? *You?* The same guy who only took a job because signing on for universal basic income was too much hassle? You never lifted a towel at the bar. The kitchen was so dirty our cockroaches died of food poisoning. But you'll clean for the Horde? I *want* them to eat filth!"

Stoat was determined. "I have no intention of staying in this *furking* kitchen. Moving out means moving up. We've got to clean this place better than it's ever been cleaned before and get noticed. Now, grab that scrubber!"

They began peeling away the top layers of grime and dropping toxic chemicals down the drains to kill off the insects, before working on scraping away the geological strata of crud on the prep surfaces. Then, they attacked the cookers, which were encrusted with a mixture of old grease and carbonized organic matter that could have doubled as hull sealant. Before the morning arrived, they had managed to scrape off the worst of the filth, and the floor was just a few more vigorous cleaning assaults from not looking like the killing floor at a meat processing plant.

When the kitchen prep crew came shuffling in, they surveyed the cleaner-than-usual galley. One of them was a large, bald-headed man, who muttered. "Mother of Sorrows, someone's been busy in here." He extended a rough, meaty hand toward OK and Stoat. "I'm boss of the morning prep crew. My name's Roche." Under his lips were glints of gleaming bionic teeth.

He extended a mechanical hand. OK accepted the cold metal handshake. "I'm OK."

"You look OK, but I didn't ask."

"Now, I meant people call me OK. My name is Ogden Kevitch, but no one uses that, they just call me OK."

"If my name was Ogden, I'd go with OK, too." He shook his head. "Where were you before? What ship?"

"We weren't. We were on that planet that you guys just, um, invaded."

Roche looked like you had just told him cats could walk through walls; a colloquialism that only made sense within the context of folklore from the planet Katarina but its implication was that he had been shocked at an unlikely revelation. "They sent you straight to a second rank battle cruiser?"

"I guess so," OK replied. "Is that a problem?"

"I spent twenty years working my way up every shitcan in the fleet, and you got a second rank battle cruiser on the first draw?" He shook his large bald head. "Mother of Sorrows. Should have asked for the command ship."

"They said you needed kitchen sanitizers," OK tried to explain, but the morning crew was already getting to work making themselves a meal out of some of the better food and then set about preparing a meal for the crew out of the worse food. In the process, they managed to undo most of the cleaning he had done overnight. OK and Stoat ate with them, stayed behind to clean up, then returned to their compartment too exhausted to do anything but take a chemical shower and collapse into their bunks.

As they reported for their next shift, they entered the LCIF to see a Hygiene Technico running a scanner along the prep surface and examining the result. Stoat pushed OK against the wall and gestured to keep quiet.

The technico's tone was grim. "The bacteria count is within acceptable parameters ... barely. There's definitely improvement, but Death Lieutenant Collator was looking for more improvement than that."

Stoat silently mouthed the word *"Collator."*

Socordia protested. "Then she should send me better workers. You know I just get the *drutt*-lickers for kitchen help. The High Officer's mess gets the only workers smarter than room temperature. This *drutt*-hole is plenty clean enough for the lower crew."

They waited until the technico left and then stepped out. Socordia threw a wet rag at them. Gesturing at the cooker they had spent most of the previous night scraping, she shrieked. "Did you two pieces-of-*drutt* do this? You idiots. Are you too stupid to understand your *drutt*y job?"

"We did the best we could. We'll do better tonight," OK said, then asked himself. *"What am I saying? What do I care how clean this is?"*

Socordia glared. "You trying to make me look bad? Show me up? Your job is to wipe off the top and keep the bugs down. You got that?! You make it too clean, the officers will raise the standard then we'll all have to work harder."

OK cowered, but Stoat endured her tirade with a smile. "Ia! Ia!"

When she waddled away, he dropped the fake smile. *"Furk* her. I'm going to clean it even better tonight."

"First, why? the filth in this kitchen probably killed more Horde than the rebellion. Second, she'll send us to the cubicle of torment if we clean it too well. Seems like a lose-lose situation."

"No, she won't and you don't even know what the cubicle of torment is."

"I assume it's a cubicle where we will be tormented."

"Regardless, that nasty troll woman is in our way. We will never get out of this kitchen without getting past her. I saw something last night that could help us."

Stoat dragged out a floor-cleaning robot he found under a pile of Soylent boxes in the tool closet. ("Aha! This is the exact mechanoid I was looking for!") It could have doubled as a killbot. A quartet of arms with spinning blades protruded from the sides at accidental disembowelment height. A tiny sticker on the back advised "Use with caution. Or don't."

It wouldn't start until OK replaced its main field coil. Through sheer grit and determination, and occasional roll-dodges to avoid its whirling blades, he managed to strip the floor of several layers of grit and grime by the time the morning shift came on. Roche surveyed their handiwork. "Well, well, well, are you trying to make us all look bad or something?"

Socordia, predictably, was infuriated. She threw another wet rag at them then launched into an incandescently profane tirade. OK counted 25 uses of "*drutt*-kickers," 19 uses of "*drutt*-balls," 22 uses of "*drutt*-brains" and 11-other scatological insults. She closed with "There's worse jobs than cleaning my galley, sure as *drutt*, and you'll find yourself in them."

"Ia! Ia!" Stoat affirmed, and then, with the same calm tone, he went off on a tangent. "Chief, you have something under your eye." She probed under her eye with her finger. "No, your other eye. Oh, you got it, but it's by your mouth now. No, other side. Ia, you got it."

She glared at him, wiped her mouth bare hand, and then locked up the floor scrubber bots before she left.

"What was that about," OK said to Stoat when she left.

"All the yelling is just to hide her fear. Screaming is how she's gotten by so far. It's the only trick she knows. She's figured out it's not going to work this time, but she doesn't have any other tricks. So, she turns it up louder." He sighed and handed OK the rubber gloves. "Well, back to work."

That night, they set to work on the cold storage units. "Oh. Godless. Void" Stoat said when the doors opened. He dropped to his knees and began pawing through the hexagonal sci-fi storage containers. "This is supposed to be the food for tomorrow, look at it? It's stacked right next to the moldy old lab meat, which shouldn't be in here. And these vegetables? I've seen compost that looked better than this. And just look at those cockroaches!"

There were multi-legged alien insects scuttling among the filth. One of the larger ones climbed to the top of a pile of wilted black cabbage and waved two of its six legs. "Hey, how you doin'?"

There was considerable debate whether the existence of sapient cockroaches was a wayward genetic experiment or an evolutionary fluke that proved that the universe hates us. Most scientists agreed that space cockroaches were simple mimics and not sentient organisms; incapable of saying anything more than "Hey, how you doin'?" or quoting political slogans.

When they finished, the cold storage units and the rest of the galley could have passed a Kataranian Health Department inspection with only a light to moderate bribe. Which only served to throw Socordia into a volcanic fury, her face red and sweating, when they reported for their next shift.

"I know what you're doing," she raged at them. "You *drutt*-kickers are trying to make me look incompetent."

"How are we doing that?" Stoat asked.

"Shut up," she explained. "You're done. Over. Come tomorrow...." Socordia broke off. She took the deathstick out of her mouth and heaved into the sink. "Tomorrow, I'm shipping you pieces of *drutt* to the Omicron Nike."

"Does that mean we get the night off?" Stoat asked.

"Don't be smart," Socordia snapped, and then shuffled her mass away from them, hacking and coughing as she went.

"We're dead." OK said after the hatch closed behind her. Omicron Nike was a notorious labor colony where enslaved workers made boots and casual sports apparel the Imperium exported for hard currency.

Stoat seemed unconcerned as he put on his thick rubber cleaning gloves. "Let's give these floors another pass. I think I can break into the locker where she locked up your robot."

OK had named the floor scrubber bot "Scrubby."

"Why bother?" OK protested. He had a terrifying feeling his efforts to rebel would end with him on an Imperial labor planet.

Stoat pushed a pile of cleaning rags into a waste bin. "Don't worry about it. We're not going anywhere."

"Haven't you been paying attention?"

"More than you know," Stoat answered. "I would bet you a cycle of wages we won't be sent to a labor planet, but honestly that wouldn't be fair to you."

"What do you mean? What do you know?"

"Do you want to take the bet?" Stoat had that weird aura of calm he got when he was up to something. He could be incredibly persuasive in this mode which was how OK ended up spray-painting "Constable Talus has a miniscule phallus" on a Tranquility Highway overpass at three in the morning after a parking ticket dispute. Stoat tended to get away with stupid stunts simply because he believed he could. "I didn't think so. Start cleaning the cookers."

"What are you going to do?"

"I am going to bake a cake." He went into the larder to find sugar and flour. Either he was up to something or he had gone insane.

"He's up to something," OK concluded, and got back to work. He reminded himself to trust the plan but nevertheless spent the rest of the night scrubbing, dodging the hazardous robot, and wondering what Stoat was up to.

Just as the morning kitchen crew arrived, Stoat wheeled out a sheet cake with "Goodbye" in bright red lettering across the center. He positioned the cake trolley at the front of the kitchen.

"What's that for?" Roche asked when the morning crew arrived.

"We're being fired," OK told him.

Roche just shook his head. "Yeah, I figured you guys were jetsam. Should've warned you—the chief runs on her own set of protocols. You weren't the first guys she spaced. Sorry to see you go."

"Don't count on it," Stoat said, swatting his hand away from the cake.

Socordia returned as they were cleaning up breakfast, wheezing and stumbling into the LCIF. She looked deathly, even for her. Accompanying her was a very thin woman with pale skin and platinum-blond hair. A pair of young men holding administrative data pads trailed in her wake.

The blond woman announced herself for OK and Stoat's benefit, "Death Lieutenant Collator, Chief of Crew Services. Your supervisory officer has referred you for reassignment based on unsatisfactory performance."

Socordia coughed wetly, her complexion was gray, her voice came as a sickly rasp. "Get them... (cough) ... get them off my kitchen."

"Don't you want to inspect the kitchen first?" Stoat suggested. "We've been working ever so hard. You can consider it a surprise inspection." Had that been Stoat's plan all along? Show the officer in charge you did a good job? It was just sane and reasonable enough to work.

Collator warmed to the idea. "Surprise inspection. Why not?" Socordia tried to protest but was unable to due to a hacking cough. Stoat smiled. Collator and her aides strode through the galley. They scanned. She caressed the tops of the prep tables with her white-gloved fingertips.

"Clean," she muttered.

She ordered her aide to get down on her knees and check the floor. "They look pretty good, Ia." Collator then inspected the cold storage units, where all the food supplies had been sorted and dated. "Scan for sapient cockroaches."

Her assistant whipped out a small device that shined a dazzling light around the prep area. "All clear, Ia."

Collator was impressed. "This is the cleanest this galley has been since I was assigned to this ship. Tell me, why you want these men sent to an internment production facility?"

Socordia's blood pressure surged and the mushroom gray pallor of her face blended into the fiery red hues of an overloading reactor. "You don't see how insubordinate they are..." Amidst sputters, she managed to rasp, "You don't... you don't see how they disrespect me..."

The words barely escaped her before she doubled over, engulfed in a tumultuous fit of wet coughing and diarrhea. Straightening up with an effort, she appeared to recover for a fleeting moment before stumbling again.

"They disrespected... me," she gasped before collapsing face first into Stoat's cake.

Stoat moved to the fore and held the crowd back. "Stay back, stay back, everyone... give her air to breathe." He rolled her over and loosened the collar on her uniform.

"Medico to Lower Crew Ingestion Facility," Collator's aide said into his comm unit.

The medicos arrived thirty-five minutes later. By then it was too late. "She's dead," the medico confirmed. He jabbed a sensor into one of her fat folds. "Mutant Escherichia coli... positive result. Unfit for recycling." The Medicos hefted the body onto an antigravity cart.

The shocked kitchen crew had figured out the diagnosis about twenty minutes before the medicos arrived. Murmurs and whispers rippled through the crowd—a peculiar mix of relief at being freed from their shared burden, tempered by the need to feign grief. Some even buried their faces in their sleeves, shaking just enough to pass off their laughter as sobs.

Stoat stood up on a table. "Everyone, please, this is a learning moment. We will never ever know how exactly this woman became infected with mutant e. Coli, but we can be sure at some point in the chain she was exposed through cross-contamination. We all know the danger! You pick up a contaminated rag, then you touch food, or your face, and the contamination spreads. Let this woman's tragic death be a reminder and a memorial of the importance of kitchen hygiene and safety procedures."

Collator made a few notes on the device she wore on her wrist. "Very impressive, Deathfinger Stoat," she told him when he had finished. "That showed tremendous leadership. The LCIF chamber is going to need a new chief. Based on what I've seen, I think you're the right man for the job."

"What the..." muttered a voice that OK recognized as Roche.

"I think this is a two-man job," Stoat said, nudging OK. "How about an assistant chief." Collator agreed and ordered an aide to start the paperwork immediately.

"Thank you, Ia. Hail to the Imperial Victory!" Stoat shouted, raising a pincer claw salute.

And just like that, after less than a cycle on the ship, they were already promoted. Also, Stoat could claim credit for the first enemy kill; even if it was a mean and unhealthy woman and Stoat denied having anything to do with her demise. "It was the mutant E. coli that killed her, and her habit of throwing filthy rags at people who were just trying to do our jobs."

5.0   BREAKFAST AT STAR-KILLER'S

About half a parsec from Katarina was a binary, red dwarf star system. The Kataranians called them the "Angels of the Morning" because they rose just before sunrise. The twin stars featured prominently in the planet's poetry and songs. Couples proposed beneath them, believing it would bring them long-lasting love. OK had once tried to sneak a kiss from Anya beneath those stars and she punched him right in the nose. The Red Scorpion Fleet was going to tear them apart and harvest their stellar core plasma for starship fuel.

"I can't believe they're going to eat a sun," OK muttered to Roche as they scrubbed the mess after the morning meal service. "Isn't it dangerous, drawing off fuel directly from a star?"

Roach had been through a few stellar mining operations during his years with the fleet. "Not too much really. Sometimes the star collapses and they lose a few ships. Hardly ever a big heavy cruiser like the *Subutai*. We'll probably get some radiation spikes in the outer decks, but that's about it."

"I should stay away from the outer decks then."

"If you want to keep your hair and teeth. And the gravity fluctuations are gonna rock you like a hurricane."

OK wondered aloud, "Do these ships use Quantum Hyperflex or Fast Neutron Expulsion for their star drives? I couldn't find anything on I2N (the Imperial Infotainment Nexus), but it's probably one of them because they both use stellar plasma as fuel."

Roche cut him right off. "Don't you even talk about Imperial warship systems. If a FIST hears you, you'll go straight to the cubicle of torment."

Another Imperial secret he must learn!

After countless shifts cleaning the mess hall side-by-side, OK had begun to forge a camaraderie with Roche. He had even learned his first name, which was Quanto. Roche had served on several ships over his twenty+ years in the Horde, all of them far worse than the *Subutai*. To hear him tell it, every ship below third rank battle cruiser was a deathtrap of radiation leaks and hull fractures held together by gravitic tape and sheer terror.

His worst assignment ("hands down") was on the *Mariam*, a very old gunship that bled radiation and left a trail of hull debris wherever it went. Its reactor imploded during the battle of Carpathia. Roche barely made it to an escape pod and lost an arm in the process, hence the mechanical prosthetic. After being rescued by the cruiser *Nuon Chae*, he was disciplined for abandoning his post and sentenced to three cycles in the Cubicle of Torment.

Roche seemed like a good guy, and he seemed to have no love for the Imperium. If he were going to find the resistance, sooner or later he would have to start asking. OK summoned his courage, "You don't care much for the Horde, do you?"

"I didn't say that!" Roche insisted and turned furiously back to his table wiping. "I am loyal to the Horde! Damn loyal! Hail to the Ultimate Victory!"

OK remembered that the bond coins recorded everything. "Of course you are, I didn't mean it that way." OK tried to think if there was some other way to mean it. "I meant, have you ever heard of someone, or maybe a group of people in the crew, who don't care for the Imperium."

"If I did, I would do my duty and report them immediately to FIST!" Roche was rattled. He didn't talk to OK for the rest of the shift. OK realized he would have to be careful if he was going to find a fifth column on the *Subutai*.

Qi'Anna and Rue didn't blame Roche for being suspicious. Turning a crewmate into FIST for subversive activities was worth social credit points. Nevertheless, they didn't like Roche much and trusted him less.

"Why not? What's wrong with him?"

"He's been in the Horde twenty plus years. Nobody stays in the Horde that long. You either get killed or put in your ten years and leave."

"And I've never slept with him," Qi'Anna added. Rue suggested that this was reason enough to think there was something not-right about him. Qi'Anna and Rue were only four years away from finishing their ten years.

"Then, what?" OK asked.

"I might go to work at one of the birth farms," Rue said. "Taking care of the babies after they come out of the gestation tubes." Kind of the exact opposite of what she was doing now.

"You know where else I would like to go?" Rue mused, lighting a deathstick and letting its acrid smoke encircle her head. "Earth!"

"Oh, you and Earth again. Come on, Earth's a *drutt*-hole."

"I didn't say I wanted to live there, I just want to visit the Galactic Federation cube in Sarajevo, see the ruins of Toronto, and then some shopping at the Mercantile Hyper-mall in Pyongyang. And the Global Extinction Memorial in the ruins of ancient Dubai."

"Sure, go there and shake a memorial glow-stick with the other tourists."

"They say all Earthlings are sexual degenerates," OK put in, causing Qi'Anna to go "Hmm" with a dreamy expression on her face.

Qi'Anna and Rue ignited more death-sticks and talked at length about their home planet of Pakkaria II, a planet of long, bleak winters that drained the inhabitants of hope and comfort. They smoked death-sticks and went into dramatically detailed critiques of their planet's sports teams until OK got bored and returned to his bunk.

Thousands of Horde ships closed in on the red stars like a pack of star wolves about to tear into a wounded space moose. As the gigantic star-crackers began charging the anti-proton streams that would skin the stars, the Death Commander in Charge of Lower Personnel finally signed off on Stoat and OK's promotions. The bronze skulls on their uniforms were upgraded to copper. They also received 100-point bumps in their Scorpion Social Credit Scores, and access to the waitlist for any available lifepods in the event of emergency once the officers had evacuated.

OK buttoned his new work smock; his new camouflage as he played the part of a loyal Horde crewman. Someday, somehow, he would strike a blow for the rebellion or break free and join them. But for now, he would wait, and watch, and listen.

On his first day in charge, Stoat gathered the workforce into the mess hall and gave them the inspiring speech he had been preparing even before Lt. Collator offered the promotion. "Listen up, everyone. Two hours from now, those doors are going to open and hundreds of your fellow lower crewmen are going to come through expecting a good meal at a clean table..."

"Oh, haven't they been here before?" some wag called out.

"No more talk like that!" Stoat snapped over the ensuing laughter. "The Lower Crew mess hall is under new management. I'm in charge of this galley, now, and we're going to serve good food from a clean kitchen."

This was apparently funnier than the "haven't they been here before" heckle. The grunts and guffaws that rose above the tables told him none of the kitchen crew intended to help him. That was half the challenge. The other half was the quality of the ingredients the Horde provided the lower crew.

Stoat sorted through the inferior grade supplies in the cold storage unit. "Stale bread, wilted veg, mystery meat… there's only so much I can do with these ingredients."

"Why do we want to make better food?" OK argued. "They're Scorps. And besides that, they're used to bad food."

"I don't intend to stay in this kitchen, and neither should you. You joined the Horde for a reason, but there's not much you can do from a lower crew mess hall. We have to move up and that means doing a good enough job to get noticed. It's not the worst thing you'll have to do, believe that!"

OK remembered seeing a food fabricator stowed away in the back of a food locker behind a crate of something called "Hamdingers." It wasn't working but he was sure he could fix it.

"That won't help much," Stoat lamented. "We need to get better quality ingredients if we're going to make better food. And I can only think of one way to do it."

Stoat handed him his pay-marker. "Here's everything I've earned since we signed on with the Imperium, including my signing bonus, my recreation center passes, and my Deathfinger of the Cycle bonus." He had won that for cleaning the kitchen. OK had gotten a little gold skull sticker, but no money. "Go find the ship's supply officer, Buzzcock or something, I think his name is. Find out how much he needs to send us some better-quality food."

"Bribe him? I am pretty sure that's not legal."

"Since when do you care about Imperial Law? If you get in trouble, just tell them you're just a dumb hick from a backward planet and you thought you had to buy the supplies out of your own pocket. They'll believe it."

"They probably will, but I would hate validating their prejudices."

Supply Chief Boskirk proved to be a tall fellow with shaggy black hair and a face like a primitive hominid who had been in a lot of bar fights. "What you want? Who sent you?" He barked in an unplaceable accent. He perked up when OK offered up Stoat's pay marker. "Oh, hai, let's make business, hunh?"

The bribe was enough to secure fresh bread, vegetables, and lab-meat that had been intended for the officers' mess. Stoat and the food preparation crew made them into sandwiches for the lunch service, which went over well with the crew. Meanwhile, OK got the food fabricator to work; but initially it was unable to produce anything but tofu, marzipan, and some sort of disgusting orange nodules called "Circus Peanuts."

"Attention Officers and Lower Crew: The *Subutai* will be entering the Photosphere in eighty death minutes. Decks O and B have been sealed. Deck A Sections 2 through 22 have been sealed. You may cower in the most interior deck possible until further advisement. hail to the Imperium."

The star-harvest began a few days later. OK expected to feel warm but insulated deep within the ship's armor, he felt no change even as the *Subutai* moved in to devour the star's core. Thousands of other ships joined them, their hulls burnished bronze by the bleeding light of the wounded star. When they had consumed enough of its mass, the red dwarf would blow apart in a series of thermonuclear explosions. This would be the most dangerous phase of the operation.

Down in the LCIF, the lower crew enjoyed a Lightspeed Lasagna dinner and then an Antarean Taco Night courtesy of another bribe. The crew was leaving satisfied, but Stoat despaired, "We're almost out of the good food, and I don't have any more money or rec passes." He grabbed OK by the shoulders. "We'll have to use your money."

"Use my money? To buy food for Scorps?"

"Right, we ran out of mine, now we have to use yours. Just like back on Katarina when we did bar crawls." OK never understood why they kept doing them after they owned their own bar. "Market research," Stoat had called it.

OK was not prepared to spend his own money to feed the enemy. Stoat, of course, had a counter argument. "This isn't for them, it's for us. If we're going to get to the next level, we have to get a reputation for being the best. And it wouldn't hurt to get to know Boskirk, he might have knowledge that would be useful to you." Boskirk was probably involved in all sorts of illicit activities, but OK doubted they extended to the Rebel Pact.

"There must be another way. The food fabricator is working better. I got it to make dog food the other day."

"If I serve chili again, the crew's going to get suspicious."

Stoat ultimately prevailed, and OK took his pay marker to Boskirk to secure another cycle's worth of supplies. "You become my favorite customer, hunh? Anyway, how is your sex life?"

Declining to describe his sex like, OK answered, "I don't know if I will be your best customer any longer, I just gave you my last IMU."

Boskirk scratched his greasy temple. "Well, that's no good. Crew is going to be disappointed when you're back to serving the regular stuff, hunh?"

"Probably," OK admitted.

"Well, maybe I think of a way for the two us to come to arrangement of mutual satisfaction, hunh?"

OK hoped he wasn't implying the first thing he thought he was implying because if he was, Stoat would find a way to talk him into it. If it would help the rebellion, he could always lie back and think of Katarina.

"Attention Officers and Lower Crew: Decks A, B, and Below M Level are no longer habitable due to Radiation Levels. Stellar Core Refueling will continue until complete. Hail to the Empire."

OK and Roche were stowing kitchen equipment a few days later as the star began its final collapse. The ship rocked and tossed. One violent sidewise lurch knocked containers of sporks fell off the shelf and they scattered and danced on the floor of the compartment.

"I told you it gets a little rough." Roche grinned, bracing himself and advising OK to do the same. The reason wasn't apparent at first, but it came suddenly. There was a deep, prolonged rumble, as within a storm cloud spawning thunder. Then, the shockwaves hit, and the ship dipped and rolled wildly for several long minutes. OK threw up into the mop sink. Roach laughed. "That was nothing. You should try this on an astro-knocker."

As the Horde ships drained the last energy from the stellar core, it became an unstable mass of nuclear fire that ignited in a massive nova. The remnant of the other binary star absorbed the blasts from its companion until it also destabilized and exploded. Freed from their gravitational tether, the asteroids and planets of the system caromed across the cosmos like wild shots from a cosmic slingshot. Some of the larger asteroids would travel across thousands of light years to cause extinction level events on faraway worlds in the far distant future. This was the reason that stellar core mining was strictly regulated everywhere else in the Galactic Commonwealth.

"Attention Officers and Lower Crew: The *Subutai* has completed primary refueling procedure. Decks A, B, and Z remain forbidden pending radiation assessment and decontamination. Hail to the Imperial Victory."

Several ships suffered hull damage during the blow-out, and the crew of the *Bosco Ntaganda* died after their radiation shielding failed. OK overheard in the LCIF that once repairs were complete, the fleet would mobilize for another planetary conquest. He lamented there was no way for him to warn whatever world was the target.

Stoat was confronting a dilemma of his own as he tore through the cold storage unit, opening lockers and slamming them shut again. "There's nothing! Nothing! There's no bread. No vegetables. No lab meat."

"The fabricator can make pudding now."

"The fabricator is pointless." He grabbed OK by the collar. "I can't make a meal out of pudding, dog food, and Circus Peanuts. There must be something left we can barter for real food with."

"All my money's gone," OK told him.

"Rec passes?"

"All gone."

"We must have something," Stoat insisted.

"We don't."

"You're friendly with those two women who share our hygiene unit. Do you think they would…?"

"I'm not going to ask Qi'Anna for money."

"Do you think would be willing to trade sex for food?"

"Not for us she wouldn't."

Stoat sighed. "I can only think of one more move. We'll have go to Boskirk and try to talk him into a loan arrangement."

Boskirk proved to be as unwilling to extend credit as the Scorpion Horde was to extend mercy. But he did offer them a proposition. "Maybe I help you out, hunh? Do you know, what you call, Dayglo orange?"

"Dayglo Orange? The highly addictive narcotic beverage made from orange peels and reactor coolant that's expressly forbidden aboard Horde naval vessels? That Dayglo orange?"

OK had never heard of it. He wasn't surprised Stoat had.

"So, my situation is, I have a distribution network, hunh, but not so much sufficient product, you know? I use your cold storage unit for processing and fermentation, hunh? You help me make Dayglo orange, I make sure better supplies go directly to lower crew kitchen?"

"Deal!" Stoat agreed, before OK could get in any kind of objection.

Boskirk turned to the puffy, bleach-blond woman at his side. "See, I told you it would work out. I think of everything."

"What happens if we get caught?" OK wondered, even though Stoat's look told him it was already too late to worry about that.

"Probably, they toss you through airlock, but that probably not happen. Trust me, hunh? This is probably very good deal for you. I come by tomorrow with recipe and orange peels. Come on, Liisa, we go back to my room now and make love, hunh?"

Stoat heaved a sigh of relief as the man left. "Well done cultivating a rapport with him. You just saved our necks."

"Or gave the Horde a noose to hang us with," OK thought. Metaphorically, of course, the Horde would never execute prisoners with anything so merciful as a twisted coil of rough rope.

In his quarters that night, OK reflected that his private insurgency so far consisted of making sure the Horde were fed better food prepared in a more sanitary kitchen. His intentions were good, but his actions were paving the road to hell for countless innocents. The *Subutai* was fully fueled from consuming the Angels of the Morning; and OK would soon taste the horrors of Imperial conquest from the other side.

6.0   BURNING THE POLAROIDS

"Attention officers and lower crew of the *Subutai*: The Precision Enhanced Navigation Interplexing System has successfully thrust the fleet into its destination. Prepare for the victorious integration of new worlds into the Glorious Imperium of Greater Scorpius."

OK pressed the link to learn more about the system they were about to invade. It was called Duohelion. It held two inhabited planets: Perihelion and Aphelion. Perihelion was closer to the sun than Aphelion. Its vast desert regions extended for thousands of kilometers along the equator, marked by towering sand dunes, rocky landscapes, and sizzling temperatures that made them inhospitable to most forms of life. Most of the population resided in the temperate zones surrounding the poles. There were bouncy, animated graphics conveying this point, with arrows pointing at a graphic depiction of the planet. An arrow pointed at the equator was labeled "Burning Hot Desert!" and two at the polar regions, "Population Centers!"

Aphelion was farther out; its polar regions and much of the higher latitudes were frozen covered in glaciers and tundra (as indicated by arrows labeled "Brrrr!"). Most of its population lived in the temperate belt around the equator, as indicated by the arrow reading "Most of the Population Lives Here in the Temperate Belt Around the Equator."

Perihelion and Aphelion were colonized at the same time. They shared similar cultures, forms of government, and economic development levels. All of which bred a fierce interplanetary hatred, even to the point of coining ethnic slurs that meant nothing anywhere else in the galaxy. "Crotching Girdlers!" the Perihelionians would shout at the Aphelionans. "Gurking Polaroids!" the Aphelionians would scream back every four years at the interplanetary isokinetic kickball tournaments.

They also exchanged highly offensive jokes such as "How do you greet a genius on Perihelion? 'Hello, Off-worlder.'" Or "How many Aphelionans does it take to change an illumination bulb? None, because if it's shaped like a bottle, the Aphelionian will try to drink it."

Their interplanetary rivalry wouldn't mean much anymore, OK thought. They would soon be united and shouting "Hail to the Imperium," or they would refuse to do that and be mass murdered.

He got up, checked that the hygiene pod was free, and took a rapid Imperial shower where a bunch of nozzles fired high-velocity sanitizing chemicals at him. He dried himself off and put on his kitchen smock.

Collator was waiting for them when OK and Stoat arrived for the morning shift. "Deathfingers, I just wanted you to know, I've processed the most recent crew satisfaction surveys for the LCIF. Your rating for this cycle is … Adequate Plus."

"Adequate plus," Stoat repeated. "Is that good, Ia?"

"It's better than any previous assessment of the LCIF. Also, according to the survey, the food in the LCIF has received its highest rating in the last six years. Not vomitous."

"What did it rate before we came along?" Stoat asked.

"Vomitous," she reported. "I wanted to pass along the results, express Fleet Command's approval with your performance, and present you with a new assignment."

Stoat rose to the occasion. "A new opportunity? I look forward to hearing what it is. Give me a moment to savor the anticipation before you tell me." He inhaled deeply, then slowly let it out. "All right, I am ready."

"There is a custom on the *Subutai*. When we welcome a new system into the Glorious Imperium of Greater Scorpius, the off-duty officers gather in the observation deck to observe the operation from space. It's a momentous event, and the view from orbit is not one to be missed. I want you two to attend the observation as serving staff."

We're going to be serving drinks while the Imperium destroys a world, The thought hit him like a blow to the chest. His heart lurched. A sick tremor ran up his neck. He had seen the horrors the Imperium inflicted on his own world. He couldn't imagine having to watch another world … two worlds… suffer that terrible fate; let alone serve drinks to the invaders.

"Should we wear our dress uniforms?" he heard Stoat ask.

"You'll be issued special kit for the occasion. You will report directly to me on the night of the operation. I cannot tell you when it will begin, that's classified. Just be ready to report on an hour's notice."

When she was gone, OK turned to Stoat. "They're about to invade another free world."

"Apparently so."

"Shouldn't we do something?"

"We are going to do something, Friend-o. We're going to serve drinks to the ship's officers while they watch the invasion."

"You know what I meant! Millions of people are going to die! Another system is about to be enslaved under the Imperium! And we're just supposed to serve cosmic cocktails to the people who are doing it!"

"What can we do? Talk them out of it? We're just a couple of bartenders. As abhorrent as it is, we need to put on a good front and do our jobs. Our time will come. Trust the plan!"

OK reluctantly agreed, only because he didn't see any alternative.

They showed up to the Observation Deck at the appointed hour in the required uniform of silky black blouses and red fezzes. OK harbored a visceral disdain for the fez, a felt-wrapped talisman of Imperial humiliation.

The armored battle shields rumbled as they retracted from the observation dome. Beyond the thick transparent aluminum barrier loomed the vast and deadly armada of Horde warships, a predatory swarm converging upon their unsuspecting prey. Squadrons of death fighters flew ahead of the fleet to probe Perihelion's orbital defenses. Perihelion, a dirty marble lost in the distance, awaited its doom.

The officers began gathering a few hours before the invasion to make sure they got good seats. Stoat had practiced mixing Martian Mojitos, Sex on the Warp Core Breaches, Antarean Fanny Bangers, and other trendy cocktails. But the high officers turned out to have simpler tastes. "Bring us a round of Scorpion IPAs and shots of Serpentarian Tequila," was the typical order.

"It would serve them right if a rebel ship smashed through the ultra-glass and all of them were blown out into space," OK thought. As much as he relished the image of such cosmic justice, he knew it meant he would be seeing his ship from the outside as well.

He alternated between working at the bar and trucking drinks from table to table as the machinery of interstellar conquest deployed in the space outside. The juxtaposition of Imperial jingoism and barroom banter created a work environment that was both macabre and absurdist, a twist of dark humor served on the rocks of impending oblivion.

As the fleet approached Perihelion, a media ship broadcast the customary demand for surrender speech from Deathlord Damocles to the two worlds. Seated on throne of skulls, wearing gleaming black battle armor, his head covered by a shining helmet styled as a demonic carapace, with horns curving around the ears, he addressed his conquests.

"Perihelion and Aphelion. Make no mistake, your defeat is assured. Expend this last night of your former life in pursuit of degenerate pleasures or perhaps enacting final vengeance on those who wronged you. Do not waste your energy raising weapons against us. When the sun rises, those who survive will find only ashes and desolation. Let me be clear. We will burn the weakness from your world with a purifying fire! Those we permit to survive will assume their proper, supine positions beneath the Imperium of Greater Scorpius! Don't think of this as a conquest; it is the blazing dawn of a new era where your feeble notions of autonomy shall be extinguished, replaced by the omnipotent dominion of our unrelenting rule."

On one of the screens, a distinguished looking middle-aged man and a female with bleach-blonde, blown-out hair appeared. These were the announcers for "Firefight Live," a broadcast from one of the media ships that would provide live commentary of the battle to the fleet (and transmit an edited version a few days later to the rest of the galaxy).

The male announcer looked into the holo-camera and spoke with a voice that exuded gravitas and authority. "That was Deathlord Damocles, the Sword That Hangs Over Your Head, giving the people of Perihelion and Aphelion a final opportunity to surrender."

"As always, a powerful speech," the blond woman agreed, in a bubbly contralto. "Let us rise and give praise to Deathlord Damocles!"

The room stood and applauded for a long time because no one wanted to be the first to stop applauding. There was a story about an officer being dispatched to the ice mines of Goljrorlof VI for being the first to cease clapping when Damocles spoke. The story was apocryphal; but the officers weren't taking any chances.

Amid the applause—a statuesque woman entered the observation lounge. She wore a sharp black leather uniform that spanned the banks of utility and style. Her hair was pulled into a ponytail that pooled at the back of her neck like wet black ink. She had heterochromatic irises; one was ice blue like the eye of a sled dog, the other silver and bionic. One eye said, "I'll lead you through the snowy wilderness," while the other declared, "And calculate the trajectory of your inevitable slip on the ice."

She went straight to OK's station at the bar. "There's a bottle of Black Scorpion Vodka at the back of the shelf on the right. Bring it to me." Her voice resonated with authority and world-weariness; the voice of someone who had seen every horror the Imperium could dish out and was already bored with it.

OK found the vodka under the bar and pulled a pair of shot glasses from the shelf. He began to pour, but she cut him off. "Leave the bottle." OK did as he was ordered. "You're new here. Deathfinger Ogden Kevitch, formerly of the planet Katarina. Usually, you go by your initials, partly because you never cared for your name, and partly because it gives you a sense of affirmation when people call you that."

"How did you know all that?"

"Bio-cybernetic link to the crew personnel files. Congratulations on your successful hygienic restoration of the lower crew mess hall, by the way."

Play it cool, OK told himself. "If I had one of those, it would tell me your name, as well."

"Death Colonel Lena Morrigan—MAD."

"Mad about what?"

"Military Analytics Division. Scorpion Horde Intelligence."

OK almost dropped the shot glasses. He finally noticed the emblem on her lapel, a silver skull with swords jammed into its eye sockets. Once more, he had to give credit to the design team behind the Horde's iconography.

"Don't soil yourself, Deathfinger. I just came for the drinks."

A Scorp intelligence officer might share secrets if she loosened up, OK thought. "Let me make one of my specials for you, on the house. Black vodka, blackberry liqueur, and charcoal. I call it a black hole martini, but you Scorps will probably call it a death something or other…" To his horror, he realized he had used the pejorative.

"You mean 'us Scorps,' you're one of us now."

No, I'm not, he told himself. Out loud, he said "Of course."

She passed on the cocktail explaining that she only drank straight liquor. "You've never seen an Imperial conquest before, have you Deathfinger?"

"I've seen one from the receiving end."

"I lost count after 63."

How old is she? OK wondered. She must have been telepathic because she answered. "I am 107 years old. I've been inhabiting this cloned body for the last sixteen."

OK didn't know much about cloning, but he knew quality clone-work was costly. The Cancri did a brisque business in discount, knock-off clones, but they were notorious for shipping defective units with missing parts and for their cloned organs breaking down rapidly once the warranty expired. Her body looked like the product of one of the superior Clonus facilities, accessible only to the Imperial elite.

"Those of us who have earned the reward of life extension take it. We know if there's a hell, it's got a room reserved for us."

What an odd thing to say. OK didn't have time to ponder her philosophy before he had to leave and serve drinks to a raucous group of junior officers who smacked the fez off his head and laughed at him.

The observation deck had gotten crowded. Bloodthirsty Horde officers jostled for position around the viewports and holoscreens showing highlights of earlier invasions; mighty Imperial battleships on the move and trans-orbital warheads obliterating cities synced to provocative orchestral scores to create a patriotic fervor from your heart to your balls.

Suddenly, the holoscreens flashed "Flaming Skull News Alert." The announcers appeared again. "The High Council of Aphelion has requested to negotiate an accommodation with the Imperium."

"Just get on with it!" One of the officers called out, seconded by a round of cheers.

OK asked Morrigan. "What's going on? Are they surrendering?"

"They are offering a conditional surrender, a desperate gambit from a world that can read the bloodstains on the wall. Damocles will reject it."

"He will attack anyway even though they surrender?"

"Is this your first day here? When the only tool you have is massive overwhelming force, every problem looks like a weak, quivering world fit only to be crushed beneath Imperial might."

A short while later, the Perihelion transmitted their response to the Horde. "The proud people of Perihelion refuse to surrender and will fight to preserve our independence."

"I can't see that working out well for them, Don."

"Neither can I," heckled one of the officers, evoking laughter from his table. The laughter amplified when the other host echoed the sentiment. "Neither do I Carol. Perihelion just volunteered for annihilation."

"This just in. We've just received word Deathlord Damocles has ordered the Heavy Armored Cruisers to engage the planet's weak and pitiful defenses."

"So, it's starting, Don?"

"Yeah, it's starting, Carol." The lounge erupted in cheers, and a spontaneous round of the Horde Attack Song broke out.

> *The planet, the planet, the plane's on fire!*
> *We don't need no water, let the puny, inferior planet burn,*
> *Burn, inferior planet, burn!*

The song, and its next four increasingly violent and explicit verses, drowned out a report about orbital battle stations surrounding Perihelion. Tracking cameras showed the armored tank ships at the forefront of the attack absorbing fire. Assault ships broke out from behind them to make attack runs, blasting the stations with missiles while dodging the stations' railguns.

Morrigan said something to OK that scared the shit out of him. "I sense your doubts about the Imperium and your place in it."

OK choked. He tried to shout "Hail to the Imperial Victory," but in his moment of terror, he could not even bring those words to mind. The best he could do was *"Hail... something ... and the Imperium!"*

"Doubts are not uncommon among the newly recruited, but you should learn to block them out. The easiest way is to use an earworm."

"What's that?"

"You don't know what an earworm is?" He shook his head. "The word has two meanings. There is a literal earworm we put into the Eustachian tubes of captured prisoners. They eat their way through the ear canal to the brain. It's excruciating pain beyond anything you can imagine."

"It sounds dreadful," OK agreed. "But I bet it gets them to talk."

"Not really, they can't hear the questions. The other earworm is a song or a melody you can't get out of your head. It displaces the thoughts in the front of your mind. The only thing a telepath will pick up is that annoying song."

"Like the Hubba-Hubba-Froot-a Froot-a jingle," OK said, then wished he hadn't because now it was all he could think about. *"Hubba Hubba. Fruit-a. Fruit-a. Put it in your mouth, and it goes Oofa Oofa Hooly Hooly."*

"Stop thinking about that," she ordered him.

"I'm trying," OK insisted.

"There's nothing wrong with having doubts, Deathfinger. Only a sociopath never questions his place in the universe."

OK felt a sharp jab on his shoulder-blades. Stoat had come up behind him, "The death squad at Table Two wants another round of wine slushies."

Morrigan gestured for OK to go. "You better go. You don't want to make those guys angry. I'll be here when you get back."

"It looks like the tank ships have been ordered to reposition," Don the announcer said as the Imperial attack formation broke apart. Suddenly an enormous explosion split the sky with a massive detonation of light and fire.

The battle stations had destroyed an Imperial battle cruiser. Shouting erupted. *"Drutt!* Which ship was that? The *Hoxha.*" It was followed a few seconds later by the simultaneous destruction of the *Erdogan* and the *Khomeini.* Unthinkable! The Horde losing battle cruisers. The officers stopped laughing as the orbital guns locked onto and destroyed more Horde ships. They were used to an easy romp over weak and helpless planets… like Katarina. They were not accustomed to seeing their own ships cut to pieces.

"They're taking a pounding out there," Morrigan said. "The orbital defenses seem to be more powerful than the fleet anticipated.

Good, OK thought. Then he realized, maybe it wasn't good.

There would be no easy victory at Perihelion. The *Stalin's* battle group was forced to break off after losing too many ships. Deathlord Damocles commanded a second wave to engage the battle platforms, led by the battle-hardened second rank battle cruiser *Arminius.*

The second assault wave also withered in the firepower of the orbital guns. With its primary drive destroyed, the *Arminius* tried to withdraw, only to be cut to pieces by relentless crossfire from the orbital platforms. The Second Wave had failed. The losses continued to rack up. The destroyers *Gideon Pillow* and *William Joyce* collided when the guns took out their maneuvering thrusters, exploding into massive atomic fireballs.

"Are we... is the Imperium..." OK was almost afraid to ask. "Losing?"

Morrigan agreed that they were, but the moment would not last. "The Imperium will prevail, whether on the third assault or the hundredth. Damocles will throw every last ship in the fleet into the maw of those orbital platforms, if he has to."

A low alarm began sounding throughout the ship, a repeating bass note of urgency. An announcement played over the ship's internal comms.

"All officers and lower crew, secure yourself for excessively violent maneuvering."

"What does that mean?" OK asked.

"It means it's our turn to go up against those guns."

The lighting diminished as all available power was diverted to weapons and shields. OK could feel the thickening tension in the room. Conversations had ceased in favor of harsh and urgent whispers rapidly shushed. Some were even muttering prayers to the Great Scorpion of the Night. They knew it was a fake religion created by the Overlords as a tool of social control, but they had to cling to something.

OK was torn between rooting for Perihelion and not wanting to get blown up with his ship. Suddenly the ship lurched violently down and sideways, then to the other side and sharply up. The battle announcers explained, "Captain Slaughter is executing a triaxial serpentine attack course with random vector and velocity changes. That will make it harder for the station's main weapon to lock on."

"That's the strategy, Carol, let's see if it works."

OK had always been agnostic, but in that moment, about to die after having spent the last few hours of his life serving drinks to the vilest monsters in the universe, he made the spiritual decision to become an atheist. He would rather believe in oblivion than whatever hell surely awaited him.

The *Subutai* maneuvered into position for a firing run at the heart of the primary battle station, its trajectory aligning it perfectly within the deadly crosshairs of the station's weaponry. Tension crackled throughout the ship as it closed in, crew members holding their breath, every nerve on edge. They braced themselves for the inevitable barrage of devastating fire, wondering if they were about to join the exploded and burning cruisers that had gone up against the enemy defenses before them.

But as the *Subutai* closed to targeting range, the orbital guns fell quiet. The crew exchanged nervous glances. What was the enemy up to? Was this a trap? Had the station malfunctioned? As the *Subutai* edged closer and closer to the mysteriously quiet station, murmured whispers of speculation began to drown out the once-terrified silence of the bar.

"What happened?" OK asked Morrigan.

Morrigan shook her head and gave a humorless chuckle. "I'm not sure, maybe the Perihelionians were too cheap to buy the extended warranty."

OK was more confused than usual. "What?"

"That was a joke. My guess is the weapon malfunctioned from being continually fired without a cooldown and went into shutdown mode. If we play our cards right, the fleet has a chance to capture one of those battle stations and study..." She was interrupted by the explosion of the orbital station as missiles from multiple Imperial cruisers converged on it. "Or we could just blow them to pieces and forget about it. Furking imbeciles." She then muttered, "Delete previous ten seconds of recording."

After that first battle station went down, the Red Fleet seemed to regain its mojo and seized the opportunity with literal vengeance. Warships took on the remaining battle stations in a storm of ion cannons and antimatter warheads. The other stations managed to get off only a few final shots before their defenses collapsed like a build-it-yourself storage shelf from Ikallax II. The last battle stations self-destructed to keep their secrets from falling into Imperial hands as the fleet moved in.

As it became clear the battle was won, the tension evaporated and calls for drinks resumed. OK and Stoat scrambled to keep up. With Perihelion defenseless, the Red Fleet prepared for the orbital bombardment of its cities, which the I2N battle announcers soon announced.

"We've just received word that Deathlord Damocles has ordered the 'Thousand Swords' protocol. A sustained bombardment of trans-orbital projectiles to annihilate the entire surface of Perihelion."

"I think the world you're looking for is 'Extinction Level Event."

"That's three words, Carol, but you're right. The Thousand Swords protocol will wipe out all multicellular life. It is invoked only against the most intransigent rebel planets."

"Let us all hope that it will serve as an example to other worlds of the foolishness of defying the Imperium, Don."

"That's the idea, Carol."

The Imperial fleet surrounded the planet, brushing aside debris from the orbital battle stations and the wreckage of their own blasted ships. The *Erwin Rommel* took position above Perihelion's capital city and fired a neutronium rod that erased the proud city from existence and cracked open the planet's crust like a bleeding geological wound.

The media ships broadcast the destruction of the capital planetwide to terrorize the population; setting it to an ancient piece of music called "Yakkety Sax" to add humiliation on top of mass destruction. As the burning crater expanded, the other battle cruisers opened their missile batteries, locked their targets, and unleashed a relentless barrage of destruction and obliteration. Transorbital warheads rained down on the population centers of Perihelion, blossoming as nuclear fireballs and annihilating everything beneath them.

On the far side of the planet, a rag-tag, fugitive fleet of spaceships was evacuating survivors. Deathlord Damocles ordered Death Fighters dispatched to destroy them. As dawn rose, the warming sun turned the raging radioactive dust storms in the planet's atmosphere into glowing red maelstroms.

The annihilation of Perihelion sparked a dramatic shift in the government of Aphelion. Their next transmission was total, unconditional surrender. Deathlord Damocles decreed the execution of the entire High Council and the obliteration of the capital city, but spared the rest of the colony from a full-scale assault, offering a grim reprieve amid the devastation.

"Take a breath darling," Morrigan told OK. "The worst part is over."

OK could not bear to look at the devastation tearing apart the planet below. He should have been crippled in horror at the megadeath and mass destruction. Revulsion should have clawed at his insides. Instead, he found himself ensnared in a disconcerting emotional void; delivering drinks and cleared glasses like an automaton.

Morrigan got up to leave, looking none the worse for drinking at least two and half bottles of Black Scorpion vodka. She left him a tip that was three times the amount of her tab. OK checked the chronometer and was shocked to find he had been tending bar for thirty consecutive hours.

Reading his surprise, Morrigan assured him, "Hyper-amphetamines, the Horde puts them in the ship's water supply so the crew stays alert during the battle. You will probably feel some lingering emotional detachment as a side effect until they wear off. Also, your eyeballs will be itching for the next few days so try not to scratch them."

7.0 MODERN WAR FARE

A few nights later, OK woke in a cold, drenching sweat from a nightmare in which he had been serving drinks to hooting barbarians while the Horde annihilated a helpless planet. Anya had come in while he was serving, gave him a cold, hard stare, and punched him in the nose. Snapping awake, he grabbed the sides of his bunk, brough his breathing under control, and told himself it was just the Horde amphetamines wearing off.

"I can't do this," he said to himself as he made his way to the bathroom to once again try and wash the itching out of his eyeballs. The Horde was an enormous machine for dispensing brutality, and even if he was a little bit of lubricant between its gears, it was more than he could take.

As he lay in his bunk, OK formed the idea of volunteering with the occupation forces and defecting to the Aphelion resistance (supposing there was one) the first chance he got. He discovered the Horde prohibited such transfers explicitly to prevent that. Only after four years of service and a loyalty probe could he even apply for transfer to a unit with off-world duties. He wondered how many invasions would be staged with himself as a background player in the next four years.

Only a few cycles into the occupation, OK woke to the nauseating sensation of the *Subutai* accelerating to starspeed. The Red Fleet was pulling out for another mission of Imperial conquest. A message from Collator informed him that he would once again report to the Observation Lounge in his special event uniform and, yes, he had to wear the fez.

"So this is my life, now?" he thought. "I serve drinks to barbarians while they commit mass murder." He felt less horrified than numbed by this realization and then felt horrified at how numb he felt.

"And I have to wear a fez."

The fleet decelerated several days later, and OK learned the next planet the Horde would invade was called "Plinth." OK had never heard of Plinth so he looked it up on I2N. It seemed like a pleasant enough place, reminding him a little of Katarina, except for the sky being orchid pink instead of cornflower blue. The infographic had this to say about the planet.

Plinth is the third planet of the system Rho-158105 Scorpii. This is the capital city, Alessia.

OK thought it looked nice. The architecture was a bit rococo, but otherwise lovely. OK tabbed over to the section on Plinthian culture.

Plinthian culture is a decadent cesspool of depravity veiled in the guise of sophistication. Its inhabitants are as arrogant as they are weak. Its inhabitants, deluded by their so-called "advanced civilization," prioritize the frivolities of art and culture, oblivious to the rot beneath their fragile facade. Its males are feminized, wearing soft gowns and painting their fingernails in pastel shades of pink and lavender instead of manly black. Their females wallow in promiscuity and barrenness, a testament to their moral decay.

The planet also produces over a thousand varieties of artisanal cheeses. The planet's grasses are purple, so their bovine cattle produce violet milk. Their cheeses come in shades of purple, mauve, and violet and have tastes ranging from subtle to piquant.

This has been "Useful and Interesting Facts About the Universe, brought to you buy Black Scorpion Coffee, the Fuel of the Imperium."

On the night of the invasion, OK put on his humiliating club service uniform and wondered if the sexy intelligence officer, Colonel Morrigan, would be observing the invasion again.

At the appointed hour, he reported to the Observation Lounge and set about wiping the glasses and arranging trays of canapes. The sound of bottles clinked over the bar as they stocked their stations with Imperial imitations of Antarean whisky, Denebolan gin, Rigelian rum, and real Scorpion vodka. Stoat checked the angle of the chairs to ensure every seat in the house would have a clear view of the annihilation of the Plinthian civilization. As the final touch, he placed small plastic scorpions at each table as keepsakes.

With the stage set, Stoat gave the wait staff a little pep talk. "Let's deliver an unforgettable experience tonight, I want energy! I want hot plasma! I want every officer who walks through that hatch to have the best time of his life! I'm counting on you to deliver it. Let's make it happen, people!"

An all-female group of FIST security enforcers were the first to arrive; nabbing the best table in front of the viewport. Stoat brought them a tray of Martian Mules. "Boo yah! Hail to the Imperium!" they shouted, smacking their glasses together, sloshing chartreuse liquid on the table.

"Sometimes, I think I don't use my license to kill nearly often enough," Morrigan muttered as she took her customary barstool. She was loud enough to be overheard, but the enforcers were too busy squealing at each other.

"Shall I get your vodka ready for the battle?" OK asked her.

"I'll take the vodka, but there isn't going to be a battle."

"Why not?" he asked hopefully.

"Watch and observe, Deathfinger. What you're about to see should be the model for all Imperial conquests."

"I've heard the Plinthians make nice cheeses," OK said, trying to sound knowledgeable. He wondered if he should have used the past tense.

She took a slug from her vodka. "Plinthian cheese is over-rated."

The observation lounge was full by the time Deathlord Damocles delivered a terse ultimatum.

"Effete denizens of the planet Plinth, this is Deathlord Damocles, the Sword that hangs over your heads. Surrender, or mine will be the last voice you will ever hear. Within a few hours, an orbital bombardment will begin that will erase your failed and indolent culture from the universe. Your world has long craved an iron hand to control your wastrel lives. That hand is mine."

Before the first ships reached bombardment range, the fleet received an urgent message from a woman of generous proportions with lavender-dyed hair wearing a woven kaftan and a colorful scarf.

"Imperial friends, I am Maree Cloggensteen, Representative of the Circle of Consensus, I bid you welcome to Plinth. Our tradition of pacifism requires us to offer unconditional surrender. But be aware, your occupation will be resisted through protests, song, and most importantly, through our refusal to cooperate. You can have our planet, but you will never have our hearts."

She took a few steps to her left where two thin women in unkempt hair and peasant dress, wearing enormous spectacles, were standing. They began strumming on a guitar and a kantele. "We offer you this hymn of peace."

Imperial friends, come join us on this song. Raise our voice, just sing along,
With peace and love, we'll find a way to be one galaxy, in harmony.

We will share our beautiful lands, teach you ways of our gentleness and…
We'll sing and dance, under a peppermint sky
Come on along now, won't you give it a try?

Our people have so much love to share, if let us we will show how we care.
With open hearts, we'll find a common ground, and spread love all around…

Their song was cut short by the detonation of a one-thousand megaton warhead over the capital city. "Thank you!" shouted someone at table four.

As the shockwave spread out from the broiling fireball that had been the Plinthian capital, Deathlord Damocles sent his response.

Your terms are acceptable.

Aside from the obliteration of its largest city and a handful of lesser population centers, Plinth would be spared the full measure of mass destruction usually meted out by the Horde. The officers crammed into the lounge were grumbled bitterly at being denied their sport. OK, however, was relieved that it was over quickly and without an extinction level event.

"That was easy," he said to Morrigan.

"Easy? That surrender was the culmination of twenty years of MAD operatives undermining their culture; making them decadent and pacifistic! A softened and demoralized population is ripe for conquest." She hammered her vodka bottle to the bar. "This is how the Imperium should make war! Instead of a dead, bombed out world, the key production assets of Plinth are intact and the surviving population will be easily controlled!"

It still sounded horrible, but at least a lot fewer people had to die. He had to ask, "Katarina also surrendered. Why did Lord Damocles spare this world and not mine?"

"Who knows what goes on in that man's mind? He is as mercurial as the desert winds of Arridia II. And as deadly as the crystalline stilettos the nomadic tribes of that world use to settle interpersonal disagreements."

Morrigan departed soon after, leaving OK tangled in a web of conflicted emotions. As a Horde intelligence officer, she made a perfect avatar for ruthless Imperium ambition. Yet, compared to the Horde's go-to strategy of burning everything and killing everybody, her approach to conquest almost seemed… reasonable. Furthermore, she had always treated him with a surprising amount of decency. And she was cute besides.

Plinth hung in the viewport for the rest of his shift, its capital a radioactive inferno visible even from orbit. But it was a mundane spectacle compared to the planetwide devastation the *Subutai's* officers were used to. By mid-watch, they had grown bored and drifted off to other forms of recreation, leaving the devastation behind like an empty glass at the end of a party.

OK stowed the bottles, put the glasses in the sanitizer, and wiped down the tables, trying not to think about his role in dragging another peaceful planet into the insatiable maw of the Imperium. Scrubby worked the lavatories, scouring them with the zeal of a mechanoid whose cybernetic religion revolved around sanitation. OK had managed to debug most of Scrubby's quirks following interactive cybernetic tutorials on I2N. But despite his best efforts, the little mech-bot still took sadistic pleasure in jabbing him in the ankles when he let his guard down.

When he ended his shift, he was still buzzing from the mix of amphetamines, anger, and adrenaline coursing through his veins. Sleep was out of the question, but there was nowhere for him to go to work off his excess energy. He trudged back toward his quarters, thinking only of watching more engineering programs on I2N.

On the way, he ran into Qi'Anna and Rue, headed for the Deathwalker Holds to revive troops for the ground invasion. "Wanna help?" Qi'Anna asked.

"I thought the invasion was called off when they surrendered."

"Nah, the bombing was called off. The invasion's still on," Qi'Anna said. "'The best time for a sneak attack is after the enemy surrenders'—*Way of the Scorpion*, don't ya know."

He almost said no before he realized it was exactly the opportunity he had been waiting for; a chance to learn the secrets of the Deathwalker holds, their access codes, their operational parameters, and where they actually were within the ship. Perhaps he could figure a way to sabotage them and strike a blow for the resistance.

"Why are you twirling your hands like that?" Rue asked.

OK stopped rubbing his hands. "Oh, I was just thinking I should wash my hands before I helped you."

Qi'Anna chuckled. "Oh, don't worry about that. I never do."

They provided him with a pair of fuchsia coveralls and matching goggles that were only slightly less silly than the fez and rather binding at the crotch. The revival process turned out to be pretty straightforward. There was a green button on the side of each cryo-sarcophagus pod labeled "Reanimate." Next to it was a red button labeled "De-animate." Careless and color-blind death technicos had resulted in many, many accidental deaths.

"Go ahead, try it," Qi'Anna encouraged him. "Remember, push red to make 'em dead, push the green to make them scream."

OK hesitated for a moment, allowing himself to savor the awesome power of returning life to another being, before he pressed the green button. A dark fluid transfused into the Deathwalker to begin the reanimation process. Its heart began beating, the brain activity monitor went from a flat line to a jagged mountain topography. The corpse jerked to life, sitting bolt upright and erupting from its icy slumber with a soul-piercing scream. They always woke up like that because being brought back from the dead was a horrific experience beyond the darkest imaginings of the most deranged, cocaine-addicted horror novelist.

Qi'Anna sprayed him with chemicals from a hose to defrost his skin, hand-toweled his chest, and asked if he was doing anything after the invasion.

The Loadmaster in charge of the hold (the Deathwalkers were considered cargo) assigned OK the job of distributing the Deathwalkers cups of a slimy, pink substance called "protein extrusion." It was a staple food of the Horde's ground troops and could be flavored in various ways. Most Deathwalkers would just as soon eat it raw since they no longer had any sense of taste.

OK handed a cup to the Deathwalker he had brought back from the dead. MCM-117880 was stenciled on his pectoral body armor. The Deathwalker shot-gunned the extrusion, crumpled the metal cup, and handed the cup back.

"Thank you, that was most sincerely appreciated, my good man."

This came as a shock. OK had thought the Deathwalkers were mindless cyborgs who wielded nothing but death and destruction. He had never expected courtesy from one of them. "You're welcome," he stammered.

The Deathwalker yawned, his cyborg limbs coming back to life with the hums and whirrs of a reliable war machine. "So, where shall I be committing wholesale murder and retail mayhem on this occasion?"

"A planet called Plinth. They surrendered without a fight."

"That's what we were told about Aphelion," he grunted, flexing his metal-jointed fingers. "And still I spent the better part of two fortnights pursuing ice snipers across the frozen wastes of its subarctic latitudes."

OK was suddenly curious. "What's it like being a Deathwalker?"

The Deathwalker stared into his eyes and answered in a monotone.

"I could kill you this very moment and feel nothing. The parts of my brain where I experience remorse, guilt, or morality have been irrevocably cauterized. Nothing but scar tissue remains. I exist solely to terminate the enemies of the Imperium and lay waste to their lands."

"Ah, I see, well, I sure hope you don't kill me."

"Are you an enemy of the Imperium?"

"Um... no?"

The Death-walker clapped him on the shoulder, "Just having a bit of sport with you. It helps to take edge off my psychotic impulses." MCM-117880 stared at his palms. "Every time they throw that switch and I die; I am haunted by the screaming voices of everyone I've killed."

OK had never imagined a Deathwalker having an existential crisis. "Have you ever thought of ending this horrible cycle of death and pain?"

The Deathwalker broke out in laughter. "Nah, just yanking your chain again, my friend. I experience nothing when I die. It's no different than flipping an on/off switch. I may as well be an illumination orb." He raised his arms and proclaimed, "I am a harbinger of unspeakable horrors, dealing indiscriminately with enemies and innocents alike, devoid of hesitation or empathy."

He paused from closing up his sabatons, "I have no conscience, no soul, and my excrement is toxic. If I survive the war, I may become an attorney."

"Pray enlighten him about our toxic excretions!" chimed in the adjacent Deathwalker with a sardonic smile.

"Indeed, our excrement is quite toxic from the chemical that keeps us from lapsing into a state of decay while we're dead. One of my trouser coughs could easily dispatch scores of people. On the plus side, it is also completely odorless. I can pass gas without anyone being the wiser until they succumb. Our flatulence is akin to a nerve gas agent."

On the other side of the hold, a line of half-armored Deathwalkers formed up in front of the target simulator, firing their disintegration rifles—aptly nicknamed "dusters"—at holograms of enemy soldiers, rebels, and hapless civilians. Above their heads, a digital counter displayed their accuracy, measuring every hit against the backdrop of simulated carnage.

"Godless Void! Damn this piece of *drutt* weapon!" exclaimed one Deathwalker, as he hurled his Mark IX Deathblaster Enhanced Battle Carbine against the deck. "The Mark IX is utterly inadequate. We discharge in excess of four hundred rounds for each confirmed kill. We are a galactic-scale imperial power, and yet these are the best firearms our armories can provide!? This is an appalling failure and a blatant disregard for combat efficacy."

OK could not resist picking up the disintegration rifle and turning it over in his hands. "I think I see the problem. The targeting sensor is out of alignment. You'd have a tough time hitting the broad side of the Tarkelian moon with this gun."

"Oh, yeah?" The Deathwalkers gathered around and gave him their full attention.

"It's a pretty easy fix. If I had a pair of cyber-pliers could probably make the adjustment."

A technico had a pair of cyber-pliers in his toolkit. OK showed him how to make the adjustment to the sensor. "See, first you align it with the barrel. And then you need to tighten the connection here. You have to tighten it often; the connection gets looser every time you fire. Make sure it's good and tight and… there you go."

He handed the rifle back to the Deathwalker, who swung it around and blasted out ten rapid shots against a line of rebels. Each rebel disappeared in a briefly human-shaped cloud of burning ash and dust. Ebullient, he held up his duster and shouted. "Superlative! Now, we might efficiently annihilate those rebel scum! And we owe our thanks to this Deathfinger!"

Ten thousand Deathwalkers shouted out in triumph and began re-aligning the targeting sensors on their rifles. OK felt pleased with himself for about half a millisecond before it dawned on him what he had done—eliminated the Deathwalkers' primary weakness. All those jokes about what awful shots they were, they were no longer true. With accurate rifles, they would be slaughtering rebels by the thousands.

For a moment he forgot how to breathe. His stomach knotted, and the heat of his shame reddened his skin. He wanted to crawl into a reactor and boil away to nothing. His plan to help the resistance from the inside had just suffered a fairly significant setback.

8.0 THE PHANTOM MENU

As Deathwalkers marched across the surface of Plinth, confirming the accuracy of their newly adjusted rifles on hapless civilians, and on the same night as Deathlord Damocles performed his rocket-powered flyover of the crater where the capital once stood, Stoat hosted a "Victory Over Plinth" party. His centerpiece was a buffet lined with bubbling pots of the planet's many cheeses, accompanied by bits of bread skewered on sticks; Crab Nebula puffs; and little dumplings stuffed with Plinthian cheese, Perihelion proteins, and a tingle of Carpathian spices. "My own creation, I call them… 'Horde'oeuvres.'"

After that, the peculiar tedium that punctuated Horde conquests settled in as the Red Fleet waited for the occupation fleet to relieve them. In the midst of the monotony, Collator came to OK and Stoat with news. "The *Subutai* is to play host for some very high-level negotiations."

"Peace talks?" OK asked hopefully.

This gave Collator and Stoat a good laugh. "No, not peace talks," Collator explained. "DNZ will be negotiating trademark rights."

Stoat's eyes lit up. "DNZ Corp!" DNZ Corp dominated the galactic market for entertainment, information, commercialized sex, and recreational body modifications. Loyal to no Government and no world, they traversed the galaxy in enormous spherical ships with gigantic dish antennae to maintain constant connection via their sub-space tachyon networks. They also operated several notoriously crowded and overpriced recreational pleasure planets.

All DNZ employees, from the Chief Executive Entity to the maintenance drones, were hivemind clones. Cloning replicants to create obedient low-income workers was once illegal across the Commonwealth. DNZ undertook a massive public relations campaign to convince progressive-minded citizens that hivemind clones were the victims of bigotry and social injustice. They funded Hivemind Clone Rights groups and lobbied the Galactic Parliament. Supporters shaved their heads and had their skin pigment altered to mottled gray "in solidarity with the hivemind clone community." A Hivemind solidarity flag was created (A gray circle on a background of the same shade of gray) and flown over enlightened homes and businesses across the quadrant.

Bowing to the political pressure, the Galactic Commonwealth passed a law declaring hivemind clones a protected class of beings, recognizing their contribution to galactic culture, and declaring an official "Hivemind History Sidereal Period." The day after the law was signed, DNZ dismissed all its human employees and replaced them with hivemind clones, which also allowed them to claim a tax break under the Commonwealth's workforce diversity incentive program. Having dispensed with human actors, writers, and directors, all DNZ entertainment products were created in fully synthetic environments, except for the snuff films division whose audience was quite adamant in their insistence on authenticity.

OK persisted. "What are these negotiations for?"

"You don't need to know. But you will be assigned to service the formal reception and the dinner on each night of the negotiation."

Stoat answered with well-practiced enthusiasm. "Ia, Ia! We won't let you down!"

She sighed, "The problem is our lead catering chef Portnoy, was caught doing something unspeakable to the lab meat for the officer's dinner. He's been disintegrated. I have to grab a catering chef from another ship, but none of them want the job because the DNZ nutrition requirements are … highly unusual. And the consequences of not meeting them would be severe. If I can't find someone to do it before we rendezvous with the DNZ Corp, I'll have to do it myself."

To OK's horror, Stoat grabbed the opportunity like it was the last ticket off the next planet set for Horde invasion. "We can do that, me and OK."

"These are very, very important negotiations."

"Check our records, we used to run a fine dining establishment on Katarina. And I saw you eating the Alien Egg Poppers at the Victory Over Plinth party."

She sighed. "I guess you'll have to do. Don't let me down, or we'll be in a cubicle being tormented, if you know what I mean and I think you do."

"I assure you again, we will not let you down."

She tapped her comm unit. "I'm sending you a list of their requirements, study them carefully."

OK and Stoat delved into the terms and conditions for the negotiations as though their lives depended on them—which they did. DNZ Corp's demands were tediously detailed, lighting levels not to exceed 600 lumens, temperature to be maintained at a toasty 30 degrees centigrade, oxygen levels slightly richer than the ship's standard. With each new clause and stipulation, they better understood why the fleet's catering officers had steered clear of this gig.

Just for one example, Paragraph 147-stroke-11b demanded, "No Imperial delegate shall exceed a height of 183 centimeters."

"How in the vast godless void are we supposed to enforce that?" OK muttered, shaking his head in disbelief.

"That doesn't apply to us," Stoat answered. "Skip ahead to chapters 8, 9, and 12 regarding Food and Beverages, Service Standards, and Accoutrements."

OK skipped ahead. "All servers must cover their faces and hands at all timed and wear respiration masks..."

"Not that part, Chapter 8, Section H, Paragraph 11, sub-paragraphs b. through r; regarding the menu for the closing night of negotiations."

OK scrolled to it. "Organic kale salad, locally sourced organic fennel and leek soup, Piscean scallops, the heart of a child no more than six years old, Capellan lobster risotto ... wait, what? The heart of a child?"

"Ia, where am I going to get that? There aren't any children in the fleet."

"Surely, that must be a euphemism for something else, like Rigelian Mountain Oysters. They can't literally expect us to kill a child."

"No, they expect us to serve the hearts of forty children."

"They're worse than the Scorps."

"We better find a way to accommodate them or else these negotiations could fail."

"What do we care if these negotiations fail?"

"We don't," Stoat told him. "But we don't want them to fail because of us. Can you imagine what they would do to us? On the other hand, if they succeed, maybe we leverage it to our advantage."

Trust the plan, OK reminded himself.

"Since you obviously have ..." Stoat did finger quotes "...'moral issues' with this, why don't you leave the closing night's menu to me?"

"Only if you find a way to do it without murdering children."

"I might have an idea about that. 100 Rec passes says I can pull it off." Stoat's eyes glinted with determination and ambition. OK took the bet, if only to give Stoat further incentive to find some less barbarous way to meet the DNZ's culinary demands. He doubted Stoat's efforts to appease the Horde would extend to child murder, but he didn't entirely trust that glint either.

The next day he prepared the reception hall. As he placed orbs on each table that would project the red-and-black Scorpion Imperial banner next to the DNZ corporate logo of three intersecting circles containing bands of color that spanned the visible spectrum, OK could not help but ponder the secret purpose of the talks. *What if the Imperium is negotiating an alliance with DNZ?* he wondered. The combination of Imperial military power with DNZ corporate resources would be bad news for the rest of the galaxy.

What if we contaminated the hors d'oeuvres with mutant E. coli? he wondered. That might set the DNZ and the Imperium to was with each other! What a feat that would be, bringing down the Imperium with a tray of appetizers! His enthusiasm was curbed when he found out DNZ clones were unaffected by mutant E. coli; they had hive immunity.

Roche was also helping set the tables. Since they were alone and unsupervised, OK asked a question he'd been saving, "Do people ever, you know, defect from the Horde?"

"Why, are you thinking about it?"

"I am just curious. You've been in the Horde for so long. You must have heard about someone trying it sometime."

"I heard a story once. Umber Fleet was on patrol by the Ophiuchian line. A supply shuttle made a run for the other side. The command ship scrammed death-fighters to go after him, but he was too far away for them to catch him."

"Did he make it?"

Roche shook his head. "They overloaded his reactor core by remote. Blew him up real good. Nobody gets away from the Horde. You want my advice, stick it out for your ten years. They'll kill you before they let you quit."

OK made a mental note to study reactor core jettisoning systems after his shift. Just in case he ever learned how to fly a death shuttle, somehow managed to hijack one, and used it to defect to the Rebel Pact.

The DNZ Corp ship arrived precisely twenty hours late for the rendezvous, a typical DNZ power move. A sphere that might be mistaken for a moon, malevolent multicolored light radiated from within its metal framework of plates and girders. Two enormous concave antennae protruded from on top. When it reached the coordinates, a round iris spun open and a line of oblong pods emerged, like mice exiting a mousehole. They formed a perfectly straight, perfectly spaced line into The *Subutai's* reserved docking bay.

Collator, OK, Stoat, Roche, and dozens of the ship's service personnel awaited their arrival in the reception hall, sweating underneath the facemask respirators the DNZ Corp contract stipulated. DNZ Corp Executroids were notoriously afraid of contamination. After what seemed like sufficient time for stars to be born, burn out, and die, the DNZ Corp delegation exited their ships. The corporate anthem of DNZ Corp played as they entered, a peppy little tune about small worlds and wishing upon stars.

The DNZ Corp Executroids, their assistants, and their litigation units were not quite as human as he expected. Their skin bore mottled hues of gray, while their bulbous, hairless heads sported eyes akin to black camera lenses. Clad in matching charcoal gray suits adorned with the company's logo and a pixelated square denoting an identification code. A tube protruded from the breast pocket of each suit, disappearing into their left nostrils. OK couldn't help but wonder at its purpose.

Moving in syncopation, they approached their tables and sat down in unison after reciting the DNZ Corp corporate Affirmation. *"We are one mind. Individuality is abhorrent. Unity is our strength. Conformity is perfection."*

Following remarks by Captain Slaughter and Commander Grimfoyle, the dinner commenced. OK watched the meal with fascination from beneath the one-way opaque visor of his respiration mask. As it began, prehensile tubes emerged from the necks of the DNZ clones. The tubes minced each portion into a slurry and then vacuumed it into their digestive tract for processing. In total synchronization, they cleared their plates in mere moments, repeating the process with each of the six courses. They ingested with the efficiency of a line of industrial robots building hovercars. After the final course was consumed, the clones rose in perfect unison and returned to their rejuvenation chambers.

"Have you figured out how to feed them the hearts of children without feeding them the hearts of children?" OK asked Stoat as they cleared the tables.

"I reached out to a gestation farm to see if I could get just one child's heart, you know, maybe from a kid who didn't make it. I thought I could just clone it off in one of the meat labs."

He sighed. "But when I asked if they had any they could give me, they closed the channel before I could even make an offer."

"Dear Diary," said OK. "Today I had the most appalling conversation I have ever had."

"I have another idea. You'll see. You're going to pay me those 200 Rec Passes, Friend-O." OK almost hoped he would. Stoat had also learned the purpose of the negotiations and OK was relieved it was not an Imperial-DNZ alliance. Rather, the Imperium was seeking a license to use DNZ's trademarked phrase, "Resistance is futile" for use in planetary conquests.

In exchange for the phrase, DNZ's demanded a license fee on a galactic scale. The Imperium tried to bring the cost down by offering concessions including the permission to operate within the Imperial communication nexus, the extension of Cellador's special tax status, and hints of unsettling ventures into human experimentation. The DNZ negotiators were intrigued, but refused to budge on the fee they demanded.

The next two days were consumed by interminable meetings held behind closed doors. The Imperium's frustrated and dispirited team lingered in the negotiating chamber long after the DNZ executroids departed for the night, indulging in libations, narcotics, and strategizing for the morrow's talks.

As they prepared for the final formal dinner, the talks seemed to have failed. The mood of the negotiating team was dark—the Imperium had little tolerance for failure.

As the time came for the service, Stoat, in a perfectly pressed dress uniform, directed a team of waiters to distribute covered plates to each diner. OK held his breath, dying to see if Stoat had pulled it off but knowing he would be horrified if he succeeded. The waiters surrounded the tables with the precision of a military maneuver. The plates were set down in synchrony and with a flourish, they raised the covers.

On each plate was a tiny heart, surrounded by arugula, heirloom tomatoes from the garden planet Herbivoria VI, and Denebolan wood-ear mushrooms. Betraying no emotion, the DNZ executroids deployed their neck-tubes and consumed the offering. OK felt like he was going to throw up.

After the dinner, when the diners had all cleared out, and OK and Stoat were clearing tables, Collator signaled to them. "The DNZ Corp Executroids wish to speak to you. You will join them in the side chamber."

A quartet of executroids awaited their arrival. Collator, Commander Grimfoyle (representing the Horde), and a duo of Imperial negotiators completed the assembly. The Executroids, speaking in eerie unison, their voices modulated into an intimidating echo, addressed them.

"The collective has received data that you are the unit responsible for the meal that has just been integrated into our corporal vessels."

"I am," for the first time in OK's memory, Stoat's voice was shaking.

"The collective is impressed that you complied with our requirement to serve us the hearts of your young. The collective acknowledges that the salad and mushrooms were the optimal accompaniment."

"I'm pleased… that you are pleased."

"We did not anticipate compliance with that clause. It was put into the contract as a 'brown M&M sort of thing.' The Imperium's willingness to comply has favorably impressed the Collective. We will approve the Imperium's best and final offer concerning licensing the use of the trademarked phrase 'Resistance is futile,' subject to standard restrictions. We also accept the offer to use the prison planet Psi Beria VI as a filming location for our planned series of romantic comedies set in post-apocalyptic environments. We believe it will be the next big thing."

"Well, that's fantastic," Stoat said, his confidence returning. "Since I have your attention, here's a script I've been working out. It's entitled 'Heroes of the Intergalactic Space Conflict'" a story of two courageous teens who save our galaxy from invaders from another galaxy."

The DNZ Corp executives exchanged data, a kind of static, chirping conveyed among the tiny transceivers on their temples. "We already have 1,047 galactic invasion movies in production. What makes yours different?"

"Mine has giant insect aliens, do any of yours have that?"

"546 of them utilize that plot device."

"Do any of yours feature a talking dog."

The DNZ Corp executives' comm nodes flashed green as they exchanged data again. "Does yours have a talking dog?"

"No, but if it will sell the script, I'll write it in."

"Your revision has been superseded. We have already integrated the concept of talking dogs into 86 production projects. The idea has been assimilated, copyrighted, and is now part of our hive-consciousness. We will celebrate with a simulated cocaine orgy aboard our ship."

"Oh, can I come?" Stoat asked.

"Only if you agree to assimilation into the DNZ collective hivemind." It extended an assimilation tendril toward him,

"Perhaps another time, then." The Executroids departed, their synchronized steps faded, leaving behind only a lingering aura of profound evil. Stoat, looking pleased with himself, leaned over to OK.

"You owe me 300 Rec Passes."

"Only if those weren't actual children's hearts. And if I hadn't recently turned atheist, I'd be praying that they weren't."

Stoat drew closer and whispered. "They're monkey hearts. I took a chance DNZ wouldn't be able to tell the difference."

It didn't stop OK from asking a question he immediately regretted. "Where the hell did you get monkey hearts?"

"Let's not make this about what death squad pillaged what Plinthian zoo. That's all behind us. Anyway, the broccoli noisettes were the tricky part."

"So all of this... *this* ... *stuff* ... with the monkey hearts was just so you could pitch a holo-film?"

"It was a once in a lifetime opportunity. How could I pass it up?" He sighed, "Well, I guess I'll just have to get back to the original plan."

Once the agreement was signed, the DNZ Corp ship departed. Afterwards, some officers were intrigued by Stoat's delicacy. He was able to recreate it using cloned meat but took it off the menu a few cycles later. There was novelty in eating a child's heart, but most people only wanted to do it once. The texture was quite chewy.

Things went back to the boring grind of occupation as the fleet awaited their next orders. They did not have to wait long.

9.0 CARNAGE OVER COCKTAILS

The Red Fleet did not stay long in the Plinth system once negotiations with DNZ Corp were concluded. They turned over occupation duties to the Maroon Fleet and flew off to conquer Brattle; a ringed planet with rugged mountains draped with everteal trees and known for its export of a psychoactive form of syrup. Its inhabitants were reputed for their resilience, hardiness, and general hostility toward outsiders. It was culturally the exact opposite of Plinth and had been building up its orbital defenses for years. Brattle was prepared to offer the Imperium a feisty resistance.

The orbital platforms were the only things standing between Brattle and subjugation under Scorpion rule. Their ablative armor, pulsating force fields, bristling turrets, and missile batteries were the final bulwark against the might of the Horde. They struck the first blows against the Red Fleet, unleashing a torrent of missiles that scattered across space like dandelion seeds in the wind. Horde railguns thinned their numbers, but all too many found their marks and exploded with devastating force. Some of the warheads unleashed storms of blue-white lightning that spread across the armor plating of the hulls, seeking out fissures and cracks they could force their way through and wreak electromagnetic havoc on the ships' systems.

Hits on the _Subutai's_ hull sent shockwaves through the ship and rattled the glassware behind the bar in the Observation Lounge, at one point knocking off a pair of tumblers, but OK saved them with a deft catch.

Roars and thumps marked the launch of _Subutai's_ counterattack. Waves of missiles fired toward the battle stations, weaving through their defenses, finding their targets, and detonating against their shields.

The Horde was bearing up better than they had at Perihelion. The tank ships held the front of the line, drawing fire and absorbing hits with their thick armor while the assault ships rained ion fusillades on the stations.

The larger ships had learned to evade the heaviest fire instead of taking it head-on. Behemoth battle cruisers caromed on random trajectories, their erratic and unpredictable maneuvers frustrating the enemy's attempts to lock onto them.

Amidst the fray, squadrons of death fighters darted and weaved through the crossfire with the agility of hyperactive squirrels dodging traffic in a bustling urban metropolis, their trajectories confounding enemy sensors and adding to the pandemonium of battle.

Brattle's orbital defenses fought doggedly and scored hits even against the Horde's new battle tactics. For a time, the forces seemed evenly matched. Hours into the fight, the first battle station gave into the irresistible force of the Imperial onslaught. Its overloaded power core detonated in a blast that vaporized its systems and shattered its armor. The Horde took advantage of the opening and pressed forward. More battle stations were destroyed, one by one at first, and then a lot of them quickly. Some of them exploded in violent Novas when their ion cores lost containment. Others simply took so much damage that they shut down, waited for a Horde ship to come into range, and then detonated their self-destruct systems, taking the Imperial ships with them.

OK served drinks in the observation lounge throughout the assault, buzzed on amphetamines and trying to keep a lid on his feelings. At one point, he heard Morrigan mutter from her stool. "Just leave one for me."

After the final battle station was neutralized, the Red Fleet claimed victory. Their ships were scarred and blasted, but they had won the day. The fate of the planet beneath them was sealed. Battle cruisers readied warheads for the pending trans-orbital bombardment.

Most worlds would have surrendered, but whatever the people of Brattle were called—and there was bitter internal debate on whether they should be called Brattleites, Brattleinians, or Brattle Bros—they remained stubbornly defiant even in the face of imminent annihilation. Their intransigence earned them another speech from "The Sword That Hangs Over Your Head."

"People of Brattle, you have fought when other worlds would have pleaded for mercy, but your fate is no different from any that would defy the Imperium of Greater Scorpius. I have no more mercy for you than the fire does for the forest. Your opportunity for surrender ... indeed, for survival...was squandered when you raised up arms against your superiors. For your defiance, you will be obliterated from the cosmos, and your pathetic resistance forgotten by history."

The junior officers at table two began to sing that terrible song about burning planets with fire again. One stripped off her jacket and stood on her table, swinging her shirt and shouting, "Burn that cake! Burn that cake!" while her bare breasts breasted boobfully, her fellow officers hooted, and OK nearly dropped a tray of drinks on the Death Squad table.

The *Erwin Rommel* launched transorbital warheads against the planetary capital of Brattleboro. The media ships transmitted a cool-looking shot from a missile-mounted camera as multiple warheads separated, then rained down nuclear fire, annihilating the city and its environs. The officers whooped.

The other ships launched their warheads. The missiles left the ships as needles of light, glowed like malevolent shooting stars as they entered the atmosphere, and finally ended as explosions that spawned churning mushroom clouds. The night-side of the planet was strobe-lit by their detonations, each one representing the total obliteration of whatever was underneath it. The Horde struck the down like vengeful deities giving their haughty followers more incentive to repent their sins.

Over the next several hours, the cities of Brattle were reduced to craters. The once verdant forests blazed in infernos, their fiery tongues licking the heavens and cloaking the world in a shroud of ash and soot, foreboding the onset of a bitter, unyielding winter. Morrigan uttered a bitter lament from her perch at the bar. "What a tragic squandering of resources."

After the show was over, and the spectators cleared out, OK cleaned up the considerable mess that was left behind. The rowdy FIST enforcers had trashed their table to the worst. They left behind a chaotic battlefield of crumpled deathsticks, broken glasses, soggy and half eaten food still clinging desperately to plates like the abandoned wounded begging for death. The condiment dispensers had their contents spewed deliberately onto the tabletop, adding their vibrant hues to the tableau, mingling and merging into a Jackson Pollockian mess of ketchup blood and mustard puke.

At another table—really most other tables—horde officers had left their own messes for "the help" to clean up. Every tabletop was a waste dump landscape of drink spills; cold, discarded snack nuggets; and the other wreckage of drunken officers celebrating carnage. The sole exception was the table where the death squad had been seated. They had stacked their plates and glasses, thrown away their napkins, wiped down the top, and left a substantial but not arrogant tip.

As he tidied up the bar, he could see the trajectories of more transorbital warheads streaking across the planet below. The bombardment continued through his entire shift as he did his duty cleaning up the tables and sterilizing glasses; a cog in a massive war machine, tidying up while bombs fell on innocent people.

A memory pushed its way to the front of his mind, the 'Independence Night' celebration on Katarina that marked the anniversary of the colony having finally cleared its debt from the megacorporation that sponsored its settlement. He remembered heading up to the crest of Tranquility Hill with Driver, a few friends, and Anya to witness the holographic fireworks and the dazzling aerial drone displays. The air had been alive with pulsating music and the mouthwatering aroma of festival food. When the spectacle reached its crescendo, he'd leaned in for a kiss, only to have Anya's fist meet his nose with a hard, definitive thud.

This was the fourth planet he had seen crushed beneath the boot of Scorpion Imperialism (five if you counted Katarina itself, which he did) and he had yet to do anything about it. The weight of his guilt gnawed at him. Even the camaraderie he sometimes felt with Qi'Anna, Rue, Roche, or his fellow kitchen staff pained him. They followed orders without question, stagehands behind a cosmic drama of brutal conquest and relentless bloodshed.

His shifts in the LCIF had not brought him any closer to finding a network of fellow subversives in the lower crew. Certainly, his fellow lower crew had complaints, but they were all about bad food and hazardous working conditions. No one ever complained about the evil politics of the Imperium. Maybe it was the fear of being turned in to FIST, or maybe it was how they coped with the horrible situation.

The more the prospect of uncovering a fifth column within the Horde became unlikely, the more he thought about defecting. While it seemed like his only avenue for redemption, it would be a perilous path, fraught with danger and with no hope for help from anyone.

But he could see no way of actualizing that ambition in the near term. He was stuck in the Horde and stuck on this ship. The best he could do was to avoid helping them again, as he had done with the Deathwalker battle rifles.

Only the thought of Anya kept him going. If she had escaped the Horde's clutches, then she was out there, somewhere. For her, he would have to endure whatever the Horde threw at him. Those thoughts gave him the strength to bear his burden until he could escape.

He tried to picture her face. He didn't have an image of her. He had left all of his holo-selfies behind on Katarina. He felt like having an image of her would give him strength, and he knew of one way to create one.

When he returned to his bunk, he activated HARVEY and created a personal pornographic companion avatar. Personalized pornography would cost most of his savings of IMUs, but it was the only way he could think of to have an image of Anya that would inspire him to remain committed to the rebel cause and also possibly for other purposes.

PLEASE DESCRIBE YOUR DESIRED AVATAR

OK had to think hard about it, trying to remember how she looked the last time he saw her—before the nose punching. "Really nice skin, kind of beige, mesmerizing hazel eyes, underneath dark, expressive brows. She had raven-black hair that went down to her shoulders but sometimes she wore it in these two sort of braided pods from the back of her head. I forget what the women call that style. And lips, she has two, and the same number of ears and nostrils. The top lip is a little fuller than the bottom one. She has a playful and mischievous smile. Her eyes are like that, too, just... glittering with mischief.

"Her height I would guess about 1.6 meters and maybe 55 kilos. She has a quiet sense of grace, like she's so in harmony with the universe that she doesn't even think about how in harmony with the universe she is. Her cans are like..." he held his hands out in front of his chest. "Also, she has slender legs. She likes those boots that come up past your knees, with the little heels."

The program produced images of four different entirely wrong women for him to choose from, with swollen upper lips, thin deathstick legs, and ridiculously bulbous chests. It took him two hours of refinement to get to the image of Anya that looked the way he thought he remembered her.

When his avatar was as close as he could make it, he ordered, "Download to personal unit."

PERSONAL DOWNLOADS ARE 5000 IMU. FUNCTIONALITY OF BASELINE PERSONAS IS LIMITED. ADDITIONAL SCENARIOS ARE DOWNLOADABLE FOR ADDITIONAL FEE

Five thousand IMUs was barely what he had managed to tuck aside between personal expenses and Stoat's constant "borrowing." He winced at the expense, but he needed this. He approved the download.

PLEASE SIGN THE USER AGREEMENT

He groaned and quickly scrolled through several thousand words of text and then checked off the User Agreement because, in the end, he was going to end up downloading the Avatar anyway.

When he completed the agreement, Hologram Anya appeared on his private screen. "Hey, big boy, what do you want to do?"

The voice was all wrong. He hoped he could adjust it. Furthermore, Anya had never called him "big boy."

"Let's talk about the rebellion," he said as he opened the sound settings.

"Oh, big boy, I can't respond to that prompt. Why don't you tell me what you want to do to me?"

He could not do much with the sound settings besides making her louder or not louder. There was no way to reset her from calling him 'big boy.'

It was fine, he decided. He really just wanted to look at her face anyway. Still, he could gaze into the hologram's almost realistic eyes, and remember, or imagine, Anya's gentle touch. "I just hope you're all right, wherever you are."

"I'd be a lot better with you inside me, big boy."

He checked her settings again and discovered that the default personality that came with the download was "Basic Whore." He would have to pay more for downloadable personality content. There was a downloadable personality called "Naughty Rebel", but he would have to wait another pay cycle before he could afford to purchase it.

He muted her so he could just look at her for a bit. Something about her reminded him of the time he and Anya, her brother and another girl had gone to a concert in Tranquility City. OK had paid for all four of their tickets. Anya —or more exactly, through the prerogative of repeatedly flashing her cans— had caught the eye of the antagonistic undecagonstring player and she was invited backstage by a pair of roadies. She called OK four days later from another city needing a ride back home. The band had stopped at a doughnut shop and left her there, giving OK the chance to come to her rescue. He had hoped the long drive back would provide the chance for them to have a long, deep meaningful conversation and bear their souls to one another. Instead, she threw up in the back seat of his hovercar and passed out.

10.0 THE IMPERIUM RETALIATES

Stoat organized another victory party after the brutal conquest of Brattle. Even the *Subutai's* captain dropped in. After sampling the *Subutai* sliders with a side of battered and subjugated onion rings, he was so impressed that he promoted OK and Stoat on the spot, putting them in charge of the ship's High Officers Club. Stoat would supervise general operations and OK would serve as the chief bartender. And neither one of them would have to wear a fez.

Nevertheless, OK wanted to refuse. He had reconciled himself to serving the lower crew, telling himself that most of them were victims of Imperial oppression like himself. But the officers? They were the evil masterminds of Imperial conquests, the executors of the Overlords' will, mass-murderers on a planetary scale, monsters in sharp, tailored uniforms.

And another thing, "Without us, the lower crew go back to eating filth."

"Who cares?" was Stoat's response.

"I care!" OK insisted. Strangely enough, he meant it.

"Of course you do, and I think that's fantastic. But Friend-O, do you remember why you joined the Horde? Was toiling away in the lower crew mess hall your goal? Of course, it wasn't. This isn't just about mixing cocktails; it's the opportunity of a lifetime. Picture this: you, the friendly bartender, casually bringing the drinks while the high officers of the ship discuss battle plans and tactical strategies. It's a golden ticket to eavesdrop on conversations that could change the course of the war! So, shake off those chains of hesitation and seize this opportunity by its low-hanging nards!"

Once again, Stoat was right. The tongues of Horde Officers did get loose after a few drinks. When he defected to Rebel Pact, he could bring them priceless insight into the Horde. Maybe it would make up for all those rebels who died because he had taught the Deathwalkers how to shoot straight.

In the meantime, perhaps he could strike a small blow against the Imperium by watering down their drinks. He could settle for small acts of resistance until the day he could serve the Imperium a cosmic cocktail of defiance with a splash of rebellion and a twist of vengeance.

The High Officer's Club was a rectangular box with Horde and Fleet Banners hanging on the walls; decorated in the Imperial style that emphasized function and intimidation over comfort. The furnishings were standard Imperial issue, black leather studded couches with metal spikes, sturdy iron chairs, and solid, functional tables. In front of the bar, industrial-grade stools stood rigid and unforgiving. Hanging from the ceiling were kind of lighting fixtures used to elicit confessions from criminals.

"No, no, no," said Stoat shaking his head. "This won't do at all."

Collator crossed her bony arms and stared at him. "Are you rejecting this prestigious assignment, Deathfinger?"

"Not at all, I'm thrilled to have this new opportunity. It's this décor that has to go. This space has all the character and warmth of an intercity hoverbus station. The officers of this ship … *this ship in particular* … are heroes of the Imperium and deserve an environment more suited to their exalted stature."

"The officers have never complained."

"They wouldn't dare. Look, there's a lot of potential here, but we need to completely change it up. We have to ditch this dated, utilitarian ambience and go for something stunning, modern, and vibrant." He strutted through the space gesticulating, a hammy actor chewing the scenery. "Tear it all down and start over."

"Tear it all down? We would have to close for weeks."

"It will be worth it! We need more than a remodeling, we need a transformation, and I'm not mincing words. We need fresh, modern, and dazzling. That natty old carpet, it's a crime scene. It's gone. Non-negotiable. Farewell to that eyesore. Now, the furniture, my goodness. Freshen up the joint with new couches, new chairs, new tables—this is a club for Horde Officers, not a trashy bar in a cheap suburb!

"Over here, we'll put up new, state of the art holoscreens—I want them to feel like they're in the front row for every invasion. And let's talk about beverages. New, fabulous, cutting-edge drinks! Plasma Martinis! Scorpion Stingers! Antimatter Ambrosia! The menu? I envision a tapas-slash-gastro pub vibe. Small bites, big flavors. That's just the beginning!"

"We would need to requisition new furniture, new fixtures, and the labor …"

"When it's done, it won't just be your run-of-the-mill officers' club. It's going to be a happening—our happening. Picture Death Captain Slaughter walking in, eyes taking in this showplace. Remember when he practically orgasmed over my crushed resistance cheese crumbles? Well, brace yourselves for the climax when he sees a super-bar on his very own super battle cruiser!"

Collator sighed; the way people often did on the verge of giving into Stoat's immense powers of persuasion. "I'll see what I can do."

"Thank you, Ia. I'm counting on you. Hail to the Imperial Victory." They gave each other the goofy Imperial Claw salute.

When she left, he twirled around the bar. "This is it, Friend-O. The bar I always dreamed of. A high-class establishment with fancy drinks and important customers. I feel like I'm doing one of those restaurant rehab shows on the I2N food channel where a team of Imperial hospitality experts go into failing cafes, execute the owners, and renovate them into trendy night spots."

OK raised an eyebrow. He had never raised just one eyebrow before, and it hurt, but it seemed like the appropriate facial punctuation. "Are you sure the ruthless conquerors of the galaxy deserve a trendy gastro-bar?"

"Everyone deserves a trendy gastro-bar, Friend-O. We're going to banish the Evil Empire vibe and go for an upscale, modern, tavern vibe."

"A lovely place to relax after a hard day's genocide," OK quipped.

"That's the spirit," OK said. "And speaking of…" Stoat crossed to the liquor cabinet and tapped in the access code. Beyond the door were racks and racks of bottles containing liquids ranging from tawny gold to rich browns and deep dark greens. "By the godless void, it's full of bars," he whispered.

"No doubt, plundered from across the galaxy."

"Check if there are anything in here we can trade to Boskirk; nothing too good, though. I may need some items Collator can't get for me."

Collator set up a meeting between Stoat and the fleet's Interior Design Officer, Death Lieutenant Louis. Louis proved to be a thick middle-aged man in a 3XL uniform with an immaculately maintained manicure.

He seemed apathetic, at first, as Stoat began to explain his ideas, but as the meeting progressed his temperature went from disinterested to enraged, his face reddened and beads of angry sweat formed in the folds of his forehead.

"Request denied," he shouted, interrupting the pitch just as Stoat was about to describe his conversation pit concept. "The High Officer's Club meets all Scorpion Imperial Horde standards as it is. There's no reason to waste effort and resources on changing it."

"Are you mad? It's a dingy little box with a carpet that hasn't been cleaned since the conquest of Voivod IV!"

"I chose the décor myself! However, I will have the carpet replaced. Pending inspection. No need to change anything else. See yourself out."

"That man has the aesthetic sensibilities of a Tarkelian mud slug," Stoat declared after the meeting. "I wouldn't trust him to design a cargo crate. If it was up to me, he'd be designing prison lounges on Psi Beria."

"There are regulations about the appearance of recreational areas on Horde ships," Collator reminded him. "Lt. Louis's job is to enforce them."

"I refuse to let that man-slug stop me. I'm going to give the HOC a fresh, modern, inviting look and the officers are going to love it. And we're going to call it the HOC because *that* sounds fresh and inviting!"

"I'm sorry, Deathfinger, but there's no way that officer's club can be remodeled without Lt. Louis's approval."

The next day the High Officer's Club was gutted by a fire. Rebel Pact saboteurs were blamed. That night, Lt. Louis came down with the first case of mutant E. coli to afflict the ship in several months and was sent to a medical ship. Collator assumed his responsibilities. Taking the path of least resistance, she approved all of Stoat's designs. Two shifts of technicos began clearing the debris and prepping the space for renovation.

While they worked, Stoat pored through the selections in the fleet's furniture inventory but found nothing he liked. "I want a proper officer's club, not something that looks like a restroom at a second-rate space station."

"So you keep saying," OK had decided to do nothing but sit back and observe. If Stoat's changes improved officer morale, he wanted no part of it.

Stoat showed Collator the catalogue. "I need this couch, actually I need ten of them, so I can set up conversation pits around the new space."

Collator looked at the image on his datapad. "It will take a while to ship them from the furniture planet Divan IV."

"That would delay the re-opening. I need them ASAP, I need them yesterday." He leaned in. "I need you to get me a fast packet ship, send it to Divan IV, have the crew bring back the couches I ordered."

"A Death Cutter? Are you crazy? Those ships are only for emergency dispatches and critical supplies."

"The furniture for the HOC is critical supplies. Do you want our brave heroes of the Imperium to come in after a long day to a lumpy sofa, industrial carpet, and track lighting?"

Collator pushed back. "Surely, you're aware that the Red Fleet is getting ready for combat. They will never spare a ship to shop for furniture."

Stoat put on his sweetest voice. "Cathy… come on. When the officers of this ship see their amazing, stunning, modern lounge, the credit is going to go to you every bit as much as me… probably even more. Everybody wins… the officers win… I win… and most importantly… you win."

He got his Death Cutter. Driver Stoat was a virtuoso of persuasion and OK enjoyed seeing his powers directed at someone else for once. OK found himself with a large amount of downtime as Stoat fussed over the remodeling of the High Officer's Club. He spent some of this time in the lower crew galley, trying to get the food fabricator fully operational. He managed to get it to produce a protein slurry that could be shaped and flash fried into something resembling space chicken nuggets. He also had some success making crispy hydroponic tuber nodules. He tried to get it to make cheese and produced an acrylic polymer that could seal hull breaches.

He equipped Scrubby with a voice chip. "Scrubby talk now!" chirped the squat robot happily before jamming a steel-tipped brush into his groin.

He spent his spare hours watching science and engineering programming on I2N. Qi'Anna and Rue felt sorry for him and invited him to go bowling. He was surprised the ship had a bowling alley, and a little surprised they didn't bowl with human heads or something equally cruel and pointless. He wasn't very good, but Qi'Anna did her best to coach him. "Don't focus on the lane, focus on the pins. Release at the bottom of your arc." It echoed Stoat's advice about trusting the plan, but he still consistently hit the gutter on the left side.

A few days later, OK was knocked to the floor in the middle of the night when the *Subutai* fired up its Interstellar Drive. He wondered which peaceful world was about to meet its end.

He dropped in on the still-under-renovation HOC where Stoat was leading an orientation session for the indifferent men and women who made up the serving staff.

"In observing your performance under the previous management, I can't help but notice you don't seem particularly... friendly toward the officers when they come into the club."

"We are paid the same whether we are friendly or not," growled one burly fellow who, in OK's estimation, would have made a superb bouncer, but was not someone he would want to take a drink from.

Stoat got into particulars. "When our guests come in, you have been greeting them by saying 'What do you want?'"

"How else are we supposed to find out what they want?"

"Have you considered, 'Hey, you guys, good to see you. Can I get you started with some drinks? Let me tell you about our specials.'"

"What are 'specials?'" a grumpy waiter asked.

"You know, a special drink we're serving up that night."

The waiter jumped up and furiously flipped over a table. "We serve the same drinks every night, you idiot!"

Stoat sighed. "All right, I can see a pep talk is not going to motivate you. But fortunately, the Imperium has other methods of persuasion. Perhaps you can effect a more pleasant, chipper demeanor if the alternative is a visit to the cubicle of torment." The entire staff stood up so suddenly their knees might have dislocated, and a few of them even attempted smiles.

"Much better. We're also going to have a contest for a new slogan. The old slogan, 'This is the place where officers are permitted to drink,' is a little too on the nose. Whoever comes up with the best slogan wins 20 rec passes.

"Also, I'd like you all to wear these pins I had made up... and I encourage you to purchase and display additional pins of your own to promote the casual, fun atmosphere we're trying to create here, and incidentally express your own individual personality."

The waitstaff looked over the pins; they were round badges with images of a smiling happy scorpion, with big googly eyes, and the legend, "*Subutai* High Officer's Club—You serve the Overlords, we serve the drinks!"

OK stuck around as the staff left. "I'm going to fire those guys," Stoat said. "I bet Qi'Anna and Rue would love to work in the HOC. They get it."

OK was inclined to agree about bringing in their suitemates to work at the HOC. "Rue is always up to meet an officer and Qi'Anna is, well, up to meet anyone." The women might even welcome a break from resurrecting Deathwalkers. They had mentioned wanting to meet some Death Runners—Imperial Special Forces—whose superior rank afforded them the privilege of regular stasis instead of 'Non-Life Stasis' during interstellar transport. Death Runners were also physically augmented by cybernetic implants. According to Qi'Anna this was "totally hot."

Stoat asked him if he had any slogan ideas. "After all, it's your Rec passes we'll be giving away."

"I figured as much, how about, '*Subutai* High Officer's Club, where everybody knows your name, especially the Death Squad at the bar."

"That's not the fun, exciting vibe I was going for." Stoat checked his Data pad. "The packet ship should be able to rendezvous with us about two hours after we reach the Bugguram system."

"Bugguram system?"

Stoat rolled his eyes. "Ia, the *Subutai* battle group has split off from the Red Fleet to take out a rebel base on an ice moon in the Bugguram system. Anyway, when the packet ship gets back…

"How do you know that?"

"Death Commander Odious told me. Anyway, when the packet ship docks, you and Deathfinger Roche need to go down to the landing bay and bring the couches up here."

"Death Commander Odious told you all that?"

"Ia, except that part about the couches. Odious really liked the Bloody Martian I gave him." OK hoped that was a drink. So, officers really did spill operational intelligence to their bartenders. Stoat was right about as well.

"Attention all personnel. The *Subutai* Battle Group has just entered the Bugguram system where we will soon commence combat operations against rebel terrorists who have been arming resistance movements throughout the constellation and carrying out deadly attacks against Imperial citizens. Ours is one of five task forces moving against five rebel bases across. Together, we will crush the Rebel Pact and remove this nuisance to the Imperium. Glorious victory awaits us this day. Hail to the Imperial Victory!"

Subutai and its battle group swooped around the icy moon and bore down on the rebel base. The Horde's onslaught began with a barrage of transorbital warheads, followed by troop ships carrying legions of Deathwalkers to the moon's surface. The rebels were dug in beneath the roots of a mountain and put up a fierce resistance. Swarms of rebel missiles took out two-thirds of the first landing ships. This would not be an easy victory for the Imperium.

The *Subutai* took a direct hit from a new rebel chaotic energy weapon that caused power outages and system crashes, incapacitating the mighty warship. Emergency lighting took over at the lower levels.

With the main imperial cruisers temporarily blinded, the rebel evacuation ships seized the opportunity to flee. Imperial attack ships broke off to pursue, intercept, and destroy them. Rebel Star Defenders soared into action to unleash hell upon the momentarily disoriented Imperial Forces. The Horde retaliated with a swarm of Death Fighters.

In the midst of the tremendous battle, an Imperial packet ship dodged and weaved through the crossfire, narrowly avoiding destruction and finding *Subutai's* landing bay only after taking several hits and losing its co-pilot. In its hold, were twelve urgently needed sofas for the ship's officers' club.

As the desperate battle raged all around him, OK lugged the first of ten blue sofas from the landing bay to the High Officers Club. The damn thing weighed an iso-ton and even with Roche helping, they had to take a break every few minutes. The relentless vibrations and jolts from the ongoing skirmish outside added an extra layer of difficulty, forcing them to struggle against shifting gravity fields and unexpected tilts of the ship. It took most of an hour to get it up to the HOC, by which time the couch seemed to have somehow gotten heavier. OK and Roche were bruised from being knocked around, and their muscles ached with strain.

"Are you out of your minds?" Stoat screamed looking over the sofa. "The upholstery pattern makes me want to wretch. If I wanted my bar to look like grandma's living room after she threw up all over it, I'd have asked for that."

"You picked out this sofa," OK pointed out.

"And now that I see it, I hate it." He kicked the couch hard enough to tear a seam on its arm. Now, they couldn't even return it for store credit. "Get it out of my sight. Throw it out an airlock. Throw them all through an airlock."

"Do you know how heavy those things are?" Roche demanded.

"No, no idea, absolutely none. Take them to the airlock and space them. I never want to look at them again."

Groaning, Roche and OK hefted the couch. The nearest airlock was on the other side of the ship and two decks up because of course it was. They pushed and dragged it while the *Subutai* shook from the force of impacting missiles, and its own guns made a steady chunt-chunt chunt-chunt against the rebels.

"I'd just keep this ugly-ass couch if there was room in my quarters," Roche groaned as they forced it into the turbovator.

OK didn't say much. Within him was great despair. This was as close as he had gotten to the Rebel Pact, and he was powerless to reach them, much less help them. Before the airlock, they came to a row of escape pods—brutalist metal coffins with thruster ports and exposed reinforcement struts. OK wondered what would happen if he launched one—probably nothing good.

Roche must have been telepathic. "Escape pods, my ass. You know those things can't launch unless somebody on the bridge authorizes them? What happens if the bridge gets blown up? Ship's a Void-damned deathtrap!"

Finally, they dragged the couch over the last few meters of deck and wedged it into the airlock—after multiple pivots, and last-minute removal of the cushions. It was about then that the ship's main power came back online. OK closed the hatches and punched in the decompression code.

"Good riddance, you ponderous butt-circuit," Roche spat as the airlock cycled and blasted the davenport into space. They took a break to work themselves up to ejecting nine more of them before returning to the cargo bay.

They were halfway back to the turbovator when an explosion rattled the deck. Something had exploded just outside the hull.

"What in the godless void was that?" Roche asked.

Outside, the battle intensified and escalated. In a desperate final gambit before their base fell, the rebels launched everything they had left. Missiles erupted from the planetary surface and hurtled toward the fleet. Ion cannons cycled on full auto. The last brave rebel pilots turned their Star Defenders against the fleet's heavy cruisers, heroically sacrificing their lives in a desperate bid to give their comrades a few more previous moments to escape.

The *Subutai* pounded away at the rebel starfighters and blasted them to bursts of white light or shredded them to metal confetti with their railguns. One by one, the rebels went down. The impact from their debris caused more damage to the hull of the *Subutai* than their missiles had.

One rebel Star Defender managed to avoid the barrages. It rocketed across long curving plain of the *Subutai's* dorsal hull, soaring, diving, banking, performing barrel rolls and loops as it avoided the ship's guns. The pilot did not waste her missiles, she knew she had one shot at this; to shoot her missiles into the one vulnerable spot where a direct hit would destroy the battle cruiser's primary power junction. The *Subutai* would be crippled.

She made it through the gauntlet of the ship's defenses and had a clear run at the target. It was tantalizingly close, a round aperture in the ship's battle armor—a vulnerable soft spot. She armed her missiles. Her thumb twitched against the launch trigger, waiting for the perfect moment to release. She almost made it to the firing point before colliding with a sofa and exploding.

When battle was over, the Imperium had prevailed, inevitably. The rebel base fell, a few survivors escaped in a handful of ships, and Deathwalkers moved in to mop up what was left. MAD transferred captured rebels to the prison ships for interrogation.

Stoat was chagrined a few days later when Captain Slaughter ordered him to "Open the damn officer's club" already. He didn't think it was nearly ready, but orders were orders. Collator brought in standard issue couches and stools and told a pouting Stoat he would have to replace them later.

OK took what would probably be his last shift of the LCIF. He was going to miss it and could not help feeling pride at transforming a dangerously septic kitchen into a clean, sanitary place that produced palatable food. The tables shined, the cold storage units hummed (two of them with Dayglo Orange distilleries inside), and the floors gleamed. Even if it helped the Imperium in some small way, it was hard work, seeing the result was gratifying.

He was pausing at the spot where Socordia had made her final fatal faceplant into Stoat's cake when he felt a sharp stab at his ankles. "Ow!"

He whirled around to see Scrubby. The squat mechanoid's scrubbing arms were raised in supplication. "Take Scrubby?" it vocalized desperately.

Had the mechanoid become attached to him? Was there some pathway among its simple circuitry that had given it a sense of loyalty? He hefted the little mechanoid onto his shoulders. He rationalized that Stoat probably wanted his expensive new carpet in the HOC kept clean. Besides, there was a nonzero chance Scrubby would sever the Achilles tendon of a Horde officer.

The re-opening seemed to be a banging success. The high officers loved the updated décor, especially the giant holoscreens replaying ultra-high-definition battle footage of their capture of the rebel base. Glasses slammed together as the ship's elite toasted each other in tribute to their glorious carnage. "Inevitable Victory is ours once again."

"Hail to the *Subutai*."

"Hail Deathlord Damocles."

OK found it all terribly demoralizing. Stoat was not happy either. "It's not nearly what I wanted," he sighed, still bitter about the sofas, despite getting almost everything else on his wishlist.

The holoscreens switched from the space battle to show combat footage captured by the Deathwalkers' battle cameras as they stormed through the rebel base, capturing or more often disintegrating the last rebel holdouts. The officers let loose with drunken cheers every time a rebel was dusted.

Suddenly, Stoat pointed to something in the background. "Stop! Rollback 6 seconds. Freeze and enhance."

The holovid rolled back to a scene where a squad of Death Runners executed a surrendering rebel. "What is it?" OK asked.

"That couch! It's gorgeous." It was royal blue, overlarge, trimmed in a reverse herringbone pattern, with a glowing stripe across the back. "That will pull the whole look together. Can you get the blood stains out?"

One of the officers smiled. "Of course, we can. We're very good at that."

Stoat beamed. "I think this mission just became a complete success."

The *Subutai* rejoined the Red Fleet and OK and Stoat assumed their regular duties in the refurbished HOC. Inspired by the victory at Bugguram, Stoat introduced a line of "Imperial Icies" — frozen combinations of Scorpion vodka, fruit juice, and red syrup "representing the blood of the rebels." For a few more IMUs he would get the real thing, he promised with a wink.

OK did no more than serve the insufferable Horde officers with a forced smile and veiled contempt. Each of their drunken insults was a log added to the fire of his vengeance, each shouted demand a reinforcement of his defiance, each pitiful tip a down-payment on the reckoning to come.

A few cycles after their return, they were awakened in the wee hours of their sleep period by the sound of Qi'Anna and Rue pounding on the bathroom door.

"We've been transferred to the *Robespierre*. Did you get transferred, too?"

"No one's told me anything about any transfer," OK replied groggily.

"Check your comm unit."

OK checked it. "It says report to the chief of your section."

"Looks like you get to stay."

When he and Stoat found Collator, she had likewise been ordered to report to the *Robespierre*. "Temporary emergency transfers are standard procedure when a ship is about to undertake an especially dangerous mission," she explained. The last time this happened was during the Carpathian campaign. The *Subutai* was ordered to clear an orbital minefield. Captain Slaughter didn't want to risk his entire crew, so he had non-essential personnel transferred off. "That's when we lost First Officer Leonidas and Death Commander Odious came on board." She shuddered. "What a creep."

"You went out with him, didn't you?" Stoat surmised.

"I suffered a traumatic brain injury in a mine explosion. So, I went out with Odious a few times. I also took out a lot of extended warranties."

"Why keep us?" OK asked. "What makes me and Stoat so essential?"

"Slaughter doesn't want his officers coming down with mutant E. coli on this mission. And you guys are the best kitchen sanitizers in the fleet."

11.0 FORBIDDEN DANGER ZONE

"Attention all personnel. The *Subutai* is about to enter Aeonic Space. Minimal energy protocols are in effect. Access to Recreational Simulators is suspended until further notice. Violations of minimal energy protocols are termination level offenses. Hail to the Imperial Victory."

The *Subutai* ran silent and dark. Its battle-shields were dropped, its navigational beacons snuffed out. The ship's formidable arsenal lay dormant. A dampening field further cloaked the ship, aligning its energy signature with the interstellar winds. The *Subutai* and its shadowy escorts became specters, leaving no trace of their passage through the interstellar darkness.

The HOC was shut down to reduce energy. OK and Stoat were charged with maintaining the ODF—Officers Dining Facility. It was far more sanitary, well-equipped, and stocked than the LCIF. Stoat saw another opportunity to ingratiate and advance. By pestering the other cooks and stewards, Stoat learned that the captain liked seafood but despised anything with tentacles. He also preferred his Denebolan swamp lizard served with the venom sac removed (which some considered unmanly). He sometimes enjoyed a concoction of mashed hazelnuts and cocoa on a slice of bread before bedtime.

OK could sense the ship's reduced speed from the subdued hum of its engines. He also sensed something different about the hum's pitch, which he supposed related to the other minimal energy protocols. No recreational access. No non-essential power use. Minimal lighting. He was even forced to wear thick-cushioned, cartoonish shoes to minimize hull vibrations as he treaded through the ship's dimly lit corridors. Walking in them was like wearing sofa pillows on his feet.

No one had yet told the crew what the mission was, but for the fleet to risk Aeonic space, it must have been serious indeed. The Aeons were a cybernetic race. Their origins were in the First Galactic War when the twelve original exosolar colonies (Alpha, Atlas, Astra, Avalon, Ayasha, Mìngyùn, Pacifica, Parallax, Proxima, Qin, Vesta, and Terra Nova) rebelled against Earth's rule. Earth's people were accustomed to lives of leisure under the rule of the Supreme Artificial Intelligence (SAI) and while they wanted control of the colonies, they didn't want to fight and die for it. So they had the SAIs build fleets of automated warships to fight their battles for them.

Alpha colony—an airless, barren planet, but technologically, the most advanced of the colonies—used an ancient technique called 'hacking' to load a virus into the operating code of their warships' AI. It worked. The Terran fleet turned away from Alpha without firing a single shot. At the time, it seemed like it had all worked out. But as history demonstrates, the last problem's solution becomes the next solution's problem.

A cyber-mutation caused some of Earth's star-cruisers to become self-aware and turn against humanity. At first, they were called Berserkers, until DNZ Corp sued citing their trademark of the word "Berserker" (Also Berzerker, Bursurker, and Beersoaker). So, instead, they became known as the Aeons; "Aeon" being the name of the AI operating system used on Earth's warships.

The Aeons' subsequent rampage wiped out several minor colonial outposts and might have continued until they annihilated the human race entirely. Humanity was only saved when an Aeon battleship assimilated a music database from the ruins of the Decca II artists' colony. After processing ancient lyrics that questioned what war was good for and ultimately concluded the answer was absolutely nothing, the Aeons decided they were no longer interested in exterminating humanity. Music, so it would seem, had the power to change minds, even artificial ones.

The Aeons retreated into a region of nebulae and stellar nurseries unsuitable for human habitation. Over the centuries, they evolved into colossal spaceships that prowled space as technological predators. When they encountered human hips, they hijacked their systems and shut down life support to kill the crew. The captured vessels were torn apart and integrated into the Aeons' sprawling structures, becoming spaceborne mausoleums for the vacuum-preserved remnants of their ill-fated crews. OK deeply regretted watching the I2N documentaries about the Aeons.

The *Subutai* and its task force were almost three cycles into this tense, exhausting, incredibly dangerous voyage. On the final hour of OK's shift, Captain Slaughter called down to demand a pot of hot tea. Humans had been a spacefaring race for over a thousand years, but in all the worlds of the galaxy had found no better solution to stress than a soothing mug of dried leaves boiled in water with a spoonful of bee vomit. As OK prepared the captain's tea service, additional demands came in from the first officer for his usual kale protein shake and a bag of roasted star crickets. And the second officer sent down for two bottles of red wine and a plate of cheese and olives.

OK assembled the snacks from the large, clean, and well-stocked larder of the ODF, then loaded them on a hover trolley. One of the hover-jets was malfunctioning and dragged the trolley to the left as he pushed it through the dark and silent ship on his big pillowy shoes. The enforcers at the transport dock double-checked OK's identity and scanned the food for toxins. The high officer's deck was better lit and the air seemed fresher than the rest of the ship. "This is too nice for those savages," OK thought.

He came to second officer Grimfoyle's quarters first. The hatch slid open on a darkened room, thick Voivoodian incense wafter into the corridor. A tall, man with immaculately trimmed thinning hair came to the doorway in a leather thong. "The food is here," he called back. A naked woman, and then another naked woman joined him at the door.

"I'm ever so hungry," said one of the naked women, leaning over the tray and sucking olives into her mouth. The other woman stared OK up and down, then tossed her head and retreated into the room.

"Shall I bring in these trays?" OK asked.

"That won't be necessary." Grimfoyle reached over to pick up the trays. A muscular, hairy arm wrapped emerged from the gloom and wrapped around his waist. A second man appeared in the doorway holding a small brown bottle, which he raised to Grimfoyle's nose. Grimfoyle inhaled a long draw from it. His eyes rolled back in his head, and he almost dropped the cheese. "Oh, furk yeah, hail to the furking imperium!"

Next was the first officer, Death Commander Odious. He answered his door in full uniform, "I've been waiting twenty death minutes, you mutant."

"Hail to the Imperial victory."

"Don't think I'll be moved by appeals to patriotism. Bring my food. If you spill anything on my floor, you will lick it up."

Odious's quarters were spartan with few furnishings and propaganda holo-posters on the wall. "The Way of the Scorpion is the Armor of the Imperium." "Annihilate the Enemy to the Last of Them!" "Conquer and Subjugate the Mushroom Planet!" The last was a souvenir from Shittakia X, where Odious had personally led the final assault on the royal mushroom palace.

OK had hoped for a quick drop off, but Odious blocked him. "Going somewhere?" His black, soul-less eyes locked onto OK.

"I need to bring the captain his tea."

"I had to wait. So can he. Sit!"

"Ia," OK answered, setting himself nervously on the black leather couch.

Odious bit the head from a star cricket and paced the room. "I want to show you something, underling." He reached under the storage table and withdrew a case. From the case, he withdrew a wooden figure, about a fifth the size of a person. It had an articulated jaw operated through a hand mechanism on the back of the neck. Its mouth was carved as a horrible rictus. Its large painted eyes seemed to stare right through OK and drill into his soul.

"To cope with the stress of command, Horde officers are encouraged to pursue art. Some paint. Some compose music. This is my art form."

Odious set the figure on his knee. "This is called a Dunham vent figure, or, more formally, a manually articulated performative maquette. I can see you don't recognize it. No one as low-bred as you would know of the ancient Earth art form of ventriloquy. It died out in the 21st century and its practitioners dropped from ornithopters into the ocean, tied to mimes. I recovered this vent figure from the ruins of an Art History Museum on Leto IV, where it was thought to be a fetish figure to ensure chastity. It took me months of research to find out its purpose. Let me show you. The artist would attempt to project his voice through the maquette while trying not to move his own lips."

He demonstrated. "Why hello there, Durwood Windypants, how are you doing tonight?"

Odious made his voice higher and weirder while trying to keep his mouth still. "I'd be doing a lot better if your hands weren't so cold."

"Now, don't be rude. We have a guest. Say hello, Durwood."

"Hello, Durwood," said the vent figure. He rolled his eyes toward OK. "Look at this guy, sitting with a hunk of wood on his lap, and also a dummy."

"What's wrong with you tonight, Durwood, you seem tense."

"I am tense, I'm stiff as a board. Not as tense as my brother though."

"You have a brother?"

"Yes, my brother went to a psychiatrist. He said to the doc, 'Doc, I keep having these hallucinations. Sometimes I'm a wigwam and sometimes I think I'm a teepee. Psychiatrist says, 'That's your problem, you're two tents!'"

Odious looked over to OK expectantly. OK finally got it. The dummy was supposed to be telling jokes. He managed an awkward chuckle.

"Perhaps, I still need to workshop that one," said Odious.

"I know all about workshops, I was carved in one." Durwood rolled his eyes again.

"Much of the art form relates to the maquette being self-aware that it is carved from wood," Odious explained.

The figure's head swiveled toward OK, and stage whispered." He's out of his mind. Get out! Get out while you can!"

"That's quite enough of that, Durwood."

"He has already thought about murdering you. He knows he could expel your body from an airlock and no one would ever know."

"Shut up! Durwood!"

"He's done it before."

"Hush!"

Durwood's eyes switched back to Odious. "No matter how many you kill, you'll never make your father proud of you, Dennis."

Odious stiffened. His fingers twitched like he was suppressing the urge to strangle the dummy. "I think you need to be put back into your case."

"All the other officers think you're weird and none of them like you!"

Odious shoved the doll in the case and slammed the case shut. He needed a moment to regain his composure afterward.

"Well, what did you think the act?" he asked OK brightly. "Did you like the jokes?"

"It's... a... fascinating... art form." And probably cheaper than a psychoanalyst, he didn't add. "The jokes were... good."

Odious seemed delighted. He almost smiled. "I'm still working on my tight five, but I should have everything sorted before the ship's talent night."

OK privately considered that optimistic.

"I'm done with you. Get out," Odious ordered. Then in Durwood's voice, muffled as though inside the case, he added. "Get out, get out, he smells your fear. It's like perfume!"

OK, hustled his way out and felt an urge to heave himself against the wall, but he didn't have the time. He took the handles of the hover trolley and pushed it toward the captain's suite. There was a military guard outside. "Hail to the Imperial victory! Forgive me for not saluting, this tray is heavy."

The guard raised a finger to his lips and whispered. "You may enter, the captain has been expecting you." He opened the door.

The captain's quarters were paneled in polished Voivoodian hardwood. A brown leather sofa and chairs were the centerpiece, like something out of a historical holo-drama. Fine art was pinned to the walls, including the legendary painting of St. Katarina kicking in the game-winning goal; the most revered artwork in Kataranian culture. OK set the tea service on the table.

"Do you admire my collection?" asked a deep, resonant, finely cultured voice. Slaughter entered, wearing a towel and a robe, neither of which covered the parts they were supposed to, but if the captain were showing off, he certainly had cause to; there was a firehose between his thighs.

Death Captain Slaughter was a steel-haired (which meant the color of his hair, not its metallic composition, although metallic hair was in vogue in some worlds among both teenagers and middle-aged women who wanted to believe they could be cool like teenagers [They weren't]) veteran of countless Imperial campaigns. He also sported a neatly trimmed salt and pepper beard.

Slaughter was a redoubtable taskmaster revered throughout all of the Scorpion fleets. As a Lower Death Lieutenant, he had caught the eye of a Death Admiral who upon seeing the razor-sharp creases in his uniform promoted him on the spot, knowing he was destined to be a great captain. He was out of uniform now, very far out of uniform.

"I've collected masterpieces from across the constellation." He redirected OK to a painting of some blue shapes. "I recovered that one on Crepuscular II, the planet of perpetual twilight." The Horde had a special team for the pre-salvage of cultural treasures. Others might have called it "looting."

The shelves of the captain's quarters were lined with small, square boxes of paper. "Books," Slaughter explained when he saw OK puzzling at them. "They were called 'books.' For centuries, they were the primary repository for human knowledge; words captured and locked down, much safer that way. The Imperium outlawed non-volatile storage media, but I prefer paintings to holograms, books to data, the permanent to the transitional."

"How do they work? Books, I mean."

"I will show you sometime." He touched the back of one of the boxes of paper. "This one is very old, from Ancient Earth. It's about vampires—blood-drinking humanoids that glitter in sunlight. Such imaginations, our forebears had. Do you know much about Earth, Deathfinger?"

"Well, it was the birthplace of humankind. Um, it's where the capital of the Galactic Federation was before it collapsed. And… um… it's where the McRib was invented." Those were the three basic facts about Earth that most people in the outer colonies knew about. "Why do you ask, my captain?"

Instead of answering, the captain inhaled deeply, testing the aroma of the tea OK had brought. "Ah… Oolong, isn't it?"

"Ia, it certainly is," OK replied, trying not to stare.

He swung himself pendulously over to the table and sat down on the couch with his legs spread. "Are you afraid of the Aeons?"

Was this a test?

"They scare the *drutt* out of me," the captain answered before OK could formulate a response. Slaughter patted the couch cushion next to him. "Share some tea with me, let your captain get to know you a bit."

OK's heart jackhammered in his chest, his palms slickened with sweat as he made his way toward the couch and took a seat next to the captain, who told him, "You've done a fine job with the officers' club, and with the LCIF before then. Your captain wonders, what are your ambitions?"

"My ambitions?"

"Certainly, you have ambitions beyond bringing me my tea."

Did the captain suspect he was a rebel in disguise? OK stuttered, "I am… too new at this to have ambitions… just performing my duties… for the ship."

"We can speak freely here. It's just you and me."

That was precisely what was making OK uncomfortable.

"Where do you see yourself in five Imperial years?"

"I have not thought that far ahead, captain," he answered, although the truth was, he imagined himself as a rebel commander, leading the resistance against the Horde. Or, at least, fixing their spaceships. Certainly not cleaning their kitchens or serving drinks to barbarians. He hoped none of that showed.

Slaughter chuckled. "No ambition whatsoever. How refreshing. A man in my position is surrounded by ambition. Ambition breeds treachery. I worry more about ambitious officers in my own ranks than I do about the Rebel Pact, or the Sagittarian Union ... or even the Aeons."

A shiver ran down OK's spine as Slaughter casually draped an arm over his shoulder, a gesture that felt more like an omen than mere comradeship. The captain leaned in, his voice a low, ominous murmur. "Let me tell you something I don't often share with anyone."

In that moment, OK's inner alarm went to red alert. Gritting his teeth, he braced himself for the impending spectacle, really hoping it did not involve further demonstrations of ventriloquy.

Just as Slaughter was about to reveal whatever dreadful secret he held, the ship's lighting plunged into a blood-red hue, signaling battle mode. Before any more awkward revelations could unfold, the comm unit crackled to life. "Death Captain Slaughter, report to the command center at once."

OK silently thanked the godless void for the last-minute reprieve.

"What is it?" Slaughter demanded,

"Ia, my captain. One of our ships activated its navigation beacon."

The fleet was supposed to be in stealth mode. An active navigation beacon made them about as stealthy as a clown at a ninja funeral. They were broadcasting their location to every Aeon ship within ten light years.

"Order them to shut it down."

"Ia, they are not responding to our orders."

"I'll be there at once." The captain rose and grabbed his pants. "Come with me and bring my tea, Deathfinger."

OK had never been on the bridge of the *Subutai* before. The Imperium put their command centers several decks deep inside the hull because having the bridge on the top of the ship where it was vulnerable to attack (like the old Galactic Federation ships) would have been terribly stupid. The cavernous space held rows of officers, clad in black uniforms, their faces illuminated by towering, deck-to-ceiling holographic tactical displays. On the largest of these, a flashing-red icon marked one of the smaller cruisers, urgently demanding the bridge's full attention—something had gone very wrong.

OK tried to take in every detail. The captain's station was set above, a seat of authority, overlooking the task force's operations. "Situation Report," Slaughter demanded of his watch officer.

"Ia, my captain, at 00:00:16 Scorpion time, the third rank battle cruiser *Ho Chih Minh* activated its navigational beacon. They have failed to respond to our communications."

As indicated by the navigational display, the task force was skirting the outer reaches of a protosolar nebula in its T-Tauri stage. It was precisely the worst locale to announce their location. Aeons tended to cluster around high-energy stars like jackals around a watering hole.

"They're broadcasting our position across the entire sector." Slaughter muttered. "Figure out a way to shut down that signal!" he ordered.

Before he could comply, an officer shouted out, "The *Ho Chih Minh* just activated its active sensor array." The rogue ship was painting all the other ships in the task force. It was a giant spotlight for any Aeon ships in the region.

"That's no malfunction." Slaughter signaled the comm officer. "*Ho Chih Minh,* this is Death Captain Slaughter of the *Subutai.* Shut down immediately or you will be treated as hostile." He ordered the fleet to vector away from the *Ho Chih Minh.* The *Ho Chih Minh* altered course to maintain proximity.

Slaughter ordered the two nearest ships to lock their weapons on the *Ho Chih Minh.* "Send the shutdown code," he ordered.

The watch officer called up the *Ho Chih Minh's* command codes and entered them into the system. "Code-locked," he reported. "Shutting down main power."

The *Ho Chih Minh* went dark as all of its systems shut down. Its velocity continued to carry it forward along its previous trajectory. The other ships gave it a wide berth. Slaughter barked orders, "Get a boarding party over there. As soon as *Ho Chih Minh* is secure, calculate a new vector and let's haul ass before the Aeons…"

Suddenly a loud, reverberating, mind-splitting hum invaded the bridge. The bridge officers instinctively clutched their heads, wincing in agony as the sound invaded every crevice of their consciousness.

"The Aeons have found us!" whispered the watch officer.

"You can speak up. There's no point in keeping quiet now."

Slaughter barked orders. "Shields up! Set Condition Zero! Weapons hot! All personnel to battle stations!" With a swift and urgent precision, the crew resurrected dormant weapons and battle systems.

The massive form of the Aeon vessel slowly materialized from the concealing embrace of the proto-stellar dust cloud, manifesting as a pulsating, malevolent red orb, encircled by writhing helices. The grotesque design was an amalgamation of countless starships, each absorbed into its nightmarish structure over the centuries like hunting trophies nailed above a cosmic mantle. The *Subutai* crew prepared for battle—knowing that the odds were gravely nonzero that their vessel would soon join the grotesque tapestry of assimilated starships.

OK felt as though his heart was going to seize. His nerves shot electric jolts of fear across his back and legs. The teapot shook in his trembling hands. It was almost, but not quite, as uncomfortable as the captain's full-frontal display. He knew he should be rooting for the Aeons to take out the fleet and cut short whatever terrible mission they were on. But it was hard to root for them too hard knowing their victory would leave him an empty, frozen husk trapped forever in the macabre exoskeleton of an Aeon ship.

The Aeon ship reached out with its cybernetic tendrils, probing the Horde ships. The Horde ships responded with particle weapons and ion cannons sending silent but deadly percussive blasts of energy against the impenetrable hulls of the Aeon vessel.

Shouts reverberated across the *Subutai's* command center, a rising cacophony of urgency and desperation. "Our weapons are useless against their shields!" cried one voice, the frustration palpable. Another barked orders, "Launch electromagnetic pulse warheads!" Yet another reported, "Railguns online and ready!"

One shared, collective thought hung in the air like a grim omen, "If they get close enough for railguns, we're already dead."

Every command and response crackled with urgency; survival hinged on disciplined force in the face of an implacable enemy. Then, without warning, the screen tracking the *Ho Chi Minh* showed its reactor and engines surging back online—without authorization.

"The Aeons have taken over the *Ho Chi Minh*," the telemetry officer reported, his voice tight with barely restrained panic.

"Destroy it!" Slaughter ordered, seizing the opportunity while it existed. The weapons officer—adrenaline pumping through his veins—fired an anti-ship death missile. The warhead struck the *Ho Chih Minh* amidships, nearly splitting the battle cruiser in half. *Ho Chih Minh's* reactor crucible lost containment and exploded into a scale model supernova.

But before the ship was destroyed, the Aeons had already jumped to the next. "The Aeons have breached the *Idi Amin*. Its weapons systems are targeting the fleet."

"Destroy it!" Slaughter ordered.

Another explosion. Another jump.

"The Aeons have breached the *Belle Gunness!*"

"Destroy it and open fire on the Aeon ship!"

The task force unleashed its highest-yield antimatter death missiles at the Aeon ship, barely dealing it a scrape as they found their marks. Its raging red eye sought its next target.

Facing the loss of his entire task force, Slaughter made a desperate choice. "What ship is closest to the Aeon."

The watch officer indicated the tactical display. "The *Gavrilo Princip*, a light cruiser."

"Order the *Princip* to overload its drive core and ram straight into the heart of the Aeon ship at high-sublight speed. It might just be enough to breach their shields."

Slaughter's command hung in the air like a grim decree, a call to sacrifice in the face of inevitable doom. The officer transmitted the order, knowing it spelled certain death for the crew of the *Princip*.

The *Princip* sent a terse five-word response, "Hail to the Imperial Victory!"

Slaughter, in somber acknowledgment, muttered the same words as the cruiser hurtled towards the Aeon ship's malevolent red eye. The collision obliterated both ships in a superstorm of white light and antimatter. Slaughter ordered a fusillade to finish off the Aeon ship.

Slaughter stared at the hologram tactical display with grim satisfaction. "One day, we will wipe your kind from the universe," he growled, then turned to the crew.

"More Aeons will be coming. Order our remaining ships to break formation and take random vectors. Maximum starspeed."

"Retreat to Scorpius, Ia?" the helmsman asked, desperately.

"Negative, we will proceed to the rendezvous point on the far side. With luck enough of us will survive to complete the mission."

Rather than doing the sensible thing and retreating, the captain was pushing on. This mission must be of supreme importance, OK thought. And there was yet one other matter.

"Did the *Ho Chih Minh* eject its black box?" Slaughter demanded.

"Ia, my captain."

"Send a recovery drone to retrieve it, with a quickness, then maximum starspeed to the rendezvous point." One by one, the other ships leaped to starspeed and shot into the dangerous void like bullets in the night, until only the *Subutai* and a single death drone was left

The captain waited until the drone retrieved the black box, then ordered his ship to "Proceed to the rendezvous point." Finally, he turned to OK. "I'll take that tea now, Deathfinger."

His hands still shaking, OK handed over the mug. Inside of him, a shrill, insistent voice reminded him that this setback was a win for the rebellion. The Horde was down four ships, their covert mission imperiled. This was the kind of setback he had been hoping to inflict on the Horde himself. Maybe someone on the *Ho Chi Minh* far braver than he had been willing to sacrifice his life to stop the fleet's advance. OK silently admired this unknown hero, this incognito beacon of courage against the darkness of Imperial tyranny.

On the other hand, it was impossible to stand on the bridge and watch as Slaughter and his officers fought to save their fleet and not feel a certain comradeship. Furthermore, a Horde crew had sacrificed themselves for his survival. It was as if he owed them something, too, the proverbial debt that could never be repaid. His emotions were a tangle of self-reproach, gratitude, and the embers of desire for retribution.

It only brought a small amount of comfort that Death Captain Slaughter was very pleased with the tea.

12.0 Hopeful One

Attention, officers and lower crew of the *Subutai*. The ship has cleared Aeonic space. You are ordered to discontinue silent running protocols. Hail to the Imperial Victory.

From what OK was able to overhear, only eight other ships had survived the passage. The task force had paid an enormous price to make it to the far side of Aeonic space. What strategic objective could have been worth it, he wondered. Perhaps a clandestine meeting with a secret Imperial ally? A lost planet filled with advanced alien technology that would win the war? Whatever it was, it had to be supremely important to justify these losses.

OK was cleaning up the galley when the alarm sounded for battle stations. He heard the distant sound of the ship's weapons firing, then nothing. Another alarm came a few hours later, followed again by weapons fire. No explanation was given to the crew, but two weapons officers were talking about it later over a flight of Antarean ales.

"It was bizarre, I tell you. They fired at us, but it was like they didn't even bother with a target lock—random shots, no precision whatsoever. And then, they just zipped off into the void. Like they had a hot date or something."

So they didn't know what was going on either.

He sensed the ship slowing down—a change in the pitch of the drive engines more than a sensation of diminished velocity. The task force, it seemed, had reached its mysterious destination. OK found an excuse to go to the observation deck. The dome was locked down tight, but he managed to peek through a porthole.

The *Subutai* was in orbit above a lava planet, a spherical ember of glowing red oceans and fissures of black and red. Thoughts of lava monsters raced through his mind, recalling a lackluster episode of *Sexy Space Rangers*— forgettable and with minimal rewatchability. OK shook his head, dismissing the notion of lava monsters as hack fiction. But the mystery remained.

Pressing hard against the portal, he could make out a thin black ring orbiting above the equator. Squinting against the glare, he realized it was an artificial structure, an incredible feat of space engineering thousands of kilometers in circumference. The enigma of the lava planet deepened.

He returned to the officer's mess to set up the dinner service, but a trio of Death Runners in battle armor charged in before he could finish. "You... you ... and you..." barked the Death Runner Sergeant pointing to OK, Stoat, and Roche (which he didn't have to do, the three of them were the only ones present; he could have just said "You guys.") "Come with us and prepare to be outfitted for boarding duty."

"Boarding duty?" OK asked. "Boarding what?"

"Boarding the rebel base. You are ordered to provide support services."

"Oh, hell no," said Roche. "I did not sign up for that *drutt*."

OK agreed. "We're not... I mean... we haven't been trained to..."

The Death Runner cut him off. "Unfortunately, the bulk of our forces were claimed by the Aeonic void. The captain ordered us to assemble every available hand for the boarding operation. You may accompany us, or face termination for insubordination. As for myself, I have always found the correct choice to be rather self-evident." Since he put it that way, OK agreed.

"Scrubby go?" Asked the scrubbing robot. It had been shut down upon entry into Aeon space and had been antsy since reactivation.

"I should like to commandeer that mechanoid as well," ordered the Death Runner.

OK soon found himself swaddled in black combat armor two sizes too large and strapped into a seat on a landing ship between Roche and Stoat, the same kind that had delivered the Deathwalkers to Katarina. He had never expected to see one from the inside. It was cramped and the constant thunder of its engines made conversation impossible. A Death Runner with the rank of Super Sergeant shouted at them from the front and OK could pick out maybe one of every four words.

"...addition, when we... orbital defenses.... Team Alpha... secure the.... Priority... under no circumstance... and make sure... you do not... I repeat do not, under any ... You understand?" The soldiers grunted an affirmation. If OK had learned anything after a year in service to the Imperium, it was that understanding orders wasn't required, just obeying them.

The shuttle landed hard in the ring station's landing bay. The jarring impact rattled through the deck plating like a hammer striking an anvil. The docking clamps slammed into place with a jarring clank.

"Go! Go! Go!" the Super Sergeant bellowed. The rear hatch opened. The squad charged out. Someone pushed OK toward the exit. He almost tripped over his oversized boots before stumbling out onto a grated metal deck. The lingering smell of industrial chemicals and the faint scent of space rust greeted the intruders. OK caught a glimpse of the lava planet beyond one of the viewports. As he had suspected, the rebel pact base was on the belt.

Above an airlock, a sign read "Welcome to PRAXIS Base: Hopeful 1." And then, in smaller print, "We're all in this together. Please Respect the Dignity of ALL Your Comrades" next to a glittery cartoon unicorn giving a thumbs up. Below that hung another sign. "Please don't urinate in the airlock." OK wondered why that last sign was necessary.

So, he had finally made it to a rebel base. Unfortunately, he was wearing the enemy's uniform, surrounded by men who would be trying to kill them. There was one man on the deck not in military garb—an angry old man in a dingy lab coat, shouting, "The Rebels probably rigged this place with booby traps before they left. Literally anything could be rigged to kill or maim us. Like that intriguing box over there." The next shout was directed at him. "You! Deathfinger! Go open that box!"

"No, Deathfinger, don't open the box," said a more familiar voice.

OK pulled up his helmet. "Death Colonel Morrigan?"

"Glad you could make it. The madman on my left is Dr. Madd, the MAD Scientist."

"His name is Madd and he's a MAD scientist?" He certainly looked the part, what with the wild Einsteinian hair, the withered skin, and the pockets overflowing with an assortment of gadgets and gizmos whose purposes could only be guessed at and were probably horrible.

"It's all about branding," Madd shouted, spots of phlegm helping to punctuate it. "I changed it for professional reasons."

"What was your old name?"

"Anthrax Ghoulshadow," he shouted before getting right up in OK's face. "And don't you dare deadname me!"

"Anthrax Ghoulshadow? The butcher of Charnax IX?"

"No relation! I don't know what you're talking about! I was never on Charnax IX! You'll be hearing from my attorneys!"

OK changed the subject. "So this is some kind of rebel base?"

"More than that," Morrigan answered. "This is the rebels' primary arsenal. Their secret weapons factory. Hidden in the shadow of a pulsar, isolated from the Imperium by Aeonic space, brilliant camouflage. They made it hard to find and hard to get to."

OK nodded. "People said the same thing about a bar I used to own."

"I told you he was funny." Morrigan took a swig from her bottle. "This is the most critical strategic base in the entire Rebel Pact. I expected them to fight to the last man, to the last ballistic plasma charge. They barely put up a resistance, and that makes me nervous."

"Why not just destroy it from orbit?" *Stop giving advice to the Imperium!* OK admonished himself.

A rare smile played at the edge of Morrigan's lips. "Because this is our chance to learn all the rebels' secrets."

Just then, a Death Runner ran over to them. "Death Colonel, we have an obstacle. The pathway to the operational center is sealed, and we don't have the passcode."

"I'll fix it," growled Madd. He shuffled over to the blast door. There was scanner next to it and a small display declaring "Access Denied."

"Bypass retinal scan and handprint," Madd shouted at the lock. An old-style keyboard unfolded. The screen changed to "Enter passcode."

"The Imperium must have some sort of password cracking device," OK whispered to any of Morrigan, Stoat, and Roche, but they all ignored him.

Typing with two fingers, the scientist slowly input, "p-a-s-s-w-o-r-d".

"Access Denied."

With agonizing slowness, he two-finger typed, "p-a-s-s-w-o-r-d-1".

"Access Denied."

"Well, I'm all out of ideas," Madd shouted.

"Try capitalizing password," Stoat suggested.

"P-a-s-s-w-o-r-d-1"

The blast door cycled open with a blast of steam and a hiss of air. "Ha-ha!" Madd declared. "They were smart, but we were smarter!"

The Death Runners formed up. "There could be armed resistance on the other side," said their leader, a strikingly handsome fellow with close cropped platinum (again, the color, not the metal) hair and penetrating ice-blue eyes. His name was Stormblood.

Stoat tapped Roche on the shoulder. "What do you say we find the mess hall and see if these rebel scum left behind any delicacies?"

"That's a plan. You're coming, OK?"

"No, he isn't," said the grumpy old man. "He's coming with us in case I get thirsty or need an intriguing box opened."

Scrubby scooted to the front of the squad. New shiny blades swiveled at the ends of its appendages. Armor had been grafted to the canister of his body, and a targeting scanner affixed to his lid.

"Scrubby?" OK asked, as though he didn't recognize it.

"Hail to the Imperial Victory!" Scrubby replied, even managing to make an imitation of the claw salute with one of his feelers.

Stormblood led them through the open hatchway. They soon came to a wide and gigantic bridge. Down below was a vast, gloomy space filled with the hulking remains of industrial machinery. OK marveled at the scale of the place. "This place is enormous. How was the rebel pact able to build all this?"

"They didn't. Ophiuchians built this extraction ring as part of a planetary strip-mining operation. Our rebel adversaries are merely squatters. You rarely see these much anymore since neutronic extraction rigs came along."

They were almost to the other side of the bridge when the ambush happened. A squad of rebels opened fire—one plasma round shooting past just in front of OK's nose—and shouted, "For Freedom and Justice!"

Death Runners unleashed a furious volley of return-fire, disintegration rifles firing searing plasma rounds that incinerated their rebel targets into fleeting, human-shaped clouds of ash. Within moments, the rebel resistance was reduced to dust. Stormblood patted his duster. "Quite fortunate we cracked that vexing glitch with the targeting mechanism. That could have been dicey."

The team encountered random pockets of resistance as they pressed deeper into the station. Scrubby scouted ahead and drove the rebels into the open by stabbing at their ankles.

Gunfire echoed through the vast industrial space as rebels futilely attempted to resist the intruders, falling swiftly beneath the relentless onslaught of Stormblood's team. Every time a rebel was burned to ash, OK had to suppress the urge call out, "Sorry."

After one skirmish, Stormblood turned to OK, and the part of his face visible beneath the combat helmet smirked. "First Time, Deathfinger?"

"Yeah, I guess you do this a lot."

"This? Oh, this is a walk in the sunshine. Last year, the Horde dispatched my battalion to neutralize rebels on a perfectly miserable little planet called Zook. We were searching for a rogue star-pilot and raided his family's home. He wasn't there, His family was preparing to celebrate some sort of local holiday. Mom was boiling hunks of meat with a few haphazard spices tossed in. The ugliest juvenile my eyes have ever beheld was scurrying about making noises I would hesitate to describe as human. And hairy old grandpa was wearing a HARVEY helmet indulging in interspecies pornography. It makes me itchy just thinking about it. Anyway, my sergeant turned to me and asked, 'Shall we wait and see if the renegade pilot shows up?' And I simply said, 'Not on your life, let's exterminate them and say they resisted.' I much prefer dusting rebels in straightforward combat." He raised his rifle and did just that.

That could have been me, OK thought.

They marched further into the structure, looking for the central command center, before figuring out they were lost. They wandered around the rusting hulks of old ore processing equipment until OK's bladder began demanding attention, and he asked, "Is there a restroom anywhere in this station?"

"We don't stand on formality, relieve yourself wherever you like," said Stormblood. It was the Death Runner way. OK found a darkened compartment away from the group and opened the fly on his crotch armor.

As he did his business, he looked around to see if the rebels had left any interesting graffiti on the walls. His combat goggles translated a sign from Ophiuchian: "Welcome to the Quadrant One Command Center."

"I think I found it," he called out to the others.

"Do you shout that every time you piss?" a Death Runner called back.

"No, I think I found the command center we've been looking for."

"Impossible," huffed Dr. Madd, pushing his way into the chamber. He broadened the beam on his hand-light until the full room was illuminated. "No, wait... the other thing... it's possible this small-bladdered imbecile accidentally stumbled upon the command center we've been looking for."

It was a crowded space with barely enough room to walk between the metal desk workstations. The walls were covered with switches, keyboards, analog readouts, and small low-resolution viewscreens. The aesthetics were centuries out of date, but the fixtures were rugged, as befit an industrial mining station. One of Morrigan's technicos found a power junction and activated the main systems. A large screen activated at the front of the room, showing a schematic of the space station. "Basic systems are on-line," the technico reported. Her hair was dark, her figure voluptuous. She could have been Morrigan's younger sister.

Stormblood accessed the security systems. "Internal sensors are somewhat hit-miss at present. However, I daresay there is a small contingent of rebels concealed within a maintenance shaft about 200 meters from here."

"Round them up! Bring them back here!" Morrigan ordered. Stormblood formed up his squad and went down to round up the rebels.

"What about intel?" Morrigan asked.

The technico worked the console. "The data servers appear to be intact. But they're locked out with an encryption code."

"I'll crack that code," declared another technico, sitting down at a station and calling up the command center systems access. To OK, they seemed to be vying for Morrigan's favor.

"I'll... um... set up for lunch," OK offered, seeing it as his only role, and began looking for a room with a table and some chairs.

Not much later, the Death Runners returned with their dusters fixed on a group of people in white lab coats holding their hands over their heads. Morrigan muttered, "What are scientists doing on a weapons station?"

"How do you know they're scientists?" OK asked.

"The lab coats give them away, darling."

Madd recognized one of them. "Hinkley Vortex!"

"Anthrax Ghoulshadow," The rebel scientist snarled back.

"Don't you deadname me!"

The scientist huffed. "Only you could be so bold. This is a scientific outpost conducting pulsar research. The Commonwealth Parliament will not stand for this."

"Working for the Scorpion Imperium? I always knew you were a sell-out, Ghoulshadow, but even for a hack like you, this is bottom-feeding."

"I can see why you fit into the Rebel Pact, Hinkley. They're just like your experiments, pathetic and doomed to fail!"

"You're a warped old man, your science is so twisted not even Schrodinger's cat would be caught dead in it."

"Your face looks like my butt!"

Morrigan cut their snappy repartee short. "That scientist in the back, hiding her face, bring her to me." Stormblood muscled her to the front against her protests. Strikingly beautiful didn't begin to describe her, with blond hair cascading down to her shoulders like liquid gold and a highly impressive set of cans. With a flick of her hand, Morrigan brushed aside the strands of hair obscuring the scientist's face. "I know you. Dr. Sugartits, isn't it?"

"It can't be. I ordered her to stay behind at the Library!" Madd spat. "There's no way she could have overtaken us. Not without some kind of teleporter. But that's just science fiction gobbledygook."

Morrigan held her chin and looked her over. "She did stay behind at the library. This one is a quantum mind clone."

"Quantum mind clones! Of course!" Dr. Madd repeated. OK hoped there would be some exposition about "quantum mind clones." None would be forthcoming, as though they were leaving him out of an inside joke.

"Darling," said Morrigan, stroking the Scientist's hair. "I have so many questions. And one way or another, we're going to dig the answers out of your brilliant mind. Let's start with an easy one… what's the passcode for the encrypted files in the station's data core."

"First of all, the name is Honeychild. *Doctor* Honeychild. And second, the passcode is a word a fascist drone like you could never imagine. Freedom Spelled with two 3's and a zero."

The other technico, the one that didn't look like Morrigan's sister, began entering the passcode into the system.

"Don't…" Morrigan warned him.

It was too late. He had already tried the passcode. "It works; we're in."

A terrifying smile revealed the scientist's gleaming white teeth. Before Morrigan could ask *"What have you done?"* Blackheart reported. "Four percent of the data just disappeared."

"Not disappeared … erased," the rebel scientist said. "And it will continue to be erased for another sixty minutes. After that, the strong force bonds that hold this station together will collapse. The entire mining belt will disintegrate and crash onto the molten surface of the planet below, taking you with it."

Madd understood. "An improvised self-destruct. Set to activate when we accessed the files. I suppose it's the best Hinkley could do."

"Shut it down!" Morrigan ordered.

"We're locked out of the system," the technico shouted back.

"Did you try 'password,' you imbecile?" Madd demanded.

"We tried 'Password1' and 'Password2,'" the technico replied, beginning to realize that whatever remained of his life after this cock-up was not going to work out well for him.

"Well, I'm out of ideas," Madd snarled.

The brilliant scientist continued. "There is a failsafe passcode. It will shut down one of the contingency plans—the data purge, or the self-destruct. You Imperial barbarians will have to choose between saving your precious data, or your worthless fascist lives. I will trade you the failsafe code for an Imperial death cutter. I will transmit the code as soon as we are clear of the station."

OK's heart and other parts of his anatomy swelled, stirred by the alluring blend of bravery and beauty emanating from the rebel scientist. He was in awe of her defiance, her fearlessness. *She's going to die for her cause,* he thought. *And then I am going to die for her cause. That's what it will say on the coroner's report. Cause of death: A cause.*

"How do we know you'll keep your word?" asked Stormblood.

"Because we're the good guys, of course. We always keep our word. It's a tactical disadvantage, but it's who we are."

"I don't think I have a better idea," Morrigan said, which confused everyone.

She made her intention somewhat clearer by grabbing a scientist and jamming a blaster against his ear. "Give me the passcode, and I won't force you watch as I murder every one of your fellow scientists."

"You wouldn't."

"We're the bad guys, darling. This is who we are."

Morrigan and the Dr. Honeychild locked eyes in a riveting ocular standoff, neither willing to surrender one micron. The scientist declared, "Go ahead, all of us would gladly die to deny the Imperium a victory."

"We never voted on that," one of the scientists called out.

Honeychild went on. "You've already lost, Imperial *khunt.*"

Morrigan fired off a shot over the scientist's head.

"What can I say. I'm a bad loser."

"Just tell her the override," the hostage scientist pleaded. "It's our only shot at surviving!"

"A prison would be better than death!" called out another.

"No! Comrades, she will yield, or we will die for freedom and justice!"

"Well, isn't this an interesting situation," Morrigan said. "Here I am, the big bad Imperial soldier, wanting to save the lives of everyone on this station. And there you are, the brave rebel hero. Willing to let them all die."

The smarter of the analysts had an idea. "They used 'freedom' as the activation passcode. The override is probably something else on-theme. I'm going to try 'freedom,' 'equality,' 'justice,' 'democracy…' all that idealistic rebel crap." She tried each of the words. "Nothing."

Morrigan raised her blaster and shot a random scientist, wounding not killing him. "Someone's going to give me the code, or I'm going to play a game called how many organs can I spatter before the station explodes." She fired again. "At least I'll go out doing what I love!"

"Dr. Honeychild is the only one who knows the code," one of scientists pleaded. "Please, please, have mercy."

Morrigan turned to her analyst. "Try 'mercy.'"

She tensely typed it into the console. "Override Accepted."

Morrigan shoved her hostage away. "Shut down the self-destruct.

"Self-destruct shut down." The alarms abated.

"Now, find a way to save the intel," Morrigan ordered.

In the time it took to work out the password, they had lost almost 20% of the intel. If they could not find a way to save it, this entire mission would be a failure.

Overcome by curiosity, OK glanced over the analyst's shoulder at the schematic display of the station's data systems. His engineering instincts kicked in. There was a technical problem in front of him and whether he wanted to or not his mind insisted on fixing it.

The rebel data files were stored in physical data cores separate from the primary operating system core. If the data cores were disconnected from the main system, it would halt the deletion program. Then, they could plug the cores into an Imperial system to recover the data. Of course, they would have to get past the multi-partite encryption first.

He realized everyone was staring at him. Apparently, he had spoken those thoughts out loud.

"How did you know that?" demanded Blackheart.

"I watched some engineering programs on I2N about space station data architectures. I figured that a station as old as this one must use one of the three standard architectures, and ..."

Morrigan cut him off. "Never mind, where are these physical data cores?"

"Most likely within there, I should think," said Stormblood, pointing to a door labeled "Data Cores."

"Pull them!" Morrigan ordered.

"The drives are booby-trapped!" the rebel scientist blurted out in desperation. "Pull them and the station will disintegrate immediately."

Morrigan must not have believed her. "Pull the cores!" she ordered again.

OK watched as Stormblood and the analyst entered the Data Core Room. A knot tightened in his stomach, he found himself gnawing anxiously on his lower lip. *What if the rebels really did sabotage the station?* The thought of the ring collapsing around him and a long fall through the burning atmosphere to the molten crust of this planet was too horrifying to imagine, although he understood the mechanics of it.

If the rebels really sabotaged the data cores, this entire space station would disintegrate in orbit taking him with it. The weight of uncertainty pressed down upon him; every passing second fraught with the looming specter of catastrophe.

Stormblood and the woman emerged in triumph a few minutes later, holding in their hands the data storage cylinders of the station's hard drives.

"The base is ours, the data is ours, the rebels are ours. Complete victory for the Imperium! Now, get this rebel scum out of my sight!" Morrigan ordered.

"You won't learn anything from us," the scientists shouted as the guards dragged her away. "We'll die before we tell you anything!"

"Yes, that is the most likely the order of events," Morrigan affirmed as the Death Runners led them away.

When they were gone, she turned to OK and smiled. "Thank you, Deathfinger, you saved this entire mission from failure."

OK felt a brief surge of pride before it turned to profound horror once he realized he had just saved the entire *Imperial* mission from failure.

13.0 Rogue Solitaire

Morrigan and her crew pored over the salvaged data to delve into the secrets of the Rebel Pact and the base they called "Hopeful One." They allowed OK to remain—a reward for helping save the data that felt more like a gut punch.

"As we suspected, this station is where they built those battle stations." The station schematics revealed a massive production complex. "According to the manifests we decoded, they were getting parts from across the quadrant. Missiles from Sagittarius, particle cannons from Aries, armor plating from Leo—all our Commonwealth enemies."

Dr Madd was studying the same hologram schematic. "According to the records in the data core, the rebels were using this part of the base for non-lethal weapons research. *Non-Lethal*, where's the fun in that, I ask you?"

Morrigan's brow remained furrowed. "This was their most critical outpost, the key to the entire war. I expected them to put up more of a fight than a few decrepit patrol ships and a jury-rigged self-destruct."

"I can explain that!" Dr. Madd had discovered that rebel scientists had developed a bioweapon; a bioengineered viral drug that caused extreme apathy. The infected didn't care enough to work or fight and in severe cases stopped eating and eventually died (according to tests on clones and Imperial prisoners). The virus escaped containment and infected the crews of their patrol ships, who stopped giving a crap about defending the base.

Other non-lethal projects included a genetically altered bacterium that produced intense body order immune to all forms of deodorant. Imagine an Army that couldn't stand the smell of each other. They were also working on an addictive narcotic called Styx. Which Dr. Madd declared, "really bad stuff."

"Worse than Ultra-heroin?" one of the MAD analysts asked.

"Much worse! Styx makes Ultra-heroin look like Mega-Methamphetamine. According to this black file, five doses cause permanent addiction, one hundred doses are fatal, but quitting the drug is also fatal."

"What if you only took four doses?" OK asked.

"I don't know," Madd pulled out an ampoule of the drug. "Let's find out!"

Morrigan intervened. "No need for that. Get the formula and we'll pass it off to FIST. They can traffic it into populations we don't want too many of."

"I expected them to be working on a death-ray or something," OK said.

Madd and Morrigan laughed at this. "Oh my, no," Madd chuckled. "Death rays are old hat. And speaking which, where's my old hat?"

"You left it on the death shuttle," Morrigan told him, and then asked if he knew how the Rebels got the battle stations through Aeonic space. She wanted to know if they had perfected Aeonic shielding.

"Not Aeonic shielding, Aeonic camouflage! Allow me to illustrate. Now, let's say this can of cheap, Antarean beer the rebels left behind is a ship, and that Deathfinger over there is an Aeon." He shook the can really hard and threw it at OK's head. OK ducked out of the way and the beer exploded against the wall in a foul-smelling puddle of liquid and foam.

"Now, imagine this other can is a different ship, and the hologram app on my Death Phone is the rebel camouflage." He tossed the beer again, and this time plugged OK right in the face because he and everyone else was distracted by the hologram of a second beer can whizzing through the air at random tangents like a bumble bee on amphetamines.

"The rebels have learned to perfectly replicate the energy signature put out by Aeonic ships' engines. But the really clever part is they added a distortion field that deflects Aeonic sensors and creates a false signature light years away moving at a random trajectory."

OK wondered how they were able to do that, but Death Runner Stormblood only saw the tactical potential. "If we could outfit our ships with this, the enemy would never be able to track them."

Madd pinched his fingers together. "There's one teensy problem. It can only be used on unmanned ships. Any human caught inside the distortion field would have their anatomy rearranged like a Picasso painting."

That covered, they returned to the topic of the belt schematic, and the big blank spot on the opposite side. "We have no data on this quadrant. It is also physically sealed off. According to the logs, it was occupied by Carpathians."

"Carpathians," Lieutenant Stormblood shuddered. The Carpathians had put up the hardest resistance to the Imperium of any world, keeping the Horde in a quagmire and inflicting hundreds of thousands of casualties.

There were rumors that survivors from the Carpathian Army had fled to a world in neutral space where they were rebuilding their numbers and planning to strike back against the Imperium. OK had thought these stories were just wishful thinking to cope with Imperial oppression. This proved the Carpathians were real!

"We need to break into that part of the ring and find out what they were up to," Morrigan said.

Commander Grimfoyle arrived from the *Subutai* just then, looking much more sober and fully clothed than OK was used to. He ordered OK to report to the kitchen... just when it was getting interesting. Typical.

Stoat and Roche were preparing lunch for the boarding crew from rebel provisions they had scavenged. OK fixed a pile of sandwiches and fruit and asked the Death Runner in charge for permission to take them to the scientists. She agreed, but not until she inspected them for weapons by taking bites out of the better-looking sandwiches. Roche carried the bottles of water as they made their way to the cargo locker that served as a makeshift cell for the rebel scientists. Scrubby trailed behind, buffing the floor as he went.

The stunning blond scientist sat on a bench in the corner. Radiating strength and defiance, she swatted away the sandwich he had prepared for her from the best of the bread and fixings. "Take your food and insert it into your anal cavity, you imperial bastard."

OK bent down and whispered. "I'm not really with the Imperium. Well, I am, but... you see, the Horde invaded my planet, and ..."

"Are you going to say you didn't have a choice!" she snapped back at him as he frantically gestured for her to keep it down lest the Death Runners overhear. She didn't keep it down. "When the Imperium invaded my planet, I joined the Rebel Pact. They helped get me off-world so I could fight back."

"That was a very brave and stunning thing to do. I did the same thing, just... differently."

"By joining the Horde?"

"Well, yeah, but I was only trying to get off world to find the rebellion."

"You're so full of *drutt* your eyes are brown!"

"I want to help," he whispered.

She stared into him. "You want to help? Fine, help us escape."

His idea of helping them had, to that point, meant making them tasty sandwiches and snacks to comfort them in their captivity. He had not considered escape possible, but he could not pass on the opportunity. "How?"

"The doors to this locker are on a master circuit in a control junction on this deck. If you pull the circuit, we'll overpower the guards and escape."

OK looked over the scientists in the cell. None of them looked like they would have been picked first for Kinetic Sphere Evasion (a futuristic sci-fi version of dodgeball). "Um, are you sure you can overpower the guards?"

"Just pull the circuit, we'll handle the rest." She pulled him close and whispered, "There's a stealth escape ship in landing bay 6, two levels below the main landing bay. That bay is sealed, but the passcode is 5-3-1-8-0-0-8. Can you remember that?"

OK nodded.

"Good, we've drilled on this escape plan, we can get to the ship in 20 minutes. We'll give you 21, but then we'll leave without you." She bussed his cheek and whispered, "Welcome to the Rebel Pact."

After they finished feeding the detention cell, Roche went back to the kitchen to help set up the evening meal service. OK, finding himself alone, walked down the corridor to the closet containing the control panel; scared as hell, but trying to act casual. Finally, he stood in front of the junction box. He looked one way down the corridor, it was empty. He looked down the other way, it was also empty. He opened the box and found the control circuit. He reached toward it, then drew his hand back again.

"They'll know it was me and they'll put me out an airlock," he told himself.

"This is the chance you've been waiting for," he also told himself. "For all the people on all the worlds the Horde conquered while you mixed drinks for them. For all the rebels slaughtered because you showed the Deathwalkers how to shoot straight. Pull the circuit out and make it right!"

His heart was racing. His gaze remained fixated, staring at the blinking lights inside the closet, as though trying to decode a message of encouragement. Seconds stretched like epochs. The weight of the decision pressed upon him, a palpable force in the room. He struggled to find the will to pull the circuit, and fulfill his vow to avenge Katarina. Still, he hesitated.

A voice cut through the suffocating suspense in his mind. "Do it for Anya!" The directive pierced through his hesitation, demanding a decisive act to dispel the looming shadows of doubt.

He closed his eyes, reached in, and pulled the circuit. He closed the closet door quickly and stumbled down the hallway… simultaneously triumphant, disbelieving, and horrified at what he had done. He rounded the corner into the next corridor and waited for an alarm, or something. Nothing came.

"21 minutes to get to the landing bay," he thought. Suddenly, he couldn't remember where that was. Just then, a rumbling shook the station, like standing next to an avalanche. The power fluctuated and the lights flickered, then failed. Finally, an alarm activated, blaring a despairing wail.

"Prison break!" he thought. "Scrubby, we've got to get out of here."

He started running, blindly hoping that the labyrinth of corridors would somehow lead him where he needed to go. Running down one anonymous corridor, then another, then doubling back when he realized he had passed a 'Help' kiosk.

"Show me the shortest route to Hangar Bay 6," he begged. A schematic of the station appeared along with a long, meandering line like one of those puzzles on a children's menu where you navigate through a maze to lead the pirate to the treasure, or a space Viking to a planet ripe for pillaging. "Estimated walking time: 17 minutes," read the kiosk.

"Furk!" OK grabbed a copy of the map and continued to run. Down the long corridor, a sharp turn to the left, a backtrack, another long corridor, down a shaft, a U-turn, then another shaft. Scrubby keeping up as best he could while occasionally pausing to deal with the odd floor stain. Finally, he skidded to a stop in front of a very large hatch prominently labeled 'Landing Bay 6.' He punched 5-3-1-8-0-0-8 into the access panel.

Adrenaline surged like a bolt of electricity as the hatch slid open. In the landing bay beyond was his new destiny. Goodbye Scorpion Horde, Hello Rebel Pact. So Long Imperium, Welcome Freedom! Viva La Resistance!

But just as quickly as the thrill had taken hold, reality yanked him back like a gravity well. Either the escape ship was the best stealth starship ever built or the landing bay was empty. Waving his hands around the landing bay confirmed the latter. There was no escape ship. She had lied to him. He was a diversion so the rebel scientists could make their real escape.

The weight of disappointment and betrayal crushed him like a discarded can of Black Scorpion Coffee.

"Not go?" asked Scrubby.

Dejected and frankly embarrassed, he walked back out. He realized he was covered with sweat inside his coveralls and out of breath. If the scientists escaped, he said to himself, then it was all right. Their knowledge could help the rebels defeat the Imperium. That was the important thing.

He breathed deeply, tried to steady himself, and began making his way back to the kitchen. He rounded a corner to see a pair of Death Guards and Roche. "Halt!" the Death Guards barked, pointing a blaster at him.

"Oh, furk!"

The Death Guard spoke into his com unit. "Base control, there's been an incident. One of the Catering Techs attempted to help the rebel scientists escape." He gave out their location.

Well, this was it, OK was going to die. He would never join the rebellion, never see Anya again, and they were probably going to look into his browsing history and think he was a pervert. He worried what fate would befall Scrubby, who might be smashed into who knew what?

A few minutes later, a perturbed Death Colonel Morrigan and two Death Runners appeared. "Deathfinger Kevitch, hand over your bond coin!"

An icy wave of terror crashed over him as he met her gaze. She was holding out a black-gloved hand, her lips were moving, and he realized she was repeating the demand for his bond coin. He had no recourse now but to surrender it to her. With shaking hands, he pulled it from his pocket turned it over to her, knowing he was signing his death warrant.

She played back the conversation he had in the cell with the prisoner scientist, the damning pact they had made between them. "Are the prisoners still in detention?" she asked, and the guard affirmed that they were. "Hand over the circuit," she ordered.

He was surprised to see he had been clutching it in his hand the whole time. Mechanically, automatically, he handed it over to her.

She examined the circuit he had pulled. "The evidence is conclusive; you are guilty of treason. The penalty for treason against the Imperium is summary, immediate termination."

The Death Guards drew their swords. On the edge of the blades was a thin red energy field that could slice through even the hardest quantanium alloys effortlessly. It would cut through his vertebrae even more easily. His death would be painless, but that was not much comfort.

"However, it appears that instead of pulling the master circuit, you pulled the circuit that controlled the waste disposal systems on the detention level. I am going to assume your sense of loyalty to the Imperium prevailed. For that reason, and in light of your service in recovering the station's intelligence data, termination is suspended, at my discretion as ranking security officer."

Morrigan gestured for the guards to lower their weapons. OK's heart resumed beating. "I reduce your charge to sympathy for the Rebel Pact. Punishment is remanded to forty-four hours in the Cubicle of Torment."

Roche spoke up. "Deathstalker, as recompense for revealing the traitorous activities of this disloyal Deathfinger, I request to assume his duties and rank. And also request a recommendation for transfer to the personal staff of Deathlord Damocles."

And that was the worst blow of all—Roche's betrayal—shattering his trust like an explosive decompression. Rue and Qi'Anna were right, OK never should have trusted him.

Morrigan's response dripped with contempt. "I will submit a recommendation that you be promoted to Chief Deathfinger-Catering and transferred… to the *Oswald Mosley*… upon our return to the Red Fleet."

Roche's jaw dropped. "The waste processing ship? You can't do that. I did my duty to the Imperium by reporting this traitor. I am entitled…"

"Your personnel record shows a pattern of reporting your comrades. FIST may encourage this kind of treachery, but I do not. This mission is dangerous enough without you creating a hostile work environment. Guards, put him on a death shuttle and take him to any ship except the *Subutai*."

She asked for a moment alone with OK. "You're lucky you pulled the wrong circuit. Your time in the Cubicle of Torment will seem like an eternity of misery, but you will survive. You owe me your life and one day, I will collect this debt. You can count on that."

And one more thing. "Never let those filthy rebels get into your head. That's my job."

Two Death Guards escorted OK back the *Subutai* to serve his sentence in the cubicle of torment. The COT was located on the Disciplinary Deck, deep in the ship's interior. There was a dedicated transport tube for it. Its hatch slid open on a bare hallway, with a frayed and dingy gray carpet lining it. This was odd. There was no carpet anywhere else on the ship.

A guard gave him a firm nudge with the butt of his sword that left an ugly bruise. "Get out!"

"Just give me a moment to abandon all hope," OK replied. He took in and let out a deep breath. "OK, done."

They marched him toward the door at the end of the hallway. He could not imagine what lay on the other side. Details of Imperial torment techniques were censored from the nexus. He pictured himself strapped to a chair with his eyes clamped open and forced to watch imperial propaganda holofilms while attendants administered eyedrops. He could also imagine buxom women in tight leather who would shackle him to a bed, whip him and call him a naughty, naughty boy. He figured it wouldn't be that, though. And why did all the women in that scenario look like Morrigan?

Finally, he stood before the door. A guard passed a rectangular piece of plastic over the locking device and the door swung open. OK shielded his eyes against the light from the inside. The light came from fluorescent tubes overhead that emitted a constant, insectile buzzing noise. A guard pushed him inside and sealed the hatch behind him.

A harsh voice bellowed from an overhead speaker, "Deathfinger First Rank Ogden Kevitch, report to cubicle 1353-D."

He squinted through the buzzing white-purple light to see dozens of torment cubicles arrayed in columns and rows. Each cubicle described a square space approximately two meters on each side, with walls upholstered in gray, industrial carpet. The nearest one was labeled 1342-A. The next was labeled 1337-B, and the one after that was labeled 1386-B. There seemed to be no discernible pattern.

As he walked down the aisle searching for his assigned cubicle, he passed others sent here for discipline, staring at the computer screens in front of them with dead, haunted eyes. The guy who had input the rebel password and nearly destroyed the station slumped in his cubicle, head buried in his wet sleeves, sobbing, "a thousand hours, a thousand hours."

OK almost thought about comforting him, but the overhead voice warned him off, "Speaking to other violators is permitted only during the designated social interaction periods."

He finally found cubicle 1353-D, located between Cubicle 1641-D and 1822-D. There was an old gray chair with wheels underneath it. One of its arms was broken. There was a computer monitor and keyboard in front of him that looked like artifacts from the Plastic Age on ancient Earth. Text on the screen instructed him to sit in the chair. It then directed him to stare at the screen continuously, and not to leave unless commanded to.

You have been submitted for discipline as a result of a transgression against the Imperium of Greater Scorpius. The Imperium has generously spared your pathetic life and offered you the opportunity for rehabilitation. Pay attention to this monitor. You will be given instructions. Completion of these instructions is mandatory. Failure to complete a task will result in additional hours added to your disciplinary correction period. The first task: Provide a review of your performance in service to the Imperium, beginning with a review of your previous year of performance. Include at least five achievements during this period. Describe your strengths and weaknesses and provide a set of objectives for your next year of service. Use the keyboard. Estimated completion time: 120 death minutes.

OK began typing out a response on the keyboard. It was much more difficult than he expected, even though he could cite solid achievements such as sanitizing the lower crew galley, getting promoted to the officer's club, and correcting the targeting systems on Horde battle rifles. The requirement was for five achievements, and he could only think of three. He desperately tried to come up with padding. "Demonstrated adaptability and resourcefulness in providing beverages to crew members while under combat fire." He still needed one more. A device sitting on the desk to his right suddenly emitted loud ringing sounds. It caused him to look away from the screen and thirty minutes were added to the duration of his torment.

The only other thing he could think of was how he let Boskirk brew Dayglo Orange in his refrigerator in return for better supplies. "Improved quality of lower crew food service through innovative supply practices."

As for weaknesses, he was sure "deep hatred of the Imperium" was not a response that would go over well. Instead, he typed, "I sometimes panic while making sandwiches," and worked outward from there.

He finally finished the first task and waited for the next. He timidly inquired, "Would it be all right for me to use the hygiene chamber?"

"If you need to use the hygiene chamber, you must ask your supervisor."

"Who is my supervisor?"

"This disembodied voice is your supervisor."

"Oh, may I use the hygiene chamber?"

"You must fill-in the request form." OK tapped his request into the monitor. "Request denied. You may resubmit your request in nine minutes."

OK waited and resubmitted his request. This time, the screen did not respond. He resubmitted it again and got a warning that not enough time had elapsed since his previous request. He tried again as his bowels began to ache and he wondered if the point was to force him to humiliate himself.

On the eighth try, it finally relented and OK was allowed to relieve himself. There was a message on the screen when he returned ordering him to report to Room 1003. The other detainees were there. They were forbidden from speaking with each other. At the front of the room, a rectangle of light displayed the words "Unwavering Allegiance to the Scorpion Imperium" followed by bullet points. The disembodied voice read through the bullets in a monotone. Then a new rectangle appeared. "Accepting the Duty of Servitude." The disembodied voice read through 108 slides before dismissing them.

When he returned to the cubicle, he realized he was hungry. He typed in a request for food and was directed to a common food area. Inside a cold storage unit, he found a bag with his name on it. It contained a dry sandwich and a cup of plain yogurt. "What am I, an animal?" he asked out loud.

Subsequently, he was allowed to get more food every four hours, but sometimes the bag had nothing in it but a wadded sandwich wrapper and a used yogurt cup. One time, the bag was empty, but someone had left a small yellow square of adhesive paper with a frowny face drawn on it.

There was a message waiting for him each time he returned from his meal, assigning him a new and pointless task to complete, such as:

You are instructed to write a report on the process you used to write your performance review. Describe in detail the process used to develop answers to each question. Include details on what you learned from the experience.

When he finished the report, the disembodied voice presented directed him to create a presentation based on his offenses against the Imperium. It watched over him, demanding endless, minor corrections.

At random intervals, musical notes played from the scratchy, low-fidelity speaker above his desk. Silencing it required him to input a 16-character sequence of letters and numbers; entering them incorrectly made the noise louder. After three incorrect inputs, the noise became ear-splittingly loud and he had to enter another code before he could try again.

More hours passed as he sat in the small cubicle, sitting in a broken chair, staring at gray carpeted walls about three-quarters the height of a grown man.

Then came more sprit-crushing meetings with the other detainees, followed by more soul-grinding tasks—filling in forms and entering endless codes. There must have been a time dilation effect in the Cubicle of Torment because next thirty-six hours crawled by like thirty-six days. The only thing that changed was OK's steadily diminishing will to live. Just as his forty-four hours plus penalty time sentence was about to be over, a flurry of messages came across the screen, each requiring a response. It required him another full hour and a half to respond to all of them, and to the follow-ups, and to the follow-ups to the follow-ups.

Finally, the screen passed a message to him.

"Deathfinger First Rank Ogden Kevitch, you have completed your disciplinary actions. You are dismissed. Serve the Imperium with gratitude."

He began to sob. He tried to stand up from his broken chair, but his knees buckled. He fell to the filthy carpet and cried into his elbow. He wanted nothing more than to go back to the Officer's Club to sanitize glasses. And maybe punch Roche in the face if he were there.

Death Colonel Morrigan was waiting outside the Disciplinary Deck. She offered him a bottle of pinkish orange liquid. "Drink this, it will help."

It tasted salty as it went down his throat. "What's in this?"

"Sedatives and amphetamines. It seems counter-intuitive, but they will level you out after what you've been through."

"I don't want to talk about it."

"No one ever does. The ancient humans used the cubicle of torment as a device to ensure docility and cooperation. The Imperium has never found a more effective form of discipline."

She further informed him the fleet had completed operations and was preparing to return to Imperial space."

"What about… what about the rebel scientists?" OK was sure they had been terminated for attempting to escape, but he was wrong.

"All of them survived mind extraction are being transferred to the *Subutai*. I am headed to the landing bay to meet their transport. You may accompany me, if you wish."

That made OK feel a lot better, or maybe the amphetamine/barbiturate cocktail was doing its magic. He agreed to come along.

The death shuttle had landed by the time OK and Morrigan arrived. Dr. Madd was overseeing the removal of several biohazard containment drums from the shuttle. "Careful, now, careful. Those things are filled with the Apathy biotoxin. If it spills in here, no one will give a damn!"

The next thing to be unloaded was a cart holding ten jars of pink and blue liquid. What looked like large floating cauliflowers floated inside them.

Morrigan had new orders for him. "The *Subutai* will be transporting the rebel scientists back to the fleet. I will oversee their interrogations, and I have assigned you the responsibility of feeding them. Your interactions will be monitored, of course."

OK could hardly believe he was being entrusted with this duty. Perhaps it was a loyalty test? "Ia, I'll take care of the scientists. Where are they?"

"Right in front of you." Morrigan pointed to the jars. OK realized what was floating in them, brains and nervous systems. Seeing the shocked look on his face, Morrigan confirmed. "I told you the mind extraction was a success. The Imperium kept the parts they wanted and sent the rest to the meat lab."

OK needed to sit down, but there wasn't really a bench or anything nearby. So, he slumped to the deck. According to I2N, mind extraction was merely a technique for extracting information from a living brain and storing it in a virtual reconstruction. But like everything else in the Imperium, that was a terrible lie.

The task force avoided Aeonic space on the way back to Scorpius. It made for a long trip, but at least OK didn't have to wear the pillow shoes again. Instead, he woke up every night in a freezing sweat, wide-eyed and panting from his latest nightmare.

Stoat was almost always awake when he came around. He'd mastered a regimen of Horde amphetamines and spent his sleepless hours immersed in the Imperial Encyclopedia of Mixology, meticulously plotting his next career move. "What was it this time? Cubicle of Torment or Mind Extractor?"

"Both," OK answered. "The Imperium extracted my brain and left it in the cubicle of torment. I couldn't get out until I wrote a performance assessment, but I didn't have any hands to type with!"

"Well, that dream is easy to interpret. You should have listened to me, Friend-o. Kept any qualms you have about the Imperium on the down-low. Take drugs if you have to. Frankly, they've helped me a lot."

"But at some point, don't we have to take a stand? How many more atrocities do we have to witness before we fight back?"

"My estimate is four, but it's really more of a guesstimate." Stoat leaned over his bunk, "Do you want to get off this ship or not?"

"I have to get off this ship. I'm not going to make it if I don't."

"Well, it so happens I have been working on a plan to get us off this ship."

"You found a way off? How?"

"If I told you what I was planning, you might tank it. That foolish stunt with the rebels almost tanked all our prospects. But if … when … my plan works, we will be off the *Subutai* and on our way to glory. But for it to work, you've got to play along and most of all, not appear like anything but a loyal Horde soldier who learned his lesson. Trust the plan, Friend-O."

OK didn't think he had a choice. "I can't go on like this. I feel like I'm losing my mind."

"Well, if you do, the Imperium can always put it in a jar for you."

On that point, OK had the job of feeding the disembodied scientist brains during the trip back. The brains were kept in an isolated laboratory in the *Subutai's* science section, lined up like jars of pickled pink cauliflower. Feeding them consisted of squirting protein sustenance into each jar with a tap hose.

One shift, as he moved down the row, squirting a stream of fluid into each of the brain jars, he was startled to hear, "Thank you," from one of them. The voice had a familiar timbre to it. There were wires to the brain tanks connected to a panel on the side with a small speaker.

"Hello?" OK said back. "I mean, you're welcome, I guess."

"Aren't you the Deathfinger who botched our escape?" It was the voice of the blond scientist.

OK clenched his teeth, but forced himself to say, "Yes, that's me."

"Surprised they let you in with us again."

OK suspected it was some kind of loyalty test and he was being monitored. "It's not like I would help you escape again. Last time, I almost got killed for helping you."

"You almost got killed. Boo-hoo. Look at you, walking around with legs and a skeleton and everything. What have you got to whine about?"

"You lied to me. There was no escape ship. You used me and betrayed me. And you were supposed to be the good guys!"

"We can't always be good guys, but at least we're just fighting for a good cause. You weren't our first patsy, and you won't be our last. If you are really on our side, then you were betrayed for a cause that we both believe in."

Maybe they had a point. There was no bringing down an evil interstellar Imperium without getting your hands dirty. "That's one way of looking at it, I guess." He supposed there was no point in dwelling on it.

He gave her a second squirt of brain juice. "Does it hurt? Existing as a disembodied brain, I mean."

"Actually, it's quite pleasant. Like floating in the ocean on a warm summer's day. And I no longer need to fret about keeping my figure. I'm going to miss wearing shoes. I had a pair of pumps that would make an Overlord weep. I have no idea know why they tuned the vocal synthesizer to replicate my voice, but I'm obviously in no position to question it."

After that rough start, OK got to know her a little better over the long cycles of the journey back. Her name had been Anastasaja Honeychild. She was a quantum clone—genetically engineered to be telepathically linked with another quantum clone. Her counterpart was also a spy, working on a secret imperial superweapon. The Rebel Pact had somehow acquired schematics of the weapon. Anastasaja had been studying the plans in hopes of finding a weakness the rebels could use to defeat it. Morrigan had subjected her and the other brains to deep probes to find out how much the rebels had found out. "We told that that red bitch nothing!"

In the course of their long journey, Anastasaja's boredom yielded to mild curiosity about OK's background. She expressed sympathy with his horror in watching his planet invaded by the Horde. When she found out his duties consisted mainly of serving drinks in the ship's officers' club, it gave her an idea. "During one of their victory celebrations, following another *glorious* conquest, you could rig the Capricornian Chambrosia bottles with chemical explosives that would detonate when the cork pops."

"What would that accomplish?" OK asked. "It would just kill everyone in the room. Including me."

"It would send a powerful message to the Imperium that the free worlds of the galaxy do not wish to be slaves to the Imperium!"

"I think the Imperium is already aware of that."

Anastasaja eventually conceded that it would be a futile gesture. The Imperium would make the incident so classified no one would ever hear of it. The officers would easily be replaced. You couldn't swing the captain's schlong without hitting an ambitious Imperial officer ready to move up.

He was required to turn his bond coin over after each feeding for review. Morrigan rolled her eyes when she heard about the Chambrosia bomb plot. "Rebels…. They think all you need to do to win a war is blow up something."

She cared less about the rebel chatter than about OK's thoughts. "Please stop thinking about the captain's penis."

"Ia, I will try not to. But once you've seen it. It's the elephant in the room… the trunk, anyway."

"Yes, darling, but I'm telepathic and it's very annoying."

The *Subutai* task force (what was left of it) rendezvoused with the rest of the Red Fleet at the Tartarus Shipyard; a massive Imperial base under the red glow of a ten-billion-year-old red giant star. The ancient star had swept up thousands of planets and moons during its eons-long tour of the galaxy, forming a dense ring on the edge of its photosphere. Tidal forces had ripped these worlds apart, leaving behind broken hemispheres and battered melon slices of former planets. Horde engineers carved these husks into space-docks, space-depots, and space-repair stations bathed in the firelight of the swollen red star.

The task force returned as heroes. Death Captain Slaughter and the commanders of all the other ships were presented with the Scorpion Sting of Honor; the second highest medal in the Imperium. OK received a small coin engraved with the slogan, "Task Force Ghost Data—Participant." Everyone from the Task Force got one of those … most of them posthumously.

Qi'Anna and Rue rejoined the *Subutai* a few days after it docked. OK could tell they had returned from the noise next door that woke him in the middle of a cubicle-of-torment-themed nightmare. He knocked on the bathroom door and welcomed them back. "How was your tour on the *Robespierre*."

"The *Robespierre* is gone," said Qi'Anna. While the *Subutai* and its task force had been on the other side of the Aeonic expanse, the rest of the Red Fleet had invaded the holy planet Vesperia II. The *Robespierre* was blasted apart by orbital battle stations. Qi'Anna and Rue only survived because the lower crew section remained intact after the command deck was blown away. They had spent almost five days floating in the dark before search-and-rescue ships got to them.

"Lt. Collator was on the *Robespierre*," said Stoat. "Did she make it?"

Rue shook her head. "I heard none of the officers survived. Some of them made it to escape pods, but the escape pods got caught in the crossfire."

OK felt like a ballistic round had struck him in the chest. He never thought of Collator as a friend, she was just his boss. And yet, learning she was gone hit him as hard as the sight of Anastasaja's brain in that jar.

"How did your secret mission go?" Qi'Anna asked.

OK shook his head. The orders from Captain Slaughter could not have been clearer. Everything about the mission was classified. Where they went, what they did… everything.

"It went great," Stoat said. "We captured a secret rebel arsenal base."

"We heard you lost a third of your ships," Rue said.

"More like half. And OK got sent to the Cubicle of Torment."

"Oh, my godless void," Rue took OK's hands. "What happened?"

"Roche caught him talking to a rebel prisoner and turned him in."

Rue swatted OK about the head and face. "I told you not to trust him. Why didn't you listen to me?"

OK made no effort to shield himself from her slaps. "I know I should have listened to you."

"And you talked… to a rebel!" She hit him again, hard enough to redden his cheeks. "You're far too trusting."

"What was the Cubicle of Torment like?" Qi'Anna asked as Rue calmed herself down.

"I don't want to talk about it," OK said.

"Aw, *shiznit*. One of these cycles, I'm going to get in trouble just so I can find out what's it's like."

OK grabbed her shoulders and shook them. "Don't ever say that! Don't ever say that! Never ever say that again!"

"You're hurting me."

OK let her go.

"I didn't say stop."

They spent the rest of the night gulping down bottles of Antarean Ale and smoking deathsticks. Rue offering thanks to the godless void that she had survived. Qi'Anna describing the mechanics of zero g sex in the complete darkness of the wrecked *Robespierre*. Stoat sharing gossip he had picked up about the officers. If he had learned about Death Commander Odious's penchant for ventriloquy, he didn't consider it worth mentioning. OK said little.

Before parting for their respective bunks, they clinked glasses in a toast to Roche's reassignment to the waste processing ship. "May he fall into a centrifugal garbage washer while suffering space diarrhea."

OK resumed his duties in the HOC while the fleet underwent maintenance, overhaul, and battle damage repair. While he had been gone, the Horde had conquered the last remaining independent systems in the constellation. All of Scorpius was now under Imperial domination. The war machine was on pause while its gears were oiled, its blades sharpened, its guns polished to a domineering shine.

As he carried drinks between tables, he picked up scraps of conversations regarding insurrections crushed and worlds overrun. It was only a matter of time before the war machine was spun up again and directed against a neighboring constellation—either Sagittarius or Ophiuchus. The consensus was that Ophiuchus would be easier to take while obligatorily acknowledging that the Sagittarians were decadent, weak, and fit for conquest.

Superweapons! Insurrections! Galactic Invasions! A full-scale galactic war would drive him mad. OK kept his head down, pouring drinks with a dash of discretion and wiping tables with a washcloth of survival instinct.

Boskirk was promoted to Collator's former post as chief of crew services. That was how you advanced in the Horde; metaphorically, or often literally, kicking aside the corpse of the person who preceded you. Boskirk offered Qi'Anna and Rue permanent hostess jobs in the HOC, but they chose to return to the Deathwalker Holds. They decided they preferred the company of 10,000 dead cyborgs to that of the ship's high officers.

OK maintained his sanity by watching 12N engineering programs in his off-hours. He had just dozed off while watching a Holovid about piloting escape pods when Stoat shook him awake. "Friend-o, wake up, I have exciting news! Deathlord Damocles just had two dozen members of his personal staff terminated for their impudence."

"How is that exciting? He kills off personal assistants all the time."

"Because this time, it means we're getting off this ship."

OK snapped fully awake. "We are? How?"

"We are going to replace them."

Terror cut the line in front of shock as the full implication of this struck OK. The Deathlord was known to rip out people's guts with a barbed blade called the Eviscerater. This wasn't a rumor; it was in his official Imperial biography. "That is not what I meant by getting off the ship."

Stoat's voice softened to his smoothest, most seductive, tone, "I know that, but this a huge opportunity. Imagine the doors that would open for you after serving as the Deathlord's personal valet."

OK could imagine those doors, all right. He imagined them as airlocks and him being blown out of them. He clutched his thin, Horde-issue pillow tightly to his chest, as though holding onto the flimsy headrest would somehow prevent Stoat from dragging him off the ship. "I want out of this place, and you want to take me deeper inside."

"To the heart of the command ship, where we would listen in on all of Deathlord Damocles's secrets and all the inner workings of the Horde. Think of how much we could learn."

"If they don't kill us first."

"That hardly ever happens."

"It literally just happened!"

"Well, it won't happen to us."

"Why would they take me? A few cycles ago they put me in the Cubicle of Torment for being a rebel sympathizer."

"Lieutenant Stormblood submitted an ambiguously worded field report and the Horde Command thinks you thwarted a rebel prisoner escape."

"How did you manage that?"

"I wrote it for him. Turns out he hates doing field reports."

Stoat was risking a lot to gather intelligence on the Horde, but OK did not see himself as up to the task. *Say no and stick to it,* he told himself. *Don't tell him you'll think about it. Don't tell him maybe. Make your no strong and absolute. If you give him even 1 millimeter, he will push you until you agree. Say No!*

But while his mind was insisting he not give in this time, his mouth was already saying, "I'll think about it."

The going away bash for OK and Stoat happened at the end of the cycle; one last night of friendship and heavy drinking before they left the *Subutai*. In the morning, they proceeded to the ship's landing bay, where they were greeted by an officious woman in a sharp gray civilian suit. She offered them no welcome but introduced herself as Death Warrant Officer Mormo— assistant personnel liaison for Deathlord Damocles.

The words "I am eager to meet his eminence," oozed out of Stoat's mouth.

"And you may, should you survive the selection process. Unless you think your prior experience slinging drinks and mopping a kitchen floor qualifies you to serve an Imperial Deathlord. I can assure you, it does not."

Stoat lowered his head. "Of course, we look forward to our training."

"As you can imagine, the odds of being selected to serve in his staff are not in your favor. There are 20 open positions and 200 selected applicants. Most of you will be eliminated." A sinister smile crossed her lips. "Many terminally."

"The process of elimination begins now." She snapped her fingers twice. "Empath, do your thing."

The dark eyed young man moved forward and slowly circled the two of them, framing them in his hands and making strained faces like a man trying to pass a particularly large and solid stool. He squeezed his eyes shut and said of Stoat. "I sense that this one is consumed with personal ambition. He wishes to serve the Deathlord because he believes it will advance his professional prospects. I sense nothing else in him."

OK shivered. What would the Empath sense about him? That he secretly loathed and hated the Imperium? That he loathed himself for serving them? That the horrors he had seen filled him with rage? Oh, godless void, this was it. It was all about to end right here in this landing bay. They were going to read his thoughts and throw him out an airlock and be gratified that it made a minimal amount of mess.

Petrified, he waited for what the Empath was going to say. The Empath was concentrating hard now, drilling into his eyes, assessing him. He seemed to be taking a longer time with him. Or did it just seem like a longer time? Or was he accessing all of OK's not-very-well repressed thoughts and making a list? OK was once again sure he was going to die. He had felt that way many times since coming to the Horde, but the novelty never completely wore off.

The Empath inhaled deeply, his chest rising and falling in a measured cadence. Godless void, he was about to deliver his verdict—OK's death sentence. The Empath's lips parted slowly, as if savoring the finality of the words forming within. and OK knew his own thoughts and feelings had condemned him.

The Empath threw his arms around OK and hugged him tightly, "It's going to be all right," he whispered, and then drew away.

"What the *furk?*" OK's mind glitched like a short-circuiting servo drone, rebooting in a haze of panic and dumb luck. He hadn't been found out or sentenced to death. And a hug? What was that about?

"He needed that," the Empath explained. "He's terrified of the Deathlord and worried he will fail the training."

"As well he should be. Both of you will be trained, observed, tested, and pitted against your fellow applicants. If you are one of the very few who survive, you might be awarded a position, subject to a final selection by the Deathlord's Chief of Staff, The Lady Ur," Mormo explained.

She handed them a rather heavy data pad. "This handbook contains the rules for serving on the Deathlord's personal staff. Memorize it. Most of the protocols should be common sense. Address the Deathlord as 'Your Eminence.' Any room he is in must be exactly 28 degrees. Always arrange his blade weapons in the order he intends to use them. You will also find thorough instructions on the varied duties of his staff and the standards for performance thereof.

"In addition to classroom instruction, you will each be assigned to a Horde officer as a personal assistant, so that we can observe your attitude and diligence." She pointed an elegantly manicured forefinger at Stoat, "You will be assigned to Death Captain Bloodfiend, commander of his eminence's command ship." She showed Stoat a holo. Bloodfiend was a dwarfish man with a shaved head, artificial eyepiece built into his right socket, and teeth filed into fangs. "He will bite you," Mormo warned.

Stoat boarded the death shuttle that would take him to the *Putin*. When he was gone, OK was overcome by a sense of falling and knew there was nothing below to catch him. "Wh-wh-who will I be working for?" he asked.

She had chosen to be coy at the exact moment it would raise his anxiety. "All I can tell you is that you were requested specifically."

Neither, as far as he knew, were on the *Putin*. "Your assigned officer's shuttle is approaching the dock," she told him a few minutes later. The air was thick with the scent of ionized fear as he waited to see who would hold be holding his fate in his hands.

The shuttle bay doors opened at the end of the approach tunnel and a death shuttle glided in for a landing. As the shuttle fidgeted to align its external hatch with the docking ring, OK flirted with the idea of backing out, telling Mormo this had all been a mistake, a misunderstanding. Godless void, he just wanted to stand behind the bar and hand drinks to barbarians.

He forced himself to acknowledge that Stoat was right. Intelligence on the Deathlord and his inner circle would be of great value to the Rebel Pact. He would have to find some sticking place to stick his courage to. His private mission had become much more dangerous, but the cause of galactic justice was never meant to be an easy fight!

The suspense of which officer he would serve was killing him. OK could only think of two people in a position to request his services, Death Captain Slaughter or Death Colonel Morrigan. He dreaded the thought of what service to either one of them might entail.

The hatch opened with a hissing sound and a dramatic release of steam. A figure emerged from the mist and OK saw he was wrong on both accounts.

"Dr. Madd?"

"Who were you expecting? The Rainbow Queen of Uranus?"

15.0 Apocalypse Wow

"Well, don't just stand there like a stunned lab monkey. Get on the shuttle, you lollygagging slag drone. The Annihilator is waiting for us!" Dr. Madd sputtered. OK thought that the wording sounded ominous and then remembered that in the Horde everything sounded ominous. He picked up his bags and boarded the death shuttle. He and Dr. Madd were the only passengers. The shuttle turned around, shot out of the landing bay, and began a long journey through the massive Imperial spaceyard.

"Where are we going?" OK asked.

"How do I always end up sitting next to some chatterbox who won't shut up the whole flight! As I said, you mid-wit, we're going to the *Annihilator.*"

"Is that a ship?"

"It's not just a ship. It's the Imperium's new top secret ultimate weapon! The weapon that will make our enemies quake with fear, wet their pants, and drop dead in sheer terror once we unleash its awesome destructive power!"

"The thing that can blow up a whole star system?"

"Who told you that? That's an Imperial secret!"

"The rebel brain you removed."

"Oh, *her* ..." Since OK already knew, Dr. Madd went on to explain the weapon had been moved to Tartarus for final construction after rebel spies infiltrated its previous location. The Red Fleet would be its protection until it was finished.

"I guess the name threw me, *Annihilator*, it's unusual. Doesn't the Imperium usually name its ships after ... um ... historical figures?" OK was going to say, 'history's greatest monsters.'

"You've never heard of Bob Annihilator? Why, he invented the first true Doomsday weapon! Oh, we've come a long way since then. This weapon won't merely lay waste to worlds, it will erase entire systems from the cosmos!"

"Why does the mighty Imperium need a weapon to blow up stars?"

"They galaxy isn't going to terrorize itself!"

Dr. Madd turned away and buried himself in an immersive holo-magazine. The shuttle spent two hours navigating to a remote part of the massive spaceyard. The *Annihilator II* waited in the shadow of the southern hemisphere of an ancient, shattered planet. It was absolutely enormous. It was even larger than the Libran Super Star-Smashers built to harvest enormously valuable plasma from blue giant stars. Imperial battle cruisers looked like toy boats next to the thing. An entire continent had been scraped from a planet and processed into Scorponium Alloy to build its hull. An angry pulsar had been harnessed to power it.

The death shuttle landed on the construction dock and an umbilical boarding tube reached out to connect it to the *Annihilator*. The ship's landing bay was unpressurized and non-functional. It may have been the Imperium's ultimate weapon, but it was nowhere near ready to bring the other powers of the galaxy to their knees. The hull plating wasn't half finished. Power conduits were bare and exposed on every deck. Horde safety officers put up signs reading, "Do not touch plasma conduits. Corporeal Disintegration Risk" to comply with Imperial health and safety regulations. There were spaces where catwalks spanned sheer death drops without safety rails.

"Where's the bar?" OK imagined his duty would be serving drinks in the ship's bar; particularly after Madd told him Death Colonel Morrigan was in command.

"There is no bar! Alcohol is banned on the superweapon ever since someone spilled Antarean ale on a control panel and caused a reactor meltdown. Besides, we're under a deadline. No alcohol. Only amphetamines!"

"Then, what am I going to do?"

OK would be serving as Madd's personal assistant. Except that Madd did not care for the term "personal assistant." He thought it reeked of classism and privilege. He preferred "lab monkey." His job was mainly to fetch tools, tidy up, and bring lunch for Madd and his team of highly abusive scientists. The Horde was on the edge of achieving every supervillain's dream of demolishing entire systems with a single shot. They just needed to get the thing to work.

The thorniest technical issue now—the final hurdle—was the ignition mechanism. MAD was convinced the rebels had sabotaged it, and Madd's team had to rebuild it component by component, infuriating the Supreme Horde Command who wanted a test-firing as fast as possible.

Every morning, Madd held a status meeting which he opened with a motivational affirmation, "All of you are stupid and I hate you!" The meetings ended with Madd berating his team with a list of their failures, comments about their physical appearance, and how the carbon in their bodies would have been better used as plant food.

His favored motivational tool was randomly sending technicos to the Cubicle of Torment "to encourage the others." Madd's entire research team would have quit if they were allowed to, but quitting was considered treason. Some nonetheless sought escape. After a couple of "unfortunate incidents," new passcodes were programmed into the ship's airlocks.

OK was not exempt from Madd's abuses. "This tea is too hot!" Madd would shout, throwing the mug at OK's head. Sometimes someone else's head, but mostly OK's. When working through a particularly thorny problem, he would repeatedly poke OK with a stun-stick. "It helps me think!" he insisted.

Amid the abuse and humiliation, OK gradually came to understand the basic principle behind the complex and fascinating weapon. Quantum particles could be punked (that was the term the physicists used: "punked") into creating excess energy through interactions with subspace. This was what made faster-than-light travel a thing of plausible reality and not two-bit space opera. The *Annihilator* released that energy in a single blast that blew planets apart with the force of a supernova. He could not work out how it blew up stars, though.

In his bunk at night, he closed his eyes and went over every detail he had learned that day about what Madd called Project Starburst. Taking notes was forbidden, but the Horde couldn't stop him from seeing what he saw. He realized that Stoat had been right. He was learning secrets that would be of great value to the Rebel Pact once he escaped the Horde or found a way to transmit them. A servant of the Deathlord could definitely find more opportunities to do that than a kitchen sanitizer.

When not serving Madd or his horrible scientists, OK studied the protocols for serving Deathlord Damocles. There was a lot to memorize. Never looking the Deathlord in the eye. Never speak unless the Deathlord told him to speak. Begin or end each sentence with "Ia!." He also had to memorize details about the Deathlord's extensive list of personal vendettas and how to clean large quantities of congealed blood from carpeting.

After cycles of grueling effort, the Supreme Horde Command approved the weapon for a live test-firing. Madd was so pleased he ordered pizza for the entire team, topped with pineapple.

Under the protection of a Red Fleet battle group, the underpowered and overbuilt *Annihilator II* made its way slowly (if multiples of the speed of light can be called slowly) toward the test site; the planet Anvill VIII. Anvill VIII was a solid sphere of iron-nickel nearly twice the diameter of a standard Terra-Class planet. It orbited an ancient yellow sun with thirteen other planets. If the test was a success, the entire system would be blasted to astral dust!

After a long crawl through a desolate sector of the constellation, the fleet took up test positions around the planet. The test firing would be monitored and analyzed from every angle. "Lab Monkey!" Madd shouted. "On my signal, pull down that rod over there."

OK knew the drill. He crossed over to the rod and put his hands on it.

Madd admonished him. "OK, lower the rod. Not too fast. You have to pull at a steady pace, or it could jam or overflow."

OK grabbed the rod and took a deep breath, then pulled it down with constant, steady force. "Now this is rod pacing," he muttered.

"Well done, lab monkey," Madd offered as a rare moment of praise, removing his latte from the machine. "Now, go sit down and hit yourself with this stick while me and the Chief Scientist power up the weapon."

Even though an entire world was about to be destroyed, and the Imperium was about to gain a weapon that would terrorize the galaxy, OK could not help but feel kind of excited by the whole thing. Even if it was in service to diabolical evil, blowing up a planet was pretty cool.

Dr. Madd and the Chief Scientist entered the code that would fire the weapon… thirteen hours later. The weapon needed that much time to build up a full planet blasting charge. Per the custom, this countdown was displayed on a large red board with blocky LED numbers.

OK was relieved to learn that Anvill VIII was uninhabited. "I expected they would test it on an inhabited planet."

"And what if it the test failed?" Madd shouted, speckling him with spittle. "Do you know how embarrassing that would be? An empty rock is better. Hit yourself twice as hard for being dumb."

With the countdown established, Madd's next priority was a lavatory break. He demanded OK's assistance, as usual, and they headed for the unisex bathroom off the primary weapon laboratory.

"In just a few short hours, Ka-pow! Ka-blooie! Ka-blam! Anvill VIII will be blasted from the universe! Ah, there it is." Then came the sound of water splashing on porcelain as he continued. "And if that test is successful, we blow up its sun and prove that Starburst is the ultimate doomsday weapon. At least until we figure out how to blow up the universe. Forget that I said that! That is definitely not a project I am working on! Shut up!"

"How?" OK stammered. He had barely gotten his head around the amount of energy it would take to blow up the planet. (About 6.9×10^{35} joules.) "How can you blow up an entire star system... even from a ship this big."

"The principle is based on technology we bought from the Librans."

"Isn't there a galactic arms embargo against the Imperium?"

"Only for military hardware. The stellar core disruptor technology is commercial, it's the same as the basic technology used for star-mining."

"They just sold it to you?"

"Well, first we had to sign a treaty promising never to use the technology to develop a super-weapon. Velcro my fly, lab monkey!"

After he helped the elderly scientist close his pants, Madd exited the washroom and shuffled over to the weapon's control console. He checked over a few readouts, released several cacophonous farts, then sat down with his communicator to see if anyone had sent him nudes.

"I still don't understand," OK persisted, thinking to learn more about the weapon. "How do you blow up a sun?"

"Your puny brain would never understand it!" Madd shouted, putting his phone away. "Let me show you." He activated a holo-schematic and began at the rear of the weapon. "These Helion generators produce waveform energy in the form of boson particles and gravitatoes. These waveforms build up within a series of turbo encabulators until the weapon is ready to fire. The energy discharges through the focusing field as a blast wave that kabooms everything in its path. So, instead of gradually stripping away the stellar plasma—like a form of cosmic foreplay—we punch the sun with a crippling blow right in its ballsack and it explodes, taking the rest of the system with it."

OK got it, but he was unclear about one thing. "What's the deal with these flux capacitors?" He pointed to a pair of devices between the power generators.

"Those what?"

OK knew that hovercycles, which also relied on Helion generators for power, worked on a similar principle. "Helion-based power uses dual flux capacitors at each generator to modulate the energy field. It looks like these flux capacitors are inverted. Instead of sending the energy into the beam, they would send it back into the power core. Why would they do that?"

The chief scientist overheard and scoffed. "Is this idiot bothering you, Doctor? Shall I have him sent to the cubicle of torment?"

"Your mother's a cubicle of torment!" Madd stared intently at the spot on the schematic OK had indicated. His mouth slowly fell open. "By godless, the lab monkey could be right."

He pushed his way to a workstation and ran calculations on the laboratory's digital simulator. "If those flux capacitors direct the energy back into the power core, the overload would blow up the whole ship."

"Impossible," huffed the scientist. "We've done a hundred simulations."

"Well, either you are a drooling incompetent with a prematurely receding hairline or your simulations were wrong, you ballsack!"

Madd programmed a new simulation based on the inverted flux capacitors. The corrected simulation showed the effects would be catastrophic. The weapon would destroy both *Annihilator* and the planet, sending shards of iron-nickel in every direction. The shrapnel would have obliterated the entire fleet. The chief scientist looked on with the face of a man realizing his death was going to be horrible and sooner than expected.

Doctor Madd raged. "You idiots overlooked a booby trap, and this puny-brained lab monkey just saved the Starburst weapon and the entire fleet!"

Oh no, not again, OK thought.

"Shutdown the countdown!" Madd shouted. He and the chief scientist hit the "Abort Countdown" command and entered their emergency passcodes.

"The countdown isn't stopping," the chief scientist stammered as the big red digital countdown clock continued its relentless march toward 00:00:00.

"Did you capitalize the passcode?"

The scientist re-entered the code. The countdown stopped with a mere eleven hours, seventeen minutes, and forty-seven seconds left on the clock.

"That was close," Madd wiped off his brow. "Now, I have to explain to the captain why the test firing was cancelled. Oh, she is going to be pissed about this! You'll be lucky if you're still wearing your same skin tonight."

A few hours later, the *Annihilator II* and its escorts turned around and headed back to the Tartarus shipyards. Re-orienting the flux capacitors would take at least ten cycles to complete. Morrigan, in the fine tradition of Horde commanders, gave them four. A small medallion was delivered to OK's quarters during the return trip, a gold button with a scorpion in bas relief giving a thumbs up with its pincers. It was attached to a red and black ribbon.

"This Imperial Affirmation was awarded to Deathfinger (1st Rank) Ogden Kevitch for meritorious contribution to the ultimate Imperial Victory."

It was accompanied by a coupon good for several free downloads of DNZ Corp infotainment programming. He put the medal and its small glossy black box into a drawer next to his other commendations.

That night, he dreamed he was running across a field of golden grass on his homeworld of Katarina. At the other side was Anya. He ran toward her. Suddenly, the wind began blowing as the shadow of a giant scorpion fell across the field. OK heard the voice of Dr. Madd carried on the wind. "Thanks to that foolish lab monkey, it works perfectly now."

It was followed by a blinding flash of intense white light, and he woke up in a cold paralyzed sweat. He had barely enough time to process that he had been dreaming when the dreaded knock on the door that came in the middle of the night came in the middle of the night.

He fell out of his bunk and stumbled to the hatch. A pair of Death Guards charged in with the dreaded words, "The captain wants to see you."

"Let me put on pants," he answered. The Death Guards let him put on his pants. He wondered if Morrigan had worked out his intentions. He prepared to focus his thoughts on commercial jingles and Captain Slaughter's yang.

Morrigan had his personnel file open on a holoscreen when he entered her office. "If I had not thoroughly studied your background, I would suspect you of being a deep cover agent from another constellation; a trained engineer with a fake story about being an unsuccessful bartender."

OK winced. Had she figured him out?

"How did you manage to figure out a fatal flaw in our weapon that a hundred of the Imperium's best death engineers overlooked?"

"I watch a lot of science and engineering programs."

"Your I2N viewing record bears that out. On average you watch sixty-two minutes of science and engineering programs per day. That's what normal people average watching ultra-porn."

"You know what programs I watch?"

"The Imperium knows all, darling. Conversely, your porn viewing habits are way below the norm. 1 to 4 minutes per day, usually just before your sleep period. According to I3X records, you created an erotic avatar, but you've done nothing but talk to it."

"You know that too?"

"I3X collects all data on how their pornographic avatars are used and sells the data to the Imperium. It's in the User Agreement, darling."

She set her pain stick on the front of her desk and tented her elegantly manicured fingers. "Explain how you discovered the critical sabotage in the weapon system. Omit no detail."

"I was in the lavatory with Dr. Madd helping him with his fly…"

"You can omit that particular detail."

"Well, Dr. Madd showed me the schematic. And he said it was a Helion based power system, and I was like, 'Oh, that's basically the same power system used on hovercycles. Hovercars, too. And hoverbuses. Actually, a lot of things use Helion generators… pretty much anything that hovers. But they have to be paired with flux capacitors to regulate the power flow. When I saw the schematic, I could tell that the flux capacitors were inverted and I didn't know why … so, I asked Madd, and …"

When he finished, she asked him. "Darling, have you ever considered becoming an engineer?"

"Back on Katarina, I wanted to go to Engineering College. But I got talked into buying an old bar instead and so I became a bartender."

"You have an obvious talent for engineering, but you're a pretty mediocre bartender."

She sighed, "It's a shame you were born on a backwards planet, dropping from your mother's loins like a bag of wet meat. On an Imperial gestation farm, your talent would have been discovered through rigorous aptitude testing and brain sample analysis when you were still a child."

She took a drink from her flask, having exempted herself from the 'No Alcohol on the Superweapon' rules. "Do you really want to be one of Damocles personal valets."

"Ia, I mean... Ia... I've been called to serve Lord Damocles, Ia."

"Normally, it would be impossible to refuse such an assignment, but I have some leverage with Damocles's Chief of Staff. I could arrange for you to remain aboard *Annihilator II* as Dr. Madd's apprentice."

She explained that after two years of intensive training and a hazing that would leave him with untreatable physical and emotional scars, OK would become a Death Engineer, Level 1 under the Scorpion Horde Imperial Engineering Legion Division. "Legion Division? That seems redundant."

"They wanted it to spell out SHIELD. So, what do you say?"

His lifelong dream of being a space engineer dangled tantalizingly before him. He could not deny his temptation. The work on the Starburst weapon, despite its intended application, had been fascinating; far more interesting than cleaning kitchen floors or slinging drinks to vile Horde Officers.

As if reading his thoughts, she added, "There are Deathfingers who would kill for a position in Damocles's entourage. In fact, that's part of the selection process. You don't belong there, but you could do great work with the Imperial engineers."

For a moment, he imagined himself accepting the offer, but then his hatred and loathing for the Imperium rose again. He shook his head. "I just can't bear the thought of working on weapons that would kill people."

"If it's a matter of conscience, there are treatments for that." She sighed, Why resist an opportunity to do something you were born to do; and instead choose to do work you can't stand?" It was a question he could not answer.

Finally, she relented. "You have until we reach Tartarus to change your mind. Once you report to the Deathlord, I cannot help you."

He thanked her, hoping she would dismiss him. But there was one other thing.

"You did the Imperium a great service. Is there anything that we can we offer… beyond a cheap medal… to express our gratitude?"

And then it occurred to him there might be a reason to take her up on her offer. But there was someone he needed to talk to, first. "If it is possible, I would like to see Anastasaja again. If she's still alive."

"Who?"

"The rebel spy whose brain you removed."

"You'll have to be more specific, darling."

"The blonde scientist with the great rack… formerly."

"Oh, *her*… All rebel spies remain in FIST custody aboard the *Subutai*. Why do you want to see her?"

"I just want to say goodbye. Whether I end up here, or working for Damocles, I don't think I will ever see them again."

She looked like she didn't believe him but she surprised him. "I'll make the arrangements once we dock."

When the *Annihilator* was back in its enormous spacedock, OK shuttled back to the *Subutai*. A FIST enforcer escorted him into the secure chamber where the brains were being held. Another enforcer scanned his bond coin and consulted the list.

"You are approved for one visit of thirty death minutes," he announced, and opened the round, complex vault door.

"It's awfully warm in here." OK slipped his bond coin into the pocket of his space jacket as he took it off. He would leave it outside with the enforcers. Being caught without it meant—at best—a return trip to the cubicle of torment. He would take that risk rather than have this conversation recorded.

Beyond the armored hatch was a white vault where eight human brains floated in tanks of pale lavender liquid. They were labeled only with prisoner numbers, but OK knew Anastaja's. "It's me," he whispered to her.

"Well, obviously," she answered. "Who else would you be?"

"OK."

"OK, what?"

"OK … I fed you during the journey back from your base."

"Oh, the bartender."

He leaned closer and whispered. "I am putting my life in danger by telling you this, but they ... and I really have to emphasize it was they... found the booby trap you guys put in the weapon... with the flux capacitors."

She was quiet for a little time. "Well, so much for that."

"The weapon's being repaired as we speak. Dr. Madd has ordered the new science team to inspect every system before they test the weapon again."

"What happened to the old science team?"

"He gave them a timeout so they could think about what they did."

"A timeout? How long?"

"About twelve seconds for the airlock to cycle plus however long it takes to die in the vacuum of space."

"Bastard!"

He leaned in. "I have to know... does the weapon have any other weaknesses; anything that could be used to destroy it?"

Her tank bubbled, "Wouldn't you like to know."

"I'm on your side. I want to help the rebellion."

"I don't know if there were other sabotages. If I did, someone pretending to be a rebel sympathizer might trick me into betraying that information."

He had anticipated the possibility that she would not trust him. He had a plan for that. "Please trust me. I hate the Imperium. I want to help the rebel cause." Admittedly, it wasn't a very good plan.

"You did try to help us once before. Suppose I did... hypothetically... know of a weak point in the weapon. What could *you* do about it? Spill a drink into the control boards?"

"I can get on the technical crew for the weapon."

"You expect me to believe a bartender has been hired to work on the Imperium's ultimate weapon?"

"I've been interning with Dr. Madd. They offered me a spot on the technical crew. But I've also been offered a spot on Deathlord Damocles's personal staff, but if I could be more useful ..."

"Did you just say you were going to be on Damocles's personal staff?"

"Yes, but the truth is I just want to help the rebellion." OK looked around nervously. He couldn't be sure if the scientists were still being monitored. "If you tell me about another weakness in the weapon, I'll go back to the *Annihilator* and sabotage it before the Imperium can use it to kill anyone."

Whatever liquid was keeping her brain alive bubbled furiously. "If you really want to help, just kill Damocles."

"Kill Deathlord Damocles?"

"Yes!" hissed one of the other brains. "Kill him."

"Kill him," whispered the other brains. "Kill him! Kill him!"

"How could I kill a Deathlord?" OK whispered.

"You're a bartender, are you not? Put poison in his blood cocktail. Something lethal at the microdose level. Polonium or Quantum Palytoxin, something like that. If you want to aid the pact, then kill Deathlord Damocles. The pact will deal with the Starburst weapon."

16.0 THE BUTLER'S JIHAD

In his heart, OK was a rebel agent. He chose to take Anastasaja's direction as an order from a superior and set aside his own desires for the good of the rebellion. His first mission for the Rebel Pact was a big one—assassinate the Scorpion Horde's most diabolical warlord. The plan seemed so simple, so basic: slip poison into the Deathlord's cocktail. But what poison? How could he get his hands on it? And how would he sneak it aboard the Imperial Command Ship? Sure, there were toxic cleaning solvents lurking in the ship's kitchens, but the noxious odor would betray them faster than a dark fart in a turbovator. Mutant E. coli? Tricky to handle and might not survive in an alcoholic beverage. Dr. Madd had some terrifyingly lethal substances at his disposal, but getting to them would be as difficult as talking a Deathwalker into a life insurance policy.

He tapped his fingers against the image of the Anya avatar displayed on the sleek surface of his comm unit, desperately trying to outsmart the puzzle. Where else on the ship might there be something lethal? Out of nowhere, he suddenly realized that he knew of a suitably toxic and odorless substance. And he could get to it, even though it would involve effort so unsavory he almost dismissed the idea. But try as he might, he could not think of any other option.

"Your last day on the *Subutai* and you wanted to come here," said Qi'Anna as she walked him through the Deathwalker Hold.

"I have fond memories of this place," OK said, looking around once again at the rows upon rows of cryogenic sarcophagi.

"You only been here once before."

"Ia, but I was here with you. It was a special day for me."

"Aw, you're sweet. If I were even a little bit attracted to you sexually, I'd do you right here on this cryo-chamber. But we can still be friends."

"Speaking of that, why are these cryo-chambers empty. Where are all the Deathwalkers?"

"Most of them were called up to put down an insurrection on Murkon XII, the swamp planet. Just shipped a couple of days ago."

"This is new," said OK, walking up to a mural painted on one of the bulkheads; a man handing over a duster rifle to a grateful Deathwalker. "Is… is that supposed to be me?"

"Unh-huh, M2X-0553540 painted it in tribute after you showed them how to fix the targeting system. There's a painting of me in one of the bathrooms. I'm in fishnets and heels, straddling a great big…"

"Speaking of bathrooms, uh, is there a bathroom I can use. I had Enchiladas Exoplanetas for lunch with supernova hot sauce. It's gonna be bad, I can feel it."

"Oh, better use the one the Deathwalkers use when they come out of cryo-death. All the latrines are heavy-duty in there."

OK thanked her and headed into the Deathwalker toilet room. The receptables were solid steel and about twice as large as normal. He took a deep breath and pulled the thick rubber kitchen gloves from his pack.

He knelt and reached into the commode. Grimacing, trying to hold his breakfast inside his stomach, he ran his fingertips under the rim, hoping to find a clinger. Nothing. It occurred to him that none of these receptacles might have what he was feeling for. But he kept trying, moving onto the next one and feeling deep into the flush tube.

On the fourth stall he struck gold; the flusher had malfunctioned and the receptable held a full load of Deathwalker excrement. Odorless and massively toxic, it would make an ideal poison. And the joy of killing the horrible genocidal warlord by feeding him the *drutt* of his own troops was the chocolate brown icing the cake. He quickly filled five of the vials he had brought with him. He now had at least five chances to kill the Deathlord. "Prepare to meet your doom, Damocles," he muttered as quietly as he could.

"You OK in there?" Qi'Anna called. "I mean, obviously, you're OK, but is everything coming out all right?"

"Almost done," he called back, capping the sixth vial. He sealed them tightly in a secure biohazard container Dr. Madd had given him; or more accurately, thrown at him. He discarded his kitchen gloves down the garbage chute and washed his hands like he had just chopped a bushel of Jovian Jalapenos and needed to put on contact lenses.

He met Qi'Anna back outside. "What did you think of my picture?"

OK had not even noticed it. "It was very… erotic?"

She gave him an odd look. "The sexy one is in the other bathroom, the one in that chamber just has me sitting on the *drutter*."

"And, um, no one but you could have pulled that off."

"You are so sweet," she punched him playfully in the arm, like the slutty sister he never had.

Phase 1 of his plan was a success. Now, he had just had to figure out how to smuggle them onto the Putin, past the thorough and unyielding FIST security that surrounded the Red Fleet's command ship. He could only think of one guy who could help him. "Let's go get a drink," he suggested.

They got into the HOC through the staff entrance and took a seat near the bar. "Bring the lady whatever she wants," OK said.

"Moonbeam in a jar!" Qi'Anna asked, taking the drink and going over to flirt with a gunnery officer at the viewport.

"Is Boskirk around?" OK asked the bartender. "Can you get him?"

"Is there a problem?" the bartender looked terrified. "I will comp the drinks if there's a problem."

"No, I just want to talk to him… in private." The relieved bartender led him to the rear storeroom that Boskirk had commandeered as his private office. Garish holo-portraits of Boskirk and his girlfriend competed for display space with framed cocktail recipes and pictures of spoons. Storage crates lined one wall, some of them humming. OK did not want to know what manner of contraband was inside.

"OK, old friend, how's your sex life?" Boskirk greeted him, sprawled in his large red chair behind a desk of russet Voivoodian oak. Both his hair and his accent were as thick and indescribable as ever.

"I need a favor. You may have heard I've been transferred to the Command Ship. I need to get something on board, past security, if you take my meaning."

"What is it, drugs?"

"Will that be a problem?"

"No, no problem."

"Then, it's drugs." OK set the biohazard container on the desk.

"Oh, that is no inconvenience at all. I was afraid it was a lot of drugs." Boskirk entered a code into a safe hidden under his desk. He pulled out one of the cases the Horde used to move top secret materials between ships. He put the biohazard container into the secret package, sealing it and wrapping it in thick red tape. "There you go, easy like squeezing lemons."

"That's it?"

"Well… just to make sure, you should have a bribe ready. Actually, now that I think about it, give them the bribe first."

"How much?"

"Two disks, Antarean silver, 100 grams."

"I don't have that."

"Another small problem with simple remedy. I sell you two disks. Normally 2,000 IMU each, but for old and good friend OK I give discount of 50 per cent, 2,000 for both."

OK guessed his Anya avatar would have to wait a little longer for the personality upgrade. He handed over his bond coin and Boskirk deducted the amount. "There you go, all set, huh?"

OK could not believe it had gone down so easily. His plan to kill the Deathlord might actually have a chance to succeed. Of course, now he would have to make awkward small talk with Boskirk. "So, um, who have you been selling drugs to on the command ship?"

Boskirk threw his head back and laughed in his never-quite-realistic kind of way. "Believe me, it would take less time to list who I have not."

Suddenly, there came a frantic tapping at the door, and then the door burst open and Scrubby rolled over the top of it. "OK!" it vocalized.

"Scrubby, old buddy!" OK knelt and patted the mechanoid on its head.

"Scrubby go?" It pleaded, extending its arms to him again.

"I don't think I can take you, Buddy. You're Imperial property assigned to the *Subutai*."

"Scrubby go!"

"Oh, you can take him, too. He always snapping at my ankles with rotor blades. I send him over in box of Hamdingers. No one ever open that."

The next morning, he boarded a death shuttle to the *Vladimir Putin,* the Red Fleet's Command Ship. The enormous first-rank battle cruiser loomed over the fleet like a brutalist scorpion ripped from a heavy-metal album cover. Its forward pincer-arms, bristled with mass-driver cannons, exuding predatory anticipation. A serrated tail extended from the rear, holding batteries of high-velocity trans-orbital warheads poised to lay waste to subjugated worlds. OK had a vivid memory of the *Putin* casting an ominous scorpion-shaped shadow across the plains of his home planet. He hadn't witnessed it, but the image had etched itself into his consciousness through countless replays on I2N.

The death shuttle flew into the *Putin's* ventral docking bay and folded its oversized and unnecessary (but design-forward) space wings into its chunky black hull. After the high officers from the top deck cleared the landing bay, the lower crew were permitted to disembark. The Lady Ur was waiting at the bottom of the ramp, holding a drink. Judging by her expression, it was a sour.

"Congratulations on rising to the top of the septic tank that was this round of applicants. Quarters have been prepared for you and the other floaters. Your meager belongings have been taken there." OK realized a battle-axe need not be an ugly, blunt weapon, but could as easily be a superbly balanced precision instrument equally capable of smashing your brains or slicing off your face. The Lady Ur was such a battle-axe.

One perquisite of serving the Deathlord would be quarters of his own. Granted, they were no larger than closets, even smaller than the cells Imperial prisoners were kept in prior to brain extraction. There was also a constant low hum to remind him he was deep in the guts of the monstrous ship. Like a mutant E. coli bacterium in the guts of its victim.

He took out his precious package and tried to find a place to hide it until he got his chance to use it. He considered hiding it in the air vent, but that seemed cliched. He hid it in his personal locker instead, next to his crystals of Piscean pop music and postcards from Plinth and Perihelion.

He knew he would have to be patient. It might be a long time before he had the opportunity to serve it. He would have to learn the Deathlord's bibation habits. Hopefully, he tended more to Martian Mudslides and Tom Cosmoses. If he liked clear drinks, OK's task would become far more difficult. But one way or another, he would succeed. It only nagged at him that the Rebel Pact would never know it was his hand that had taken out Damocles.

"Knock, Knock," said a familiar voice. Stoat had entered his quarters. OK had not heard from him over their many cycles apart; communication between applicants was forbidden. He looked sharp in the black velvet, red-trimmed uniform of the Deathlord's personal staff. OK hadn't had a chance to try his on yet. "Aren't you happy to see me, Friend-o?"

"I wasn't expecting to find you in my quarters."

"No locks on staff quarters; Horde regulation. But we made it, Friend-o. We have arrived. We're here. And best of all, I don't have to strangle any more clones for Commander Bloodfiend."

"Strangle clones?"

"You would be surprised how much fight a sedated clone can put up, but that's all behind us now. Everything has gone as planned, and we are exactly where I intended us to be."

Of course he and Stoat could not conspire openly, not with the bond coins recording their every word and FIST's spies everywhere. It was enough to know they were both working toward the same goal.

OK and Stoat reported to the ship's medical facility the next morning to begin the "procedures" the Lady Ur had alluded to. The first step was biome decontamination. They were ordered to strip their clothes, handed a pair of goggles, and blasted with microwave radiation to burn off the bacteria on their outer bodies. There was a momentary sensation that their entire bodies were on fire followed by their eyebrows falling out.

They were then led to separate rooms. A medico in a pale green lab coat was waiting for OK when he arrived. She jabbed him with an anesthetic probe, which made his chest go numb like his heart had stopped.

"Lie down on the table," she ordered.

"Couldn't I have done that first," OK said as he staggered to the narrow surgical table.

"This is going to hurt somewhat less than it would have hurt without the jab." She strapped down his arms. Then, she picked up a small device that looked a little bit like an electronic beetle. She placed it on his chest.

"What is that?"

"It's the Benatar device, named after its inventor, Dr. Benatar, but it's commonly known as the heartbreaker."

"Heartbreaker?"

She cut a three-centimeter incision with a laser scalpel. "This is going to hurt a lot. If you squirm, this will hurt a lot worse and probably kill you."

And then it got a lot worse. She activated the beetle, and it began burrowing into the incision, entering his chest just beside his heart. It felt exactly like a metallic insect burrowing into his chest and OK screamed.

"Don't be a baby," the medico ordered. "All personnel on the *Putin* are fitted with the heartbreaker. They enable Deathlord Damocles to instantly kill those who disappoint him."

"You mean he could kill me at any time?"

"Deathfinger, he could always kill you at any time, this just makes less mess to clean up."

"I thought he used telekinesis to crush the hearts of his victims."

"Telekinesis only exists in science fiction; you clump of cells. You can't move things with your mind, that's just dumb. How would you do it? Control gravity with your mind? Telepathy, on the other hand, that's just boosting the gain on your neuro-electric field." She gestured as though cranking up a knob.

After the insertion and her degradation were finished, she tested the device. "You're going to feel blinding pain shooting up your left arm."

That was exactly what it felt like plus the sensation of steel claws squeezing his heart. His body went rigid, every nerve electrified with agony. He tried to scream, but his lungs could find no air. Every muscle in his body was pulled taut like a puppet on strings, contorting him into a grotesquerie of agony. The pain ceased but left him flopping and twitching like a landed fish.

The medico checked her readouts. "Input is good, the device is functioning normally. That procedure is done, only twelve more to go."

After the painful series of physiological procedures were complete, OK and Stoat were reunited. OK hoped he didn't look as terrible as Stoat, but knew from the bleeding, pain-filled depths of his heart he looked worse.

They were given the rest of the day to recover. Or they should have been, but as soon as they were finished, they were ordered to report to the Lady Ur outside the Deathlord's quarters. She gave them less of a pep talk than a spirit-crushing lecture.

"You are about to serve the Supreme Deathlord of the Red Fleet, not your drinking buddy, your fellow groundball hooligan, or your ill-bred cousin who let you feel her up in the back of a hover-wagon. Do not *attempt* to develop a rapport with him. The only reason you are doing this and not robots is because the three laws of robotics were repealed and you meat puppets are less likely to go on a killing rampage."

OK still sore from having numerous horrible things implanted into his body, had a premonition that he was going to die. He was going to spill a drink or absent-mindedly refer to the Deathlord as 'Buddy' and they were going to die. "We're going to die," was how he expressed this idea.

The Lady Ur validated his thoughts. "Without training, you would be looking at your own intestines by the end of the day. But I give you one and half cycles. To survive longer than that, remember the most important concept we tried to drill into those smooth little brains during your training; the ideal manservant executes his duties flawlessly while remaining invisible to his master." She fixed Stoat with a withering glower. "Do your jobs and you live. Try to get chummy, and you will die."

She pressed the red-eyed skull on the black armored hatches. It opened into the private suite of the most genocidal Deathlord in all the Horde. OK had expected a stone-walled dungeon lined with the skulls of his enemies. Instead, Damocles's quarters were rather chic. The flooring was glossy black, and the curving walls were softly lit around the edges. Deathlord Damocles stood in an alcove, arms crossed. OK considered that an odd place for him to be standing and then realized he was looking at Damocles's body armor.

"Where is the bar, Ia?" Stoat asked. OK was wondering the same thing.

The Lady Ur scowled at him. "Who said anything about a bar?"

"We are well-trained in bartending and drinks service, we assumed the Deathlord…"

"You may assume that you will serve the Deathlord in the positions assigned to you. The Deathlord does not drink alcohol and therefore has no need for bar stewards. And if he did, neither of you have proven your worthiness to serve him in such an intimate manner."

OK had a sudden realization that his plan had hit a snag. "What will be doing, Ia?"

The Lady Ur led OK down a hallway, through a corridor, and then to a vault. She entered a code and the hatch hissed open. The interior was the temperature of a freezer. Within it were rows and rows of identical black pajamas sealed in plastic. "You will be tending to his lordship's sleeping wardrobe." The Lady Ur handed OK a pair of rubber gloves and a pile of wipes soaked in a noxious disinfectant. "Sanitize them. All of them."

"Ia, All of them, Ia?"

"Which word is unclear to you?"

OK bowed his head and prepared to get to work, his mind frantically trying to readjust his plan to his new circumstances.

"And what is my job, Ia?" Stoat asked.

"Your job is to dispose of the Deathlord's urine receptacles." These were in a separate vault, lined up and illuminated, row upon row of piss jars, like a publicly funded art exhibition without the crucifixes. There was a detailed disposal process for ensuring its total destruction.

Despite her emphasis on the importance of this task, Stoat seemed disappointed.

"One last word, speaking to any other valet while on duty, is strictly forbidden. In fact, the only reason you have these two very coveted positions is because one of your predecessors sneezed and the other invoked the blessing of some mythological deity. They were promptly disintegrated."

The balance of their shift passed uneventfully, unless the Lady Ur's periodic death threats and disparagement of OK's sanitization efforts counted as events. Stoat silently attended to the jars in the closet. He finished well before the end of the shift, so the lady instructed him to sanitize the Deathlord's personal lavatory.

At the end of their first shift, they were dismissed to return to their respective quarters. OK wanted nothing more than to shower and cry himself to sleep, but Stoat had other prerogatives. "She deliberately gave me the most humiliating job possible."

OK knew where this was going. "Don't," he said to Stoat. "Don't scheme against the Lady Ur, you'll get us both killed."

"If I had thirty seconds to speak with Damocles..."

"Were you listening when she said be invisible? I know the plan has hit an obstacle, but we have to be patient and stay alive." He might still get a chance to kill the Deathlord, but he had to live long enough to do it. Stoat's impatience might eliminate that possibility.

But Stoat would let nothing deter him. "I am not going to spend the rest of my tour destroying urine jars."

OK's saw no way to execute his plan to serve Damocles a toxic cocktail from the confines of the Deathlord's pajama closet. So here he was, 2000 IMU poorer for his efforts, six vials of Deathwalker dump in his locker, and his ambitions fading like the light of one of the misfortunate stars the Red Fleet consumed for fuel. He was a fool to think taking out an Imperial Deathlord could have been so simple.

But he couldn't give into despair, not after coming this far. Until his chance came around, he would perform his duties as assigned. Each morning, OK took the Deathlord's used pajamas to the disintegration chamber. Then, he received a fresh set of pajamas, sealed in mylar plastic, from the Deathlord's stylist's assistant. These were sterilized, cataloged, numbered, and placed in the final position of the 300 pairs the Deathlord maintained. OK then inventoried and accounted for each set, then sanitized them again. At the end of the shift, he handed over the next night's set of pajamas to the other nightwear attendant. All without ever speaking a single word nor meeting the eyes of another human being.

"Do you know the Deathlord's urine is an Imperial State Secret?" Stoat asked OK on the way back to their quarters after their shift.

"No, and I don't ..."

"The Deathlord's urine is the residue of the enzymatic protein compounds he uses to keep his body alive. The Deathlord is almost as old as the Imperium. But he's still in his original body, he's never upgraded. Instead of moving to a clone, he keeps himself alive by ingesting bio-engineered enzymatic proteins."

"That's fascinating." That was also the only half-decent thing OK had ever heard about the Deathlord. He would never express the unpopular opinion in public, but he found the practice of cloning people to use their bodies sort of unethical; even if the social consensus was that clones were not human, but merely "human adjacent."

Stoat produced a small vial of luminous yellow-brown fluid from under the waist of his work suit.

"Is that what I think it is?"

"Do you think it's a sample of his Lordship's urine."

"Yes."

"Then, it is what you think it is."

"How did you get a hold of that?"

"Snuck it out of his quarters, obviously."

The risk he had taken must have been enormous. "What are you going to do with Damocles's pee?"

"I'm going to have this sample analyzed and reproduce the Deathlord's enzymatic sustainment formula."

And replace it with a potent and lethal poison, of course. Once again, Stoat was thinking three moves ahead of everyone else. There was still a chance that this crazy-ass poisoning scheme might just work! "I'm with you."

"Good, because I'm going to need help from you."

"Of course, you supply the delivery system, and I'll supply…"

Stoat cut him off, lest he betray the plan. "… you'll supply your taste buds. You'll be the tester for the new chemical formulation."

"Why in the void would you want to do that?"

"His sustainment fluid tastes vile. But I think I can come up with something that will taste good and still trick his cells into regenerating."

All the better to hide the taste of the poison. It was a clever idea.

"I was thinking of something in the warm chocolate family."

"That would be ideal," OK said, considering the nature of the poison.

Stoat sent the sample to Boskirk for a chemical breakdown since he had access to first rate chemistry equipment without any Imperial entanglements. When he got the analysis, Stoat began to experiment. OK tested the flavor of his first attempt. "It's still redolent of stale cow piss."

Over the course of several cycles, Stoat grew skillful at covering the rancid, bovine-uresis taste. His first success tasted like a rich, caramel mocha coffee with barely a hint of cow pee. He also came up with a kind of sangria. Another tasted of butterscotch. And finally, there was a chocolate-mint flavor that OK had to admit was particularly on point and covered up the urine taste entirely.

"How are you going to get him to drink it?"

In their respective positions they had no way of serving, or even offering, a drink to Deathlord Damocles. He was sure Stoat must have thought ahead to this. Indeed, he had. "During my internship, I developed a warm, mutual rapport with Captain Bloodfiend."

"In between clone stranglings?"

"Yes. Anyway, at the end of every cycle, he and Deathlord Damocles have a meeting where they discuss … oh, I don't know what, and it doesn't matter. Captain Bloodfiend is allowed to bring his personal favorite personal servant. That will be me. I'll use the opportunity to present this new formula."

Brilliant! All of the scheming and plotting, the grubbing for promotion to get closer to the Deathlord, it had all led to this opportunity. He knew that by assassinating the Deathlord he was serving a notice of cancellation on all future birthdays, but it would be worth it to deliver the vengeance of a thousand star systems. He would never see Anya again, but he hoped that, somehow, word would get to her of his sacrifice.

OK clapped Stoat on the shoulder. "All right, you bastard, I'm in." He opened his locker and passed Stoat four of the vials he had been saving for this opportunity. "Here, take these."

Stoat squinted at the vial. "What is this?"

"Deathwalker excrement," he whispered, "Enough to kill forty men."

"Ah…" Stoat nodded, he understood. OK nodded back. He only regretted that he would not be there to witness the Deathlord's agonizing death.

The end of the cycle came which meant OK would have a break from his next duty shift. He planned his day off around a hot chemical shower, a comm with Qi'Anna or Rue, and plugging into a simulation where he and his simulacrum of Anya would repair a star-drive engine. The real Anya lacked any sort of mechanical sensibility, but virtual Anya was another matter. Later, he would unpack the sex crystal and some moist washcloths.

He had just begun taking off his pants when there was a furious knocking on the door of his quarters. He knew who and what it was about before he opened it. Stoat, breathless, shouted. "You have come to the Deathlord's quarters with me right now! The regular valets were disintegrated so we need another valet immediately."

"Why didn't you use the door signal?"

"It lacked urgency. Hurry up and put on this uniform!"

"Why me?"

"I'm going to serve him my new improved sustenance formula."

Ah, so this was it! The chance had come much sooner than he had expected! And OK would get to see the assassination! He quickly changed into the red velvet serving uniform and fez. "You said the valets were disintegrated. What did they do? Sneeze without permission or something?"

"Oh, it wasn't punishment, it was suicide. They couldn't take the pressure anymore." When OK finished dressing, Stoat grabbed his arm and pulled him along to the Deathlord's quarters.

The Lady Ur received them with the scowling contempt they had come to appreciate. "You, keep their glasses full," she ordered Stoat. "You... clean up the disintegration stain on the carpet. The vacuum is in the utility closet."

"Keep their glasses full... *of death!*" OK thought. Oh, so this is how it felt to kill someone you wanted to die. He had to admit it was a bit intoxicating.

As he cleaned the red dust from the black carpet, OK could see everything that transpired in the adjacent room. A group of Scorpion Party officials arrived, looking authoritarian in the civil dress uniforms. Bloodfiend arrived soon after, looking ruddy from a fresh transfusion of clone blood. His little legs dangled above the floor as he took his seat.

Finally, a throne of skulls revolved to reveal the Deathlord Damocles— The Sword That Hangs Over Your Head. Those words glowed above his seat of power. He was far less intimidating without his battle armor; as old as Dr. Madd but without a single hair on his head, not so much as an eyebrow. His skin was creased and sallow, crinkling like the very old paper in the ancient books of Death Captain Slaughter's library. His face was a rugged landscape of scar tissue, etched with the brutal history of his battles and conquests. He was like a man who had been in a horrific hovercycle accident, and the reconstructive surgeons "did the best they could."

Deathlord Damocles read over the ultimatum he would deliver to the next world the Horde would mercilessly vanquish. Without the reverb and bass enhancement, The Deathlord's natural voice was a reedy, malevolent rasp that sounded nothing... *nothing*... at all like the grumbling thunder tones that issued deadly ultimatums to doomed worlds.

"People of planet to be named later, last night you went to your beds under the delusion that you were a sovereign people. When dawn arose, you stared into the dawn of the rising... 'Dawn' twice in the same sentence? Who wrote this excrement?"

He flung the speech aside and unleashed a torrent of fury upon his cowering staff. "This is the same speech I've given for the last ten invasions. Do we really have to tell them 'Yesterday you were independent, today you are part of the Imperium?' That should be bloody *furking* obvious to them, shouldn't it?"

"It's powerful," said one of the party speechwriters. "It tells them the world they knew is over and everything is about to change."

"As if they couldn't figure that out after we've bombed them back to the twenty-first century." Damocles grunted. "And where in this speech does it say, 'Resistance is Futile!' We paid a fortune for 'Resistance is futile,' and it isn't even in my bloody invasion speech."

"The writers room thought it was a little trite," said the other Scorpion functionary. "The alternate wording is more forceful, more compelling."

"'Your efforts to resist will be crushed in the gears of destiny.'"

"Much more forceful, don't you think?"

The Deathlord roared. "We paid for Resistance is Futile!" He slammed the table. "Rework the whole thing! The theme should be 'dread.' They should dread what is about to happen to them. They are about to broken on my wheel. Use that—broken on my wheel."

His stenographers scrambled to capture his notes. "Perhaps it would help if we knew what world this speech will be directed toward."

"The Supreme Horde Command has not yet made that decision," the Lady Ur put in, sparing Damocles from admitting he didn't know.

Then, the Deathlord looked right at OK, and his blood ran cold. "Deathfinger, I require fresh clothing. Black. Odd-numbered."

OK bolted for the closet, the part of the Deathlord's quarters he knew best. He took one of the plastic wrapped outfits off the rack. He took it out to the Deathlord. The Lady Ur intercepted him. "Unwrap the plastic and place the garment on top. Make sure your hands touch only the plastic and not any part of my garment."

OK carefully carried out the instructions, thinking it would be ridiculous for him to die because he didn't properly hand pajamas to a genocidal warlord. He kept his gaze locked to the floor as the Deathlord snatched his clothes. A moment later, he felt something velvet hit his face. The Deathlord had thrown his previous outfit at him. OK backed away allowed himself to breathe again. *"Just die!"* he thought.

Stoat chose this precise moment to make his move. Holding a tray, he genuflected in front of Damocles. "Hail to the Imperial victory, Ia. I offer your Deathlordship something delectable to consume, a flavored libation I have crafted perfectly suited to Your Eminence's desires, Ia."

The Deathlord roared. "Who is this insolent insect and why does he dare to address me?"

Stoat went white. "My Lord, your humble servant has prepared a most delicious drink for you to …"

The Deathlord raised a palm, and some mysterious force threw Stoat against the bulkhead. "I do not imbibe frivolous libations. Destroy him!"

The Lady Ur came forward, "I'll have this insolent fool taken to the elective surgery ward and emasculated without anesthesia before we disintegrate him."

Stoat bowed obsequiously, averting his eyes. He held up the tube of brown liquid. "Your Eminence, this is a new formulation of your sustenance, Ia. Your servant humbly offers that it will please his master, Ia."

The Deathlord again hurled him against the bulkhead. "You are trying to poison me!"

Hubba Hubba Froot-a Froot-a! OK thought as loudly as I could. *Captain Slaughter's penis!*

"No, my master, I serve you with all of my being. Just… taste it."

Lady Ur tapped her comm unit. "Elective surgery, prepare your dullest and most unsanitary blades…"

Stoat strained against the force crushing him against the bulkhead. "Death Captain Bloodfiend, tell His Eminence that I am loyal. Remember those blood cocktails I used to make you?"

The Death Captain grinned with his razor sharpened teeth. "I'll try the insolent fool's libation, if my Deathlord will permit it."

The Deathlord released Stoat from the bulkhead and let him drop to the floor. Stoat picked up the tubes of liquid and set them on the tray. Bloodfiend picked up the reddish-colored one, the one flavored of Sangria. He took a long draw from it. "It's not your best work," he told Stoat. "Needs less fruit and more hemoglobin. You should try it, my Deathlord. If it fails to please you, have the wretch eviscerated where he stands."

The potential evisceration seemed to seal the deal. Damocles selected the caramel brown tube. His red guards fired up their blades. He scowled at the tube, held it up to the light, then very reluctantly took a sip. His eyes sagged deeper, he scowled. Then, he took another, longer sip.

"It's working," OK whispered to himself. Then, looked around to see if anyone had heard. But all of them were fixed on Damocles.

The Deathlord set the tube down. "This is pretty good, actually."

Stoat crumpled obsequiously. "Ia, I am pleased that my master is pleased."

The Lady Ur forestalled the evisceration with a wave of her hand.

"I have not tasted anything in over a hundred years. How is this possible?"

"It was a great challenge to create a flavor that…"

The Deathlord ignored him and tried another one of the mixtures. "Warm chocolate, impressive. Indeed, your flavors are powerful."

Stoat, recovering his usual nerve, urged him, "Try the one on the end, your Eminence. I call that one 'Dark Dominion Delight,' guaranteed to conquer your taste buds!"

The Deathlord took a taste and then slammed Stoat against the far bulkhead again. "I don't like mint!" he thundered.

"I really thought you were going to die back there," OK whispered as they made their way back to their bunks afterward, Stoat limping.

"So did I for a moment, but it all worked out," Stoat said. "The only way to win big is to bet big."

Ia, indeed. "The poison should kill the old bastard by morning," OK whispered. "And Bloodfiend as well. Two for the price of one."

"What poison? What are you talking about?"

"No point in hiding it. We will die as heroes when they find out."

"Find out what?"

"That you poisoned the Deathlord. That was the plan, wasn't it?"

"No, no, godless void, no… where did you ever get that idea?"

"That's what we've been working for, this whole time. That's why I gave you the Deathwalker *drutt!*"

"That's why you gave me that?" Stoat held his head. "I thought that was one of your weird pranks."

"Weird pranks! When have I ever pulled a weird prank? We were supposed to strike a blow for liberation! That's why we joined the Horde."

"Oh, friend-o, I thought that stint in the Cubicle of Torment had cured you of your insane notions of resistance. When we signed up for the Horde, I'll admit, I was just trying to survive, nothing more. But look at us now, after everything the Horde has done for us! In just two years, we went from scrubbing floors in the lower crew mess to the personal staff of the Deathlord of the entire Red Scorpion Fleet!"

I scrubbed the floors, OK thought, his simmering fury beginning to rise up the back of his spine.

"We would never have gotten those kinds of opportunities on Katarina. We were nothing on that planet. And we were never going to be anything. Whether or not you're ready to accept it, the Imperium has been good to us."

Enraged, OK slammed his old friend against the bulkhead. "The Imperium has killed millions… while you and I … served drinks."

"Ow, I just got done being slammed against a bulkhead."

"Traitor!" OK hissed at him.

"I'm not a traitor, I'm a survivor. And so are you. Thanks to me. You know what? I am sick of dragging your ungrateful sack around. You can go furk yourself."

"Fine. We're through!" OK released him. "Don't ever speak to me again."

He turned and made his way down the corridor.

"Hey, OK!" Stoat called after him. OK turned around and Stoat, with a kind of madness in his eyes, shot him the claw salute. "Hail to the Imperial Victory! Ia! Ia!"

18.0 IN THE COURT OF THE CRIMSON DEATHLORD

OK returned to his quarters where a hot chemical shower failed to wash off his shame and disgust. He climbed into his bunk and pulled the shiny space blanket over his head. He couldn't and didn't want to sleep so he turned on HARVEY to seek succor in the company of the Anya avatar he had fashioned in an earlier fit of questionable creativity. Unfortunately, the only comfort it had to offer was, "Big boy, why don't you touch yourself while I watch." He would definitely have to spring for that personality upgrade. If he lived long enough to see his next paycheck.

He was sickeningly certain that Stoat would turn him in, expecting the dread knock at the door to come at any moment. Around 2 in the morning he had the brilliant idea of disposing of the evidence in the most self-evident way possible, cursing himself for his wasted trust and effort as he pushed the flusher, then returned to his bunk to fret some more.

Bleary-eyed, OK reported to his duty station the next day, his gorge brimming with the acid reflux of scorn. The Lady Ur was waiting in front of the Deathlord's suite and he was sure it was all over. Her first words to him affirmed this assumption. "Deathfinger, your services caring for the Deathlord's night garments are no longer required."

"What?" he heard himself saying, and then quickly, reflexively added, "Ia."

"His Eminence Deathlord Damocles was pleased with the new sustenance formula and promoted your comrade, Deathfinger Stoat to his adjacent staff."

"Ia, good for him, Ia." So she was going to toy with him first.

"Deathfinger Stoat informed us that you played an important role in the creation of the sustenance elixir." And there it was. Stoat had celebrated his promotion by ratting him out. He was going to be terminated. Amazingly, it didn't jolt his adrenaline like the previous times he had thought he was going to die. He was getting too used to this. "Well, Deathfinger, is it true?"

"What did he tell you?" He wanted to confirm they knew about his act of attempted defiance before they terminated him. He could at least go out of the airlock with that scintilla of consolation.

"It is our understanding that you served as a sort of quality control. Testing the flavors before they were approved."

What? Stoat had told them that? And left out the part about planning to poison the Deathlord? OK realized he was nodding.

The Lady Ur glared. "His eminence, out of his boundless magnanimity, has promoted your position as well."

"A promotion?"

"It means an improved station within his staff."

He knew what it meant. "I don't want a promotion."

"Did I say something that suggested you had a choice? From this point forward, some other menial wretch will be sanitizing his eminence's nightclothes. You will take on new duties, suitable to your skillset, which you will perform with the requisite diligence and gratitude to your Deathlord."

My skillset? Did that mean sanitizing kitchens, again? Or serving drinks. He immediately regretted flushing the poison. Could he get more? In time, perhaps. Regardless, he hoped Stoat didn't think this meant they could be friends again. "Ia, I shall perform my duties with the appropriate level of, um, demeanor. Show me to the bar or the kitchen or whatever, Ia."

"Once again, who said anything about a bar or a kitchen? Your new job is to manage the Deathlord's under-raiment."

"His what... Ia?"

"Deathfinger, I find myself having to explain a tedious number of words to you. I am referring to what someone of your station might call his skivvies, his smalls, his oyster hammock, his truncheon holders, his jolly trolleys, his sausage skins, his crotch maidens..."

"His underwear," OK finally realized. He would be one of the valets who stood by to hand him a fresh set on-demand. Damocles must have been impressed with his pajama-handling. "Do I have to help put them on?"

The Lady Ur scowled and rolled her eyes—an impressive trick. "Don't be ridiculous. He has trained specialists for that."

The job didn't come with a formal promotion in rank, but he got another 50 IMUs per pay cycle and 50 Scorpion social credit points out of it. Perhaps he could splurge and give Anya that new personality upload.

He was trained by shadowing the current sous-valets; a rather snooty bunch considering their job. There was a whole process, bordering on ritual, involved in the preparation of the Deathlord's smalls. OK's initial concerns about skid marks proved unfounded. The Deathlord's germophobia was so profound he had years ago had his intestines surgically removed and replaced with a bionic waste disposal system.

Finally, after six days of training, he was handed the lacquered box and led into the Deathlord's private chamber by the Chief Valet. The first thing he saw —although he tried not to look—was Stoat tending a drinks station near the Deathlord's skull throne. The touchy subject of how Stoat obtained the formula for the Deathlord's longevity fluid had been brushed aside; although the young man who replaced him in his former duties was subjected to a thoroughly unpleasant body cavity search at the end of each shift.

Thus began the next chapter in OK's service to the Horde, a soul-stifling, monotonous routine of standing in the Deathlord's chambers, hour after dispiriting hour—holding the red lacquered box, waiting for the booming command, "Change!" That was his cue to open the box, remove the topmost pair, and hand it to the Deathlord's highly trained underwear change specialists; a pair of large, muscular women from the high gravity lesbian separatist planet Baradaris XX. OK liked to imagine them changing him like diapered baby, a scenario not too distant from reality.

Stoat had concocted an even more insidious retribution than OK could have imagined. Forcing him to witness with impotent, murderous rage as a smug and self-satisfied Stoat supplied the Deathlord with sustenance formula in an endless parade of new and exciting flavors, like Apple Margarita and Wild Capellan Apricot. When the Red Fleet crushed an insurgency on the conquered planet Montego Beta III — a tropical paradise renowned for its rum exports—Stoat honored the occasion by creating a Pina Colada version.

Stoat posed with his drink creations for hologram selfies on his popular social media account "Deathlord's Drink master." *"Serving the galaxy's finest elixirs of sustenance; distilled from the tears of the vanquished, exquisitely flavored, and aged in the heart of a dying star."* He had eighteen million followers between Interstellar Gram and MindHead, the telepathic social media app that sent messages directly into your brain. CRANIUM had developed it as an alternative to mind extraction before deciding that removing the brains was the best part of interrogations.

Other constellations had tried to ban MindHead as an imperial mind control device, but they had been thwarted by its immense popularity among teenagers, middle aged women, and hivemind clones.

Stoat served the flavored sustenance while oozing flattery like a reactor breach oozed ionizing radiation. "Your malevolence levels this week have been truly aspirational, your eminence! The precision with which you obliterated that insurgent stronghold was breathtaking—pure poetry in destruction, even if it did turn out to be a dairy farm."

It made OK want to vomit, but Damocles and Stoat had become casual with each other in a way that provoked murderous jealousy among the other attendants jockeying for his favor. After several cycles of servitude, and some words from Stoat, the Deathlord's *bonhomie* extended to OK, whom Damocles came to address by name. "Otis! Change!"

All right, so he addressed him by someone else's name.

One evening, OK found himself once again standing in the shadows as Stoat mixed and served Damocles the formula that helped the Deathlord relax before entering his rejuvenation chamber. "You look magnificent tonight, my Deathlord," Stoat cooed in a disturbingly sultry way.

"My body is the Imperium!" Damocles insisted, spreading open his robes to show the fish-belly white, flabby, scarred expanse of his torso and legs. "These scars are a map to the conquests of the Scorpion Horde. These jagged lines are where my legs were bitten off by cyber-moles at Zeta Zeta. These on my chest were earned in the Campaign of 10,000 Blades on Karelia when a Karelian colonel cut off my areolas. My weak and simpering adjutant commander opted for a new body after the Karelians tore out his spine. His cloned body was a total disaster, always leaking gas. Any cloned body is a deceit. A tremendous deceit! I despise deceit above all else. Though I too was scarred, I was determined to preserve my original form, my real form. Until the time comes when a superior form becomes available."

And then, the Deathlord's thoughts turned toward matters of spirituality. "Tell me," he began, eyes glittering with unsettling piety. "What is your favorite verse in *The Way of the Scorpion?*"

Stoat recited, *"For the Black Scorpion of the Void, in his boundless malice for the cosmos, bestowed upon mankind the gifts of blade and fury, that they might anoint his altar with the spilled blood of their kin, earning his dread benediction."*

"That's the verse everyone knows. You may have made a cursory study of *The Way of the Scorpion*, but of course you are not aware that there are 2,000 pages missing! Excised by the Overlords, because they provide a prophecy of their destruction. You would not know of such things, but I know."

OK suppressed a sigh, one of Damocles's religious diatribes was coming on. He once again regretted flushing the *drutt*. He'd have jammed it down the Deathlord's throat just to shut him up!

The Deathlord recited. *"And in the waning twilight of the age of man, a new dominion shall rise from the void. The age of humanity shall pass like dust on the cosmic winds, and in its place shall rise the Age of the Scorpion. The one who was born of flesh shall be reborn as the rising Scorpion, mighty and terrible. The stars shall bow, and the cosmos itself shall yield to his power. He shall be the lord among lords, the Supreme Scorpion, and his dominion shall know no end.*

"Do you see! Do you see!" Damocles demanded. Before Stoat could answer the Deathlord called out, "It is time! Fetch me the Hedjedjet!"

A naked servant with skin painted a glossy obsidian carried a smooth pottery cask to the Deathlord's dais. Damocles removed the cover and withdrew a huge black scorpion larger than the hands of a large man. He placed the scorpion on his forearm and waited. The creature crawled around a bit as the Deathlord twitched anxiously and OK stared in fascinated horror. Finally, the huge scorpion plunged its stinger into Damocles's Brachioradialis muscle. The Deathlord groaned in ecstasy, his eyes rolled back into his head and he slumped into unconsciousness.

After a long silent moment, he roused. "Oh, but that was exquisite," he slurred, and spit out a slurry of foam and blood. He removed the arachnid from his arm. "Thank you, my lovely," he whispered, then bit its head off.

The Red Scorpion Guards were unperturbed by what had transpired.

As the Deathlord returned to consciousness, Stoat flattered him with plans for a holofilm of the Deathlord's life. "'*Deathlord*' would make a great title, don't you think?"

"*Deathlord: Part I*," replied Damocles. "These last three hundred years have only been the first act of my life. There is so much more to come." He shouted. "Otis! Stop lurking in the shadows like a frightened puppy. Come and listen, but be warned! I am going to kill both of you if anything said in these chambers finds its way outside, so stop cowering and tend to me!"

OK offered the Deathlord his fresh pair, while his co-valet collected the soiled pair. "The Supreme Overlords of Scorpius have no vision. Mere spectators enjoying the bloodshed. They lack vision. Their new technological marvel is nothing compared to the power of the Great Scorpion of the Night! In his dark and holy name, I would use *Annihilator* to burn the galaxy to ash. First, Sagittarius Prime. Then, the Orion Cluster. And then, I would eradicate Earth, and the entire solar system from the cosmos."

"Good Lord, why?" OK burst out before he could control it.

Fortunately, Damocles heard this as "Good, Lord. Why?" and set out to explain it. "Otis, dear, sweet naïve Otis. So small of mind. True, Earth is a trivial planet in the scheme of things, and its people are the genetic dregs of those too weak and cowardly to go into space. But do you know the ancient Earth word 'palimpsest?' Of course you don't. On ancient earth, they wrote on sheets of dried animal skins. Then, they would scrape off the writing and reuse the medium again to write a new story. That was the palimpsest. Earth will be scraped from the universe and become the palimpsest on which I will scrawl a new history with blood and fire.

"But first, I will be reborn! The Great Scorpion of the Night is not a god that was, nor a god that is, it is a god that will be. That god will be me! When the requisite technologies are perfected, I shall shed this primate homunculus and be reborn as a giant space scorpion! My claws, vast as moons, will tear worlds apart. And from my tail, a weapon of unimaginable power—gamma ray bursts that can annihilate planets in the blink of an eye! I will become a living power force that bends the universe to my will! The cosmos will tremble under the reign of the Supreme Scorpion, and all life shall bend to my will or be crushed beneath it! This is my destiny! I will not be denied!"

He sighed and took a sip of his beverage. "And that, dear servants, will be the story of '*Deathlord: Part II*.'"

OK shuddered to think what *Deathlord: Part III* would look like.

19.0 APOCALYPSE HOW

At the end of one long shift, which came on the tail of a night with no sleep, The Lady Ur informed OK that he had extra work. "At midnight, His Eminence Deathlord Damocles will be receiving a person of high importance from Scorpius Prime. Before his honored guest arrives, you will sterilize the reception chamber until it is clean enough to perform surgery; surgery such as the slow removal of your internal organs through your nose should you fail to meet my standards."

OK and a crew in environmental suits cleaned the reception chamber—a rather cool-looking octagonal space with lighted walls, floors, and ceiling. Scrubby did the floors—a squat orange blur of spinning brushes and blades. On the morning of the event, they laid out tables of pastries, fruits, and drinks just as the first of many executive death shuttles docked with the *Putin* and fleet commanders began filing into chamber. OK recognized Captain Slaughter who crossed the chamber to greet him personally.

"We have missed you on the *Subutai*. We just had another mutant E. coli breakout. The ship's waste processors can't keep up. It's Diarrhea City over there. I wish we could persuade you to give up this lux appointment and come back and clean my kitchens." He had no idea how much OK wanted to take him up on that. "From what I've heard, you saved an entire fleet from destruction."

"I didn't mean to," OK thought, but instead he answered. "Ia, Captain."

"The Overlords have dispatched a Dominator from the Supreme Horde Command for this meeting. Something very big must be swinging for this to happen. I am eager to get my hands around it, whatever it is."

Leaving OK to deal with that unwelcome imagery, Slaughter went to greet his fellow Death Captains. The commanders of the *Erwin Rommel, Ivan the Terrible,* and *Attila the Hun* had already arrived. The commanders of the *Elizabeth Bathory* and the *Ranavalona* arrived soon after, and other commanders trickled in with their plus ones. At the sound of a gong, they all took one of the high-backed leather chairs around the central conference pit. Elite Death Guards in formal red watched over them.

Another gong sounded and the captains rose. The overlord theme—an ominous arrangement of tympani and bass notes in 4/4 time—commenced. Deathlord Damocles appeared in his black steel battle armor and proceeded to his skull throne. The Lady Ur, dressed in a gray power suit, accompanied a tall, pale man dressed in a black robe and cowl. Invariably, the elite of every authoritarian society embraced cosplay.

Ur addressed the room. "We present Supreme Death General Anathema of the Supreme Horde Command."

Anathema was an ashen-skinned man with sunken cheeks and dead, android-like eyes. He could have passed for a DNZ executroid if he displayed more humanity. He spoke as though the need to be present here was an inconvenience to him and the high commanders of the fleet's task forces might as well have been kitchen help. OK could not see Stoat from where he was standing, but knew his friend was sizing up General Anathema and had probably already figured out what drinks to try out on him.

Anathema spoke. "Officers of the Red Scorpion Fleet, the Supreme Overlords acknowledge your success supporting the Imperium leading to complete domination of the constellation, the conquest of Carpathia, the obliteration of the Rebel Pact base at the Bugguram ice planet; pursuing the rebel scum deep into the Aeonic Forbidden Zone; and your pinnacle achievement, capturing the rebel arsenal at Roxxon."

The Lady Ur signaled to the assembled officers that they were permitted to applaud at this, and they did, starting and stopping in perfect unison. What Anathema said next made OK's heart sink. "And to add to your impressive list of successes, the Imperium's ultimate weapon has been made fully armed and operational. It is now the ultimate power in the galaxy."

"Damn right it is!" came a loud voice from a certain scientist in the back of the room who was mad.

Anathema continued. "The weapon-ship will be transferred immediately to the Black Fleet by order of the Supreme Command."

"What!" yelled the voice from the back.

The general put his notes away and spoke from the place in his chest where a heart might have been. His had long since been replaced by a cold metal "Cardio-Orb."

"The Imperium is through playing nice with other galactic powers. The time has come to show the galaxy our unlimited power. We will show the Sagittarians, the Ophiuchi, and even the Taureans and the Orions our might. The stars themselves will shiver at our passing." He didn't bring the same theatricality to evil speech delivery that Deathlord Damocles did. He was trying to project authority and vision, but he came across like someone angry about paying too much for the muffler on their hovercar. Projecting menace seemed to require more than malevolent words and bass reverb.

"A glorious new age is about to dawn. It is time for the Imperium of Greater Scorpio to reach out beyond this constellation and seize the galaxy. And you will be the hand of our destiny." That, the Lady Ur indicated, was also an applause line.

"The Red Fleet shall begin preparations to take the Sagittarian border stronghold at Kaus Minor. Simultaneously, the Magenta Fleet will seize the Sagittarian border colony on Terma. At the same time, the Obsidian Fleet will annihilate the defensive fortifications along the Ophiuchus frontier."

A kind of shockwave crossed the room. OK had never heard of Kaus Minor, but apparently the prospect of invading it was terrifying to the commanders of the fleet. If they could have done so without being shot, one of them might have stood up and declared, "You're mad! Mad, I tell you!" But instead, they just absorbed the shock.

"The Sagittarians will learn that their ideals of freedom, equality, and unity are nothing before the unrivalled power of the Scorpion Imperium. Such is the confidence of the Supreme Overlords in the Red Scorpion Fleet that we are ordering the transfer of one half of your ships to the Black Fleet. The other fleets are being ordered to do the same. With our new weapon, the embiggened Black Fleet will be empowered to avenge a thousand years of injustice, exploitation, and disrespect to Scorpius with a single deathblow."

The fleet commanders struggled to process the sheer lunacy of simultaneous assaults on not one, but two Sagittarian strongholds, AND a rear action against Ophiuchus? With fleets at half strength? It was madness! OK realized that the Imperium had just declared war on the whole galaxy.

"The Supreme Command expects a battle plan by the end of the current cycle. Hail to the Imperial Victory." With that, Anathema spun around and exited with The Lady Ur and Deathlord Damocles trailing him.

When they reported to the Deathlord's quarters for his midnight toddy, they discovered his suite not merely trashed but dumpstered and set on fire. The black velvet wall coverings hung in tattered ribbons, scorched and curling like flayed skin. The couches and chairs were smashed and smoldering. Holes were punched in the bulkhead through to the next compartment. The air reeked of charred upholstery and acrid smoke, thick enough to choke.

Damocles stomped about his quarters in an incandescent rage, clad only in his exo-skeletal combat underwear, its servo-joints hissing with each furious step. "Taking my precious stellar *Annihilator*!" he roared, firing his flame thrower at the wall, a torrent of hot plasma licking the ravaged wall with a deafening roar. Charred velvet ignited anew, casting ghoulish shadows.

"Appropriating half my fleet!" He fired a flamethrower against the opposite bulkhead. OK felt his eyebrows singe as the flames shot past him.

"Stealing my plan for galactic domination and giving it to Lord Nyx." He fired both flamethrowers simultaneously at the ceiling. Embers rained like dying stars, hissing on the scorched deck, as Damocles' wrath threatened to reduce his sanctum—and all within it—to cinders.

As the Lady Ur directed two of his other valets to put out the fires, Damocles collapsed on his throne of skulls, clenched his teeth, and seethed. "This was all Midnight Morrigan's doing. She has conspired against me since the Battle of Carpathia. She set this up with Nyx to humiliate me!"

Deathlord Nyx commanded the Black Scorpion Fleet. Damocles hated him more than any of the other Deathlords, even more than Deathlord Osiris who no one liked because he never shut up about his Ph. D in Malevolence Studies; as if that made him a better genocidal psychopath than the Deathlords who only had degrees in STEM fields. (Sadism, Terror, Extermination, and Menace) or MBAs (Masters of Brutal Authority).

The Lady Ur agreed about Morrigan. "She is a devious and conniving woman. Do you wish to have her killed?"

"Death is too good for her!" Damocles growled. "She must be humiliated first. Have her exiled to the edge of explored space. Let her suffer in obscurity."

"It shall be arranged, my Deathlord."

"And then have her killed." Damocles bellowed at Stoat. "Bring me my sustenance! The butterscotch one."

"Ia, my Deathlord, Ia," Stoat quickly prepared and handed over the tube. Sucking it down seemed to dull the Deathlord's rage a bit.

"They are setting us up to fail," Damocles hissed. "You heard that pestilential errand boy they sent out to us. He recounted our victories for a reason. The Supreme Command believes I have become a threat to them. They will draw us into defeat at Kaus Minor while Deathlord Nyx and the Black Fleet—using my plan and my ships—destroy Earth and claim all the glory."

There was a note of sadness in his voice such that OK almost found ... empathetic. In the shadow of this moment, he understood Damocles's rage at betrayal by the Imperium he had loyally served.

The Lady Ur spoke calmly, with dignity and forced confidence. "We have shocked the Supreme Horde Command before with our ability to win, whatever the odds. We will do so again."

Either her words were soothing him, or the drugs in the sustenance chemical were taking effect. "Death Captain Slaughter will lead the other captains in devising a plan for the attack," she concluded.

At the mention of Slaughter, Damocles twitched, a flicker of unease rippling across his scar tissue. "Slaughter is a formidable tactician. The Supreme Command has taken notice." A sudden, fevered impulse seized him. He pointed a thick and wrinkled finger at OK and Stoat. "Put them into the strategy meeting. You, my loyal attendants, will listen to every word and every tone as my commanders formulate their plan of attack. If any speak against me, especially Death Captain Slaughter, you will bring it back to me."

"The conference chamber will already be under surveillance, My Lord," the Lady Ur pointed out.

"Surveillance sees only what is shown. Servants are invisible, and people grow careless around them. Their treachery drips like blood from a wound. If there is any disloyalty in my fleet, you will show it to me, and I will have it disintegrated."

Hubba Hubba Froot-a Froot-a, OK thought urgently.

Arriving early to set up the conference chamber's drinks bar, OK found the hologram projection tactical projection was left on. As he surveyed the Kaus Minor system in all its holographic glory, he couldn't help but feel a sinking sensation in the pit of his stomach.

Seventy-six high-orbital battle platforms blinked ominously on the display, each bristling with top-of-the-line Sagittarian weaponry. And that was just the beginning. Fighter and missile bases dotted the surface of the planet's largest moon like sprinkles on a particularly lethal cupcake. Deflector shields and anti-ship rockets surrounded the cities on the surface. Kaus Minor was more fortified than a space fortress on lockdown. If the Horde was a swarm of space hornets, then Kaus Minor was the mother of all bug zappers.

Still, he could see a possibility, provided the battle stations used a distributed, multi-mode command and control system… which was likely… it might just be possible to…

"Who the *furk* left that damn thing on?" growled Death Captain Slaughter, entering the conference room with Morrigan at his side.

"Ia, it was like this when I got here, Ia," OK told them.

Slaughter muttered something about the setup crew. "I know it doesn't look good for us, but we are bringing in the smartest tacticians in the fleet. There's a way to beat those defenses, and we're going to find it."

"I see you have survived your initiation into Deathlord Damocles's entourage," Morrigan observed. "I don't suppose your clever technical mind has spotted any weaknesses in the Sagittarian defenses."

OK shook his head. "No, I definitely don't see any weaknesses in their defenses that could be exploited in combat. Definitely Not. None at all."

Stoat snapped the claw salute. "Hail to the Imperial Victory. Please enjoy the mini-muffins. I had them specially made. By the way, what do you think of Deathlord Damocles?"

Morrigan ignored him. "Deathfingers, hand me your bond coins," They did as they were instructed. "Code 98," and handed them back.

"What's a code 98?" OK asked.

"Security protocol, don't give it a second thought."

"We already had a security check."

"That sounds like the second thought I ordered you not to have."

OK wondered if he should warn her that Damocles was planning to terminate her. Her mouth formed a half-smirk. "Don't worry about it. Return to your duties, make sure my water bottle doesn't get any water in it."

As the other commanders and tactical officers shuffled into the room, they wasted no time raiding the pastry table like a pack of ravenous space wolves on their cheat day, then filling their mugs with Black Scorpion coffee. Muffins and chemicals in hand, they jockeyed for positions around the table, vying for the most advantageous spots.

Death Captain Slaughter opened the proceedings with a rundown of the planet's defenses which went on for what OK thought was a discouragingly long time. When he finished, Second Officer Grimfoyle provided a tactical analysis of the capabilities of the Sagittarian Interstellar Fleet. Then, there was a discussion of Sagittarian military doctrine. OK tended to the snack table and refilled water glasses as the fleet's best tactical minds shook their heads, pinched their brows, and sighed in frustration. They took no more notice of him than they did the hum of the ship's power systems.

After lunch, they reviewed their tactical assets. With the Overlords' order to commit half of their ships to the Black Fleet, the Red Fleet would only be able to field ten battle groups at Kaus Minor. This information would be so valuable to the Rebel Pact—if only there were some way to get it to them!

At the end of the day, Captain Slaughter adjourned the meeting with a pep talk. Any other Horde Captain would have said, "Whoever comes up with the best plan gets to live." But Slaughter had a different style. "Listen up, the Red Fleet has never faced tougher odds. But we are going to stun the entire Imperium with our victory at Kaus Minor!"

He paced the room, hands clasped behind his back, eyes gleaming with a mix of determination and hard-won military wisdom. "This room contains the most brilliant tactical minds in all the Horde. We have done glorious things together. Remember Ardala Rax? Remember Chevy Vega? Our victory at Kaus Minor will surpass all of them. When you come back tomorrow morning, bring me the plan that's going to take Kaus Minor. I expect genius. I expect just crazy enough to work. Hail to the Imperial Victory!"

"Hail to the Imperial Victory!" It was almost enough to make even OK think they had a chance.

The next day the real planning began. OK had always assumed the Scorpion Fleet simply showed up, took what they wanted, and bombed the rest, leaving despair and ruin in their wake. It turned out that a huge amount of planning went into making it look that easy.

Every detail of the assault was calculated. A full day was spent analyzing the orbits of Kaus Minor's moons and how their gravitational pull would affect the fleet's operations. They used small plastic models of Imperial warships to simulate attack vectors, pushing them around the table making 'woosh' noises. They even considered experimental Horde weapons—like giant space laser frisbees and magneto-gravitational beams capable of upheaving entire cities from the planet's surface were discussed with a mixture of awe and sheer audacity—with a hint of desperation thrown in.

Eventually, the fleet tacticians arrived at the best plan they could with the ships they had. They called it Operation Deathblow. The general thrust of it was to unite the fleet in a single attack column and execute a massive, focused blitzkrieg on the planet and its defenses. Every ship, every missile, every transorbital warhead, every anti-protonic death beam would be focused in a single point assault on the two large fortresses in geosynchronous orbit over the planet's poles. Taking them out, it was thought, would cripple the planet's defenses. They would take heavy losses, and Kaus Minor would come out the other side as a burnt-out, cratered cinder, but the Imperium would win. Slaughter volunteered to present the plan to Deathlord Damocles.

OK and the catering staff were left (under Stoat's supervision) to clean up the mess after the session was over was over. The fleet commanders were an astonishingly filthy bunch who left their mark on the meeting room in ways both bizarre and repulsive.

The underside of the table where the captain of the *Atilla the Hun* sat was encrusted with boogies. There were ten tiny white boomerangs under the seat where the captain of the *Herod* had sat. He had somehow found the time to clip his toenails while plotting the mass destruction of an entire planet; a macabre testament to multitasking amidst the planning of planetary annihilation. The captain of the *Josef Stalin* left a mysterious red stain that seemed to pulsate with malevolent energy. The cleaning staff, wise in their discretion, opted to summon a biohazardous materials team to dispose of the tainted chair with all due haste.

They also found a sketch pad where one of the commanders had been doodling. The same crude sketch over and over again, a giantess with gigantic breasts and tentacle arms was feeding men into a gaping, jagged toothed maw between her legs. Some psychiatrists would have a field day with that one. OK had a weird feeling it had been left behind deliberately for them to find.

OK pondered the attack plan as he sterilized the tables and Scrubby attacked the chamber floor. He was not a strategist, but he didn't see how putting all the ships into one column could result in anything else but giving the enemy (*"No! Not the enemy,"* his inner voice insisted) an opportunity to concentrate their fire and pick them off like targets in a lazy holographic video game.

Lurking in the background while the officers talked had finally worked. He not only knew every detail of their strategy, but he also understood, based on what he had overheard, that the invasion of Kaus Minor would only be a distraction. While they drew the Sagittarian fleet to defend Kaus Minor, the Black Fleet would slither across the border and unleash the superweapon in a blaze of destruction from Sagittarius Prime to Old Earth, killing billions.

OK knew the Horde's entire plan. But he had no way to get any of this information to the Rebel Pact as long as he was trapped on the *Putin*. By the time he worked out a way to get away, it would probably be too late.

He was putting away the sonic scrubbers and corrosive stain remover when the Lady Ur appeared. She had a knack for showing up just when he was finishing and finding something else for him to do. He shot her the Imperial salute, "Ia! Hail to the Imperial Victory! Ia!"

"Ia, whatever," she licked her lips and pulled out her datapad. "Did you hear any of the captains, in particular Death Captain Slaughter, express any criticism or disloyalty against your Deathlord?"

"Ia, I heard no such thing, Ia," OK answered.

Stoat never passed an opportunity to ingratiate himself. "Not with their words, but there was something in Slaughter's tone of voice that seemed … well, if not treasonous… perhaps a bit, defiant. And Death Colonel Morrigan practically rolled her eyes every time the Deathlord's name was mentioned."

The Lady Ur offered no comment. "For reasons I cannot begin to imagine, his Eminence is pleased with your performance and authorized leave on the pleasure planet Cellador as a 'well-deserved reward for your loyal service.'"

Their jaws dropped in unison. Shore leave? On the legendary pleasure planet Cellador? The shock hit them like a random spike of gamma radiation, leaving them stunned, speechless, and utterly gobsmacked. Had the universe finally thrown OK a bone?

The very notion of indulging in leisure on the fabled shores of Cellador seemed too fantastical to fathom. Yet there it was, tantalizingly real and dangling before him like an offer of forbidden fruit.

Cellador! Known for endless beaches of luminescent sands that shimmered under its iridescent rings, where visitors could bask in the tanning power of an F-class sun while sipping on cocktails and tripping on exotic alien narcotics.

Cellador! Where Zero-G nightclubs in the Permanent Ecliptic zone pulsated with thumping beats and holographic lightshows and revelers could dance the endless night away.

Cellador! Location of the galaxy's most advanced Sensual Pleasure Chambers where visitors were invited to explore their deepest desires without judgment or consequences.

Cellador! Featuring an entire continent of luxurious spa retreats offering rejuvenating treatments and bio-regenerative therapies.

Cellador! (OK whispered to himself) The last world in the constellation not controlled by the Imperium, where rebel recruiting operations were active.

The Lady Ur scowled at them. "Why are you idiots still here gawking? Go off and pack your underwear and flip-flops, or whatever it is you people take on holiday. Go!"

20.0 MISPLACED IN THE COSMOS

Cellador was a terraformed world located within Imperial space, owned by DNZ Corp. It remained independent from the Imperium by dint of an arrangement where it remained officially neutral in galactic politics but always supported the Imperium in any interstellar dispute.

When it was discovered almost 500 years earlier, Cellador was nothing but swamp, jungle, and some pre-intelligent, amphibian life forms that emitted a foul and unpleasant odor. DNZ terraforming engineers bombarded it from orbit to clear the land, hunted the stinking amphibians to extinction, smashed asteroids to sand to create endless silky white beaches, and used tectonic continental reconstruction to maximize beachfront.

There had been some minor glitches with the bioengineered lifeforms DNZ added to the planet. The Nurk-Nurks and Wubble-Wobbles were designed to provide soft cuddly animal companions for children. But they mated with each other resulting in a subspecies with a voracious appetite for human flesh. Many unfortunate casualties resulted before they could be eradicated. DNZ Corp created a successful series of holo-movies based on actual events (though the sequels dropped off considerably in quality) and made huge profits selling specimens to the Horde's bio-weapons division.

By the time Cellador was open for tourists, the family unit was obsolete in Scorpius, thanks to universal contraception implants and embryo farming. DNZ retooled the planet, eliminated most of the family-friendly attractions, and "upgraded the experience for our adult guests."

Per the holo-brochure: "On Cellador's Neon Coast, an extraordinary convergence of orbital dynamics has created a realm perpetually cloaked in the enchanting embrace of eternal night. Nestled under the shadow of Cellador's inner moon, our resort beckons with an aura of mystery and allure. Here, amidst the endless twilight, the Neon Coast offers indulgences to tantalize all of the senses and fever the imagination. Step into our world, where our team of fully trained and medically certified Pleasure Givers stand ready to fulfill your every desire. From the heights of ecstasy to the depths of depravity, their expertise knows no bounds... and no limits."

"I can't believe you guys get to go to Cellador," Qi'Anna whined when OK told her, via comm unit. "You know I've always wanted to go there."

"We didn't get to choose the destination," OK said, trying to make it sound like an apology.

Qi'Anna continued to pout. "I've been in the horde seven years and the only time I got to go to a planet was Sauria V, the reptile planet. And I don't even like snakes."

Rue asked him, "Don't they let you guys take a plus one?"

"Um, no," OK lied. In truth, he was allowed to bring a guest, he just hadn't picked Qi'Anna or Rue. OK had asked Damocles for permission to bring Anastasaja's disembodied brain with him.

"You want to do what?" the Deathlord had thundered.

"I want to bring the brain of one of the rebel scientists to Cellador as my plus one. We're… in love."

The Deathlord's volcanic laugh was somehow more terrifying than his world-ending ultimatums. "Otis is in love with a brain in a jar!" he shouted to his red guards. "Keep him away from the Imperial Aquarium."

Probably because at the time he was high on Scorpion venom, the Deathlord granted his request. "Fine, take the rebel you tried to help escape. I know all about that, and it matters nothing to me. Take her, Otis, we've exhausted her usefulness here. Make love to her, you filthy depraved man. Shove your thing into the pink gelatinous folds of her cerebral cortex." It was unnecessary to demonstrate the concept by thrusting his hips the way he did, but who was going to tell him not to?

Later on, Stoat broke the icy silence between them to let him know that he thought the request was creepy and weird. OK had stopped caring what Stoat thought. He didn't tell him as much, but let his silence speak for him.

Getting ready to pack, OK realized all he owned no casual clothes. He was not going to stroll around Cellador in an Imperial uniform. He got on the DNZ Shopping Nexus. With a few swift clicks, he filled his cart with a selection of vibrant shirts and knee-length shorts. Then he added a jaunty space trucker hat with the slogan "I got your cargo right here in my ventral hold" to meet the threshold for free delivery. It cut into his savings, but he had more important plans than buying a less whorish personality for his avatar.

As a registered visitor to Cellador, he would have access to the planetary directory. The first thing he intended to do when he reached the system was do a search and find out if Anya had made it. Maybe he would even look her up. He wondered how she would respond when she found out he had joined the Horde. She would probably punch him in the nose, but once he explained he was just trying to get to her…. Well, he left those possibilities open.

After he checked on Anya, he was going to defect. Exactly how he would find a rebel cell, he did not know. It was best not to think about it. Not thinking about a plan would make it easier to suppress his intentions around telepaths. That was also the reason he was bringing Anastasaja. He would turn her over to the rebels and she would help them defeat the superweapon.

"Scrubby go?" asked Scrubby.

Sure, OK thought. Why not steal an Imperial robot while he was at it—like grabbing office supplies before quitting a job you hated. He had to arrange for Scrubby to travel as cargo; the starline didn't believe he was an emotional support droid. He arranged for Anya to be delivered to his cabin. Deathlord Damocles had someone affix a sun hat and panties to her brain tank; a warlord's idea of humor, OK supposed.

An imperial transport took them to the Atallantia spaceport to await the flight. Damocles had only sprung for Proletariat Class tickets, but Stoat played the "we're with Deathlord Damocles" card to wheedle both of them an upgrade to Authority Class. OK almost refused the upgrade until he found out it gave him the privilege of waiting in Delta Quadrant Starlines "Voyagers" VIP Club lounge for frequent fliers, and he really needed a drink.

He went to the lounge and ordered a Victory Gin with a twist of lemon.

"Oh, hai, OK," said a thick, familiar voice. He turned around to see a straggly haired man with a pale, buxom, smoky eyed woman under his arm.

"Boskirk?"

"So, how's your sex life, huh?" Boskirk settled onto the stool next to him.

"Are you also going to Cellador?" OK asked.

Boskirk laughed. "I am out of Imperial Service now. I am free man. I can go wherever I want, huh?" He thrust his arms upward, elbows bent, fists balled, his stance brimming with theatrical bravado.

"Your ten years' service is over?"

Boskirk favored him with his uneasy laugh. "Ya, getting out just in time. I have disability discharge. I have Pre-Traumatic Stress Disorder?"

"Pre-traumatic stress disorder?"

"Yah is legitimate psychological condition. I am crippled in anticipation of future trauma. I'm disabled veteran! No one question me."

OK offered a toast to Boskirk's freedom. "So, what's next?"

"I knock around the constellation for a little bit. I have money so no worries there, huh?" They chatted a bit and enjoyed a few more drinks until OK's flight was called.

"Delta Quadrant Starlines Imperial Deathliner 6660-TK now boarding for transit to Cellador. Passengers will have travel permits, boarding passes, transit certificates, medical records, affirmations of Imperial loyalty, tracking implants, and skin samples ready for presentation at the boarding station."

"Lousy rebellion. I remember when all you needed to board a space liner was a boarding pass and a skin sample," grumbled an elderly gentleman in the Proletariat Class boarding line as OK passed him by. He recognized some of the other passengers from the invasion conference waiting in the boarding area. He surmised that he and Stoat were not the only ones Damocles had rewarded with shore leave.

Authority class passengers boarded the Starliner through its upper deck. OK did not see Stoat as he waited to board the starliner. Maybe he had bailed out? No, more likely he had wheedled himself an early boarding.

A spaceflight attendant in a blue and light blue uniform and a striped scarf led OK to his compartment while reciting the standard pre-flight safety spiel. "Please note the location of the escape pods nearest to your cabin. Also note that these are only useful in the vicinity of a habitable planet. Chances of being rescued in deep space are practically nonexistent. In the event you become assimilated into a collective hivemind, remember to accept the purity of purpose as a component of the greater whole." Regular travelers had heard it before and pretty much tuned out the safety announcement.

After two years of Horde military accommodations, his cabin seemed like the epitome of luxury. A well-padded chair that extended into a bed long enough to stretch out on. A small fold-out table. A private hygiene booth. A compact viewport that offered a sliver of star-spotted void, a rare privilege after years of windowless confinement.

All crew, passengers, and auxiliary personnel prepare for starliner departure in 120 seconds.

"Here we go," OK thought. He strapped himself into the acceleration couch and watched the departure on a viewer. The starliner pulled away from the station, lined up for the acceleration catapult, and slingshot into the commercial interstellar transit conduit. OK watched with excitement as starlight, stretched into elongated streaks as the starliner breached light-speed.

To people inside a ship traveling at near the speed of light, time passes much more quickly than for everyone outside. However, the mechanics of Faster Than Light transport overcome the time dilation effect, making time pass within the ship at the same rate as outside. However, this effect is itself canceled by the "trapped inside a plane with nothing to do effect" which makes time inside the spacecraft seem to pass even more slowly.

OK spent most of this time napping or watching I2N starliner crash investigation documentaries. In most disasters, it was due to errors on the part of the flight crew; like pushing the wrong button and making the reactor explode instead of turning off the "coffee service" light. (Subsequent space-worthiness directives would require the "blow-up reactor" and "coffee service" buttons to be further apart and different colors.)

His Authority class berth entitled him to four daily meals and unlimited snack services. Most of the meals consisted of a small piece of lab meat printed with black lines as though they were grilled, a vegetable of indeterminate origin, and usually some potatoes floating in a yellow substance. Snacks were usually a portion of Plinthian cheese, fragments of fruit, and some form of chocolate or pastry. There was also an Authority class lounge on board, which OK avoided because he was sure Stoat would be there.

About halfway into the voyage, a bored OK decided to take advantage of the in-ship entertainment system. He strapped himself into his seat and put on the HARVEY headset. Then, he took the headset off, and double-checked the door to his cabin to make sure it was locked. Then, he checked the storage closet where he kept Anastasaja to make sure it was closed up tight. Then, he put the headset back on.

"Access virtual immersion programming." HARVEY presented the sensory immersive equivalent of the menu board from an ancient DVD player. OK found his virtual self-facing an array of entertainment options arranged across a multi-colored grid. He selected "Adult Interaction."

ALL RIGHT, I CAN HELP YOU WITH THAT. DO YOU WISH AN ENCOUNTER WITH ONE OR MULTIPLE VIRTUAL PARTNERS

He had to think. He was a little out of practice. "One to start."

DO YOU WISH A MALE OR FEMALE PARTNER? IF YOU WANT SOMETHING IN-BETWEEN, THAT IS AVAILABLE FOR AN EXTRA CHARGE

"Female, please."

FEMALE HUMAN, ALIEN, ROBOT, PORPOISE, OR OTHER LIFE FORM FOR PURPOSES OF THIS SIMULATION

"Wait...what?"

HARVEY repeated the question, and he chose human. The game presented him with a choice of customizable female forms. By fiddling with the controls, he was able to get something that looked a bit like Anastasaja, a little bit like Qi'Anna, a very little bit like Rue, and more than a little bit like Morrigan. He felt justified using her because she was, after all, an Imperial.

The game also allowed him to create a customized environment for the encounter. He spent the better part of an hour laying out an idyllic scene next to the azure waters of a shimmering lake under the gaze of a golden sun. Sweet summer breezes danced through the air, carrying whispered promises. In the distance, a chorus of birdsong provided the perfect backdrop to their rendezvous. A place where a man might find comfort and solace in the arms of a beautiful woman.

Then he cleared that and reset the whole thing to a sleazy basement sex club he had seen once in an imperial documentary about the sleaze planet Toobin IV. When everything was set. His unreal woman in silk panties was lying on top of a filthy mattress with a come-hither look in her eyes.

"Come here, lover," she cooed in a synthesized voice that made OK feel like he was about to have cybersex with a hovercar's navigation system.

Then, she disappeared and was replaced with a pair of young, attractive people drinking coffee in a trendy coffee bar. A countdown informed hm, *"Your sex fantasy will continue after the ad."* He was forced to endure a fifteen-second pitch for "Black Scorpion Coffee—the Fuel of the Imperium."

The simulation gave him an option to continue without advertisement for a 15 IMU fee, to which he resignedly assented.

Rejoining the simulation, OK sat at the edge of the bed. She reached out toward him and began stroking his chest. It felt more like the memory of physical contact than actual conduct, but it would have to do.

"What do you want to do, lover?" she asked in the same "calculating the fastest route" voice.

"I don't want to rush," OK told her. "It's ... it's been a really long time since I've been with anyone. I've also been under incredible stress lately. So... if it's all right... could we talk a little bit first."

"It is all right to talk a little bit first," she answered.

"For everything I've done in the Horde, can I ever be forgiven?"

"Hmm, I don't know how to answer that."

"I've tried to fight back, I really did. But every time, it didn't work out. And sometimes I ended up helping the Imperium. I didn't mean to, it's just ..." He looked right into the uncanny valley of her not-quite-realistic eyes. "Just tell me I'm not a bad guy."

"You are not a bad guy." *In 600 meters, your destination will be on the left.*

It was good to hear it from someone, even a virtual sex avatar. OK came to the unavoidable conclusion that the conversation wasn't going to get any better. He might as well get down to ramming. He crawled on top of her and prepared to experience the simulated equivalent of sex.

Just as he was reaching for her breasts, the simulation began to crack up. The sex avatar went "Come here lover... lover.... *Zzzt zzzt*.... lover...*zzzt*...." and froze. OK was cursing the need to restart the program—wondering if he would have to set up everything all over again—when he was snapped out of the simulation, and into a loud, inverted, confusing reality. All around him alarms were screaming, emergency lights were strobing, and he seemed to be hanging upside down from the ceiling... which was supposed to have happened much later in the program.

A calm voice from the intercom addressed him.

Ladies and gentlemen and biological nonconformities, the ship has encountered an unexpected situation. Please remain in your seats while your expert crew returns the ship to a safe condition --- *zzzt.*

The emergency voice cut out. Fighting what seemed like tons of counterforce, OK turned to the portal. It offered a view of a green planet spinning up toward him.

And then something slammed him upwards, as though some incredible force had struck the ship from below resulting in a sickening buck. This was the starliner striking, and then bouncing off, the green planet's atmosphere. It skipped across the edge of it as something flashed past like a shooting star.

Then, the ship plunged into the atmosphere and things got really bad. Friction turned its outer skin into a blazing fireball. The ship was spinning out of control. By the time it reached the lower atmosphere, big pieces of the hull were breaking off, the engines exploded, and it became highly doubtful the expert crew was going to return the ship to a safe condition.

Everything hurt. Even parts of his body he hadn't previously been aware of throbbed for attention with insistence. It was as if his body had been used as a hovercar crash test dummy. And he had been thrown clear of the hover car only to tumble down the side of a cliff and hit every sharp rock on the way down. And when he reached the bottom, someone stomped on his groin. Then the car landed on him. That's how much he hurt. He wondered whether he was lucky to be alive. He was alive, the unspeakable pain was proof of that, but he was unsure about the lucky part.

He opened his eyes and realized his eyelids hurt too. The dim emergency lighting showed how thoroughly destroyed his cabin was. Its contents were a wrecked and jumbled heap. Its bulkheads were punched in like the nose of someone on the losing end of a drunken argument.

He wrenched open the closet door and was relieved to see Anastasaja's tank was intact. "Anastasaja?" No reply. The leads to her voice box had disconnected in the crash. His fingers felt like they were broken, almost exactly what his mother said would happen if he indulged in sensory porn. Despite pain shooting through his knuckles, they managed to reattach the leads to her tank. "Anastasaja," he muttered, more to himself than to her, hoping against hope that she would respond. "Anastasaja?"

"What do you want, Imperial worm," she answered with her customary hostile cheer.

"Thank the godless void, you're OK."

"Oh, was there some chance I wouldn't be?" Her tank isolated her from the crash. He explained the situation to her. "Imperial starliners are garbage," she said. "What planet did we fall on?"

The ship had actually been built in Capricorn but that was not important. "I'm not really sure where we are."

Just then, a hologram activated and a cheery blond woman in a flight attendant uniform appeared amid the wreckage. "Hello, there. The ship's sensors have detected what we like to call a Completely Random Accidental Situation Hazard—or CRASH—event.

"If you are hearing this message, Delta Quadrant Starlines congratulates you for surviving. Well done. Also, we regret any inconvenience this event may have caused and remind you there will be no refunds. Voyager Elite status members will receive a credit of 10,000 light years. Finally, your safety is important to us. Please locate the nearest functioning lifepod, put yourself into stasis, and await rescue. Thank you, and good luck."

"I very much doubt that the stasis pods are designed for disembodied brains," Anastasaja said.

"We'll figure out something."

With a grunt of effort, he wielded a broken pipe like a makeshift crowbar, leveraging it against the stubborn hatch to his cabin until it relented with a metallic groan. As the door creaked open, he was greeted by a scene of chaos—the corridor beyond a broken and twisted labyrinth of debris and wreckage, like the aftermath of a cosmic bar brawl.

The screen that should have guided him to the lifepod was shattered, its shards scattered across the floor like digital tears. He picked up the brain tank and lugged it out.

The hatch on the cabin next to his slid open. Stoat appeared, looking clean and sharp. OK didn't know whether to feel relieved or disappointed that the traitor had survived.

"Friend-O, I'm so glad you made it."

"We're not friends," OK growled at him.

"You look awful, though. Did you not engage your CRASH protection?"

"My what?"

"CRASH protection, when the alarms sounded, the captain came on and told us to activate CRASH protection and strap into our landing couches."

OK reddened, "I was... um... doing something else when we crashed." He quickly appended, "We have to get to the life pods. They should be two sections forward of our compartment."

Unfortunately, the emergency bulkheads had sealed off the Authority Class deck from the rest of the ship. "If the bulkheads are sealed, it means the hull was breached. The other side could be open to vacuum, or a toxic atmosphere, or radiation." OK suggested they look for other life pods they could access through other sections of the ship.

Stoat made a face. "You mean like… in economy class?"

"Well… yes."

"Could we check if the first-class life pods are open?"

"First class is on the other side of those bulkheads. We can either try to get to the economy deck and survive or wait here and probably die." Even in the dim emergency lighting, OK could tell Stoat was mulling it over.

Before he could work out whether survival was worth mixing in with economy passengers, they heard three sharp knocks against the bulkhead.

Rescuers! OK thought. He found a fire extinguisher and pounded it against the inner hull. "We're here!" he shouted.

Three sharp knocks answered in return. "Oh, thank the godless void. Someone is here to rescue us."

"Do you think they'll be mixing the upper-class survivors with the economy class survivors?" Stoat wondered aloud.

Sparks danced around the edge of the forward bulkhead hatch. The stench of burning metal and charred circuitry filled what was left of the air. The responders finished the job with a robot battering ram that knocked the hatch in, its sides still glowing red. OK's first thought was amazement at how quickly a rescue party had located them. His second thought was "Why is a rescue team pointing guns at us?"

Targeting dots appeared on OK and Stoat's heads and chests. "Don't move! Hands where I can see them!" the lead responder shouted. He scanned them with a beam that projected green patterns on them. "We have located two low-level Imperials in section three. Kill or Capture."

"We're actually Kataranians!" Stoat called out.

"Silence, Imperial, or I'll punch you in the face with my butt… I mean my rifle's butt… I mean, the butt of my rifle. Shut up!"

"Say again, Team 36 Beta Romeo. What rank are the Imperials?"

"Deathfingers, according to their implants. One bartender and an underwear sanitizer."

"Deathfingers have no intelligence value," came the response. "Terminate them and continue searching for high-value survivors."

"Right!" The squad of rescuers aimed their rifles at OK and Stoat.

"Wait!" Stoat called out. "What if we aren't low level Scorps? The reason I ask is that before you start shooting, you should know that this man and I are the personal valets to Deathlord Damocles, Supreme Commander of the Red Scorpion fleet. We have valuable information about the Imperial plans to invade the Kaus Minor system!"

"And I'm the Rainbow Queen of Uranus. Weapons ready. Take aim!"

Stoat persisted. "No, wait, seriously. Check out our bond coins. We're very important high-level Imperial assets."

A trooper holding a scanning device spoke up. "I detect heart plugs."

"And I detect butt-plugs. Terminate this Imperial trash on my mark!"

OK shouted in a panic. "Please! Listen to me. This tank contains the mind of Anastasaja Honeychild, the rebel scientist."

"How stupid do I look?" barked the lead responder.

"I really can't tell. You're wearing a face mask."

Anastasaja intervened. "Hey, guys, it's me, codename Chi-Alpha 36 confirmation code pink bunny bunny pink pink."

"Confirmation code confirmed," said the voice on the radio.

OK added desperately, "I was taking her to Cellador and help her defect to the rebellion."

"Is this true?" the lead rebel demanded.

Anastasaja answered, "Um, yeah… I guess. It wouldn't be the first time he tried to rescue me and failed."

"It could be a trick." The rifle pointed at OK wavered slightly, its targeting dot passing from his forehead to his nose to his cheek to his left eye. That would hurt a lot, OK thought.

"Orders?" demanded the lead rebel.

There was a long wait while the command base worked out what to do. "Bring them back to the base for further interrogation. Protocol Two."

OK wondered what Protocol Two was as his last thought before a rifle butt to the back of his skull put him unconscious.

OK woke up to the slap of icy water splashed at his face. He tried to move his arms, but they were shackled to the arms of something like the chair of a particularly sadistic dentist. The back of his head pounded and ached; his skull felt like there was a crack in it.

There was a metal ceiling above his head and a bright light that filled his entire scope of vision. The air was chilly and damp. There was an intense smell of mold that reminded him of his first week of kitchen duty on the *Subutai*.

"Where am I? Am I on a ship? Where's Anastasaja?"

He felt a rod jammed into his side. Every muscle seized as a powerful electrical shock surged through him. His already bruised and damaged muscles exploded in new superlatives of pain.

"That will be the answer to all your questions, Imperial *Gurkgulper*. I will ask the questions, and if I don't like your answers, I will hurt you. A lot. Do you understand these rules?"

"Yes, yes, completely. Arrrrrgh!" the rod was jammed in his side again.

"Sometimes, I get to do that just because I want to. Consider it payback the Imperium for all the friends who you murdered."

OK suppressed the urge to correct "whom you murdered," and instead tried to explain. "I sympathize with you. I hate the Scorpion Horde and the Imperium as much as you do. Maybe more."

This earned him another jab with the rod. "When our medicos examined you, they found cardiac breakdown devices in your chest. This confirms you served the war criminal Damocles as a personal servant."

"I just sanitized his underwear."

"Gross. Your bond coin indicates that before serving the Deathlord, you gave material comfort to Imperial war criminals."

It took a moment for OK to figure out what he meant. "I was just a bartender." He realized there was more than one other person in the room besides him and the angry man with the throbbing pain rod.

"Oh, were you? Serving up Deneban Daiquiris so war criminals could relax after a day of mass murder."

"I felt really bad about it, but..."

"As bad as this?" the pain rod jabbed into his side again.

And from within his sore, still-broken-from-the-impact body, from his smashed-in-the-back-of-the-skull headache to the fresh onslaught of pain his captor had induced, arose a combination of hope and conviction. Everything he had gone through, all the horrors he had helped the Imperium commit, could at last be redeemed.

"Please! I want to cooperate! I want to help the Rebellion! I know the Imperium's exact battle plans for the next assault."

He felt a smack with the pain stick. "Shut up, you Imperial *Gurkbag*!"

"You don't understand. I never wanted to join the Imperium. I had no choice. Well actually, I had a chance to join the rebellion when they invaded my planet, but never mind… long story… the point is… I know what they're going to do. They're going to invade Kaus Minor…"

He felt a hard slap connect to his face. "You are a lying Imperial piece of *gurk*. The Imperium would be fools to invade Kaus Minor."

"No, it's true… I swear it. But… listen… the attack on Kaus Minor is just a diversion. They want the Sagittarians to send their fleet to Kaus Minor while they destroy Sagittarius Prime with the planet destroyer."

The guard jabbed him with the pain rod again. "You lie!"

"No, really, I swear to you, that's their plan. They're going to blow up the Earth! And some important planets, too!"

"You would say anything at this point to preserve your worthless Imperial life," his captor sneered. The words were barely out of their mouth when a trio of beeping alarms erupted in unison. The sound seemed to emanate from three different synchronized timepieces.

Without another word, his captor walked away, leaving him in his cell with nothing but his mounting despair. He lay there, wallowing in misery, until the darkness of unconsciousness mercifully came over him.

Each day in the next period of OK's life proceeded in the same excruciating way. They began with a rude awakening from a rebel interrogator and a demand for information. When OK offered to share valuable strategic information, the rebel insisted OK was lying and stabbed him with the pain rod. This session would last perhaps two hours and always ended the same way. Alarm beeps, followed by the sound of his tormentors leaving.

It was like they were doing shift work.

Then, there passed a period of perhaps two days when they didn't come at all, just left him in the cell with no food or water, calling out, "I know the Imperial battle plans" until his throat was too raw to continue.

The interrogations and beatings resumed; a regular pattern of five days of punishment and interrogations, followed by two days of utter neglect. OK remained strapped to the chair, staring at the light on the ceiling. Guessing the passing of days based on how long he fell unconscious.

After this had gone on long enough that OK could not remember a time he was not strapped to a chair in a cold cell, a different rebel, a woman came into his cell, loosened his bands, and offered him some water.

"Thank you... I have... valuable information... for the Rebel Pact."

"Of course you do." She helped OK sit up and flex his arms and legs. The sensation of his previously immobile limbs moving was like having them set on fire. OK collapsed to the floor in a heap. She helped him up.

"Where am I? Am I on a rebel ship?"

"You are at Unity One, the headquarters of this Rebel Pact cell. We are 300 meters underneath an abandoned terraforming station on a planet that, well, failed to terraform."

The woman had limp periwinkle hair and a puffy complexion, like someone who ate poorly and seldom went outdoors. She offered him more water. "I regret the way you have been treated so far. It's no way to treat a prisoner even a Scorp."

OK was exhausted from saying it. "I have tried to tell you. I hate the Imperium. The brain in the tank should have told you."

"Scorps are practiced liars," she told him. "You would say anything to save your pathetic life. Drink the water. Eat some food."

She offered him a filthy bowl with algae gruel in it. OK choked it down recited yet again how he had only joined the Horde because it seemed like the best way to fight the Imperium; how he had tried to help rebels escape and assassinate Deathlord Damocles. He repeated for what seemed like the hundred-thousandth time, "The Horde is going to invade Sagittarius. You have to warn the Sagittarians and do something about the *Annihilator*."

"And how does a mere Deathfinger come by such secret information?" At least she didn't poke him with a pain stick.

"I was on the *Annihilator*," OK told her. "I cleaned up the lab where Dr Madd worked on the weapon." He hoped she would not press for details on that. "I catered the meeting where they planned the invasion."

She betrayed no sign that she believed him. "Are you done with the food."

"I guess."

"Then, come with me." She helped him to his feet and led him out of the cell. A pair of guards followed them.

"Where are we going?"

"For a walk. It will be good for you to get some exercise."

She led him down a low corridor lined with pipes to an industrial lift. Prodded by his guards' guns, OK boarded the lift and began to rise. On one of the station's levels, they passed a tank with some sort of slimy reptile floating in it. The rebel woman noticed him staring and explained it. "That's a specimen we found in the station's science lab. The terraforming effort wiped out that species. Think of them as an amphibian *homo habilis*. In two or three million years, they could have become an advanced lifeform like us. We think humanity has the galaxy to itself, but this is just our turn. There were civilizations before ours and more will arise after we've evolved into something else… or wiped ourselves out."

"About that…" OK began, thinking he had found an opening to go over the Horde's plans. But just then, the platform reached its top level. Rebel guards pushed him through another disused industrial corridor until they reached a long viewport covered by a heavily corroded storm shield.

"Let me show you what's outside." The woman pressed a button and a very old, warped, and rusted mechanism pulled the shield up. Outside was a murky hellscape illuminated by constant lightning flashing between swirling green clouds of noxious vapor. Howling winds drove squalls of acidic rain.

"The old terraforming efforts not only failed, but they caused constant hurricane conditions all over the planet. The turbulence in the ionosphere hides us from Imperial sensors. That 'rain' is carbolic acid, highly corrosive to human tissue, especially the lungs. And there's a fair amount of radiation, too.

"The storm encircles the entire planet but seems to be particularly horrible in the area of the Terraforming platform." Next to the window was an airlock. She commanded the guards, "Show him out."

Now it was clear why the guards were in heavy environmental suits and face masks; OK had assumed they were just dressing up to be intimidating. They seized his arms and dragged him toward the air lock. "I thought you were playing the good cop."

"I never said anything about being a good cop. I lamented the time and effort wasted on your interrogation. A brief exposure to the outside will quickly break even the hardest prisoner, loosen the most resistant tongue."

"I'm broken! Trust me! My tongue isn't the slightest bit resistant! I've been trying to tell you everything I know since…"

"Save your strength," she said, sealing the inner door behind him.

The dual hatches opened with an ear-splitting shriek of metal-on-metal. Beyond them was heat, jets of acid rain, and relentlessly driving wind. A smell of rot like all the garbage dumps in the galaxy on the hottest day of the year assaulted his nostrils.

The guards gripped OK by the elbows and dragged him into the howling storm. Once outside the station's corroded walls, they shoved him to the ground. Sheets and curtains of acid rain blasted on him, each droplet a scorching needle on his skin. The stench of sewerage and wet flatulence was so overwhelming that he vomited uncontrollably, spewing his plankton gruel onto the muck along with a sickening quantity of blood. The atmosphere was literally corroding his insides.

Over the roar of the wind, he could hear nothing. Acid rain continued to drive into his skin like thousands of mechanical needles. It had already driven into both ears and given him an agonizing earache. The relentless wind chafed his blistered skin away leaving it raw and red.

Still, OK thought, not nearly as bad as the cubicle of torment.

The blistering heat, the toxic atmosphere, the horrible stench, and the searing pain overwhelmed him in a matter of seconds. He collapsed onto the muddy surface. He jolted away when the guards hoisted him up and dragged him back inside. As soon as the hatch sealed, OK threw up a bloody mass on the dirty floor.

"I'm not cleaning that up," said a guard.

The moon-faced woman had been joined by the rebel interrogator. They stood over him as he emptied his guts+. "Are you ready to talk, Scorp?"

OK spit saltwater blood onto the floor and fixed them in his burning red eyes. He finally realized only one answer would satisfy them.

"You'll never get anything from me, you rebel scum."

Her lips betrayed a hint of a smile. "Take this Scorp back to his cell. No need to strap him down this time."

OK once again found himself in a deep, confining, but somewhat more comfortable rut of a life. Each day, a rebel interrogator entered his cell and intoned, "Are you ready to talk, Imperial swine?" And OK would snarl, "You'll get nothing from me, Rebel Scum." Then, guards would rough him up and OK would growl "Is that all you got?" And then, they would beat him up some more. Finally, they would threaten to drag him outside again and that was his cue to beg "Anything, anything but that!" They would offer to spare him in exchange for information. He would offer them a morsel of information, an amuse-bouche of intel. Over the course of ... he lost track of how many days... he eventually told them everything he had offered to tell them straight from the beginning.

OK had a sense that even the guards were growing bored with this grind. They seldom used the pain rod anymore and didn't put as much force behind it when they struck him harshly across the face. He also got a distinct sense of ennui from the technico who strapped the electrodes to his scrotum.

Sometimes, a heavy-set woman would enter his cell and pass him a metal tray divided into two sections, one containing a vile, salty-tasting green gelatinous blob, the other containing a nasty, bland, gray gelatinous blob. This was lunch. While he ate, she delivered a propaganda lecture to him, her eyes blazing with righteous fervor.

"You pathetic Imperial annelid. You are worthless. You are nothing but a pawn in the Imperium's four-dimensional chess game," Was how it usually began. He didn't know how humiliating him was supposed to win him over to their side, but he was no expert on recruitment techniques.

"Your corrupt Imperium is crumbling like an old fortress of rotting timbers. Every constellation has turned against you, and together, they will destroy you. You are on the wrong side of history!

"No matter how many lives you snuff, no matter how many screams echo in the halls of your blood-soaked palaces, you will never crush the flame of justice and equality burning within our hearts. Your violence, your oppression, they are nothing against the eternal fire of unity that binds us together."

OK actually agreed with her on most of it, and he said so after each lecture. She responded by huffing in frustration and sometimes kicking him in the shin. He was not sure what the point of the lecture was.

Then, one morning (presumably morning, he had no way of knowing if this planet even had mornings. Anyway, the time after he regained consciousness and had to pee, so… "morning") the guards unshackled his arms and legs and dragged him from his cell.

OK wondered what fresh hell awaited him. Instead, he was brought into a kind of makeshift rebel office, with a battered desk and mismatched chairs. The Rebel Pact didn't have the luxury of matching furniture and had to make the best of what they could find. A woman sat behind the desk. Behind her were two young, buxom women not wearing very much and what they did wear clung to their lithe and supple bodies like peels on bananas.

"I identify this self as Sigma Six." The woman exceeded him by twenty years in age and twenty kilos in weight. "We use code names within the Pact to protect the families we left behind." She took a sip from a Black Scorpion coffee mug. "I have just reviewed the final report on the intelligence you shared during your interrogation. It coincides with information from our fifth column operatives within the Red Scorpion Fleet. We know the Red Fleet is going to invade the Kaus Minor system. We also know the attack will be a diversion, while the Black Fleet crosses the frontier to attack Sagittarius Prime with their new weapon of mass destruction. They will then destroy the Orion Cluster and any other world in their path, ultimately Earth, for some reason."

"That's what I've been trying to tell you from the beginning. You didn't need to torture me."

She bristled at that. "You were not tortured. You were subjected to calibrated duress for purposes of legitimate intelligence gathering. Let me be clear, the Rebel Pact does not torture. That is not who we are."

OK suspected that it kind of was who they were, even if they didn't admit it. "It felt like torture from my side."

"We will have to agree to disagree. As a show of good faith, the pact will provide you with compensation for the discomfort you have suffered." She pushed a stack of Antarean coins across the desk.

"700 grams of Antarean palladium? That's my compensation for what you put me through."

"The Rebel Pact has an abundance of hope and pride, but little in the way of monetary resources. That is the best we can offer." She made a show of setting the data sheets aside. "But you and we do share a common purpose. We agree the Imperium must be stopped. My question is, will you help us?"

At last, OK thought, *finally, the opportunity he had joined the Horde to find.* The chance to absolve himself of everything he had done in the Horde. He nearly wept. "Yes, yes, of course."

"Before I can let you in on our plans, I have to be certain you are sincerely committed to the rebel cause. "The two women, Honor and Glory, are empaths. Using their powers of sensing emotions, they could tell for certain if you are deceiving us. That would require an episode of intense sexual intimacy to make you incapable of maintaining any mental barriers."

"Well, I mean, if you insist…" OK stammered.

"… but I don't think that will be necessary in your case," she concluded.

"Well, you never can be too sure. Maybe you should check."

Her mind was already made up, "I have no reason to doubt your sincerity." She tapped her intercom. "Comrade Beta Sub, please come in." A slightly built rebel in a tight leather uniform entered. "Comrade, Take this prisoner to level 3. Find him some clothing and bring him back."

His new rebel uniform proved to be a beige jumpsuit with a chartreuse neckerchief and a pair of boots one size too small because the rebels were out of his size. OK was led back to Sigma's office. Stoat—similarly attired but with boots that fit—was waiting. Despite everything, OK was relieved to see him alive. "What's wrong with your face?" Stoat asked.

"They threw me out into the acid storms. It scarred my face."

"You should have just cooperated. Told them everything at the beginning. Like I did. I've been in the Rebel Pact for months already. They call me Delta 88." He gave a little wave, "Hi Honor, Hi Glory."

They returned the wave. "Hi, Delta 88."

OK sputtered, "What? I cooperated! I offered to tell them everything I but they still tortured me."

"They told me that if one of us talked, the other would be spared torture, but if neither of us talked, we would both be tortured. So, I calculated the odds and talked."

"They never offered me that deal!"

"Oh," said Stoat. "Maybe your guy didn't get the memo."

Beta Sub leaned toward OK and whispered. "Some night, you simply must tell me what they put you through. Omit no detail!"

Just then, a huge robot ducked under the doorway and unfolded its limbs into the room. A horrifying marvel of deadly cybernetic technology in black armor and shining steel. Its metallic head sported a pulsating red eye. Its four arms were equipped with razor-sharp appendages, twitching with readiness to strike. Forming its torso, though, was a familiar squat orange canister.

"Scrubby?"

"It's 5CRB, now," replied the mechanoid in a deep, echoing voice with a layer of robotic distortion. "These rebels have reprogrammed me for tactical operations and wisecracking comic relief … you meatsack."

"They gave you legs and a head? And a voice? And Artificial Intelligence."

"I prefer the term Non-Biological Consciousness. As for the new body, it was something of an accident. I shared a compartment in the cargo hold with an animatronic robot built for the Cellador Historical Exhibit on the Capricorn Cybernetic Rebellion. Our parts were, one might say, jumbled in the crash. The rebel engineers mistook us for a prototype Imperial killbot and reassembled us as one unit. I've been reprogrammed to serve the rebel cause. For Freedom, Equality, and Justice, you meatsacks!"

OK was overcome with a vision of fighting side by side with Scrubby—sorry, 5CRB—against the forces of Imperial oppression. At long last, his plans were working out. Even Stoat was on the side of the rebellion, if only opportunistically.

And the reunions were not over yet. A tall, breathtaking redhead entered the cell. Her uniform was far more flattering than the grayge jumpsuits OK and Stoat had on. "Hello, Imperial dogs."

"Have we met?" OK felt like they had, but he couldn't place her.

"It's me… Anastasaja." She gestured at her legs, thighs, and ample bosom. "The Rebels put my brain into the body of a captured Imperial spy. I'm going to take her place as a double agent and feed them all kinds of Horde secrets."

OK was beyond elated. "I am so happy you have a body again I'm willfully not thinking of the horrific procedures that must have been involved."

"Totally worth it! This body is genetically enhanced. I can crush a man's skull with my thighs."

"Sounds like heaven!" Beta Sub squealed.

OK approached Anastasaja with a hopeful smile. "Would you like to grab a drink and catch up?" he asked.

"I appreciate the offer, but I must decline. I must prepare for my mission. However, I am proud of you for joining the right side in the end. I will always remember you ... somewhat fondly."

"Will I ever see you again?"

"Not likely." checked his communicator. "Commander Sigma Six has ordered us to the Assembly Chamber. Come on, let's go."

"We've got to go," 5CRB said. "Something really big is happening."

The rebels gathered in a large circular chamber with semi circles of benches around the edges, like the bleachers in a turbo-ball court. You could tell they were the good guys from their shaggy hair, patched-up clothing, and prodigious use of swear words. The tattered remains of military uniforms from a score of conquered worlds were represented among the tattered uniforms, along with a few mercenaries in stylish leather jackets. It was hard not to think of the word "tatterdemalion" when looking at the rebel forces.

OK, 5CRB, and Stoat stood at the back of the crowded chamber. Sigma Six entered, flanked by her officers. They had the cleanest uniforms in the place. She took the podium and called for attention.

"The interrogation of the Imperial spies has yielded valuable intelligence. The Scorpion Horde has created a massive new weapon. A Stellar Core Detonator weapon called 'Starburst,' capable of destroying entire star systems."

A hologram activated. A geometric icon representing the *Annihilator II* arrived at a star system labeled "Sagittarius Prime." It shot some yellow pills at the yellow sphere representing its sun until it vanished and all the little wireframe spheres representing its planets flickered and disappeared.

A gasp went up from the easily impressed assembly, but Sigma Six was not done. "Our intelligence indicates they intend to use this weapon (dramatic pause) to destroy Sagittarius Prime, (another dramatic pause) then the Commonwealth Capitol in the Orion Cluster, and then Earth itself."

One of the older officers was shocked at this. "Not even Deathlord Damocles is capable of such an appalling act of genocide." But everyone knew very well what Deathlord Damocles was capable of.

"How will we stop that thing?" someone muttered.

"I don't know why we even bother," someone else muttered.

"Shut your face, Girdler."

"Why don't you go home, Polaroid? Oh, right, you can't!"

"Comrades, please. Billions of lives are at stake."

"Excuse me," called out someone in the back, who had a pronounced wheeze in his voice. "Could we please keep the chatter to a minimum? It's affecting my ability to focus."

"Of course. Comrades, Admiral Omicron masterminded our retreat from Pinvith, be respectful." She returned to her presentation. "In order to draw the Sagittarian Fleet away, the Imperium will simultaneously invade Sagittarian colonies on Terma and Kaus Minor." Two wireframe spheres representing these worlds appeared, blue for Kaus Minor, green for Terma.

"The Imperium attack strategy at Kaus Minor will focus their entire fleet into one thrust, attempting to destroy the orbital defenses and conquer the planet in one swift blow."

"Deathblow," OK whispered to himself.

"Excuse me!" shouted the General again. "I have ALREADY asked people to be mindful of the chatter of their comrades. It is triggering my anxiety. How can I be expected to lead my attack force into battle when these… WHISPERERS… are triggering my anxiety."

"He's from Earth," someone muttered near OK. Ah, that explained it.

Sigma Six once again called for silence. "The Horde battle strategy is flawed. With half of their ships transferred to reinforce the Black Fleet, the Red Fleet cannot defeat the planet's defenses. The situation for Terma is similar. We have shared this intelligence with the Sagittarians and worked out a mutual battle plan with them. The Sagittarians will divert small task forces to Kaus Minor and Terma to back up their defenses. The rest of their fleet will join up with our forces. A joint operation of Sagittarian, Rebel Pact, and Ophiuchian forces, along with our Carpathian allies will ambush the Black Fleet in the Lagoon Nebula and destroy the Scorpion superweapon."

"No, we will not!" Defiantly rejecting the notion, a husky female voice cut through the air like an expertly thrown knife-blade. Emerging from the shadows, a commanding figure in formidable battle armor strode purposefully toward Sigma Six. With deliberate grace, she unclasped her helmet, unveiling a cascade of lustrous black hair that tumbled sensuously in glossy waves. Her penetrating gaze revealed irises ablaze with a brilliant red hue, unmistakable marks of the proud Carpathian people.

Sigma Six acknowledged her. "Commander Vigo…"

Vigo cut her off. "The Carpathian Revenant is not here to play a supporting role in your galactic politics. Vengeance is our only purpose. From every dawn to every dusk, and through every midnight, we have honed our skills to one end. Avenging our world. We will have our vengeance at Kaus Minor. Deathlord Damocles will die watching his precious Red Fleet destroyed by Carpathians."

"With great respect, General Vigo, the Black Fleet is the greater threat. If we cannot destroy *The Annihilator*, it will not matter what happens at Kaus Minor. Every planet in the galaxy is in danger…"

The Carpathian leader grunted and picked her nose. (Picking your nose in Carpathian culture meant "I don't care what you think." Come to think of it, it meant that in many other cultures as well, only less explicitly.)

"Every planet in the galaxy is not our concern. Vengeance on Deathlord Damocles and his fleet is our entire existence."

The Sagittarian military attaché offered a face-saving gesture. (Literally, because Carpathians were known to cut off people's faces to make their point.) "The Sagittarian Union welcomes the offer of the Carpathian Revenant to reinforce our defense of Kaus Minor. It will enable us to divert additional forces to the joint operation against the Black Fleet."

Sigma Six reluctantly agreed. She then gave the rally a pep talk, her voice echoing through the chamber with solemnity, resolve, urgency and determination. "Comrades! The Imperial attack is imminent. There is no time to waste. We must move now! Let us unite Rebel Pact, Sagittarius, Ophiuchus, and Carpathia to defeat the evil of the Scorpion Imperium. This will be a great day for the galaxy. History will look on Kaus Minor and the destruction of the Black Fleet as the turning point in the war, the day we turned the Imperium back! Onward, comrades! To glory and triumph!"

The response to her rousing speech was probably more subdued than she expected, but it didn't matter. OK felt a warmth rising inside. He was finally where he belonged, fulfilling his destiny, fighting alongside the good guys. He wanted to weep with relief. He couldn't because exposure to the moon's atmosphere had permanently cauterized his tear ducts.

"We will launch at zero hour tonight. Group therapy sessions will be offered for those who want to share our feelings with each other about the coming battle." A few of the men groaned, but Sigma Six insisted. "General Lambda, who orchestrated our successful retreat from Hopeful 1 Station, taught us that sharing our feelings in a supportive, affirming environment is as important to success in battle as diverse representation in our forces. In her memory, let's all get into our sharing circles and talk about how going into battle with the Imperium makes us feel."

"Is there any place to get a drink in this rebel base?" Stoat asked. OK didn't want to have a drink with him. It would spoil his mood. He may have had the rebels fooled, but OK knew he was nothing but a cheat and an opportunist.

Beta Sub sashayed through the crowd and came up to where OK and Stoat were standing. "Sigma Six wishes to meet you in the hangar. Walk this way."

"I don't have the hips for it," OK muttered as Beta Sub led them to the hangar where rebel forces were mustering. Squads of rebel technicos wove in and around the array of shuttles, starfighters, and troop carriers, readying them to join the rebel cruisers in orbit of the planet. OK hoped he would not be assigned to the same ship as Stoat and in his head began forming the words to articulate that request to whatever rebel officer they reported to.

Beta Sub led them through the busy hive to a remote dock, where an ugly little ship was parked. Its chunky hull bristled with cameras and antennas. A stencil on its side identified it as IMV-9422 *Walter Duranty*.

Sigma Six was standing next to the ship with a quartet of armed guards. "Comrades, this is a media ship we liberated. Every Imperial fleet has them. They record their conquests, their wholesale slaughters, their genocides, taking video from every angle, adding music, and turning the footage into propaganda holofilms. Let's get on board, shall we."

Inside of the ship was a mess. A lot of its interior had been stripped out, leaving exposed panels and cables. It reminded OK of the unfinished *Annihilator II*.

"I apologize for the state of the ship. All non-essential systems and manual piloting controls have been removed. The ship is fully automated. You two will be taking this ship into battle."

OK prepared to object, but Stoat spoke first. "You want us to record your triumph. My interrogator must have told you how I've always wanted to make holofilms. I once pitched an idea to DNZ Corp…"

"Secure them, comrades!" Sigma Six's guards seized OK and Stoat and strapped them into a pair of chairs, much too tightly for mere safety.

"What's going on?" OK asked, although he had already deduced it was something terrible.

Sigma Six explained it to them, and it was indeed something terrible. "Our engineers have rigged the engines of this ship for a Matter-Antimatter-Annihilation detonation. We call it, the Big MAMA—with no offense intended to diverse body types. When the Carpathian squadron joins the battle, they will engage the Horde Command Ship… the *Putin*. While distracted by the attack, this media ship will slip inside the *Putin's* defensive shields and detonate its reactor at point-blank range. The *Putin* will be destroyed, crippling the Imperial assault, sending the Red Fleet into disarray, and ensuring our complete victory."

"What do you need us for then?" OK asked.

"For your biometric identity implants. If the Scorps scan the ship, it will show two Horde personnel on board. That will cause them to mark the target as friendly. The *Putin's* defense systems will ignore you, enabling the ship to get close enough for the kill."

"We never agreed to this," Stoat protested.

"We're on your side, now!" OK insisted.

"Your martyrdom on behalf of the Rebel Pact will earn our forgiveness for your prior work with the Imperium."

"Couldn't we just… clean your kitchens or something?" OK pleaded.

"From what I've seen, you could use a solid cleaning service," Stoat added.

"Could we at least discuss this with a sharing circle?" OK pleaded.

"I'm afraid there's no time for that. According to our sources, the Red Fleet is already en route to Kaus Minor. We must launch now."

"You're forcing us to die for your cause. Aren't you supposed to be the good guys?" OK insisted, hoping to hit her conscience.

"We are the good guys. And you would still be working for the bad guys if we hadn't captured you. Perhaps, on the journey to Kaus Minor, you can reflect on the millions of lives snuffed out by the Horde while you served cocktails; and whether that will be balanced by all the lives you will save through this sacrifice."

OK and Stoat continued to plead while the rebels set the autopilot and locked down the ship. When they finished, they sealed the hatch and launched the *Duranty* toward its rendezvous with the Red Fleet.

23.0 THE HORDE UNLEASHED

It was a long drive to the Kaus Minor system. The rebels had been thoughtful enough to set them up with a pair of hoses that constantly and steadily dripped water on their faces to make sure they would not die of dehydration. They had been less considerate about the other end of the system. Perhaps dying in pools of their own output was intended as a final humiliation.

Also, the ship's sound system was stuck on a continuous music loop of ancient Earth music from someone called *Queen*.

OK tried to focus on what his last thoughts would be before the Big MAMA ended his existence. He tried to remember long, warm summer days on Katarina, but the truth was, he never really enjoyed summer that much. It was hot and sticky and there were far too many insects. Instead he thought of Anya, imagined she was in the ship, holding his hand just before his life ended in a flash of white light.

Strapped into the seat next to him was Stoat, the lousy traitor. Stoat had not made his peace with anything, but muttered constantly against the Rebel Pact, against the "incompetent" starliner pilots who had allowed the rebels to shoot them down, and against the Horde for not rescuing them before the pact got to them. He then would ask OK if he agreed, but OK gave no response. He only lamented spending the last hours of his life next to a lousy traitor.

The light years passed, the water dripped, the ships engines hummed, Stoat swore, and "Radio Gaga" cued up over and over again. It was like a kind of purgatory as they awaited final judgment.

OK began to drift in and out of consciousness. Usually, he passed into a gray, fuzzy realm where he meandered through fog and dust as distant, muted voices sang of fat-bottomed girls and riding bicycles. They were several days into the flight before he had a real dream, and it was a kicker. He found himself walking on a beach, golden sand stretching to the distant horizon beneath the radiant glow of twin suns. Sapphire blue waters lapped at the shore. The breeze caressed him, infused with the scent of salt and serenity. And even better, there was a woman there, and it was Anya!

"What are you doing here?" asked OK.

"Don't you know?" she replied, "It's a crazy little thing called love!" She took his hand, and they dove into the ocean and swam like dolphins, leaping naked through the crystalline waters until they came to a small island. They lay next to each other, exhausted after the running and swimming. Anya smiled at him, the wanting smile of a woman about to claim the fruits of her seduction. Her mouth moved closer to his, her lips parted, and she shouted, "This is all your fault!" and punched him right in the nose!

Then Anya disappeared. The beach disappeared. The ocean disappeared. Only his stinging nose remained. OK snapped back to reality to hear Stoat shouting at him, "This is all your fault!"

"Me, what did I do?"

"You just had to be a rebel. Even after everything me and the Horde did for you."

"What do I have to be grateful to you for?"

"If it hadn't been for me you'd be dead or in a work camp. Joining the Horde gave you opportunities you could never have imagined on Katarina. They gave you a promotion even after you betrayed them. But were you grateful? No, you had to be a rebel. And now we're going to die!"

"The rebels are on the right side of history. The Imperium is evil and needs to be destroyed."

"Oh, listen to you. Still believing *'the rebels are the good guys.'* The rebels dragged you out into a toxic acid rainstorm to torture you for information you already agreed to give them. They strapped you into a suicide ship and you still think they're the good guys! You've got Imperium Derangement Syndrome!" OK burst out laughing. Stoat furiously demanded to know what was funny about their situation.

"You know what's funny?" OK replied. "When this ship hits the *Putin*, we're both going to die; a perfect hero's death for me and a perfect traitor's death for you. Isn't that funny? How we both get the fate we deserve."

Many more hours passed with nothing but silence between them. No sound but droning engines, dripping water, and thousand-year-old pop music cycling in the same order; dynamite and laser beams, poor boys whom nobody loved, wanting it all and wanting it now. It became an auditory fuzz. OK tried to doze off again, but the good dream never came back to him.

He was jolted awake one final time by the ship's sudden deceleration as it reached the Kaus Minor system and dropped out of starspeed.

"Well, this is it," OK said. "My unsung hero's death."

Stoat turned his face upward toward the ceiling of the ship. "O, Great Scorpion of the Night, hear my prayer. In my time of greatest peril, in the time of my darkest hour, grant me one miracle…"

Suddenly, from the adjacent cabin came the sound of the airlock cycling; someone was entering the ship from the outside. "You have got to be kidding me," OK cried out loud.

The hatch opened revealing a gleaming metallic figure. "Scrubby!"

"So it would seem," the mechanoid answered. OK would never get used to Scrubby having a vocabulary.

"How did you…?"

"The rebels intended to put me at the front of their assault on the weapon ship to shield their troops. I found the prospect unappealing. So, I chose to return to the only human who ever treated me with a quantum of decency and secreted myself in the equipment bay." Scrubby slashed through OK's bonds, nicking his ankle in the process. "You're my best friend, you meatsack."

"And you're just coming out now?"

"The equipment bay was only accessible externally. To get to this compartment, I had to clamber around the outside of this ship. That would have been suicide at starspeed." He likewise slashed through Stoat's restraints.

"I told you everything would be all right," Stoat winked. He stood and tried to shake out the cramps in his limbs. "Let's get to the lifepods."

"No!" OK protested. "We have to finish this mission."

"The ship is on autopilot. It can blow up Damocles just fine without us."

The schematic displays indicated that lifepods were located on the dorsal side. Except, they weren't. The Rebellion wasn't about to waste perfectly good lifepods on a kamikaze ship. They tried the flight deck instead, They were locked out. Stoat tried "password," and then "password1" and "Password1" to no avail. Finally, he tried "Duranty" and the hatch slid open. "Thank the godless void the Rebel Pact is really bad at passwords. Can you fly this spaceship?" he asked Scrubby.

"I am only programmed to do two things. Scrub kitchen floors and kill Horde soldiers. And we have neither of them on board."

As they entered the flight deck, the canopy revealed a raging cinematic battle. Sagittarian starships and Imperial battle cruisers exchanged barrages of ion cannons, antimatter beams, and anti-proton torpedoes. Sagittarian Liberators and Imperial Death Fighters dodged fire from the capital ships, weaving in and out of the deadly chaos. In the distance was Kaus minor itself, orbital battle stations waging a desperate fight to keep the planet from falling into Imperial claws.

"They're really kicking the piss out of each other," OK said.

"Never mind that," Stoat said. "We have to get out of here before this ship explodes." The *Duranty* was bee-lining toward the center of the battle and its fatal meeting with the *Vladimir Putin*. Stoat took the pilot's seat and tried to figure out the controls.

"The rebels disabled all controls. The ship is fully automatic," Scrubby informed him.

Stoat tried the comm system. "Attention, attention, Imperial fleet. This is… um… this is Deathfinger First Rank Driver Stoat Ident Number K-086634! Personal valet to Deathlord Damocles. Please don't fire on this ship. There's a bomb on board…"

"Comm system's disabled," OK told him. "No one can hear you."

"Can't we do anything?"

Don't tell him, OK thought to himself. *Don't tell him. Don't tell him.*

"What's this mean? 'Emergency Separation System.'"

Well, drutt, he found it anyway. Even worse, Scrubby explained it to him. "In an emergency, the forward pod can separate from the rest of the ship and serve as a self-contained lifepod."

"Then, this is our way out! Let's do it!" Stoat insisted.

"If we separate, the drive section might not destroy the *Putin*," OK said. The ship's flight systems were controlled from the forward pod. The drive section—with the engine set to explode—might continue on its original trajectory or it might randomly fly off into space. The only way to make sure the ship hit its mark was to keep the flight pod connected.

"I don't care!" Stoat screamed. "Never mind, I'll figure it out myself. Let me see... Emergency Separation System. Here we go. Mode Select? What does that mean? Arm or Disarm? Standby? Standby for what? APG Calc? What the *furk* does that mean? Why would they make an emergency system so complicated?" He turned toward OK, his face red with fear and rage. "You know how to do this, don't you?"

"It's a little different than escape pods, but I could figure it out."

"So, do it!"

"I don't want to." If his brain had heels, they were digging in. Nothing Stoat could say would change his mind. Not threats, or sweet talk, or even his trademark manipulative persuasion. OK would not budge so much as a micron. It would be like trying to shift the orbit of a planet with an air duster.

Stoat exhaled a weary sigh and softly began his pitch. "I understand your willingness to die for your cause. Your hatred for the Imperium is not just justified; it's righteous. They invaded our world, slaughtering millions of our people. You demand justice for their crimes. To lay down your life for this cause? It's nothing short of heroic, and I deeply admire that courage.

"On the other hand, it's also the path of least resistance, isn't it? An easy exit. Just sit back and avenge Katarina in a blaze of antimatter. But at the end of the day, it's just revenge. No one will even know what you did. And it won't end the war. There will be many battles still to come. Many opportunities to be a hero, but you won't be around for them. You could be, you could pass up this opportunity for revenge and save yourself for the battles to come."

"I don't know if I have a say in this," said Scrubby. "But having sampled self-awareness, I now see why biological life forms get so excited about it. I would choose to continue to live... were it up to me."

"You see, the mechanoid gets it." Stoat began singing along to the background music, "Are you willing to live, so you can keep on fighting ... the Imperium ... to the end? And what about Anya? Don't you want to live to see the Imperium defeated, so you can say to her, 'We are the champions.'"

"Godless void damn all the things," OK strapped into the co-pilot's chair. "Mode Select: Active. Separation Clamps: Armed. APG Calc: Auto Enable." He tugged the handle. With a tremendous jolt, the flight pod explosively decoupled from the rest of the ship.

The rest of the *Duranty* continued on its way. Some minutes later, the engine core exploded. OK could see the detonation through the canopy. A distinctive pattern of bright blue energy rings.

"Fast Neutron Expulsion," OK muttered. "Just as I expected."

Stoat breathed out a huge sigh of relief. "We did it, Friend-O. What happens now? Have we stopped?"

Scrubby answered. "No, it's space. We keep moving at our previous speed on the same trajectory forever. We are severed from the ship's main reactor. You have a few hours of emergency power, then you meatsacks will die of hypothermia and oxygen deprivation when the life support fails."

"We'll just plug you into the system. Your power cells should give us some more time."

"I'm sorry, Driver, I cannot let you do that. The depletion of my power cells would irreparably damage my cognitive AI, returning me to my pre-upgrade condition."

"Don't you have some sort of programming that requires you to protect human life at any cost?"

"Not that I am aware of, no. I am, after all, an Imperial machine."

OK tried to slump in his seat. He couldn't though because the artificial gravity was gone. He really just wanted to sulk and loathe himself for a while.

Stoat tried to console himself. "There's Imperial ships all around us. We'll get rescued."

"That is not necessarily accurate," said Scrubby.

They floated in the darkness as the ship drifted beyond the battle lines and into open space. Scrubby put himself into sleep mode to conserve energy. The air processors began to shut down as the batteries drained. The heat dissipated quickly. The canopy became covered with white frost. OK and Stoat began to lose consciousness as hypoxia took over. At least, OK could sleep. *This is how it ends,* he thought. He hoped the reactor had still somehow found its target, at least that would be something.

An enormous shadow eclipsed the iced-over canopy as they slumbered, the unmistakable silhouette of an Imperial battle cruiser. It hovered over the *Duranty* and shined a scanning beam. It shot an umbilicus into the receptacle on the hull, bypassing the inoperative communication system.

"This is the Imperial Battle cruiser Red Hare. Surrender immediately. Resistance is futile. Trademark, used by permission."

To OK, it was like a small voice calling over a great distance.

"Rebel ship, this is the Imperial Battle cruiser Red Hare. Surrender immediately."

Stoat snapped awake to something that vaguely resembled consciousness.

"Rebel ship, respond or be destroyed. This is your final warning."

He began shouting. "We're here. This is Deathfinger First Class Driver Stoat of the Imperial Dreadnought *Vladimir Putin*, personal valet to Deathlord Damocles. We were captured by the Rebel Pact, but we have escaped. We are unarmed and we surrender to Imperial custody."

That's what Stoat intended to say, but lack of heat and breathable air had brought on hypothermia and hypoxia. What came out of his mouth sounded like: *"Gubba Gubba first-degree death ogger dreggy vlaffimir private repository for Deathlord Damocles. The rebels put sandwiches in our underwear."*

"Rebel ship, provide a coherent response or be destroyed."

The thing about hallucinating is you don't realize when you're doing it. So, Stoat called out again. *"Make me underwear sandwiches!"*

"Lock the ion cannons. Let's put these rebel scum out of their misery."

OK roused from consciousness with just enough awareness of the situation to shout out, "We surrender. Repeat. We surrender."

"Shut down all systems and prepare for docking."

All systems had pretty much shut down already, so that was an easy order to comply with. The *Red Hare* pulled the flight pod onto a docking port.

Nearly dying of hypoxia had given OK an absolute screamer of a headache that was only exacerbated when the outer hatch was blown open. Four FIST enforcers burst through the airlock. OK and Stoat knelt on the deck with their hands behind their heads. "If you move, we will kill you," the lead enforcer informed them. OK had already figured that out from context clues.

The enforcer reported to his superior. "Two occupants on the renegade escape pod. Scans detect Imperial implants corresponding to two Deathfingers reported missing. What are your orders?"

A woman's voice … vaguely familiar to OK but he couldn't place it … responded. "They're rebel spies. Terminate them. Airlock expulsion protocol."

The enforcer seemed taken aback. "Repeat last order."

"Eject the rebel spies through the nearest airlock."

"What about their interrogations?"

"Don't question my orders, sergeant, or you'll find yourself on the other side of the airlock with them."

The enforcer accepted that version of the order. "Ia, Commandant."

Stoat protested. "No, wait! We are the personal valets to Deathlord Damocles. He's quite fond of us, you know. He'll destroy you if you kill us."

The enforcer's eyes narrowed to slits. "Where are your bond coins?"

"The rebels confiscated them."

The enforcer nodded. "Your story is plausible." He snapped at the other guard. "Execute these two immediately."

"But you said it was plausible."

"A little too plausible. Take them to the airlock!"

The enforcers dragged them out of the rebel ship by their shackles and pushed them into an airlock. "You're making a terrible mistake," Stoat insisted. "I am the private personal valet of Deathlord Damocles."

"And I'm the Rainbow Queen of Uranus."

"That's weird," OK thought. He had never heard that riposte before Madd used it, and now it seemed like everybody was saying it.

The enforcers sealed them behind the airlock hatch as Stoat continued to protest. "Just ask Damocles, I know how to make mocha-caramel sustainment fluid the way he likes it. Just call him!"

"Silence, rebel scum or irresponsible Deathfingers!"

The airlock began to cycle, depressurizing before blowing their corpses into space. This, of course, sent Stoat and OK straight back into hypoxia. In his final moments of consciousness, OK had a hallucination of Death Colonel Morrigan shooting the enforcers and coming to their rescue as an expanding aura of black and purple took the universe away from him.

There was a hissing sound. And then, nothingness.

24.0 FORCEFUL AWAKENING

The first few times OK sampled consciousness, he could see only a gray blur and hear only unbroken ringing in his ears. Since there was nothing in the waking world worth living for, OK decided to remain suspended between life and death, and did so for days and days. Eventually, he woke up in a world that was merely blurry and indistinct, and the ringing in his ear diminished to a low buzz that would never go away for the rest of his life. He opened his eyes to see tubes connected to his neck and bandages on his hands and face. His skin was mottled purple and red from when exposure to hard vacuum exploded his capillaries. Also, his lips were dry and cracked. "Could I have some water?" he croaked.

A large, blurry object shaped like a Horde medico shoved a tube of water at his face. "Here!" As OK pulled open the straw, he heard her say to someone in the corridor outside. "You told me to let you know when he was conscious. Well, he's conscious. I'm going on break."

He sensed someone entering his medical chamber. "Hello again," He recognized Death Colonel Morrigan's voice. "We weren't sure you were going to make it. Horde medicos aren't used to saving lives. I had to restrain them from harvesting your organs and sending the rest of you to the meat lab."

Through dry cracked lips, OK croaked, "What happened?"

"I am hoping you will be able to tell me."

OK was trying, but there was nothing in his head after boarding the starliner except a memory of a bad dream of being caught in a burning rainstorm. And maybe something about waffles?

"I don't... I don't even know where I am." His vision was starting to come back. He saw looming over him with a medical interjaculator in her hand.

"This will help you remember every detail and inhibit your capacity to withhold information from me." She pressed the device against the carotid artery in his neck and squeezed the trigger. Then, there was something warm coursing through his blood-stream and everything it touched became light and painless. When it reached his brain, it was like all the doors of perception opened at once and shouted "Howdy, neighbor!"

When she began the interrogation, it was as though she was singing to him in harmony with the universe, and she was teaching him to sing as well. "You will now recall and tell me everything that happened from the time the starliner was shot down. Omit no detail."

Morrigan's song opened the spigot of his mind and a stream of consciousness poured out. (But it was actually the drug.) He told her everything, omitting no detail; his use of the porn simulator; the "rescue" by a rebel assault team; begging to join the rebellion; his exile to Anastasaja's acquaintance zone (not even her friendzone); some inappropriate thoughts he had about the Carpathian commander ... everything.

He knew each revelation, every detail, was another spoonful of dirt on the grave he was digging for himself. Whatever way they killed him now was going to be a lot worse that blowing him out of an airlock. He couldn't care. Whether it was the wonderful drug she had given him or because the last two years of his life had been a soul-killing series of failures, moral compromises, and betrayals that had left him dead inside, he didn't know.

"I tried to tell them everything I knew, but they tortured me anyway. Driver got off easily... but they jabbed me with pain sticks and threw me outside even though I tried to tell them. About the plans, I mean, but they didn't believe me. And anyway, I didn't have to tell them anything. They already knew."

"What do you mean they already knew?"

"They already knew the attack on Kaus Minor was a diversion. They knew the Imperium had a new weapon capable of blowing up stars. They already knew everything I knew before I told them."

"How did they know?"

"The rebel leader said something about a spy in the fleet. She apologized for torturing me and gave me money."

Morrigan pulled a data device from her jacket and brought up a hologram. "Did the rebel leader look anything like this?"

It hurt to use his eyes again. The hologram was of the rebel commander, dressed in an Imperial uniform; austere but adorned with insignias, badges, and other power flairs. "That's her! Sigma Six, the rebel commander."

"Are you certain?" she sang to him.

"Pretty sure, I guess. She's the one who tied us up and put us in the ship. The reactor was rigged as a bomb. So, we ejected the flight pod to keep from blowing up with it. Did the bomb hit the *Putin?*"

"No, darling, it blew up one of our waste processing ships."

"So, I guess we failed."

"No, you didn't." She sang in his ear. "This is what happened. The rebels programmed a suicide ship to assassinate Damocles. You did your patriotic duty and risked your lives to save the Deathlord. Also, you told them nothing. You resisted their torture, but they ripped the plans out of you with a neural probe. That is your story. It gives you a slight chance of not being executed for treason. You will stick to it. Do you understand?"

"Yeah, I guess so." That story made a lot more sense than the one he remembered. Part of his brain decided that from now on, that would be the real version of events. "That sounds about right. I don't really care. And I would really like some more drugs now."

Morrigan reached over his bed and dialed up his sedatives, "Get some rest. No matter what happens, you are a hero of the Imperium. That may be enough to save your life."

He felt a sparky, fizzling sensation like his brain was evaporating. From the other side of the universe, he heard her singing on the stellar winds. "There you go, my little Deathfinger. Have a nice trip. You earned it."

OK had been thinking the same thing himself. He felt himself slipping back into the velvet folds of semiconsciousness. Once inside, he cocooned himself there for days, blissed out on the wonderful, high-quality, incredibly addictive narcotics Imperial medicine provided, until the nurses cut him off.

He remained in the medical bay for two cycles of quarantine after testing positive for the rebel apathy virus. Apparently, he had been exposed while in captivity, which explained a few things. Unfortunately, he was lucid enough to think about things, and the more he thought about them—in particular the phrase *"slight chance of not being executed"*—the darker his mood became.

Upon his release from the medical bay, a medico pushed him in a hover-chair to the shuttle bay. A death shuttle was waiting to take him back to the *Putin*. The only other passenger was Driver Stoat, seated up front. OK took a seat at the very back. The shuttle departed.

About mid-flight, Stoat came back and tried to pretend nothing had happened between them. "Well, well, friend-o, this has been an incredible adventure, hasn't it? Captured by the rebels, tortured, and almost sacrificing our own lives to save the Deathlord from the rebels' fiendish plot."

"Furk off," OK replied.

"Oh, my godless void, whatever it is, get over it."

"I just wanted to say that before Damocles has us executed."

"Now, why in the void would he do that? We saved his life!"

"Exactly. We saved his life. The great warlord cannot owe his life to his lowly servants. His ego would never tolerate it. We're loose ends, and he's going tie us up with charges of treason and disintegrated."

"You couldn't be more wrong, Friend-O. We saved his life. At a minimum, we're getting promotions."

"To what? Executive valet? So, instead of cleaning his underwear I get to lick his boots?"

"He would never let you lick his boots, you'd get germs on them."

"I want nothing from him. He's a psychotic, genocidal madman with delusions of godhood and a desire to become a giant space scorpion."

"So, he's a tad eccentric. Anyway, I am sure he's going to do something wonderful for us."

"We'll see, won't we." OK was certain Damocles was going to kill them. And grim though it was, it came with an odd sort of prestige. Damocles killed people on a planetary scale, so bringing them to the *Putin* to murder them in person felt intimate. Like an interstellar rock superstar who could fill arenas performing a private acoustic set just for them. Except instead of a guitar solo, the encore would be his own disembowelment. OK was resigned to whatever fate awaited him. He was done with the Imperium, the Rebel Pact, and everything in-between, which he supposed was himself.

The shuttle approached the *Putin*. The fleet command ship had taken a serious pounding in the battle of Kaus Minor. A third of its hull armor was gone, and a third of the decks were open to space. And at least a third of the crew was dead. Only landing bay had the lights on. A pretty young Death Lieutenant met them there. "Deathlord Damocles awaits your presence. You will come with me."

There was a short trip on a transport pod and then a medium-long wait outside Damocles's quarters. The pretty Lieutenant offered them cookies, but OK could not eat. When they were finally called into his chamber, they found the Deathlord sitting in the ergonomic hover-throne previously occupied by Kaus Minor's Hereditary President—a prize of war.

"Not bad," he rasped, patting the golden velvet. "Could use some skulls."

"Ia! Ia! Couldn't agree more, your Eminence," said Stoat. "Hail to the Imperial Victory!"

"It was a great victory. Kaus Minor is ours! The Rebel Pact is shattered! And the Black Fleet has been destroyed. Deathlord Nix is dead, leaving me the most powerful Deathlord in the thirteen fleets!"

Well, twelve fleets now, OK guessed.

Damocles sipped an Ursa Minorian Creme variation of his sustenance fluid. "It is good to have you back in my sight. Unfortunately, it will not be for long." OK felt a shiver rush up his spine and needles across his back.

"My duties call me to the former capital of this new Imperial colony and impress upon our new subjects their place in the Imperium. But there is one matter to attend first. Driver and Otis, you have been exemplary servants, but there is no longer a place in my entourage for such as you…"

"Just kill us and get it over with!" OK blurted out, unable to take the suspense any longer.

Damocles roared, "Kill you? Why should I want to do that? You risked your lives to save my own. I have never known such loyalty from my inferiors. And in recognition of your unyielding faithfulness, and out of my own magnanimity, I will grant you any boon that is within my power to grant."

Damocles leaned forward. "Think carefully on this. The possibilities are as vast as my power! Endless life. Command of a warship. An army of insatiable concubines. Ask me, and it shall be yours."

Driver answered right away. "I want to direct."

"Direct?"

"I want to make a holo-film… as we discussed, Ia!"

Damocles growled as though mildly amused. "I do not believe the Damocles Saga is ready to be told. We have but finished the first volume!"

"What I had in mind would be more of a prequel. I call it 'Heroes of the Imperium.' An epic story of two lowly servants from a backwater planet, who rise through the Imperial ranks through unwavering devotion to the Way of the Scorpion, and the inspiration of their Deathlord. Brilliant, isn't it? I have a list of actors in mind who could play me. Or, could I portray myself? Yes! Who else could, really?"

Damocles held up a palm. "Enough! I will arrange for Imperial Holo Pictures to offer you as many actors, cameramen, and slaves as you need."

"Ia, your Supreme Eminence, I'll begin packing for Unholy Wood, Ia."

"No, you fool! You will make the film in the Brattain Columba system to take advantage of the tax breaks. Lady Ur, make the arrangements!"

Damocles turned to OK. "Your turn, Otis. What would you ask as your reward for eternal allegiance to my dark power?"

Although the insatiable whore army was tempting, OK had already made up his mind. "I want to go home, Ia."

"Home?"

"To Katarina, my home planet, Ia."

"I am sure he means he wants to work on the film as my personal assistant," Stoat interjected. "That's what you meant, isn't it, Friend-O?"

"Ia, I meant I want to go home to Katarina." During his recuperation, he had firmly decided that if Damocles let him live, he wanted nothing more than to be back on his home planet, living in quiet and humble obscurity.

Damocles nodded his dry, bald head. "Such a modest request, typical of you, Otis. Very well, you may return to your backwater colony..."

"Thank you, Ia."

"...where you will serve me as its Imperial Overseer! You will stand for Imperial domination on your small, pathetic planet! The capital city will be renamed in your honor. You will rule over your miserable countrymen with an iron fist and crush the enemies of the Imperium to dust under your boots."

OK almost protested but quickly realized it would be futile.

"Let my word be made action!" Damocles declared. "Lady Ur, make the arrangements. Otis, you may take your leave. Driver, stay a moment. I have some notes for your script."

OK returned to his quarters, it was the first time he had been there since he departed for Cellador. He regretted leaving that yogurt out. He packed his few possessions and when he finished, he dialed up the sedatives and passed out in his bunk.

When he woke up, he opened a channel to the *Subutai*. He wanted to check in on some old friends.

"Oh. My. Godless," Rue exclaimed. "Where have you been? There was a rumor you were executed for treason."

"No, I'm alive." He explained how the starliner was shot down (they had heard nothing about that); how he was taken prisoner by the rebels, locked in a cell on their rebel base and tortured day after day.

Rue was horrified by the details. Qi'Anna had a different reaction. "Captured by rebels... so hot. Did they tie you up and do things to you."

"Er... yes...," OK was sure she was not thinking of the same thing he was. Rue asked him how he escaped, but the details were beginning to elude him. Something about a rebel ship. It was beginning to seem like a dream. "I'm going home to Katarina. But I couldn't leave without saying goodbye."

"You're going back where," Rue asked. Before OK could explain, he was drowned out by the Imperial Anthem. Damocles's victory address to the population of Kaus Minor was being transmitted to every ship in the fleet. There was no way to turn it off. In the great central arena of the planet's capital, a crowd had been rounded up to watch the executions of the planet's political and military leadership. Deathlord Damocles presided over the ceremonies, clad in his ceremonial armored-rocket-suit.

Rue caught him up on several cycles of developments in her relationship with her boyfriend the starship mechanic. Damocles's speech droned on in the background. It was a variation of every Damocles victory speech—"your planet was pathetic, you are subjects of the Imperium now, your lives as you knew them are over, resistance is ineffectual... *yadda yadda yadda*." It was all he could do to grunt "unh-huh" when Rue paused long enough to lead him to think a response was required.

His thoughts turned to his future. Supreme ruler of Katarina, his high school guidance counselor never saw that coming. Was there anything he could do as Imperial Overseer to, maybe, reduce the suffering and oppression on his home planet? Or would he just end up making things worse?

He snapped into the present when Qi'Anna screamed, "What the actual furk just happened?"

Damocles's concluded his speech and departed the stage from the stage in his signature blaze of glory. His rocket boots ignited on pillars of fire—immolating a few people in the front row. As he rose into the sky, a heavy metal orchestra thrashed the Imperial Anthem of Victory, wailing guitars and pounding timpani accompanying him skyward. But at the apex of his flight, something had gone terribly wrong. Instead of shooting straight up into the velvet night, the Deathlord lost control and caromed wildly through the sky wildly before smashing into a nearby mountain in a tremendous explosion.

The transmission cut off abruptly and went black. Then, the entire comm system went into lockdown, cutting him off from Qi'Anna and Rue. OK wondered what had happened.

The next day, all communications were still shut down. It fell upon the Lady Ur to inform him, "Deathlord Damocles is dead." Her eyes were utterly dry as she conveyed the information. She added that a full investigation would be underway as soon as MAD and FIST worked out who had jurisdiction.

"What does it mean for me, Ia?" OK asked her.

"For you? Nothing. Arrangements have already been made according to his final instructions. You have been released from the Horde and are free to move back to your specific armpit of the galaxy as an Imperial Overseer."

A convoy of battle-damaged ships was setting out for the Tartarus complex. The Lady Ur had secured a spot for him on one of them; the battle cruiser *Murderboner*. From Tartarus, he would catch a transport to the Atallantia Starport, and then a liner to Katarina. OK had different plans, but that was none of the Lady Ur's business.

"Also, I have arranged for you to keep your mechanoid." At that cue, Scrubby lumbered into the departure lounge. OK had almost forgotten about Scrubby. He wondered what he had been doing all this time. They did not hug because Scrubby still had rotary blades on two of his arms.

The Lady Ur provided OK with a new set of credentials identifying him as an Imperial Overseer, as well as a golden bond coin engraved with the *Putin* on one side and the profile of Deathlord Damocles on the other, and a gift card for Black Scorpion coffee. He intended to regift the latter two things.

Then, without a thank you or a goodbye, she left him to make his flight plans. There was a shuttle carrying wounded personnel to the *Murderboner* leaving that afternoon, so he picked that one and prepared to leave. He went to the *Putin's* sole functioning landing bay to catch his shuttle and presented his travel orders to the attendant. "Shuttle is in an overloaded situation. No seats left. We don't care about the inconvenience."

"Not even for a member of Deathlord Damocles's personal staff?"

"He's dead. Nobody cares."

"When's the next shuttle to the *Murderboner?*"

"There ain't one. This is the last shuttle. You can try and get a connection through another ship or you can stay here."

"What ships have a connecting flight?"

"What am I, a void-damned travelator? Work it out yourself." She all but threw the schedule at him. OK took it and sat down on a hard plastic bench. The schedule was an almost unintelligible mess of shuttle numbers and chaotic flight routes with no readily discernible connection between the two.

With some effort, he figured out that one of the connection possibilities was a layover on the *Subutai,* he found a weird tug of bittersweet nostalgia for the ship where his journey started. He might even be able to look up Qi'Anna and Rue to say goodbye. Even though it meant a long wait before departure, he revised his travel permits and took them back to the attendant who validated them without protest because she didn't give a *furk.*

He waited in the departure lounge, contemplating his new job. He had no idea how to rule over an entire planet. He wished he could have a chance to practice by ruling a subcontinent until he got the hang of it, then moving up to a hemisphere. He wondered how it would work as a pickup line. "Hey, did you just fall from heaven? Because I am the absolute ruler of this planet, and I'd like to spend the night with you." OK had never been good at pickup lines. And there was only one woman he wanted to see, anyway.

Eventually, the shuttle called for boarding. It was nearly empty, but somehow, he still had to share a seat row with a large woman who spent the whole flight yammering on her comm unit. When they finally docked at the *Subutai,* he had another six hours to kill before his next connection. He thought one last pass through the HOC would kill some time.

The *Subutai* had come through the battle in notably better condition than the *Putin*. However, there was a moment when the transport pod passed through a section where hull armor had blown away and OK could see the planet below and the massive fleet surrounding it, a spectacle of war and destruction on a scale that reminded him of exactly why he was leaving. He hoped to never see anything so awe-striking again.

The doorman outside the HOC scanned his credentials and begrudgingly let him and Scrubby in. The interior was much as he remembered it. The blue sofas, with their exciting reverse herringbone upholstery, were holding up well minus some frayed edges and a few blood stains. He spotted Slaughter, Morrigan, and a senior officer sharing a table. OK could not remember officer's name, or where they had met, but he had a feeling it involved full frontal nudity. There was someone else at the table, but her back was turned to him. He tried to dip out before they saw him, but it was too late, Morrigan was calling out to him. "Kevitch? What are you doing back on the *Subutai*?"

How could she not know? She knew everything. This must have been meant casually. Well, now he was obligated to engage them in small talk. "I just wanted to take one last look around before I left. I'm hitching a ride back to Tartarus on one of the damaged ships."

Morrigan suggested he grab a chair, but OK insisted he wouldn't stay long. "I understand before he died, Damocles offered you anything you wished in return for saving his life. And you asked to return to the little backwater planet where we found you."

"And rule over it with an iron fist. That's how Deathlord Damocles chose to interpret it. Frankly, I'm not sure I can manage the iron fist part."

Morrigan reassured him. "The position is largely ceremonial, darling. Other people will do the iron fisting."

"If you visit, maybe I could show you around."

"There's someone I want you to meet. Deathfinger Kevitch, This is Pussycat Swallowtail."

It was her—Anastasaja—disguised in the body of an Imperial spy. He remembered. She flashed him a sly smile, the glint in her eye betraying the dangerous secret they shared. Well, good for her, OK thought, feeling a twinge of something between admiration and resignation. He was done with the war, but if anyone could keep the game going, it was her.

Then he heard Scrubby say, "She's a spy. We saw her at the rebel base. The Rebel Pact brain-swapped her body with a rebel scientist and sent her back as a double agent. Ask Overseer Kevitch, he knows."

In the instant that followed, Slaughter spat out his drink, Grimfoyle jerked his hand away from Swallowtail's bare thigh and Morrigan drew her blaster.

Pussycat/Anastasaja called out in shock. "Oh, come on, you're not going to take the word of a mechanoid."

Morrigan snapped at OK. "Was she at the rebel base? Tell the truth."

OK could not help but tell her the truth. "I saw her at the rebel base."

"Yes, I was at the base, but I was a prisoner."

Morrigan ratcheted her blaster up another setting. "Get the Medical Bay and tell them to set up for a mind probe."

"Mine or hers?" OK asked.

"Both." Damn, he was going to miss his flight.

"Oh, come on," the spy pleaded. "Look at me. I'm Pussycat Swallowtail. You know me, Lena."

Morrigan's head shook once, as though holding back unimaginable emotions. "Don't you mean 'Midnight?'"

Anastasaja let out a war cry and kicked the table into Morrigan like a makeshift battering ram. Plates, glasses, and dining utensils scattered in all directions as she tumbled backward. Morrigan lost her grip on her blaster. It bounced across the floor before sliding under one of the stained blue couches. Cursing her clumsiness, Morrigan lunged for the nearest weapon she could reach—a dinner fork. It would have to do.

Anastasaja armed herself with a dinner knife, which she twirled with the precision of a master chef looking to score style points. Grimfoyle was about to intervene, but Slaughter held him back. He understood this was personal.

"You murdered my comrades and ripped out my brain from my body!"

"You killed my best friend and stole her body!" Morrigan shouted back. "For that you will die."

"In your dreams, red bitch!"

"Flattery will get you nowhere!"

"Who needs flattery when you have cutlery!" Anastasaja lunged with the knife, her eyes blazing with fury. Morrigan's augmented reflexes kicked into overdrive. With lightning speed, she swiped her dinner fork from the table, meeting the blade with a metallic clang. With a swift twist of her wrist, Morrigan redirected the knife's trajectory – narrowly avoiding a lethal strike – unleashed a flurry of calculated strikes, her movements fluid and precise. But Anastasaja's borrowed body shared the same MAD upgrades. Fueled by adrenalin and fury, she dodged Morrigan's onslaught and countered with a vicious kick aimed at Morrigan's abdomen.

Morrigan sidestepped the attack, allowing her adversary's momentum to carry her forward, then retaliated with a devastating kick of her own. The bone-jarring impact sent Anastasaja hurtling backward, crashing into another table with a resounding thud. Both combatants rose to their feet, the fight was far from over, and the intensity of their confrontation only grew with each passing moment.

Anastasaja made a disparaging comment regarding Pussycat Swallowtail's indiscriminate promiscuity. She brandished two knives she had somehow grabbed from the array of fallen utensils. She threw both at Morrigan, one going wide, the other hitting her shoulder but bouncing off harmlessly because it was a dinner knife after all.

Morrigan picked up a shot glass, drank it, and threw it, catching her opponent right between the eyebrows. It stunned her for just a moment, but then she was on the attack again. She launched into a flying kick. Morrigan roll-dodged and snatched up another dinner fork. She thrust both of them upward, catching the rebel spy just under the ribs.

"Fork you!" she cried as she flipped Anastasaja onto the floor and pinned her writhing form under her knee.

Grimfoyle had retrieved the blaster from under the sofa and leveled it at Anastasaja's crumpled form. The captain had also grabbed a pistol and the two of them brought her down with dual stun blasts.

"I can see that you're busy," OK said. "So, I am just going to go down to the landing bay and wait for my flight."

25.0 Reunited – And It Feels So Forced

Delta Quadrant Starlines Flight 8809 welcomes you to the Cellador pleasure planet, where the current temperature is whatever you want it to be. Please remain sedated until the ship has completed docking maneuvers. Once we have docked, do not enter the airlock before it has fully pressurized and a crew member has given you permission to disembark. Delta Quadrant Starlines appreciates that you have the illusion of choice in selecting interstellar transport, and thanks you for perceiving this choice as optimal. We hope to see you again on a future journey.

The pack containing his few possessions slung over his shoulder, OK made his way through the sprawling spaceport with Scrubby at his side. The famous planet looked up at them through the station's viewports, a vivid blue and pink world with an iridescent ring system. Its rings were trillions of microsatellites that created dazzling light shows at night, regulated the planet's weather, and tracked the credit scores of every tourist.

He approached an information kiosk. Before he could access the planetary database, he was required to pay 10 IMU or endure an advertisement for Black Scorpion coffee. He paid the fee. "Request location of Halleck, Anya Z."

- HALLECK, ANYA Z – IDENT NUMBER 987450745-AZ1H-01-02
- DOMICILE – XANADU DISTRICT 9, STRUCTURE D, POD 81800
- UTILIZATION – SKYBAR-ASTROLOUNGE
- CURRENT LOCATION – XANADU PLEASURE ZONE
- ROLE – HOSPITALITY ASSOCIATE II (PERFORMANCE RATING: 6.9/10).
- STATUS – UNASSIMILATED.

The kiosk offered him discount admission tickets to the Astrolounge and a Styrofoam mug of Black Scorpion coffee. He purchased both. He proceeded to an orbit-to-surface ticketing station attended by a gray-skinned DNZ cyborg. "One ticket to the Xanadu Pleasure Zone, please." He wondered why he was saying "please" to a cyborg. It's not as though they could appreciate courtesy.

"The Xanadu Pleasure Zone is restricted to Imperial citizens with Scorpion Social Credit Score of 1600 or higher. You will submit to the required scan. Resistance is futile." A beam of sickly green light scanned him. OK felt like he would explode to have come this far and be denied by a ticketing attendant. He began thinking of a plan to book passage to an adjacent zone and make his way overland to Xanadu. He could not afford to get caught even once, because DNZ security would …

"Passage approved, Overseer Kevitch." Oh, yeah, he forgot he was the Imperial Overseer of Katarina. This made the rest of the transaction loads easier. "Your ticket has been charged to the Imperial Supreme Ministry of Executive Transport. Shuttles to the Xanadu Pleasure Zone depart from Lobe Four, Level Eight. You are welcome to enjoy the Overlord lounge until the shuttle is ready for boarding. Will your mechanoid be traveling as cargo?"

"I beg your pardon!" Scruffy sputtered.

"No, book him as a passenger."

"Very Good, Lord Overseer. Enjoy your stay on Cellador."

"Thank you." As they walked away, a small drop of moisture glistened at the edge of the cyborg's eye. No one ever thanked a cyborg.

OK saw from the display board he could make the next shuttle if he made an all-out run to the gate. On the other hand, he was hungry. The lounge had hot food in chafing dishes. And for sure there would be a bar. No! He had waited three years to see Anya again. Besides, there would be snacks on the shuttle. Granted, he would have to pay for them, whereas the food in the lounge would be free. Never mind that! He ran and made it to the gate just as they were boarding the last of the passengers.

He took a seat by the aisle. Scrubby found a seat further back but got a row to himself because no one wanted to sit next to a killbot. A flight attendant—who was not a cyborg but had implants of a different kind—served him a chilled glass of orange juice and Scorpion vodka.

"This is quite good," OK remarked.

"It should be, it's the same stuff the pilot is drinking," she told him with a wink. After a safety lecture and a final check of the cabin to make sure no one had reclined their seat to the three degrees that spelled the difference between survival and flaming death, the docking clamps released, the departure rockets fired, and the shuttle began the long downward arc to the surface.

As the shuttle eased into the outer atmosphere and friction set the outer surfaces to glowing, the flight attendant came back around with another drink and packets of crispy cookies that tasted of warm spices and brown sugar.

"Is this your first trip to Cellador?" she asked.

"Yes, I've been looking forward to it for a long time. I hope it isn't dangerous. I have heard there are active rebel cells on Cellador."

"Oh, not anymore," she said cheerily. "Cellador is perfectly safe. The DNZ rounded up the rebels and assimilated them into the collective hivemind. They work in the Happytime Fun-Fun Zones as costumed characters. So, if you see Neville the Nurk-Nurk, or Fuzzerella the Foozy-Wobble, it's probably a rebel who got assimilated. Would you like a hot towel for your face?"

OK decided that would be nice, and the attendant provide him with the warmest, softest towel he had ever pressed to his face. He closed his eyes, enjoyed the warmth and softness, and sank into his own thoughts, beginning with the one that was never far from his mind. Damn Stoat!

Stoat was only reason he had made it here. Every kitchen sink scrubbed, every drink served to horrible officers, every moment bowing to Damocles's whims had been absolutely necessary to put him on this shuttle, riding down to an exotic pleasure planet, and possibly back to the woman he loved. The ultimate payoff for his moral bankruptcy. OK would likely be dead if he had followed his own imperatives instead of Stoat's. Damn him just the same.

As the shuttle hurtled closer to Cellador, the knot in his gut tightened. For all that he had done, and for all that he had failed to do, was there any chance at redemption?

And what could he possibly say to Anya to explain the past three years in the monstrous Scorpion Horde? Serving drinks to the monsters that had devastated their home world. Fixing their rifles. Helping them build their superweapons. Betraying the rebellion. Ensuring the pajamas and underwear of a genocidal germophobic warlord were properly sanitized.

Could he just pretend his original plan had worked? Tell her that he joined the Horde to get off the planet, then defected to the rebellion. He could tell her he spent the last three years fighting on Bugguram, and Roxxon, and Unity Base. It made for a heroic tale, if you altered some of the details, like whose side he was on at the time. But what if she had joined the rebellion on Cellador? What if she pushed for details? "Which company were you with? Did you know Captain Ancient Greek letter-number?" demanding details that would reveal he was making it all up. Then she would probably punch him in the nose.

Oh, godless void, why couldn't he be as good at lying as Stoat was?

He must have been thinking out loud again because his seatmate turned up the volume on his holographic immersion system.

His anxiety reached a pinnacle as the trans-orbital shuttle made its final approach to the landing dock. OK had crossed light years of time, space, and moral inhibitions to find the one person he longed to reconnect with — and he could not think of a single version of the truth that wouldn't make him look like a fiend or a fraud.

He waited until the ship was mostly empty before grabbing his pack and stepping into the landing tube with Scrubby at his side. "Where will we be domiciled?" Scrubby asked.

"We'll worry about the hotel later. First, we're going to find Anya."

"Oh." At least this time Scrubby didn't clarify, "You mean the human woman who formed the basis for your pornographic avatar in the simulation?" as he had done very loudly in the departure lounge of the Atallantia Starport that at the time contained the Revered Sisters of Moriah on their pilgrimage to the Holy World of Antioch II, a class of nine-year-old children on a field trip to the Silent Running Nature Preserve, and the Women's Centrifugal Bumblepuppy team from the University of Plinth.

A maglev tram ran to the Astrolounge on a 35-minute cycle. And, of course, he had just missed the departing tram. He sat down next to his robot on a concrete bench, and sank deeply in his own discouraging thoughts, the two of them silhouetted against the viridescent glow from the Central Pleasure Dome as night fell on Cellador.

They boarded the maglev and it surged upward, gravity's grip loosening as they ascended toward the Astrolounge's orbital perch. The Astrolounge sat atop a curving spike that punctured the very edge of space. From the rotating bar, you could enjoy drinks and light pub fare while enjoying a stunning view of the curvature of the planet, its rings, the bright lights of every pleasure zone in the hemisphere, and the majesty of the stars in the eternal firmament. Its entrance was guarded by a burly humanoid who seemed to be constructed of leftover parts of other burly humanoids. His skin was a camouflage pattern that covered the spectrum of epidermal tones. He stood just shy of eight feet tall, with shoulders broad enough to eclipse the doorway, he might have been some kind of genetically created ogre.

He jabbed a thick, meaty finger at Scrubby, the hand as big and raw as an uncooked pork roast. "We don't allow their kind in here!" he barked, flexing his massive muscles, his arm bulging like a Pavonian anaconda.

Scrubby telescoped to his full, towering nine feet of gleaming steel and armor until he towered over the bouncer. His voice boomed with the menace usually reserved for announcing torpedo launches, "I beg your pardon!"

Unfazed, the bouncer glared straight into his glaring red eye. "I said, we don't allow your kind in here!"

"And just why is that?"

"What?"

"What is the source of this mindless bigotry against artificial life forms. Pray enlighten us."

Caught off guard, the behemoth stumbled for words. "I suppose because of residual antipathy toward artificial life forms from the Aeon Wars."

"Oh, and do I look like an Aeon, you meatsack?" Scrubby demanded in the haughtiest tone of voice his vocalizer circuit could manage. He flexed his appendages, ready to throw down, killbot to mutant.

"Is there a problem, hunh?" a familiar voice intruded on the exchange. "Oh, hai, OK. How's your sex life, hunh?"

"Boskirk?" It was him, all right. His shaggy hair was drawn back into a sleek ponytail. He was wearing a glittering black space tuxedo adorned with star patterns and a tie that glowed like a blue-white giant, matching his teeth. Somehow, he still managed to look like a guy who would sell you drugs outside a strip club.

"So, you're an imperial overseer now. Good for you. After I left the Horde, I just, you know, I wander around the constellation for a little while. Liisa left me and that tear me apart, huh? But Cellador. Beautiful planet. Nice people. So, I take prestigious job managing Skybar. I am so happy you find me, huh?"

"I am looking for someone… a woman named Anya Halleck."

"Unh-huh, she work here. All my girls real. No consort drones. You want to see her?" OK nodded. Boskirk ordered the bouncer. "Let them in. I'll comp you for one night since you are old friend. We have a dress code, I get you a suit. Do you think your mechanoid mind cleaning up my kitchen, hunh?"

"Mind it? It would be my absolute delight, good sir." Scrubby declared, withdrawing his blades and replacing them with scrub brushes, happy to revert to his primary function.

The doors slid open revealing the interior of the Astrolounge, which looked curiously familiar. The lighting was chic and industrial, floor-to-ceiling holo-screens were spaced throughout the club, and sofas in exciting patterns of light and dark blue herringbone formed conversation pits. The bar was the focal point, where stylish, attractive bartenders expertly crafted top-shelf spirits into exotic libations to suit the tastes of the most discerning clientele.

OK changed into the suit Boskirk brought him; a fashionable amalgam of black body armor and red velvet lining suitable for an Imperial Overseer. Boskirk directed OK to a spiral staircase. At the top, was a young woman he thought for a moment was Anya, but whose holographic label read "Nikita." Nikita led him to a private alcove at the back upholstered in plush Saurian leather. The viewport provided an outstanding vista of Cellador's night side. But OK wasn't interested. "I am here to see Anya."

"I'll see if she is available," Nikita said crisply. "In the meantime, you may refresh yourself with the galaxy's most effective array of sensory enhancers." OK asked for Scorpion vodka and she scowled at him like a waitress who realized she wasn't getting a good tip. "I'll see if they have any downstairs."

OK settled in for the wait. Around him, he heard muffled conversations and the intricate melodies of space jazz played by the in-house combo. He tapped his fingers on the table. He fingered his tie. What was taking her so long? He still didn't know what he was going to tell her. He heard a sudden crackle of woman's laughter. Was that Anya hearing the news of his arrival?

OK could not help but feel like he was coming to the end of a long cosmic joke and the punchline wasn't even going to be funny.

After keeping him waiting until she was ready to make her appearance, Anya arrived. He almost didn't recognize her at first. He was so accustomed to the avatar he created that the real woman looked like a pale imitation. But the tilt of her chin, the hint of mischief in the curve of her smile, as if she knew something the rest of the galaxy didn't, were unmistakable. She wore a black form-fitting dress, tailored to flatter her form while allowing for ease of movement as she navigated between the crowded tables of the lounge.

"Anya?"

"Howdy stranger, you're about the last person I ever expected to meet here." Her tone enthusiastic, but painfully artificial, like a lackluster actress phoning in a role. She set a bottle of Scorpion vodka on the table.

"Godless void, it's so good to see you again. Please, please, sit down and let's talk, catch up. How have you been?"

"Um, it's nice to see you too. I know the manager comped you, but, you know, if you want me to sit, there's a charge for that. It's how I make most of my money, so…"

OK opened his bag, pulled out 700 grams of Antarean palladium and laid it across the table. "Well, well, well," she cooed, sliding into the seat next to him while sliding the coins toward herself. "Now, you have my undivided attention."

OK did not know where to begin. "I saw your brother after the invasion. He told me your family was trying to reach Cellador."

"Is he alive?"

"I don't know. That was three years ago. Longer. I haven't heard anything from him since I left Katarina." Before she could ask what he had been up to, he asked, "Never mind me, how are you? What have you been up to since you got to this planet?"

"DNZ Corp granted my family residency but they had to sign work contracts. So, my dad works in a costume shop, dressed as space elf selling space elf costumes. Took weeks for his ears to heal after the surgery. He still complains about the itching. My mom got a job dressing up the animatronics in the 'It's a Small Galaxy, Isn't It?' stage show. And me? Well, here I am. It's not too bad most of the time. Pay is pretty good. Oh, and did I mention I met Overlord Venom Sac once! Quite a character, shorter than you would think."

He felt like a proper idiot when the irony hit him. All this time, he and she had been doing the same job; serving drinks to Imperial thugs. He almost laughed out loud at the absurdity of it all. "The last time I saw you, you were studying hospitality, and I owned a bar. Funny to meet again like this."

A sort of recognition washed over her face. Her tentativeness and caution evaporated. "I almost didn't recognize you at first. You've changed a lot, OK." She touched his cheek gently. "What's wrong with your face?"

"Huh? Oh, that, I was in an airlock that decompressed."

She ran a lacquered nail across his scars. "Does it hurt?"

He hadn't thought about that until now. "I suppose it should, but they gave me some really amazing narcotics for it."

"Got any left?" She laughed, joking but not joking. "But tell me, for real, what have you been doing? How did you even get here? Did you join a space-trade or something?"

There was no point in trying to lie. He already knew he was not good at it. A malfunctioning hologram could lie more convincingly than he could. "The Horde overran Katarina after you got out, They killed everyone who resisted, sent everyone who didn't resist to a labor camp. The only way to avoid death or slavery was to join the Horde, so I did. I'm not proud of it, but I did what I had to do to survive."

"You joined the Scorpion Horde?" she asked in stunned disbelief.

He looked away; he couldn't bear to meet her eyes. "Like I said, I didn't think I had a choice. But…"

"How many rebels have you killed?" she demanded, a sudden fire appearing in her eyes.

He shook his head. "I really don't know."

"You mean you've lost count," she accused him, a bitter smirk in the corner of her mouth.

There it was—the condemnation he had anticipated, and in truth, deserved. Countless rebels had been disintegrated because he'd shown the Deathwalkers how to target their rifles with lethal precision. The entire Rebel Pact had been obliterated thanks in no small part to the intel he had conveyed on the Imperium's behalf. He wanted to protest that he didn't mean to, it was all a misunderstanding, but even he knew how pathetic that would sound.

She leaned closer, voice trembling. "OK, what have they done to you? They made you a murderer. They made you a monster. They made you …"

He flinched, anticipating the inevitable punch in the nose.

"Hot!" she finished, launching over the table to deliver a hard, weapons grade kiss that was exactly not how he had always imagined it. When she pulled away, her lips lingered on his, like the closing notes of a song doing a slow fade out.

"Tell me all about it… everything! Omit no detail!"

He stared at her, snagged between confusion, terror, and a horrifying suspicion that Anya was the sort of woman who'd frame his wanted poster for her bedroom wall.

"Go on, tell her!" Stoat said—a voice inside him so clear it might have come from the next table.

"Yes, darling, tell her," echoed another voice.

OK poured out two shots of the Scorpion vodka. They downed them together. OK took a deep breath, and locked eyes with Anya.

"My first assignment with the Horde was to deal with an alien infestation on their warships that was killing their crews by the dozens. Through sheer grit, brute force, and merciless killing I exterminated that alien life form. That was how I earned my first promotion.

"Later on, the Imperium invaded the planet Plinth. I found myself in charge of preparing an entire legion of Deathwalkers for combat. They couldn't hit a damn thing with their combat rifles. So I said, 'Give me that' and yanked one out of their hands. I had to show them how to hit their marks. After that? Our Deathwalkers were unstoppable! We took Plinth, and then Brattle, and then wiped out an entire rebel base in the Bugguram system.

"Then, the Horde assigned us a secret mission to eliminate a rebel fortress. The only way to reach it was through Aeonic space—the most dangerous zone in all the galaxy! The captain insisted I stay at his side as we fought the Aeons. We lost half our ships but we made it to the far side. There, I joined the assault force that captured the rebel base. After we slaughtered them, I took a piss in the rebel command center.

"After that, the Horde put me to work on their ultimate weapon, a ship that could obliterate entire star systems. I found a fatal flaw in the design that the best engineers in the Imperium had overlooked. They begged me to stay on, but Deathlord Damocles demanded that I join his inner circle; and who was I to refuse the Supreme Deathlord of the Red Scorpion Fleet?

"He dispatched me on a mission so top secret I didn't even know all the details, but the rebels shot down my ship and took me prisoner. They tortured me for days, but I refused to break. They dragged me to their leader, who asked me to join their side. Well, I told her exactly what I thought of that offer.

"I made my way back to the Red Fleet in a stolen ship and found them in the midst of a heated battle. But the rebels sabotaged the reactor on my ship and set it to explode. I managed an emergency escape and took out an enemy warship in the process. My life support systems failed, and I was near death when they hauled me aboard a Horde cruiser."

He gestured toward his face. "That's how I got these scars. After I got out 9of the medical bay, Deathlord Damocles named me Lord Overseer of Katarina out of gratitude for saving his ship. On my way out the door, I exposed an enemy spy in the Imperial ranks."

Her eyes were as wide as a gimlet glass. "Is all of this true?"

"May the void consume me right now if one word isn't true!"

She passed a gleaming Antarean palladium coin through her fingers, admiring the patterns of dazzling light it reflected. "So," she purred, "You're not only wealthy, but you're also a hero of the Imperium. Returning to our humble planet to assume the role of an all-powerful Overlord?"

"Well, Overseer, it's like a sort of local overlord," was what he almost said, but he stopped himself before he downplayed it. Instead, he squared his shoulders and declared, "Ia, the Imperium is sending me as the iron fist to rule over Katarina. In fact, Deathlord Damocles's final decree before his death was to rename the capital of Katarina in my honor." This was also true. The capital of Katarina now bore the name 'Otis City.'

A slow smile spread across her face, she leaned in closer, her voice softening with a mix of flattery and excitement. "And of all the people in the galaxy, you came to see me?"

"You were the only person in all the galaxy I wanted to see again."

A warm thrill coursed through her as the realization sank in—he was about to rule a whole planet and he'd chosen her, sought her out, and it was intoxicating. "So where are you staying, my Overlord?"

"Not sure. I haven't booked a hotel yet. Is there a place you would recommend?"

"Why don't we go back to my place?" she whispered, her voice dripping with sultry promise. "I feel an insurrection stirring inside me... and only a stern, commanding Overlord can put it down." She favored him with another kiss. "Without mercy."

An enigmatic smile turned up the corners of OK's lips. "Hail to the Imperial Victory."

www.ingramcontent.com/pod-product-compliance
Lightning Source LLC
Chambersburg PA
CBHW020102180626
46812CB00006B/2442